Also by Anthony Giardina

Men with Debts

A BOY'S PRETENSIONS

ANTHONY GIARDINA

Simon and Schuster

New York   London   Toronto   Sydney   Tokyo

Copyright © 1988 by Anthony Giardina

Published by Simon and Schuster
A Division of Simon & Schuster Inc.
Simon & Schuster Building
Rockefeller Center
1230 Avenue of the Americas
New York, New York 10020

SIMON AND SCHUSTER and colophon are registered trademarks
of Simon & Schuster Inc.

Designed by Kathy Kikkert

Manufactured in the United States of America

10   9   8   7   6   5   4   3   2   1

Library of Congress Cataloging in Publication Data
Giardina, Anthony, date.
    A boy's pretensions.

    I. Title.
PS3557.I1353B69   1988   813'.54   87-23463
ISBN 0-671-62136-X

Acknowledgments

I wish to thank Creative Artists Public Service (CAPS) of the New York State Arts Council and the Northampton Arts Council for grants which assisted in the writing of this novel.

For Eileen

Where do these
Innate assumptions come from? Not from what
We think truest, or most want to do:
Those warp tight-shut, like doors. They're more a style
Our lives bring with them: habit for a while,
Suddenly they harden into all we've got

And how we got it; looked back on, they rear
Like sand-clouds, thick and close, embodying
For Dockery a son, for me nothing,
Nothing with all a son's harsh patronage.

—Philip Larkin,
"Dockery and Son"

1
LAUNDROMAT

I thought of the breaking glass. Then of his face, and
how it must have looked—the "O" my father's lips
pucker into when he is caught unaware—at the sound of
the explosion. The train was moving slowly between

Stamford and Bridgeport; I settled back into my seat, closed my eyes. Had the glass actually cut him? My aunt, on the phone, had said he'd been adjusting a sign (there was one that hung in our laundromat window all year long: "DRYCLEAN FOR WINTER," with an image of the smiling sun and two happy children in parkas). She'd also said he'd been standing on a ladder, and that would have made it worse. But under all these questions was the perverse thought of what it must have looked like to Felder, the dry cleaner next door, as he glanced up and saw the thousand shards of exploded glass, and my father among them, sailing through the window of his own store.

Then the train was stalled; the whole buckling apparatus had lurched to a stop near some tenements; black children in shades of pink played a game in a cement courtyard. We were there ten minutes or so.

"Do you know why we're stopped?"

A woman across the aisle leaned forward; an anxious face, a set of lines and angles perched over a spread of papers on the snack tray.

I shook my head; the movement felt slow, too heavy a response. I watched her take in the fact that I wasn't from her world; this delay meant no missed appointments for me. I was being called home, that was all.

When I'd first heard the news (my aunt had called me in the dorm) I'd gone directly to my room and started to pack. Then, as if I were remembering too vividly one of those old horror movies featuring neurotic spinsters in old houses, I thought the walls, the pale green familiar dormitory walls, were closing in, the room becoming several sizes smaller. I ran outside, just to feel normalcy, to pretend for a moment that none of it had happened, the laundromat remained intact, I was free to spend the day as I wanted. I was halfway across campus when I saw Mrs. Branner walking toward me, against the just-turning red and yellow trees. It was odd, her of all people; the immediate instinct had been to turn away. Instead I lunged for the fact that I knew her, or barely knew her, and shouted, in too high, too shrill a voice, "I've got to go home!"

She stopped a dozen feet before me, and there was no response beyond a curious turning, a slight tilt of the head that suggested she perhaps recognized me but wasn't sure. I stuttered, "My father's laundromat blew up! He's hurt!"

I looked at the blue dress, and the man's flannel shirt she wore over it, had presence enough of mind to wonder what destination I had interrupted her from: a cup of coffee in the cafeteria, grading papers in her office? The vast portion of the map that remained unaffected by a small explosion in Massachusetts lay spread before me. I broke eye contact, saw then that her stockings were rolled halfway down her calves.

Then: "I've got to go home"—said, this time, more quietly.

"I'm sorry."

Her lips parted slightly; one hand went up, but as though she hadn't quite found a use for it. And then, as though a tiny crack in the world had opened, I forgot for a moment the whole event; was thinking, instead, of her, the pale cheeks and green eyes, the way her hair rose off her face, the slow development of lust, over three weeks, four, the presence, in a Jesuit university, of female knees, and of the days in the lecture hall and nights spent trying to push her out of consciousness while she remained, manifestly, there.

"Your parents own a laundromat?"

She was only flustered, looking for something to say, but she had managed to land on the one thing: not the potential tragedy, but somehow the fact of it, the humiliation, announced there in front of everyone.

And because there seemed no point now, no gain, in pretending I belonged here, like these others, independent of the workings of machines two hundred miles away, machines that should have been replaced years ago, I turned and ran, ignoring the last thing she'd done, which had been to hold out her hand to try and stop me. Ignoring, too, the slowly growing look of pity in her eyes.

"Are you all right?" the woman across the aisle asked.

The train was moving again now, slowly, crawling. The black children slid from view.

"Yes, I'm fine." I couldn't imagine what I'd been doing to cause her concern.

My Aunt Rose was sitting in one of the green-cushioned chairs that lined the hospital corridor, staring straight ahead. She had my mother's long, delicate nose; the rest of her looked, from this angle, abbreviated. Her dress was black, functional. Her stubby fingers toyed with a box of Chiclets.

"Rose."

Her eyes flared up briefly before focusing. All her life, she'd been waiting for something like this to happen.

"Nickie," she said, gesturing to me with the hand holding the Chiclets. "Your father looks terrible. You'd hardly recognize him."

The hallway was long and dark, punctuated by irregular clots of light formed by open and semi-open doorways. At the very end, INTENSIVE CARE announced itself in gold lettering on a frosted, blue-tinted window, lit from within.

"The glass?"

"All over him, Nick. Your mother's in there with him."

She pulled herself back then; her features became rigid, as if she'd been newly reminded of the gravity of what had happened.

"It's terrible. It nearly killed him. You should have been there."

I nodded; I looked away.

"You kids think your parents are gonna live forever."

"I don't think that, Aunt Rose."

"He shouldn't have been there alone."

I had seen her, perhaps a month before, standing up to her knees in the soft mud in a secluded corner of Wingaersheik Beach, announcing to her brothers and sisters that she had to do "a pishada," laughing so hard she was afraid she would do it in her pants. The men planted their clamming forks and turned around. We heard the stream then, and her brother Carmen shouted, "Look out, Rose, a clam's liable to come up and bite it!" Now she sat before me, silently passing judgment on the frivolousness of a college education.

"Al will help you with the laundromat, Nickie. You've gotta help your father now."

I looked down at the floor. Someone large and heavy-stepping approached. I saw first the man's black work boots, frayed cuffs, and knew right away who it was. Herman Lieber worked next door to us, in Felder's Dry Cleaners.

"Where's John?"

He didn't bother to introduce himself, or make any of the formal gestures. Instead he stood there, pulling at the ends of a soiled handkerchief.

Aunt Rose looked up at him, suspicious.

"This is Herman Lieber," I said. "My Aunt Rose."

"He's okay?" Herman asked.

"I haven't seen him yet."

Herman couldn't stand still; he shifted from foot to foot, licked at his lips.

"I can't go in?" he asked.

"It's Intensive Care," Aunt Rose said. "They don't let anyone who's not in the family in."

Herman looked hurt. He stared down the hall at the blue-tinted glass as though he were seeing it as stronger, more impregnable than it in fact was.

"Maybe you could sneak me in, huh, Nick?"

Herman's hand went out, shook a moment in the air between us. "Say I'm an uncle, somethin'?"

He half-opened his mouth, gave evidence of a huge thirst. I marveled at the idiosyncrasy of grief, how it could take the fluid from the mouth of a virtual stranger, yet leave the son fully lubricated.

"Sure, Herman," I said finally. "I'll get you in."

The sides of his big face started to lift into what I thought was going to be a grin; then his eyes were brimming over.

"Nick, I'm sorry."

I could smell Felder's perc on the green work shirt he hadn't bothered to change. It seemed absurd to be smelling it here, in this antiseptic place. Once, when I'd first arrived at college, I'd been unpacking my trunk and, lifting out a sweater, had been hit by this same smell. Quickly, I'd hid the offending garment from my roommate, as though my entire adolescence had suddenly flashed on display.

"I just hope nobody finds out," Aunt Rose intoned, picking up and opening her pocketbook. Inside it were tissues, gum wrappers, a makeup case—the familiar stuff of aunts. Her huffiness now had a pleasurable quality to it, as though she'd been waiting for years for a situation in which she could exercise the prerogatives of exclusiveness.

I left the one small suitcase I'd brought on the chair beside her, and guided Herman down the corridor.

It was no trouble at all finding my mother. She was visible just inside the door of Intensive Care, wearing a plum-colored dress with buttons running down the front, and a frilly collar. I understood that the form under the sheets, though it was mostly invisible, was my father. My mother's face was made up, hair brushed back, her lips colored bright red. All this gave me the illusion that things couldn't really be so bad, until I remembered that my mother would not have left the house in a plain housedress, her hair uncombed, even if it had been to claim my father's body.

She looked at me, then at Herman; confusion passed briefly over her features. I felt ashamed of having brought Herman with me, as though I were hiding behind him.

"Herman," she said.

He held himself back a moment, uncertain whether he was allowed any closer. A nurse looked up from the table where she'd been taping a printed name to a wrist brace-

let. Herman moved forward as if at any second he might
have to change direction. He grasped my mother's hand,
shook it.

"Bad, huh?" I saw him look over her shoulder to where
my father was. Then my mother opened up to allow Herman to hug her. As her head touched his stained green
shirt, she looked at me and closed her eyes.

"Mom." I went forward.

She took my hand, squeezed, smiled in the odd, social
way she had of smiling at me when there was company
around.

"Say hello to your father," she said.

I looked down at the bed. My father's head lay on a
slice of pillow, the rest of him covered in white, porous-
looking sheets. His head looked nearly as white as the
sheets, except for a large, purplish blotch starting at his
left temple and covering most of one side of his head. A
bandage had been taped to the center of it. The gray in
his hair above his ears stood out, and his bald dome
looked smallish. My father did not look hurt so much as
old, and astonished, as though the news of his aging had
just reached him, and he'd been so floored by it he'd
crept into this bed, in this hospital, for protection.

"Hi, Dad," I said.

The sides of his mouth split outward into a faint smile.
It looked difficult to accomplish, and I motioned that it
wasn't necessary. Herman Lieber hunched over, leaned
on the bed, so that I was close enough to smell the perc
again.

"Bad, huh, John?"

My father nodded.

"You should have seen," my mother said. "There was
glass all over him. They had a job cleaning him up. It's a
miracle he's all right."

Her face came alive at the words.

Herman nodded. "I saw; the store." He made a dull
clucking sound with his tongue.

My father had reached up, to try to grab my hand.

"I closed up for you, John," Herman said.

"You locked the doors?" my mother asked.

Herman shook his head. "Didn't have the keys. I put up a sign. Larry's gonna watch for you. Maybe I can take Nickie over there later with the keys."

I was startled by his sudden reference to me. It was as though I'd just been elected to a club I had no interest in joining.

"No, we'll go over later," my mother said.

She looked down at the place where my father had grasped my hand, the first notice she'd taken of us in a while.

"It was nice of Herman to come, huh, John?"

My father nodded, the slow, painful movement.

Herman shook his head. The long slope of his nose seemed to widen as he looked down at my father, and the flesh on his cheeks looked as loose as a heavy woman's buttocks.

"Old machines," he said, still shaking his head. My father continued to look at the ceiling. "You gonna sue?"

"Who would we sue?" my mother asked.

Herman shrugged. "Somebody. Your cousin, he sold you those machines?"

My father nodded slowly. He'd bought the laundromat a decade before, from a cousin to whom he still paid rent.

"So?" Herman asked.

"It's not his cousin's fault," my mother said.

She smiled then, afraid of giving offense to Herman Lieber. Her failure to recognize class distinctions had always been a source of amazement to me. Once, coming home from work this summer, I had found her going over samples in the living room with the Fuller Brush man. After introducing me, she'd looked a little longer than usual at my neck and ears, then, turning apologetically to the salesman, said, "He needs a haircut."

Herman stepped backwards.

"You sure you don't want me to take care of it for you? I can shoot right by, then drop the keys off at your house."

"We're leaving now too, Herman," my mother answered. "It's no problem. How are Jeannie and the girls?"

"They're okay."

He stood, nodding vaguely. I looked at his dark, spot-ted clothes, my mother's dress, the white institutional curtains and the green radiator beneath them, then at my father's head. It looked as soft as a baby's, had the auster-ity of a newborn's.

"I'll go," Herman said, leaning down. "John, anything. Josie, you hear me? Anything."

My mother's eyes filled up.

"You've always been such a good friend to him, Her-man."

I'd worked beside my father in the laundromat all summer. I knew what their friendship consisted of: they ate doughnuts and drank coffee together, held long con-voluted discussions centered around the greed of cus-tomers. But for them, it was enough.

Lieber left, and we stood for a long time in silence. It was so clear now that my father's recovery would not be swift that it was far more painful that they said nothing, hung back, more out of their customary reticence than anything else, from saying, "You'll stay."

"How was the train ride?" my mother asked.

"Fine."

She glanced around the room, smiled at a passing nurse, as if in hopes of striking up an idle conversation.

I felt a tug on the skin of my wrist.

"Nick," my father said, "make sure they put wood over the window, a sheet of plywood."

I nodded, waited for more, but that was all.

We just stood there then, and I had the sense that we were all dwarfed by my father's business, attendants in the waiting room of *its* illness, not his. On each of our minds, I was certain, was the same image: the deserted store, with its yellow washers and lime-green dryers, its potted plants and orange vinyl benches, the stacks of old *Newsweeks* and *Ladies Home Journals*, the now blasted dry-cleaning machines. Like the descendants of some overpowering invalid father, we had nothing to say to one another in the face of its illness, save the giving and receiving of orders as to how we should go about attending to it.

"Are you hungry, Nick?" my mother asked.

"No."

"You must be starved. Did you eat on the train?"

"No. Uh-uh."

"They have a cafeteria. Rose is outside; take her with you and go get something to eat."

"I'm not hungry."

"You need money?"

I shook my head. There was something too settled, even too pleasant, in the attending to our needs now, the business of food. The possibility that I might escape the repercussions of this had fled entirely: the exact dimensions of my fate were there in the way my mother concerned herself with my stomach. I was on board.

But beyond this, they said nothing. My mother leaned over my father and smoothed back a curl of hair that had fallen over his ear. My father's face had retreated into a blank, uncharacteristic despair. He stared at the ceiling.

"It's a shame they don't allow flowers," my mother said.

Then we waited, as if to be given permission to leave him, until a doctor came in and told us he would need to sleep. We kissed him, each of us with the same relief, and left him in the white airless room in Intensive Care.

We stopped briefly, on the way home, to examine the damage done by the blast. The explosion, which had come from the machine manufacturing perc, had made a mess of the area where our dry-cleaning machines had once gleamed. The insides had poured out, stripped and blackened: any stranger would have thought someone had died there. My father's cousin, Leo, had already taken care of covering the window with plywood, so there was no reason for us to stay long. We were silent for the remainder of the ride.

In front of the house, my Uncle Al sat waiting for us in his oversized Plymouth. As soon as he saw us, he opened the door on the passenger side and slid out, his green work clothes hugging him as he stood, all three hundred pounds of him, blocking our entrance to the driveway in his lineman's pose of grief. My mother leaned against him, and I watched his big hands pat down her hair.

His eyes looked hungry when I shook his hand, as though he wanted to knock me down just for the sake of setting something loose in himself.

"Nickie, what a tragedy, huh? I'm sorry."

He placed both hands on the sides of my face. And his expression started to change.

"But what a lucky thing he's all right, huh?"

His face broke into a huge grin, tempered only by the approach of his wife. Aunt Rose had driven us here. Now she stood impatiently, as though she'd come to a card game and no one had volunteered to deal.

"You have something in the house, Josie?" she asked.

"To eat? Oh, ya."

"You sure? I could go shopping for you. I could run down to the Star." Rose made no gesture toward movement, as if it were understood that her offer would be rejected. My mother was already on her way into the house.

"We gonna eat here?" Al asked.

"Josie!" Rose called. "Come on over to our house."

My mother opened the door and stepped inside, ignoring her sister. This was ritual for them, the offers made and refused. Soon Rose followed her in.

"Nickie," Al said, when we were alone. His hands were once again on me, and the grin had returned, as if only in the absence of his wife was the whole physical side of him freed.

"You gonna stay now?" he asked.

"I guess."

I wanted to avoid him, to not have to answer this. He had a way of coming so directly at you, as if none of the human filters existed. He had always reminded me of one of those cartoon characters human in every respect except that they are, in fact, bears.

"Good boy," he said, and I looked up at the house, silently repeating his words. I looked at the brick facing, the row of windows on white clapboard, the house too big, much too big, for the three people—now two—who lived there. I imagined myself up in my room, growing fat and pale, the raw material of a future mass murderer.

"We should go inside," I said. "She might need some help."

My mother was in the kitchen, unloading a Tupperware container of frozen meat sauce into the big saucepan. I glanced at the frozen chunks of meat and lost all hunger. My aunt was placing tea bags in four cups.

"So your mother says you're going to stay, Nickie," she said.

There was something different in hearing this, even secondhand, from my mother. I watched her, working at the corners of the container, flicking out pieces of flank meat, ignoring us. The meal was what was important. My life was something to be juggled and adjusted, like the pictures she'd hung in my room, bright orange sunsets this summer, replacing the sailboats of my high school years.

"He said, outside," Al announced, behind me.

I continued to look at my mother, still waiting for her response. She turned on the heat under the saucepan. My aunt almost simultaneously turned the heat off under the teapot, and began pouring.

"Isn't anyone going to ask me?"

My mother had gone to the cupboard, to take down dishes.

"Just till your father's well," she said.

"Fine. They don't just let you take off a month in the middle of the semester, in case you don't know. I can't just show up in the middle of October."

"Oh, it'll take longer than that," she said, laying out plates.

"How long?" A new fear was starting now: she knew

things, she'd been told things by the doctor that she'd
kept hidden.

"He'll be three more weeks in the hospital *at least*.
And then you don't think he can go right back to work,
do you?"

Aunt Rose put two cups of tea down on the table, the
hot water barely tinted copper from the thin, papery bag
submerged in it.

"You wouldn't let him," Rose said.

"I wouldn't let him is right." My mother's lips
stretched out to emphasize her point, some crazy long-
hand she used in talking to her sisters. I'd come to imagine them all, as little girls, so cowed by their father's
presence at the dinner table that they'd learned to talk to
one another by means of lip twitches alone.

Aunt Rose placed the other two cups on the table. She
and my mother sat down to them immediately. My uncle
lifted his, spooned sugar into it at the kitchen counter.

"Sit, Al."

"No, I'll stand...Josie." He waited a moment before
saying the "Josie" part.

He waved her off, looked out the window at our back-
yard. There was a patio, a stand of trees, then the bird
feeder that marked the division of our property from our
neighbor's.

"Have your tea," my aunt instructed me.

"I don't want any."

I thought, for a single, frightening moment, that I was
going to cry. I could imagine, then, their faces looking up
at me in surprise: He's just a baby! Our Nickie, so tall,
with such big shoulders! The assessment would be unbearable, and to prevent anything like that from happening, I went to my room.

I had packed very little: after the humiliation on
campus, I had just wanted to get out of there as quickly
as possible. There were two shirts and a pair of pants in
the open suitcase; I had thought I'd be here for a weekend, no more. Now I sat there and considered the clothes
hanging in my closet, how they would become my ward-

robe now. I envisioned myself walking through town in the orange shirt with tennis-racquet appliqué I'd worn when I flunked my first driving test.

It was dark now, but I didn't bother to turn on the lights. There were so many ways I might have avoided this. Other boys did, made big dramatic breaks that were really overt ways of saying: I am no longer available, I have left. This summer I had wanted to go to Mexico. Fordham had instituted a project aimed at freshmen and sophomores to assist in building houses in some remote part of that country. It would cost each volunteer five hundred dollars. My friend and roommate Tommy Bevilacqua had been one of the first to sign up.

I had come home one weekend in the spring to announce this intention, and on the ride home from the train station had missed my timing, springing it on my father at a busy intersection. Moments passed before a response came, and then it was "Mexico?"—the rounded lips, a squint in my direction, and the question, "What about money for the fall? You're not gonna work?"

"Dad, it *is* work."

"They don't pay you?"

"No." I hesitated. "You pay them."

"Great," he said. "That's good for the Mexicans. That's great for the Mexicans."

I held off a moment, then said, "Dad, I need to do something for other people."

The words sounded hopelessly weak even as I was saying them. And I knew exactly how he saw me: this kid wants to go help people, in Mexico no less! Let him help me! Let him do the work that needs to be done!

And in the end, that was what had happened. Tommy Bevilacqua had gotten his hack license and driven a cab to get the money for Mexico; I'd chosen to stay the summer, to "help out."

Someone's footsteps were just outside the door. My mother called, "Nick, come have some supper."

I didn't answer, so she knocked.

"Nick."

She opened the door a crack.

"No light?"

She switched it on. Then she stood there, seemingly unaware that anything beyond the usual was happening.

"Coming?" she asked. The pleasantness in her voice was grating, as was the fact that she managed somehow to look beautiful. Without waiting for my response, she turned and headed back down the hallway.

I waited a short while, then went back to join them. My protest had clearly had no effect; they had already begun to eat, and when Rose and Al looked at me, I felt the chagrin of having behaved badly, as though I *had* cried. My arms now felt as if they had no muscles in them; the dish they had left for me felt heavy as I loaded it with meatballs and spaghetti from the pot. When I sat down, Al looked sideways at me and nodded, then speared a sausage and devoured it in two bites.

So this was it. My immediate future decided, there was nothing to do but eat, and I did so with an unforced obsessiveness that saw my plate cleared within minutes. Why not get fat now? Who would there be to impress? I was living among Italians now; my life was going to be inseparable from theirs. Why not face the brute facts? Go fill your plate again.

"Al was saying," my aunt began, a crust of Italian bread wedged inside her cheek, "maybe you could get into night school someplace."

"You got universities here," Al said. The word "universities" sounded so splendid in his mouth, I felt my heart quicken with regret.

"Sure," I said, "but I don't want to go to school at night, and anyway, it's too late to enroll."

They were silent for a moment. Rose looked at my mother.

"Jenny's boy went at night," Rose said.

I had a vision of Jenny's boy: Fatty Arbuckle in a Ban-Lon shirt.

"He sells paper now," she continued. "Wax paper."

"Oh, God," I couldn't help saying.

"What? He has a house."

"That's great, that's great," I said, going for another helping.

When I turned around, though, I thought I'd been misjudging them: their faces were open and visibly distressed, as though the desire to reduce my options to the cheesiest available had not, after all, been the sum of their intent. Instead, they looked as though they'd been making an honest attempt to settle matters equably with the materials at hand. What did they know of the difference between college life in a city two hundred miles away and night classes at B.C.? To them, it must have appeared like a freezing child shaking his head at the offer of a coat, holding out for a more expensive model.

"It would take a semester, Josie? A semester?" Al turned to my mother.

She glanced up at him, then down at her food, nodding, half-smiling. She said, "Ya."

"So a semester is not so bad, huh? You'll graduate just a little late, that's all. Unless, what do they, hire in the summer, these college scouts?"

I absorbed my uncle's image of college life: the hiring force descending en masse over the green campus. The phrase "college scouts" smacked of athleticism; he saw us all as hopping ballplayers, anxious to make a good showing, to be hired by some "club" into which a college degree was a "ticket." I had seen enough to be saddened by his misconception, but at the moment felt enough outside to be vulnerable to it: the "college scouts," whoever they were, would surely miss me now.

"I don't know." I shook my head and sat down with my plate of meatballs.

"What do you mean? You don't look around, you don't see? You haven't researched this?"

Al's hands were each three inches above the table. His bottom lip quivered a moment before he withdrew his hands, nearly knocking over a water glass in the process.

"He doesn't know yet what he wants to do," my aunt said, biting down again on the Italian bread and peering at me sideways, her head pivoting like an owl's.

In the silence that followed, my uncle stared ahead, as though he were seeing my future as a candle in the center of the table, about to go out. The movements of his lips and a sudden quickness in his eyes led me to think that at any moment he would make a decision for me. I thought it was time to change the subject.

"It's funny none of you worry that if I don't go to school this semester, I'll be eligible for the draft."

"Mother's sole support," my aunt snapped.

I looked at her a moment, astonished. She had the facts of my mother's defense laid out like a brief before her; her skin suddenly looked as cracked and leathery as an old lawyer's.

"What sole support?" my uncle half-shouted, as if offended.

"The law, Al," she said. "They can't draft a boy if it's gonna leave his mother high and dry. As long as his father can't work, he's safe."

I said nothing then: just sat there, stuffed. Once again, their looks suggested it was not enough that I accept this; I had to be happy with it as well.

"If that's the way it has to be, that's the way it has to be," I said.

They said nothing. For a moment, no one moved. My aunt's mouth looked petrified, the lines formed by the position of her upper lip as though they'd been there for years, that pose of skepticism as natural to her as sleep.

My uncle lifted his hands again, shook his head from side to side.

"Nobody likes this."

He smiled at me, in a supplicating manner, to make it nice. The kitchen light shone on his wide head; his high forehead looked formidable, bullish, almost admirable.

That night, after my aunt and uncle had gone, I did the dishes while my mother went into her room to say a Rosary. The phone had begun ringing even before we'd finished supper, and had hardly stopped since: relatives, the ones who hadn't heard of the accident immediately, and friends who were arriving home from work.

When I was finished with the dishes I sat at the kitchen table and waited for her to be done talking. From her room down the hall, I could hear the "Ya's" and "It was terribles" like cue balls bouncing against the padded walls of the house. I thought of the campus at this time of day. I remembered Mrs. Branner walking toward me, her stockings rolled down.

"What are you doing?" my mother asked, when she finally appeared.

"I'd like to talk," I said.

"You want some tea?" She went to the stove, turned the gas on under the pot, then sat down, resting her arms on the table. If anyone had said those words, "I'd like to talk," in the way I imagined I'd said them, I think I would have been frightened at what I was about to hear. But from her expression, it was clear that for her, I carried no threat.

I looked down at the table, wondering how to start.

"You're upset about your father?"

I heard her, but I did not look up to see the expression behind her words.

"No, I think he'll be fine."

Now I wanted to see how she looked. She had turned to the side; her skin, under the light of the kitchen fixture, had fallen into a long unbecoming sag of flesh. I forced myself to keep looking.

"What are you thinking?" I asked.

She glanced at me, and shook her head. Her eyes moistened for a moment, but she quickly recovered, sat straight up and threw her head back.

"I feel like Aunt Rose and Uncle Al steamrollered us into something," I said.

"Oh? What?"

"Well, all this about the laundromat. Telling us how we're supposed to be doing this."

"Do you have any other ideas?"

I stared into the middle distance, shied away from what I wanted to say.

"Are you worried for him?" I asked.

"Your father? Of course." She smoothed out an invisible tablecloth on the formica table. I watched the way her hair swooped off her forehead, exactly as she'd worn it in their wedding pictures, twenty-five years ago.

"Dad's a survivor," I said, feeling stupid.

She stared at me, noting what I'd said as if puzzled.

"I just don't see him dying, Mom. I mean...Dad? You couldn't kill *Dad*."

The icy cast her features had taken on made me stop.

"Don't say that," she snapped.

She got up and went to the window, reached into the drawer for an apron, put it on and began washing the dishes I had already set out to dry.

"Mom, I washed those."

"You never do them clean enough."

I watched her from behind, the delicate movement of her neck. I let her finish; it seemed therapeutic. When she was done, she took off the apron and poured us tea. She stood over the cups, absorbed in the task, then turned and set them down on the table, still not looking at me.

"I should call your Uncle Billy in Philadelphia," she said.

My Uncle Billy, a saxophonist and vocalist with his own band, was my father's only sibling. He would be the one relative unlikely to find out on his own. He had broken away; alone of all the relatives, he had run from daily contact.

"Before you call Uncle Billy, Mom, I want to say something."

The light caught only half her face, casting the other half into shadow. I saw for the first time then that I did, in fact, possess the power to frighten her. Something in the knowledge, though, pushed me forward.

"I was thinking maybe you could do it."

She was looking at me, and her head moved, just a fraction of an inch.

"The laundromat," I said, to make it clear.

Her eyes shifted, as if she were looking inward. I was seeing her, suddenly, her hair, her body, as a thing of angles, a geometrical sphere hovering over the kitchen table, a set of impulses opposed to and conjoining mine. It frightened me, and I worked to blot this out. I searched for an emotional response to her the way you would work at a scabbed-over wound to elicit the pinpoint of fresh blood.

"Mom," I said, to call her back.

She finally sat down, and picked up her tea.

"Mom, I'm sorry. I want to go to school."

The silence was such that I felt the intrusion of electrical sounds—the hum of the washer downstairs—and outside, the clicking hysteria of crickets.

"Say something," I had to demand, finally. I was gazing down at the table, afraid to face her.

"Oh, I don't know enough about fixing those machines."

When I looked up, it was clear from her expression that she considered my request incidental. Wherever her thoughts had gone as they'd moved away from me, it had not been toward a deep consideration of my words. Perhaps she had been thinking of a way to smuggle my father's beloved peaches into his hospital room.

"You know as much as I do," I said, not expecting a response.

But now, to my surprise, she appeared to be mulling it over.

"How would I get there?" she asked.

She sipped her tea, her lips forming a long flute over the rim of the cup. Was there really no conspiracy to keep me here, trapped? Was it only a matter of convenience? The knowledge left me feeling simultaneously edgy, nosing out the suddenly available loopholes through which I might seek escape, and sorrowful: my mother, after all these years, still had no way of getting herself around.

"What if Aunt Rose drove you?" I asked.

"She might not want to."

"But if she did. Would you be willing?" I waited a moment. "Mom, this is my life. I will be behind, do you realize, for the rest of my life if I miss this semester?"

I flinched against the exaggeration, then tried to compose my face as if I honestly believed it. My mother looked at me. Suddenly we seemed no more than two children plotting in the father's absence.

"But what about your father in the hospital? I can't visit him and take care of the laundromat at the same time. And when he's home, he'll have to have someone to take care of him."

"You can hire Ray." Ray, a footloose French-Canadian, shuttled between my father's laundromat and Cousin Leo's car wash: summers at the car wash; winters— usually only the thickest, busiest times—assisting my father.

She nodded. I felt close, but didn't want to push.

"Ya, I guess we could do that."

She finished her tea before saying anything more.

"Ya, I guess you should go."

She looked at me a little sadly. I was her one child, after all, and the prospect of having me home for several months must have pleased her.

"I'll call Aunt Rose for you; we'll see if we can't set up a schedule of when she could drive you." I was aware of hurrying now, wanting to effect things. "Maybe we should call Ray tonight and see if he's available to relieve you. Will you get tired?"

I asked the question brusquely, alluding to some deep concern and fooling no one. I regretted it right away. It would have been better to be openly selfish.

We made the calls, though, together. My Aunt Rose, on the other end of the line, sounded suspicious. She talked fast, asking all the questions we had neglected to: what about emergencies? What about my mother's lunch? In the background I could hear Uncle Al shouting questions, then the silences after Aunt Rose turned to answer him. During the silences, their surroundings came forward: the smell of fried potatoes in their kitchen and the living-room atmosphere, thick with untouched framed photographs of the valued dead.

In the end, Aunt Rose agreed—"if that's what you want, Josie"—and my mother, after hesitating for one excruciating moment, answered "Ya."

We reached Ray in the rooming house where he lived. A woman answered the phone, asking "You want Ray?" too loud and over-insistently, as if she hadn't spoken to another human being in a long time and wasn't sure where to pitch her voice. Ray had been drinking, it was clear, but he was agreeable. He spoke to my mother in the deferential tones of a servant.

"Oh, I guess I could, Josie—if it's okay with your cousin, that is."

Ray's French-Canadian accent made his words come out like marbles spit from a full mouth. I listened in amazement at how well it was going.

"How's John there, Josie?" Ray asked.

My mother's voice caught, and for a second I thought it was over. But she was only catching her breath at the end of a long sigh, as if to act for Ray the depth of her grief.

When the call was over—we'd spoken on extensions in different rooms—we met in the hallway, at first in darkness, until my mother switched on a light.

"Well," she said, smiling up at me.

"Are you sure you can handle this, Mom?"

"Well, if I can't, you can come home on weekends, can't you?"

I felt my smile start to freeze, and it was as though the electrical hum around us climbed a notch higher.

"Sure," I answered.

But something new had entered my mind during my mother's conversation with Ray: I needed money. The parsimonious budget my father and I had worked out at the end of the summer (most of it my own summer earnings) had quickly proved insufficient, if I were to do anything but sit in my room and live on bread and water. With the issue of train trips home, the need would be even greater. Of course, the discussion could wait.

"Mom, can you write checks on Dad's account, or is it something he has to do himself?"

She was moving down the hall toward the kitchen.

"Oh, no," she said, her back to me, "you know Dad. He has his account and I can't touch it. He gives me money at the beginning of the week and that's it."

She set the cups and saucers we had used for the tea in the sink, and turned on the water.

"You'll have to ask Dad if you need money."

When we arrived at the hospital the next day, my father was waiting for us.

His head was propped on the pillow, and his face was expectant, livelier than it had been the day before. He looked at us as though we were a treat he'd been promised. I saw him then as infinitely younger than the serious, work-inured man I'd been lumbering beside for years.

My mother bent over and kissed him. I watched them in the light—his pale, scarred head and her made-up cheeks.

He reached for my hand and took it. By this time the deliciousness of our arrival had worn off; he seemed already tired by us. He looked down at my hand and saw the checkbook I was carrying. I hadn't actually decided whether to go ahead with my request, but the fact that I was carrying it now made its own point. In response to it, his eyebrows lifted, and the sides of his face twitched upward. He looked uncomfortable.

"Lemme have that," he said.

He began writing out a check. My heart quickened, in response to the shock of good news. Then he handed it to my mother.

"Take it to the bank, they'll cash it. It's made out to you."

My mother looked down at the check, made no response, pocketed it. I waited.

"What was that for?" I asked.

"Groceries," he said, wincing as, one hand behind him, he tried to sit up straighter.

"Leo says you shouldn't worry, John," my mother said, smoothing out the sheet beside him. She'd spoken to my father's cousin that morning on the phone.

He looked at her; his eyes formed wide circles. I could see, beneath his pupils, the pink lip of skin.

"He put a big sheet of plywood up over the window so it's all covered. Nick and I went this morning and emptied out the machines. We made twenty-seven dollars. That's good for one day, isn't it?"

"Business was slow yesterday," my father said. I watched him digging back, recovering his life before the blast.

"So you see," my mother said, "we've got everything under control."

He looked up at her, his face elongated by the wish to believe this was really so.

"Nick's going to school tomorrow," she said cheerfully.

I knew instantly this was the wrong time to have said it, catching him unprepared. As he looked at me, a mixture of fear and disbelief dissolved over his features.

"Dad," I said, and turned away to look at my mother. It seemed everything was speeded up, starting to happen too fast. Something on his night table was dropped. The sound came up abnormally loud. I had an impulse to call a nurse.

Then things settled. I realized nothing had happened. I wasn't going to be grabbed or hit. They were sitting there, my parents, in quiet consideration of a new and difficult reality. My father stared into the space between us. Once I'd seen him cry, at his stepfather's funeral, but never again.

"I'm sorry," I said, looking at the bedclothes, the bedpan, the half-finished glass of orange drink with a bitten-down pink straw at my father's bedside.

"That's why you're hiring Ray," he said, looking at my mother. I realized he was having trouble looking at me; that was the extent of his chastisement.

"Leo told you?" she asked.

He nodded. "He was here this morning."

Finally he looked up at me. His eyes were red-rimmed, and he was looking at me in a way I hadn't seen him do before: there was a kind of defeat in this look, a lack of shame at the need displayed.

"You think your mother can handle it?" he asked.

I looked down, at the place on the floor where the edge of the metal side table reached the tiles.

"I think so. I showed her this morning how to unload the money from the machines. That was all she didn't know, really." Then, after a moment, I continued: "I think if she doesn't get tired, she'll be all right."

"You do, huh?"

I was afraid to look at him. When I did, though, I saw his gaze had turned inward, as if he were slowly working out in his head the long-range effects of some impulsive purchase.

"With Ray's help," my mother said, reaching for the orange drink and holding the straw up to his lips. "You want some?"

He shook his head. "No, it's too pulpy."

My mother sipped at the orange drink. "They must squeeze it fresh, hon. It's better for you that way."

A little later the nurse came by with the sheet on which my father was to make his selections for meals for the next few days. My mother took the menu and recited each of the choices with relish, stopping just short of smacking her lips: breaded pork chops or broiled haddock, Salisbury steak or spaghetti marinara. I listened to my father repeat his selections in a dry voice.

When that was finished, I went ahead and mentioned the additional money I would need. I didn't intend to leave until the next day, but my father insisted on taking care of business now. He wrote a check quickly, firmly. His hand didn't shake.

For the last half hour of our visit, we watched *The Match Game*. There were no regular television sets in Intensive Care, but my father had agreed to pay to have one brought in. The nurses told him that as long as he watched it quietly, and none of the other patients complained, it would be all right.

Aunt Rose drove us into South Station the following night.

I'd spent the day with my mother in the laundromat, making sure she knew the ropes. She did, she was mostly fine, but it had been depressing having to stand over her watching her neck strain as she tried to fit the key into the coin-changing machine, or get it at the right angle so that the tricky coin slots under the washers could be emptied.

In the big vaulted station there was only one newspaper stand open, selling girlie magazines and gum and candy beside the stacks of *Globes* and *Herald Americans*. We were a half-hour early for the seven-o'clock train. The only other people waiting were a soldier in a green coat, leaning against a wall, smoking a cigarette, and a girl sitting with her mother and father and a smaller girl, her little sister. The smaller girl was misbehaving; her father's shouts at her echoed in the vast hall. Between the shouts, I heard the click! our shoes made on the floor as the three of us crossed the station.

We sat on a bench behind the other family. The girls' mother turned to look at us, made a quick, uncertain assessment, then turned away.

"Nobody comes here anymore," Rose said. "They all fly."

I nodded, looked at the floor; she said this every time we came here.

"Are you going to buy a ticket, Nick?" my mother asked.

"There's time," I said.

"There might be a line later on." Rose was looking toward the ticket windows on the other end of the hall.

"Oh, sure," I answered, and heard the man behind me, enunciating every syllable slowly, say, "Shut up and wait till your sister gets on the train."

The little girl whined, and there followed a slap. She was crying as I moved toward the ticket counter.

The clerk took a full minute before looking up from his open file and stepping toward me at the window.

"Help you?" he asked.

"One way to New York."

He punched out the ticket. I handed him ten dollars and received a dime in change.

On my way back to the bench I passed the empty arcade windows labeled "HABERDASHERY," "LUGGAGE—SUITCASES" and the pole of an abandoned barbershop. An enclave labeled "SHOESHINE" was lit and appeared to be open, though with no attendant in sight. I wondered who would ever be found in this place for whom a shoeshine might make a difference. On the bench, my mother was watching me, smiling, while my aunt stared suspiciously at the empty shopfronts.

I was close enough then to see that my mother was having a conversation, her head half-turned, with the little girl's father.

"He's going to New York," I heard her say.

"Oh, yeah?" The man looked at me, only half-seeing me; there were dark pockets under his eyes and large flakes of dandruff coasting on the surface of his thick black hair.

"She goes to Providence," he said, nodding toward his elder daughter. "Rhode Island School of Design. We could drive her down there—takes an hour, hour and a quarter—but she says no, she wants to take the train."

The girl, who looked to be about my age, paid no attention to her father. She adjusted the straps on her leather suitcase. Her hair was as thick as her father's, but curly, and parted in the center. An Italian girl. I couldn't see her face.

"Will you come home soon?" my mother asked me.

"Yes. Soon," I said.

"The dorms are open so late at night?" Aunt Rose asked. "You get in, what, eleven at night? How will you get up to the Bronx?"

"I'll take a cab, Aunt Rose," I said, though I knew I'd be taking the subway.

"You're sure it's safe?" my mother asked.

"It's safe." I lifted my suitcase and moved it an inch or two.

"You know I worry," my mother said, and brushed the knee of my dungarees.

At seven o'clock exactly the gate was opened. I hugged both of them and moved off in the direction of the small crowd that had gathered. When I turned back, I saw my mother and Aunt Rose standing in the arched frame of the gate; Rose seemed to be hesitating as to how far she was allowed to step beyond the waiting area. She looked cautiously around her, as if at any moment some official would come along and brutally notify her of her territorial rights. Beside her, my mother stood absolutely still, watching me.

Only one car was open to us on the train. The Italian girl's parents came aboard with her. Her father hefted her suitcase onto the luggage rack; when he lowered his arms, his face shone darkly with sweat, and one of the buttons of his shirt had come undone. The girl, as soon as she was seated, kept her focus away from them, staring instead out the window. When they had left, she took a piece of purple cloth out of her shoulder bag and tied it around her head, bandanna-style.

There was one latecomer.

Just before the train started, a young man came running up alongside it, a thin lock of black hair flapping against his neck and shoulders. He carried a guitar, which bumped against the sides of the seats as he moved up the aisle, finally deciding on a seat across from the Italian girl. He looked at the girl and, raising his eyebrows, said, "Almost didn't make it." He sounded as though he were trying very hard to make his voice resemble Peter Fonda's in *Easy Rider.*

The girl turned to him and smiled. The train began its slow movement. On the platform, the girl's father waited, his hands stuffed into the pockets of his black pants.

In the early stages of the journey, bits of conversation these two were having reached me in the place where I was sitting two rows behind them. I tried not to listen, but it was unavoidable. Just outside Providence, the boy took down his guitar and began strumming. He looked down to where I was sitting and asked, "Anybody mind?" It took me a moment to respond. When I finally shook my head, he looked at me with the mildest curiosity, then turned back to the girl as if they were in cahoots on some secret plan. She hadn't gotten off in Providence. She had lied to her parents, and had no intention of returning to the Rhode Island School of Design.

The boy began playing a song. The lyrics to it were:

> *You have shown me how to live again*
> *But more than this*
> *I can love again*

repeated over and over. The girl closed her eyes as she listened. The boy wore a Jethro Tull T-shirt, and when he sang the bones of his skull came forward.

There was a lot of smoke in the car by the time we reached New Haven, so when we stopped to change engines, I got off and sat on a bench. I watched, from outside, the boy put down his guitar and get up to stretch. The girl looked outside, glancing at me for a second before taking the guitar herself and beginning to play. Her chin moved as she sang, and her eyes were closed. My palms were wet now; I lifted them off my thighs and tried to look away. It was late. New Haven was silent, except for a dull rumbling.

I got back on the train and took down my suitcase. My

heart was pounding because I thought they were looking at me, and I knew my behavior must look questionable.

Then I was on the bench again, with all my things, and the train was moving out of the station. When it was gone, and I experienced that terrible moment when I didn't know anymore why I had done this, I thought: it was because I didn't want to hear that boy's song anymore; I couldn't stand hearing it another second.

Then I waited for the next train, the one that would take me back to Boston, to my parents' laundromat.

D

ear Nickie,

I have had my scrotum licked.

Before you fall over dead at the news, let me inform
you that the perpetrator was picked up at a dance where
all the girls were so Catholic that I despaired of even
getting my tongue into one of their hot little mouths
without promising I would accompany her to
Communion the next morning. The girl in question is
named Mary Ellen and possesses the kind of ass you'd
expect to find under a nun's habit, two raisins joined
together at the top. That she went down at all was a
surprise but when she went so far as to attack this tender
and previously uncharted part of me I thought of Nickie
and asked: I wonder if this would fit his definition of
mature love?

Mexico seems a blur now. I thought the experience had
changed me a lot, but now I guess it really didn't. The
same old shit goes on here, and I respond to it in the
same basic ways. Still go to dances to pick up girls.
Nothing spiritual about what happens then or afterwards.
Still enjoy it with the sort of piggish verve I find it hard
to feel guilty about. If I was obnoxious to you those first
couple of weeks back, it was because I was afraid of being
tainted by rubbing too close to someone who hadn't been
to Mexico. Afraid of losing my spiritual gloss. Now I

wouldn't mind having someone in this depressing empty bed across from me, even if it was your own sorry, guilt-obsessed self (actually, I had some fun imagining you with Mary Ellen, I thought what you'd probably do was apologize for *having* a scrotum, then accompany the girl to Confession).

That's all. Nothing else new. Steinegger still insists the war would be over in five minutes if you bombed the rice paddies. We are all too listless to argue. Hurry back.

Your pal,
T. *Bevilacqua*

I put the letter down and looked above the counter where I'd been reading it to the image of my father's cousin Leo, who was sitting on the vinyl bench with an open cup of take-out coffee and a lemon Danish laid out on the table in front of him.

He looked up at me, and lifting the coffee to his lips, asked, "What's it say?"

"College news," I answered.

He slurped the coffee, his maniacal gold-veined eyes wide open, as if expecting that I would go ahead and tell him the news conveyed by Tommy Bevilacqua.

As soon as he had turned away, I actually offered, "He had his scrotum licked," but low enough so that I was sure he wouldn't hear.

Since I'd taken over a month ago, Leo had been coming in nearly every day, having his informal "coffee break" in front of me, but never offering so much as a bite of his Danish. This morning he'd been to visit my parents—my father had been taken home three days ago—and had brought me the letter.

"How was business last week?" he shouted.

"Fine."

"Tell me in specifics!" He had the crust of the Danish

in his mouth now; some of the yellow filling spilled over and landed on his pants.

"Son of a bitch," he said lightly, dabbing at it with a napkin.

"What do you want? The figures?" I asked.

He nodded. "The figures."

"We did two hundred ninety-seven last week."

I thought of Tommy Bevilacqua as I said it, the girl perched between his knees. The figure coming out of my mouth sounded ludicrous, unworthy of human concern.

"Beautiful," Leo said.

"What beautiful? We were doing twice that before the explosion."

He turned to me as if assessing my face, its relative merits.

"I know that, Nickie. I know that. But you don't understand. A thing like this, it can scare people away so they don't come back. That you're getting half you should see as a triumph."

I didn't see it as a triumph; I had watched our customers as they entered the store, the women in hairnets and rollers, children racing for the gum machines, the suspicious looks around, and then the question, "Is this the place that blew up?" or, from the more knowing, "How's your father?" They were in and out quickly, victims of necessity.

"What time did your father say he's coming in?" Leo asked, polishing off the last of his Danish.

"Sometime this afternoon." Aunt Rose had agreed to drive him in, his first survey of the store since he'd come home. They had called, a half-hour before, to tell me.

Leo balled up the paper that had wrapped his Danish, inserted it into the coffee bag, and then lobbed the whole thing into a trash receptacle, in a womanish imitation of a basketball player, one leg kicked up from behind. He looked at me and winked, took out a cigar and bit off the end of it.

"Business is beautiful," he said, looking around. There was one woman, in the back of the store, folding sheets. Otherwise the place was empty.

"You play ball out there at school?"

"No," I answered.

"Why not? You're big enough." He looked at my body as if he were examining one of the cars that had just come through his car wash, for signs that his trusted system had failed.

"Hardly anybody plays ball anymore, Leo," I said.

"Come on, what are you talkin'? The Fordham Seven? What do they call them? The Seven Blocks of Granite? You're tellin' me that's all dead?"

He lit his cigar and picked up an ashtray delicately, holding it under the cigar. He had the capacity to make me nostalgic for even the least savory of my college friends.

"All dead," I said.

"A shame," he answered, and clucked his tongue. The look he gave me was one of unveiled disappointment. Then he turned quickly, gracefully on his heel and went over to the detergent dispenser, above which there was a mirror.

In it, he patted down what little hair he still had. I remembered him behind the big organ of the roller-skating rink, the first business he had built on this plot of land, now a full-scale shopping center, which had once been his father's farm. Big and florid behind the multi-colored organ, Leo had beat out jazzy versions of "Tea for Two" and "Mala Femina." He was a bachelor, then and now.

"Who you making yourself look nice for, Leo?" I called across the floor.

He turned to me and lifted his eyebrows.

"You don't let your father work, you hear me? He comes in this afternoon, keep him down, he needs the rest."

He pointed one finger at me—with the hand that was still holding the cigar—and kept it pointed, his lifted eyebrows working a promise out of me while his cigar dripped a trail of ash on his way out the door.

Tommy Bevilacqua was getting his scrotum licked, and I was cleaning machines. People were dirty and careless; spilled bleach stuck in clumps to the white metallic finish of the washers. In a room two hundred miles away I imagined Mrs. Branner finishing a lecture. I thought of the seat I'd occupied, and though it seemed the unlikeliest of possibilities, I imagined the form reaching her, the announcement that I'd withdrawn, and her experiencing a brief pang of loss.

But who was I kidding? Quickly, I grabbed the *Ladies' Home Journal* I'd been glancing at during odd moments of the day, and took it with me into the bathroom. It was dated August 1965: five years old, but no matter. This was the general level of currency of our reading material, all donated. I'd been perusing an article called "My Life with Paul Anka," featuring a photo layout of the former Anne De Zhugeb, now the singer's wife. I loosened my pants and propped the magazine up over the sink so that it was open to one particular photograph. Mrs. Paul Anka, blond and wholesome, was not the type of woman I was normally attracted to, but for the moment she would do. She was perched on the edge of a beige couch, and her breasts looked enormous. I ignored the image of her smiling husband seated below her, a proprietary hand just touching her back.

I was looking forward to release, was in fact seconds from it, when I heard the voice of Aunt Rose, as if approaching from the end of a long tunnel. "Nickie?" she called.

"Jesus," I said, my hands going aloft. I heard my aunt's footsteps approaching.

She banged on the door. Somehow I'd known she would.

"Nickie? You in there?"

"Yes, I am. Aunt Rose, *please.*" I could hear the catch in my voice; too high: it revealed, I was sure, everything.

"Your parents are here," she said.

I could sense her waiting, a foot or so from the door. My penis made a slow, chagrined descent; I flushed the toilet to make a pretense of having been in there on official business. When I opened the door to leave, my aunt glanced down at the magazine folded under my arm— slyly, I thought.

"There they are," she pointed.

I saw my parents walking on the thin, hot strip of sidewalk leading from where my aunt's car was parked in front of the Mr. Donut to the clear glass doors of the laundromat. My father looked thin and tall beside my mother; he wore a light green shirt and chino pants, and the colors enhanced his paleness, the sense he gave of being a step beyond the warp and woof of shopping-center life. My mother, escorting him with one arm held under his, smiled and looked around as though at a waiting audience.

Beside me, Aunt Rose's face was tense, as if she were taking every step alongside him.

"Help him, Nick," she said.

I held the door open for him. He smiled vaguely at this, a response that seemed too formal. My mother waved at Felder, next door. I turned and saw that Felder was involved with a customer and hadn't noticed her.

They moved past me, and Rose put down her bag and helped to seat my father on the bench.

"You ought to get him a cane, Josie. They have nice ones now," Rose said.

My mother smiled at her; I sensed something going on under her response, some hidden communication between them.

"Not like Pa," Rose said.

Between them, my father looked exhausted by the effort of getting from car to bench. I saw that he was noticing nothing, unusual for him.

"The place looks clean, John," my mother said, and he snapped out of his trance, looking around now with quickened eyes. His gaze fixed on the empty slots where the dry cleaners had been, and he nodded.

"You're early," I said.

"We thought we'd take you out for lunch," my mother said. "You haven't eaten yet, have you?"

I thought of lying. Watching my father eat—his new slowness, the deliberateness of his chewing—had become difficult.

"No, I haven't," I said.

"We should get something and bring it here," Rose said. "I think John's too tired to go anywhere, Josie."

My mother touched my father's arm. "What do you think, John?"

My father looked down at the table.

"We'll stay here," she said.

I was elected to go to the clam bar and pick up lunch. Then Rose and I emptied the table of magazines and laid out the banquet, while my mother attended to a customer in the back. Between us, my father sat stiffly, attuned to the conversation my mother held with the customer, as if at any moment he might be called into service.

I handed him his clam roll.

"Go ahead and eat, Dad."

He just stared at the toasted roll.

"Or do you want to wait for Mom?"

He nodded.

"Can I put some tartar sauce on it for you?"

"Let him put some tartar sauce on for you, John," my aunt cut in, anxiously sitting forward, her hands in her lap, over her plate of fried shrimp.

"Yeah, throw some on there," my father said.

My mother returned to us, wearing an apron she'd put on to protect her dress from the emissions of the machines. "Lunch ready?" she asked pleasantly. How easy it was for her to move from one thing to the next! To go from work to this private ritual, which in her mind was not private at all. She kept the apron on while she ate, and if a customer were to come along with some bothersome request, I knew she'd have no trouble interrupting her meal. She'd get up and do it with a smile.

"Easy, hon," she said, wiping away some of the tartar sauce that had spilled onto my father's chin as a result of his eagerness to eat.

He nodded, contrite. Later, I saw him staring again at the gutted area where the machines had been.

"Are you going to replace them?" I asked.

"Yeah," he answered, plowing once more into the clam roll, his face lost there.

In a few minutes I got up and excused myself, went to the back of the store and locked myself in the bathroom. I'd been overwhelmed by their silence, the three of them just sitting there, eating.

In a little while I heard my mother's voice lifted in a kind of singsong manner, in conversation with a customer, not far from the bathroom door.

Between the repeated "Ya's" I thought I detected a few "he's," and piecing words together, I realized she was not talking about my father. "He's here every day," I heard, and "He'll go back to school when his father's well." Then an oddly pitched, tantalizing, "Does he to you?"

I put my ear to the door and listened harder, until I recognized the crackling, Boston-Irish voice of our customer, Mrs. Orr, and saw in my mind the ancient redveined face which had always reminded me of an old municipal pool left drained and untended for too many hot summers. Mrs. Orr had evidently said something that caused my mother's voice to ring with false concern. Though I couldn't see her, I knew my mother's head would be tipped to the side, taking in whatever Mrs. Orr said as though it were a recipe she would try this very night.

I opened the door just enough so that I could see them: Mrs. Orr with three shopping carts loaded up, my mother with her back to me, her head cocked. Mrs. Orr's eyes bugged out of her long, gourdlike face as she spoke, her neglected choppers flashing gold and silver. When she saw me, she threw me a shy smile. It made me think of her sons—big, strapping brutes, the eldest a couple of

years older than me, the youngest a toddler of five. Her
white hair was caught up today in an orange kerchief.

"There he is," she said, and my mother turned.

I knew now I'd been tattled on: this old woman standing behind my mother gloated as if she'd witnessed some
horrible act of mine and now had the satisfaction of re-
porting it. My mother's face as she regarded me was
deeply lined, her mouth slanted.

It was only a moment before she said, "Mrs. Orr thinks
you're depressed."

The announcement made Mrs. Orr's face visibly
brighten: the whiskey patches on her cheeks and nose
glowed.

"The customers don't like it," Mrs. Orr snipped. The
responsibility in speaking on behalf of "the customers"
made her roll up higher on the balls of her feet. I had
never hated a human being more in my life.

My father was at the end of a long line of dryers now,
his hands in his pockets, looking as though lunch had
given him some strength. A midday shadow cut across
the pale sculpted marble of his head.

"I'm not depressed," I said.

My mother stared at me as if the words were deflected
off some shield she wore.

I went and picked up a wet rag. I scrubbed along the
tops of the machines, working at chips of dried bleach. I
was aware of them watching me. At one point I turned
and saw them all, worried looks on their faces.

"I'm not depressed, all right?" Still nothing. "Look,
you're all fine here." I threw down the rag. "I just need to
go out for a walk, all right?"

And throwing my hands in my pockets, I left them,
ducking out the back way, so as not to make a scene.

At five o'clock on the nose, my uncle Al's Plymouth
pulled into the parking lot, and Uncle Al eased himself
onto the pavement. He looked through the glass doors at

me and, mopping his brow, made a big, floppy waving movement with his hand, smiling as though he hadn't seen me in a long time.

"Hot as a bitch," he said, entering the somewhat cooler store. He was wearing his gray work clothes, the name "Al" stitched in red over his left shirt pocket. His work was soldering parts in a defense plant ten or so miles away.

A few customers dotted the long space given over to a folding table in the center of the laundromat. Women. Uncle Al surveyed the sparse crowd. "Busy, huh?" he asked, not waiting for a response. Something was on his mind.

"What are you doing here, Uncle Al?" I asked.

"I came to see you, Nick," he said, then sat down. Immediately, though, he edged forward and his hands went out.

"What do you want, Nick? You want a cup of coffee? A doughnut, one of them curlicues?"

I knew he hadn't meant to say "curlicues." He looked confused for a moment after he said it.

"No. No, thanks, Uncle Al."

"What, you must want somethin'. A Coke?"

His chin went forward anxiously; he looked far more pleased by the word "Coke" than he'd been by "curlicue," but I knew that neither of these words connected, for the moment, with real things; both were abstractions, "treats."

"No, thanks."

I sat there, waiting for an explanation.

"Did you eat yet?" he asked.

I shook my head. Normally, I left the laundromat empty between five thirty and six thirty, to go home and eat with my parents, then returned here for the night shift.

"Well, what do you say we go out, have a pizza?" Al asked.

I looked at him. I thought he probably wanted to go home, have a beer and watch the news, or putter in his yard. Obviously they'd called him, told him I was "depressed," asked him to come and cheer me up. I hadn't said anything this afternoon after Mrs. Orr's accusation, and they had, wisely, dropped it. But here was subterfuge. My Uncle Al, of all people, with offers of "treats."

"Not pizza," I answered, scowling. I felt suddenly perverse enough to go along, to see what he would do to try and upgrade the quality of my life.

"What, then? You name it."

"Let's go to a restaurant. Let's have a meal. Someplace where we can get a beer, all right?"

He was taken aback. His upper lip curled slightly, the smile gone awry.

"You're not twenty-one, Nick."

"Yeah, but I'm with you."

I could see the idea coalescing for him: uncle—nephew, boy's night out. He was a little uncertain of it, but he nodded and laughed, as if just getting a joke.

"You're with me. That's right, you're with me."

I was eager to see what his idea of a restaurant would be. When he drove us down to the end of the parking lot and parked in front of the bowling alley, I thought it was to go inside and cash a check. He gestured, though, for me to get out.

"Here?" I asked.

"Sure." I watched him, from behind, walking up to the swinging doors. He looked huge-assed, pachydermous. "They serve."

There was a counter that ran, U-shaped, along one-half of the bowling alley on the ground floor. This, as well as the lanes themselves, and the roller rink and miniature golf connected to it, belonged to Cousin Leo.

Inside, I expected to see relatives, big-bodied second cousins with slicked black pompadours whose names were like watercolors sliding one into the next: Tommy, Louie, Joey, Fred. Instead, I saw strangers ringed around the horseshoe counter, hunched over the plastic mustard and ketchup dispensers, eating to the rhythmic swish and crack of bowling balls.

"Give us a beer," Al shouted to the redhead behind the counter. She glanced up at us.

"How old is he?" she asked, gesturing toward me.

"He's old enough. This is Leo Battaglia's cousin. This is John Battaglia's son you're lookin' at here. What do you like—Budweiser, Pabst?" He hit me on the shoulder.

I loved the choice: Budweiser, Pabst. For the sound of the word, I said, "Pabst."

"I'll tell you what," the waitress said. "You show me his I.D., he can have a Pabst. Otherwise, you can have a Pabst and if he takes a sip, I didn't see it, all right?"

My uncle nodded, clearly thinking this was a delightful woman.

"Two glasses!" he shouted, as she moved away.

"What are you gonna have, Nickie?" Al picked up the huge red menus and placed them, open, in front of us. I looked up and down the rows of Cheeseburger Specials, then at the "Fish 'n Chips," the "Spaghetti w. Meat Sauce" and the out-of-place "Greek Specialties."

"Anything," Al said expansively. "Whatever you want, you get."

He took his glasses out of his shirt pocket. He'd been consulting the menu for a time without them. I wondered what added delights he thought he'd find with the assistance of the thick lenses.

"This looks good," he said, pointing to the "Pork Chops Pizzaiola." "Your cousin Leo makes sure they do it good, I bet."

He closed the menu with a snap, placed his hand over it. The waitress was in front of us.

"What does Leo eat when he's in here?" Uncle Al asked.

"Who?" the waitress returned.

"Leo Battaglia, the guy who owns this place."

"He don't eat here," she said, and turned her head slightly to the side.

Uncle Al looked crushed.

"They use real Italian plum tomatoes in the kitchen? Progresso? They use good olive oil?"

"Look, I don't know what they use. You want to ask the chef? You want another beer?"

"The pork chops come from his cousin Tony's store on River Street?" My uncle fidgeted.

"I don't know," the waitress said, giving up, going away.

"What kind of an operation does Leo run here, anyway?" Al said quietly, as if to himself.

We finally ordered cheeseburgers, and ate them without saying much. Every once in a while Al would turn to me and smile brightly. When the check came, he folded it in two and, placing it square against his water glass, asked: "So Nickie, you seeing anybody?"

"Seeing?" I asked, playing dumb. Say *fucking, dorking,* I thought. I wanted to know his terminology. Once I'd heard his wife refer to it as "doing his business."

"You know," he said. "Going out with a girl."

"No." I shook my head. We both seemed embarrassed by the admission. He turned his water glass in a semi-circle.

"You know," he said, "I think about these guys who go up into space. They want to go up for long periods now." He lifted his hand, made a small, delicate gesture, like letting a bird go. "Weeks, they're talkin'."

He cocked his head, splayed his fingers. "They can take care of food, they got some way of takin' care of air, and sleep." He was counting these off on his fingers. "But sex, this I can't figure out what they do about."

My face had become a little hot, and my arms started to tense; where was this conversation going to lead?

Uncle Al's head went down. If he were to ask me to go to a whorehouse with him, I'd have to turn him down. But what then? Would he report it to my parents? Would they begin a subscription to *Playboy* for me?

"Anyway," he said, "I can't figure it."

Outside, the subject of sex seemed to have come and gone as quickly as the idea to see a movie that had left town a week ago. Al stopped in front of his car, seemed to have run out of steam. We had a half-hour to go before the dinner break was over, and I knew Al's fine-honed sense of duty would keep him with me for the entire time.

"Hey," he said with a visible start, "what about a game of miniature golf, Nickie? We got time?" He consulted his watch, though I was sure he'd made up his mind. "Sure, we got time."

He started off, not waiting for my approval, in the direction of the miniature-golf course.

Above him, I watched the way the red and green lights of the roller rink illuminated the night sky. At the edge of the parking lot, the white silhouette of a female bowler moved in neon to the point where she let go of the ball, then returned to her original position. I thought of how I garrisoned myself behind a closed door in the laundromat each evening, poring incessantly over the old magazines, the Times and Ladies' Home Journals, collecting the detritus of the past several years—the births of Andy Williams' children, the menu at Luci Baines Johnson's wedding reception. Out here, just a step or two beyond the door, there was a crazy kind of beauty, at least at night. Uncle Al knew how to appreciate it: he moved down the sidewalk like a ticket-of-leave man, sampling treats as though he'd been denied them a long time. I came to wonder if he'd even been forced into this at all, had instead chosen me as the object of his temporary release.

Al beamed as we chose clubs. Above us were windmills, castles; a massive water wheel hovered over a simulated brook. In some aberrant moment, Leo had decided to call this course "Journey's End."

Al just missed a hole-in-one on the first green. I watched him waddling up to where the ball was, to tap it in, his look of pleasure. He had forgotten all about sex, but now I found I couldn't get it off my mind. My shot fell way off, hit the backboard and returned halfway to me.

He laughed. "Nickie, what are you doing?"

After three shots, I managed to get it in. He clapped me

on the back. "You'll improve," he said.

Then, as I watched him move off to the next green, it occurred to me: Al had been somewhere I hadn't. A kind of irrational jealousy flared up.

What was it like, I wanted to ask, that first time with Aunt Rose, the opening of those long-guarded thighs? We were standing beside a small bridge now; a tiny stream rippled through it, the metal that served as its bed rusting, the water slightly orange. If I were to ask, what would he say? Instead, I turned my energies to trying to beat him, but the tension made me miss even simple shots. Al was enjoying himself. I would watch his forehead curl as he planned a shot. Conversation dwindled to nothing. At the seventh hole, he was beating me by six points.

Once, near the end, I watched him reach down and scratch his genitals, then sway backwards, reasserting his position. I remembered in what pristine terms his and Rose's condition had been referred to through the years: "They can't have children." As if permission had to be asked, a license acquired. "They are unable to": this was never said, the deficiency never alluded to, exactly. That there was something wrong with them was unthinkable.

He looked at me, staring down at him. I wondered if he could possibly imagine the interest I took in his inner life, the very relationship he might have developed with those malfunctioning genitals a story I'd have eagerly listened to. It could never be discussed, though. It was not only that there was a built-in code prohibiting such discussions; even if we could somehow break down the code, what language would there be for us to use? I tried concentrating harder on the game, but it was no good. He was nine points up when we returned the clubs. He asked me if I wanted another game, but I said I thought it was time to get back.

He wasn't quite ready to leave me yet.

When we got back to the laundromat, he disappeared for a moment, then returned with a pair of the big, sugar-glazed apple rings from Mr. Donut. He dug into his pants for change, plugged two quarters into our soft-drink machine and carried a pair of Cokes under one arm, grinning. "Dessert," he said.

We sat down in front of the low table; he opened the Cokes and set them down in front of us. I thought of the barometer in his head, the amount of "fun" he had promised to give Nickie, the needle rising now at the thought of the apple rings, the Cokes. I hadn't gotten much more than a sip of his Pabst in the restaurant; he must have thought better of the idea of getting his nephew drunk. The whole incident in the restaurant, in fact, once he'd found out that Leo didn't stand over the cook with a monocle, supervising his every move, had been tinged with the sense that he'd been unpleasantly duped. He was more comfortable now, with these small treasures, asking me to indulge. I wanted to oblige him, but the sugar coating on the outside of the apple rings was cloying, and I ate only half.

"What's the matter with that?" he asked, his mouth full.

"Too sweet," I answered.

He picked it up, examining it like a beloved object, an artifact of his world that I had just pointed out had a tiny crack in it.

Then he finished it for me, as I'd expected he would.

When I got home that night, the lights were still on in the house, blazing from rooms where, at this time of night, their usage could only mean company. There was a strange car parked in our driveway, a flaming-orange Chevy, and beside it, my Aunt Rose's Rambler.

I could hear them upstairs in the kitchen after I'd entered through the garage door. Their voices were not identifiable. I panicked a moment, thinking this might be yet another plan to cheer me up, Mrs. Orr and her sons ringed around our kitchen table with tankards of ale in their hands, invited here to teach me something of the Lusty Approach to Life.

I thought of hiding in my mother's sewing room, since

it was possible they hadn't heard me come in. But what was this constant necessity to hide? Wasn't this my house too? Maybe I could just slip by, offer a feeble greeting and then excuse myself.

The woman whose face I saw in the light of the dining room was not familiar to me: under red hair, cropped short, she had the sort of face I'd expect to see on a box of cookies, the Keebler elf as housewife. There was something shrewd about her face, too, the modern, overlarge glasses perched over a puckish nose: nobody's fool. A small roar went up at the dining-room table when they realized I'd arrived. My father pushed back his chair and lifted his arm: "Here he is." His voice seemed to have more strength in it now than it had had this afternoon. Company had made him lively.

My aunt and mother, on discovering me, had let out sounds that were nothing more or less than squawks: in isolation, they would have caused everyone to turn and stare at them. Next to the redheaded woman, a dark-haired girl looked up at me with an expression of intense melancholy.

"You remember Viola!" my mother half-shouted, standing up. "Viola," the name, came down to me through a long spread of names, my mother's friends and cousins, dating back to childhood. "Viola" was a name, spoken into a phone in another room, while I toyed with some jack, or coped with the boredom of being an only child whose mother is busy.

I nodded. Beside Viola, the girl looked down at a half-empty cup, lifted it so that the liquid swirled from side to side. My mother was already in the kitchen, pouring me coffee.

"Sit down, have some cake," she said.

"This is my daughter, Nicholas," Viola said. The girl was looking down at the table.

"Oh, ya." My mother blushed. "I'm sorry, dear," she said, turning to the girl. "This is Julie."

Julie smiled up at me then as though the melancholy I'd been aware of up to that time was only a shyness she retreated into while waiting for acknowledgment.

"Hello," I said. The sudden flash of teeth made her seem anxious. Other than that, she was an extraordinary-looking girl. I was surprised to find her here, in this dining room, in this house, not one noted for the array of beauties that had passed through it.

"There's nothin' at all wrong with your father, Nicholas," Viola said, talking too fast, as though her words were a load of just-bought articles she was stacking, quickly, on a shelf. "He's been tellin' us jokes, stories of the old country, makin' us pee in our pants, huh, Josie?"

"For instance," my father began, throwing his head back, "there was the lady from Ulishu."

Viola didn't wait for any punch line before she started to laugh. My father hunched forward, his hands planted on the table.

> "The Lady from Uleeshe,
> Whene'er she had to peeshe ..."

The cackle that rose up from the table was overwhelming. It gave my father a wide berth to finish, in Italian, his rhymed tale, one I had never heard before, of a woman whose skirts were so enormous that even when caught outside, she was never in need of the privacy of a ladies' room.

"Oh, John," Viola said from time to time during the story.

I thought of my father in the hospital: his ash-white face staring up at the ceiling. All the doctors had needed to do was bring in a roomful of women to tell what he called "off-color" stories to. He was in his element now. I thought of the way the house usually was at night, the small pockets of light, the absence of laughter, my father's severity as he went about the business of watching television.

When he finished, Viola said, "Where do you get them, John?"

My father leaned back, his mouth forming a comical

"O." He tapped his fingers on the table, and raised his eyebrows. This too worked a laugh out of Viola. His skittishness seemed a part of an ongoing character he'd worked out years before. It was like looking at a picture of him in one of those wide-cut, big-shouldered suits he'd sported in the forties.

"What a character," Viola said. "You must have had the nurses in stitches."

I watched Julie laugh politely, as though she knew there were undercurrents to this humor going back years, to dances at the Sons of Italy Hall, cookouts at Lynn and Nantasket, that she could not possibly be expected to get.

Coffee and cake had been placed in front of me. I was sitting across from Julie watching the slant of her chin as she watched my father.

Viola turned to me, too quickly. "They got you at the laundromat, huh?" I nodded, surprised at being addressed. The change of topic brought a silence to the table. I wanted to dismiss my state of being as a subject of concern. I wanted, instead, to listen to my father's jokes.

"So, what are you, gonna transfer to some school around here?" I couldn't quite shake the sense that Viola was measuring me, as if to classify me and place me in a file of recipes she kept constantly updated: was I appetizer or main course?

"No, I'll go back to school when Dad's well."

"Where, in New York?" she half-shouted. I was used by now to having conversations with relatives who never quite found a comfortable pitch.

"Yes," I answered.

Julie looked at me, her eyes widening slightly before her head dipped down and her view shifted away. I watched her finger toy with the red-rose emblem on the label of a discarded tea bag.

"I hear it's dangerous there." Again, Viola was shouting: did she think I was deaf?

"Oh, he gets mugged every day going to and from class," my father said. Viola's laugh this time was staccato, a mere allusion to laughter.

"Julie's boyfriend died," Aunt Rose said, breaking into Viola's laughter, as she dipped a Stella D'Oro biscuit into her tea. She stared down the table at me: you see, you think life is all fun, all jokes? It had become, apparently, Rose's personal crusade to re-educate me, lest my evening with Uncle Al had left me with too rosy a view of the prospectus.

"What?" I asked, looking at the girl whose fingernail had now broken through the wet tea bag, freeing the tiny drowned bits of leaves, a few of them sticking to her violet nails.

"A car accident," Viola broke in. "They were engaged. Up in New Hampshire."

I heard my mother draw a long breath, her expression of sympathy. Viola's features seemed to retreat behind her glasses, like clothes disappearing into a stuffed suitcase.

"When did this happen?" I asked.

"February," Julie said, looking up, the first word I'd heard her say.

"We were all set to go to the wedding and everything," my mother said. "We had the present all picked out."

I watched Julie flinch. I wanted to save her from my mother's misguided attempt to magnify the tragedy through the prism of her own ruined plans.

"I'm sorry," I said, hoping to end it. I could hear clucking going on at the table, but couldn't tell if it was honest commiseration or the sound of my aunt trying to catch the end of the wet biscuit in her mouth before it crumbled onto the table.

"Well, anyway, it's a tragedy," Viola said, glancing once aside at her daughter. My father had become silent, his hands folded in front of him, looking down at the table.

He looked up at Julie. "He was a mechanic, was he?"

Julie nodded. "Uh-huh."

That was it, until my aunt asked, "Cars?"

No one answered her. Rose held a biscuit over her tea and looked around. Finally she nodded to herself and put the biscuit down.

"You wanna go, Julie? You wanna go home?" Viola moved her napkin to her chin.

Julie looked at her watch. "A few more minutes," she said, obviously out of mere politeness.

But the visit was over as soon as a limit had been set on it. My father cracked no more jokes. My aunt had effectively dampened things by her remark. The "tragedy" hovered over the table, blunting everyone's tongue. I waited for Julie to have to get up so I could see what the rest of her looked like. I expected there would be something wrong, some physical overabundance in the lower region to make up for the grace of her facial features. But there wasn't.

"Well, John," Viola said, clearing her plate, "I expect we'll see a lot more of you from now on."

"Oh, certainly," my father said, nodding.

"We're going to have a party when he's well," my mother said. "Invite all the relatives."

"Oh, that'll be great," Viola said.

Rose and I were the only ones left at the table. She stared half-sideways at me, silently making some suggestion I couldn't decipher.

"What?" I asked, and she shook her head quickly, as if someone had heard her silent thought.

"Well, it was nice meeting you." I felt Julie's hand on my shoulder. Hearing her string this many words together, I was able to catch a certain roughness in her voice. But her gesture, the gentle touch on the shoulder, was like a subtle allusion to a world she and I shared, beyond our mothers, beyond Aunt Rose. It might have worked, but she held it too long, and I saw the effortfulness in her, that such a "world," if it existed, was more a wish than a reality.

I stood up. "Yes," I said. I saw now that I was slightly taller than her.

She slipped past me. I looked at the pocketbook in her hand: what was in it?

We moved down the staircase and stood in a cluster at the front door. Julie turned once, and gave me her anx-

ious smile as she stepped into the darkness of the driveway. We waved as the orange Chevy pulled out, Viola's
face compact behind the wheel.

"I should go too," Rose said.

She hesitated a moment, standing at the door, her ro-
tund little form surveying the front yard. "Such a nice
girl, to have nobody," she said.

I felt the remark was all for me. My mother's breath
went up, caught itself on some wordless pitch, then slid
down the scale in agreement.

J ust before Thanksgiving, my father turned a corner and found himself well.

"I feel fine," he kept saying, as if surprised by it, and newly irritated by my mother's insistence that he sit, always sit. "I'm fine," he would say, giving in to her, but uncomfortable, constipated by the denial of motion.

One night we talked about it. My mother agreed that if the doctor thought it was safe, my father could come back to the laundromat for a few hours a day, as long as I was with him at all times. The spring semester at Fordham didn't begin until late January, but I'd begun to feel anxious to settle things much sooner.

The doctor agreed, and my father came in first for short stretches, finally graduating to whole days. He would even ask me to leave sometimes, just to see how he managed on his own. By mid-December, his recovery seemed complete, and my mother decided the time had come to give him his party.

The guest list, which had started small, soon outgrew the capacities of our house. The Sons of Italy Hall was chosen, so that a crowd of over a hundred could be accommodated. The idea arrived that maybe it should be combined with a New Year's Eve party.

"But then," my mother said, "we'll have to have the noisemakers and everything. Besides, that takes away from what the party's about. It's not about New Year's. It's about Dad getting well."

As it turned out, the hall was booked for December 31. The party was to be on the next night, January 1, a Friday.

That day I worked in the laundromat until five thirty, when Ray came in to relieve me.

"Close early tonight, huh, Nickie?" he asked. I said I thought it would be all right. We hadn't customarily been open on holidays, but with less money coming in since the accident, it was considered wise to keep the place open on Thanksgiving and New Year's Day this year. "Besides," my mother said, "people like to do their wash on holidays." The logic of this had washed over both my father and me, but we'd gone along with her.

I was home just before six, and knew I would have to dress quickly in order to leave with them—the prearranged plan. My father was in the living room, already dressed, sitting with his hands folded. He wore a dark suit—charcoal gray—and a red tie. His face had color in it; he looked handsome, though a little tired.

"You all right, Dad?" I asked.

He smiled as if having been awakened out of a dream.

My mother was moving quickly through the kitchen. She was dressed in a soft pink dress, and her hair had been done up that day; teased and sprayed so that it was stiff, her hair gave her face a more formal, set look, the rosy cheerlessness of Quaker wives in eighteenth-century portraits. She was attaching an earring to one ear, an orange stone set in a gold shell.

"You'd better hurry if you want to leave with us," she said.

"I've got to shave and everything. Maybe you'd better go without me. I can take a cab."

Her eyes looked suddenly glazed, and her hand, touching her ear at the point where she'd just clipped the earring, seemed to stop there. It was the look she'd given me when I'd first asked her to take my place in the laundro-

mat: I'd learned since then that this cold, uncertain, almost paralyzing stare meant she was giving me the benefit of the doubt.

"Ya," she said finally. "But I thought it would be nice if
we all went together."

I chose not to fight. Shaved and showered, I reap-
peared before them in a jacket and tie. My mother looked
at me a moment, her lips turned down at the ends, and
said, "Oh, no, Nick."

"What's wrong with this?"

"You have to wear a suit to your father's party."

"Mom, come on, it's just a party, it's not a coronation."

"Listen to her, Nick," my father said, sounding hard,
from his chair. His authority came as a surprise.

"I've only got one suit, and the pants are too short," I
protested.

"I asked you if you needed clothes," my mother said.

"If it makes you happy, I'll put it on."

The party was being catered, so there should have been
nothing for us to bring. At the last minute, though, my
mother had insisted on preparing two hundred Chinese
Chicken Wings, a specialty of hers. "People might be expecting them," she'd said. They sat in trays beside her on
the backseat. We were quiet in the car, and my father
looked tired, almost morose.

At a stoplight in the center of town he turned to me.
"Ray showed up all right?" he asked. It was an odd time
to be asking it.

"Yes," I said.

"Maybe we should swing by," he said. "Make sure
things are all right."

"Hon, we'll be late," my mother said from the back
seat.

"Just to pass by, that's all." There was an edge of irrita-
tion in his voice. I wondered if they'd fought that day.

We found the laundromat's lights turned off. My father
got out of the car and began pulling at the front door. It
was locked. I got out and stood beside him. He was looking grimly inside, shaking his head.

"Try the back door," my mother called. "Maybe he's back there."

"The guy's a drunk," my father said. He looked around. The shopping center was deserted, all the stores closed except for Mr. Donut. Two cars sat parked in front of it.

We stood there a long time in the cold. My father kept looking inside the store, as though if he looked hard enough, Ray would appear, the lights flick magically on.

Finally I spoke. "I told him he could close up early, Dad."

"You did?" As he looked at me, his chin went up, hardened.

"I never thought he'd close up this early," I said.

He looked down at the ground.

"Dad, it's New Year's Day, for Chrissake. It's your party."

"There's no need for that," he said, about my swearing.

A car pulled into the parking lot and made a wide arc around the array of stores, stopping in front of Felder's Cleaners before pulling out again. In the light from its headlamps I could see my mother's head as she turned and watched it intently.

When the car was gone, she rolled down her window. "Did they want to do a wash?" she asked.

"I don't know," my father said. Something in his face led me to expect him to start lunging after the disappearing car, shouting "We're open! We're open!"

Of course, now the implanted idea that someone had come and, wanting to use our facilities, had been turned away by the darkness, would be enough to justify, for them, my staying here. It was not even a matter of lost money, but something else: the laundromat should be open. Even if no one came in. The point was not to be caught napping. I was prepared to be asked. I could already see myself mopping up, in these too-short pants.

"Come on, let's go," my father said.

Surprised, I got behind the wheel. We were silent for what seemed like hours: the distance from light to light was endless.

"He's a drunk," my father repeated. In the backseat, my mother sighed.

"Try to forget it, John. It's your party."

I could feel my father stiffen beside me, his profile like a silhouette etched crudely onto a penny. I knew exactly how he'd take my mother's admonition: her urging him to forget it would brand it onto his memory even harder. He would be able to think of nothing else.

We parked in the lot at the Sons of Italy Hall and watched the musicians—my Uncle Billy's band, The Philly 4—carrying their instruments up the fire stairs and into the small cone of light leading to the stage.

"Billy's here," my mother said quietly, tucking the wax paper under her chicken wings. We approached the front steps, my mother carrying the trays of chicken, my father walking a little ahead of us, with his hands in his pockets. Across the street from the front entrance, a lone pizza parlor shined its lights amidst a row of shuttered stores. It was the first day of 1971.

At the door of the hall, I watched my father's face tense before he opened it. There was a kind of molting going on in him, the public character taking over. It looked difficult to assume this now, as if he were forcing his ample flesh into a too-tight pair of pants.

Inside, long tables had been set up, leaving enough room in the middle to form a dance floor. The serving girls provided by the caterer were laying sheets of white paper on the tables. There were balloons lining the proscenium of the stage and the outlines of the high windows. Uncle Al and Aunt Rose were the first guests. They waited at an unset table. Al raised his arm. Aunt Rose was looking at the servant girls, impatient to have her table properly set. My father nodded to Al, but looked beyond him to the stage, where his brother, my Uncle Billy, was testing a microphone.

"Hey, and there he is," Billy said into the microphone, his voice booming out into the big, empty hall, but somehow not coarsened by the decibels, remaining cool, liquid and ingratiating, like a radio announcer touting the pleasures of a soft drink.

"The man of the hour," Billy went on. "John Battaglia."

I listened to the way my father's name dropped off Billy's lips and watched him motioning to the other members of The Philly 4, each of them looking up from his instrument to give my father applause. "Battaglia," the name, hadn't soared when Billy said it, the way the names of entertainers did when they were announced on television: "Steve Lawrence; Sammy Davis, Junior." The serving girls barely looked up to acknowledge us: we were indistinguishable, to them, from last night's "O'Briens," the night before's "Vincuillas."

Yet when I looked at Uncle Al, I saw his mouth open wide with delight. He looked toward Uncle Billy as though he'd said the most hilarious thing he'd ever heard, then clapped his big hands together. "Man of the Hour," he repeated, nodding.

Beside him, Aunt Rose looked tense, as though he were misbehaving at a state function. The musicians went back to setting up their instruments. Al's legs started to pump, as if the music had already started.

"How are you, John?" my Uncle Billy's voice rang across the hall.

"Fine, fine." My father was right beside me, but his voice sounded hoarse, phlegmatic in its attempt to reach out across the distance to where Billy stood. We moved down the steps into the hall. My mother smiled at the serving girls. "Everything looks lovely," she said to one in particular, who seemed not to hear her. She approached another of the girls and asked, "Where's the oven, do you know?" The girl, wearing a pair of thick glasses, just stared at my mother. "Where are they cooking?" my mother repeated. The girl looked at her colleague at the next table. They spoke in French.

"They don't speak English, Josie!" Aunt Rose shouted, her table still unset. "They're Canadians."

"I'm looking for the oven," my mother said. "I brought chicken wings."

My father moved across the hall and approached his brother on the stage. Billy stood there, the microphone still in his hand, his feet planted several inches apart, his head turned, talking to one of the musicians.

"Hold it, John's here." The microphone caught his remark, made it public. He readjusted the mike onto its stand, got down into the crouch necessary to greet my father.

"John, good to see you," I heard Billy say. Then he cuffed my father on the back of his neck, where the hairs started.

They were ten years apart, but the difference had always seemed greater to me. Unlike my father, Billy had led a representative American life in the '50s: the Army, Korea, marriage to a WASP girl who looked like Janet Leigh. He had, when young, possessed the more delicate Italianate features of pop crooners of the time, and had worn his hair in the same sort of pompadour Bobby Rydell and Frankie Avalon sported. Age had bloated him, but he retained even now the hairdo, the mannerisms I had tried to imitate when I was little: flipping the hair back with one quick motion of the head, jiggling with one thigh as he spoke, the offhandedness of gesture, the way nothing in his face would move except his lips when he spoke or sang.

We'd visited him, in Philadelphia in the '50s, just after he'd formed his band, The Philly 5; he and his wife were newlyweds then. I remembered sitting in a room in his house, watching a group of young people dance to "Wake Up, Little Suzy." Billy and his friends looked like the cast of one of those "youth movies" I was too young to see, but being there, I felt I'd entered one of those tantalizing previews where Nick Adams or Dennis Hopper grabbed Terry Moore a little too roughly by the wrist and began jitterbugging. Sitting among them, my parents looked stolid, as if they'd never had a proper youth, or had misspent it.

Later, after Billy had turned forty, gotten flaccid and pouty, after he'd left his wife and three daughters and reduced his band to the "Philly 4," he'd come over to our house one Sunday night to watch the Beatles on television. "Hey, they're great," he said, uncertain of tone, shifting in his seat. He must have realized that night that some part of his promise had faded. He'd been singing songs like "Because of You" and "Chanson d'Amour" for years.

"Is that Nicholas?" I heard Billy say, and lifted my arm to wave.

"Come on over here, Nicholas," he shouted.

I moved across the floor, watching his hard smile tighten, the lines at the side of his face crack. It was hard to watch him grow old.

"Nickie, my boy." He cuffed the back of my neck, the identical thing he'd done to my father. "Hey fellas," he said, turning around to the musicians. "I want you to meet my nephew."

I couldn't tell whether this was the same band I'd watched the last time I'd seen Billy perform, five years before. They looked, at first glance, both older and shadier. Where once Billy's band had resembled the ostensibly rough but in fact clean-cut actors who followed Marlon Brando and James Dean around on motorcycles, they now looked like those same actors after having missed the right roles for a decade and a half, forced to play minor villains, go-betweens, chumps. One in particular seemed interested in me, a bald guy with a pencil mustache, the keyboard player. He winked.

"He's from New York, fellas," Billy said.

One of the musicians said something that made the others laugh. I couldn't make it out. The keyboard player said, "Get out the black book, Billy," and everybody heard that. Even my father laughed, which surprised me. Somehow being with my father when he was alone with his brother made me feel as though Billy were some beach we were camping on, far from home.

"You've been taking care of the home fires, huh, Nick?" Billy asked.

When I nodded, he said "Good boy," as though he were already bored by the sentiment.

"John, what would you like us to play tonight?"

My father glanced down at Billy's knee. "Well, you've got your repertoire, Bill."

"Repertoire," in my father's mouth, sounded like a delicate piece of ladies' underwear.

"Anything special? Something for Josie?"

My father thought a moment. "What's that one she likes, Nick?"

I knew what he was referring to. My mother's latest favorite had made its presence known in our house not only through the several records she'd bought—Robert Goulet, the Ray Conniff Singers, Wayne Newton—but in a music box, a tiny Winter Palace she'd purchased on the one trip they'd made to visit me in New York.

"'Lara's Theme,'" I said.

"'Somewhere My Love'?" Billy asked. "Oh, sure, we do that."

"It's great you could come, Bill," my father said.

"Oh, hell, John. Wouldn't miss this." I remembered hearing my mother on the phone one night, long-distance to Philadelphia, negotiating his fee.

"What time do the guests arrive?" Billy asked. I could sense his voice moving into the slick tones he adopted for business dealings.

"Oh, they should be here soon. Seven o'clock, we said."

My mother was approaching us now. Her face looked stricken.

"They say they don't have an oven here," she said. "They cook the food and bring it in."

"Josie." Billy intruded on her distress, bent down to kiss her. She offered him the side of her face, addressed the rest of her complaint to him.

"I brought two hundred chicken wings and they don't even have an oven! What am I supposed to do now?"

"I told you not to fuss, Josie." My father, with his

hands in his pockets, was looking now across the floor. Uncle Al and Aunt Rose's table had finally been set. Rose was smoothing out the paper tablecloth. The doors at the front of the hall opened and two immense strangers appeared in black coats. The woman, walking ahead of the man, removed her kerchief, revealing a massive pale face under a coiffure that seemed composed of dark bricks piled up on either side of her head. Her husband was slightly smaller, but still formidable, with a thin mustache and hair cut with a straight razor, like an adjutant in Mussolini's army.

"The Ferranos," my father said, lifting a hand.

"What are we, early?" the woman shouted, not smiling or offering much of anything in the way of a greeting. "We were afraida traffic."

I hadn't seen the Ferranos in years, but if I remembered correctly, they lived five minutes from this hall.

Behind me, I heard Uncle Billy call under his breath to one of his cohorts, "Do you know 'Here Come the Ferranos'?" It made all the band members laugh.

By seven o'clock, the announced start of the party, the room was full. Lateness was unheard of among these people. The fear of "traffic" haunted them like the awareness of a rampant germ in winter, so they arrived earlier than they had to, more often than not before their hosts were ready. It became a habit, something they were emotionally prepared for. Watching the Cataldos enter, then the Tricones, the Antonellis, and the Bonicas, I began to notice their eyes darting quickly from left to right: who was here already? Were the tables set, or still bare? Once the joint was cased, they smiled and made apologies to my mother for their earliness, their imagined lateness, whatever came to mind. Each time (I stopped counting after the fourth or fifth), my mother greeted them with the news: "I've got two hundred chicken wings and no place to cook them!"

The caterer had arrived at quarter to seven, but since

most of the guests were already there, we had a few anxious moments, with nothing to serve the first fifty people. My mother's brother Carmen acted as bartender in a
makeshift bar at the side of the hall, so there were at least
drinks, and to cover up the absence of food, Uncle Billy
started the music early. His first selection was "Blue
Spanish Eyes."

My mother's sister Natalie, her wide hips encased in a
tight-fitting purple dress, grabbed my father and hugged
him, then swept him onto the dance floor. His mouth
opened in a big surprised smile, and he gave the circle
around him a jaunty little wave goodbye. I thought of
him outside the laundromat, pulling at the door, looking
for Ray. "Say you and your Spanish eyes will wait for
me," Billy sang.

Natalie had spawned a trio of wise-assed boys, the eldest a couple of years younger than me. They were
dressed up and standing together in a corner of the room.
I went over to them. Uncle Billy segued into "I'm Looking Over a Four-Leaf Clover."

"Hey, Nick," Larry, the eldest of the cousins, greeted
me. "This guy your uncle?"

He was referring to Billy. I nodded, expecting the
worst.

"We were just saying, now that Brian Jones has kicked
the bucket, maybe the Stones could use this guy. What do
you think?"

Larry elbowed his younger brother Davy.

"Call Mick," Davy said. "There a pay phone here?"

"Leave him alone," I said, trying to joke with them.
There was no way I could give them any sense of what
Billy had been fifteen years before, dancing in a room in
Philadelphia to the Everly Brothers.

They were unforgiving, Natalie's children. One of them
started singing "Sympathy for the Devil" in a crude imitation of Billy's voice. I moved away, to another part of
the room.

My mother was arguing with Orlando, the caterer. She
gestured toward her three trays of uncooked chicken.

"I felt sure there'd be an oven," I heard her say.

"You ordered cold buffet, Mrs. Battaglia," Orlando said, his eyes not quite fully open.

"But it's roast beef," my mother protested. "You have to cook it first."

"How could we serve it cold if we had to cook it here?"

My mother's mouth went sideways, her rebuttal halted by Orlando's logic.

"Ya," she said, agreeing against her will. She looked at me; her eyes made a fleeting plea for help before she gathered herself together. "Nick, maybe you should take these out to the car, then."

I lifted the three trays in a single stack and started to make my way through the room.

The hard, anxious, fiercely rouged faces of women in tight and unflattering dresses, each of them standing next to a stiff man in a dark suit, became like a series of waves my body broke against on its passage out. Each face made an approach, however silent: remember me? Only half of the faces connected with names, and half of those names seemed to be "Rose," as if one year in the life of the previous generation had been so exhausting they'd made a pact not to trouble themselves with thinking up variations but to give all the female children the same name.

I had suddenly become important to this crowd. They were here to honor my father, and some acknowledgement from me, as simple as "Hello, how are you?," or a cursory asking after their children's health, would confirm their presence here in a more immediate way than standing at the edge of the dance floor, waiting their turn to wish my father well. Individually, I might have done this. But there were too many of them, and I was afraid of making a mistake, addressing as "Rose" a woman who was in fact a "Leticia," a "Connie," a "Jennie." I tried to move beyond them, offering each a smile.

Outside, the night was crisp, the sounds coming from the hall softened and diminished. I thought of the way the movie Pinocchio opened with a cricket's-eye view of the world, slowly moving down over the roofs of a

town and peering into one window in particular: Ge-
petto's life, a fussing among pet fish and cats. I saw the
hall that way, as if I were a benevolent alien: a man on a
stage singing of four-leaf clovers, another man moving
awkwardly in a woman's arms to the simple beat. I felt
extremely tender toward them all, among their pet fish
and cats, their wooden boys. Their colors seemed as pri-
mary as in a Disney drawing. I was leaving them: for the
first time since I'd returned, this seemed clear and un-
mistakable. My moment among them had passed.

I placed my mother's trays of uncooked chicken wings
on the backseat of the car. Benevolence made me feel
generous toward her, and gave me an idea. I looked up
and saw the open pizza parlor across the street, then took
the trays back out and started over.

Behind the counter, a young Italian boy was smoking a
cigarette. He put it out when he saw me come in. He was
skinny, his hair slicked straight back; it looked like it
could use a wash. His face was acned and devoid of extra
flesh, and he had the air of someone who expects trouble.
He watched me stack the trays on the counter.

"Listen," I began. "I'd like you to do me a big favor."

"What?" he asked. The single word was spit out
quickly; what he wanted to say was "no."

"No, listen," I said. "There's a party going on across
the street, in the hall. It's for my father. My mother made
these chicken wings, only she's got no place to cook
them. It's really breaking her heart, and I was wondering
if I could use your oven to cook them."

The lines that had formed between his eyes seemed
solidly entrenched. It took him seconds before he could
translate what I'd said into an intelligible message.

"They don't got ovens over there?" he asked.

"No. The caterer did all the cooking somewhere else."

He looked over at the hall. "Can't do it."

"Why? You've got all the ovens on anyway, don't you?"

"Boss wouldn't allow it."

"He's not gonna see. I promise."

"How you gonna promise?"

I leaned farther onto the counter. "Look, it would make that lady so happy if I could walk in there right now with these things cooked. My father nearly died, you know."

He looked down, shook his head, began cleaning off the counter.

"What if I ordered a pizza?" I asked.

"Then I'd cook you a pizza."

"No, I mean, couldn't you just slip these things in with it?"

"Hey, you wanna know something?" He looked as if he'd had enough. "You think heat is like a thing that's just *there?* Heat gets, like, *absorbed* by food, so if there's more stuff in there, there's gonna be more heat used, and my boss walks in and sees that and I get fired, what are you gonna do for me? You gonna give me a job?"

He was out from behind the counter, straightening out chairs. I looked at his red-striped shirt, soiled apron: he was stuck here.

"All right," I said, and picked up the trays.

When I was at the door, he called to me.

"You're Battaglia, right?"

I turned. "Yes."

"No, you don't know me. I seen you in the laundromat, right, your father's place?"

"Yes."

"I know your father. This place is my uncle's. Sal Marcantonio. I been workin' here since I was eleven, cleanin' up. Your father used to mow the lawn for Sacred Heart; he'd come in here for lunch sometimes."

I looked at him a moment.

"So?" I asked.

He lit another cigarette, looked up at me through the smoke. "So gimme the fuckin' wings," he said.

He placed them in the oven. "It'll take, what, fifteen minutes?"

"That's good enough," I said.

We sat down. I accepted one of his cigarettes. It turned out we'd been to high school together, but he'd been a year behind me. He didn't remember me from high

school. When that much was said, we didn't have anything left to talk about. At the end of fifteen minutes, we
got up to check the wings. They looked done.

"Ask your father if he remembers the kid who used to
work here," he said. In the next moment, though, he rejected this. "Nah, he ain't gonna remember."

I told him I'd ask my father anyway.

"Good luck to you," he said, as I walked out the door,
balancing three hot trays in the mittens he'd lent me.

Across the street, I could see a car pulling into the hall
lot. I thought I recognized it. Then the doors opened and
Viola and Julie stepped out. I waited for them on the
sidewalk in front of the hall.

When Viola saw me, her face went rigid.

"I'm mortified we're late, Nicholas," she said.

"It's all right," I answered.

Behind her, her daughter walked delicately, nervously,
her head pointed downwards, watching her feet. When
she looked up, I could tell her expression had been
thought out, as though she'd seen me from a distance but
wanted to feign surprise now.

I looked at Viola. "My mother made these chicken
wings," I began, "but she had no place to cook them. I
just went over to the pizza parlor and used their oven." I
was absurdly proud of what I had done. I could hear it in
my voice, and hung back after I'd said it, disavowing my
own eagerness to please. Viola wasn't paying attention to
what I'd said, though. She was looking up at the hall.

Julie and I waited a moment before going up after her. I
looked at her blue coat and the way her hair was combed
—brushed—off her face, with a pink barrette holding it
back on either side. Her face looked more intelligent now
than I remembered it; sharper somehow. In spite of this,
we did nothing but giggle awkwardly on the front steps
of the hall. Finally, we followed Viola into the party.

No one noticed our entrance, a fact which seemed to
upset Viola. I tried to find my mother in the crowd. She
was at the far end of the room. I excused myself from
Julie and went to her.

"Look," I said, beaming.

She looked down at the trays. It took her a moment to realize what had been effected. Then, unconsciously, she clutched her breast.

"The wings!" she said.

In another moment she'd taken them from me and begun laying them out. No question had been asked as to the miracle of their having arrived cooked.

"Mom, don't you remember? You had me take them out to the car."

"Ya," she said, arranging them on a nearby table. "How did you get them cooked?"

"The pizza place across the street," I answered. Though she was smiling now, I could tell it was the crowd that absorbed her. They would be satisfied now; they would not go away hungry.

"John!" she called to my father. "Nickie cooked the wings!"

My father, ten feet away, talking to a man whose name I couldn't remember, saluted me with his drink.

Into the microphone, Uncle Billy announced, "We'll take a break now," but the room seemed not to hear him.

"You know, you should dance with Julie when the music starts up again."

I turned to find Aunt Rose standing beside me. She looked even shorter in this hall.

"She's got nobody, you know," Rose said.

"Aunt Rose, this room is full of men." I fully intended to dance with Julie, but didn't want to give Rose the satisfaction of thinking it was her idea. I left her to go and find Uncle Billy.

The musicians were sitting in a room just off the stage, their jackets off, smoking and drinking from plastic cups. The liquid inside the cups looked hazy and potent. Uncle Billy was not among them.

"This the kid from New York?" the bald one called out, his eyelids low, cigarette smoke obscuring part of his face.

"Yes," I said.

"You want some numbers?"

I had the feeling he had said this more for the benefit of the others than for me, but I laughed anyway.

"Come here," he said.

I approached, an uncomfortable smile plastered on my face.

"You got a pencil?" he asked, when I was close.

"No," I said.

"What part of New York you from?"

"I go to school in the Bronx."

"The Bronx? Where?" His eyes receded a bit, as though he were flipping through an internal catalogue.

"Fordham," I answered.

He raised his eyebrows. They were uneven, the hairs at the widest part of them fanning up onto his high freckled forehead.

"That's an Ivy League school, isn't it?"

"No, not exactly," I said.

"Well, you call this girl Debbie, you tell her you go to school in the Ivy League."

He winked.

"You get what I mean?" he said. "Where's a pencil?"

"Tell me. I'll remember it," I lied.

"Debbie. Forty-seventh Street. Forty-seventh and Tenth Avenue. Debbie Nuttings. You call her in the phone book. Tell her Joe from Philadelphia sent you."

I nodded. I had to get out of this room.

"Thanks a lot," I said.

Once I was out in the hall, I heard my Uncle Billy's voice, but muffled. It sounded as if it were coming from behind the curtains at the side of the stage. Then it was superseded by Cousin Leo's voice, louder. Billy had been trying to keep it low. I held still.

"You want me to cosign for forty thousand, Bill?" I could sense, just from listening, the trajectory of Leo's cigar—when it was in his mouth, when out.

"I'd ask John, Leo, you know that, but not while he's sick." I listened to the slick tone, as though Billy were introducing his rendition of "My Kind of Town."

"You need it for what, Bill?"

"A piece of property, Leo."

"What kind of property? Where?"

"It's . . . property. An investment. It's in Philly."

"Since when are you buying property?"

Orlando, the caterer, passed through the hallway, down to the party. The conversation stopped until he was gone.

"You need it to live, don't you?" Leo's voice was low, resigned.

"I don't need it to live. We're doing well. It's . . . an investment."

"You're fooling around, Billy. You're a real dickhead, you know that? Property. Property, my ass. I bet you're charging Josie tonight, aren't you?"

"We came to an agreement. It's more or less a favor."

"How much?" Leo's cigar, I could tell, was in his mouth now.

"Five hundred," Billy said.

"Five hundred is a favor? Look, you do me a favor, you go tell Josie it's free, gratis. I'll write you a check."

Billy was silent.

"You'll cosign, then?"

"Jesus." I could hear Leo breathing, this far away.

"Why don't you get a regular job, Billy? Something you can live on."

"Just don't lecture me, okay?"

The two men were silent. Then I heard a low laugh from one of them.

"Jesus," Leo said.

Billy stepped out from behind the curtain then, a drink in his hand. "Nicholas," he said, his voice full of false heartiness. He threw his arm around me. "Listen, you go back to New York when?"

I told him.

"You know, I come into the city every now and then. We could get together, what do you say?"

"Sure," I answered.

Leo appeared as well then, the cigar entrenched between his pink lips, puffing streams of smoke. He studied us a second before moving off.

As soon as he was gone, Aunt Rose appeared at the entrance to the hall.

"Nickie, you back there?" she called.

"Yes." She could see me plainly now.

"Your mother wants to see you. The chicken wings are rare, Nickie; they're pink inside. Lucy Ferrano threw up."

Her small dark eyes were on fire again: we were back in the hospital now, and she was pointing out the dark hole that was existence, the horror that ensues if you tread around it too lightly. Death and undercooked chicken were finally one.

Beside me, Uncle Billy repeated "Lucy Ferrano threw up," and laughed easily, as though this were news reported to him from another party.

I went down the stairs to where Rose waited, looked beyond her at the section of the room that had been affected by Lucy Ferrano's accident. Uncle Al was on his knees, cleaning up. My mother stood over him, handing him paper towels, as the Canadian girls, just behind her, looked on, unsure what to make of this. Al looked over to where I was standing. I watched his brow crease and go dark: why had I done this?

My mother, too, looked over at me, her mouth straightening into a hard line: "They weren't cooked!" she shouted.

On a seat behind her, Lucy Ferrano was being attended by her husband and a pair of women, cousins. Her big, overworked coiffure seemed to have moved forward: it looked like a heavy thatched roof that had come unmoored, and was threatening to crush the structure beneath it. Her face, though, even in its pale, postsickness stage, looked formidable enough to offset the blow.

"Throw it all out, Nick," my mother said.

I looked around for my father, but couldn't find him, so I took the plates of chicken wings and started to carry them out. He was coming out of the men's room at the back of the hall as I passed it. He looked down at the wings and said, "What happened?"

"I must not have cooked them enough," I said.

He nodded, and looked past me, toward the crowd.

"Lucy Ferrano threw up," I said.

"She did, huh?"

His arm was already lifted. Someone was greeting him, and he was smiling. I left the hall and found a dumpster in the parking lot. I thought my mother would want to save the trays, so I tried sliding the wings off into the dumpster. The grease from the trays stuck to my hands, and some of it got on the cuffs of my shirt.

"Shit," I said loudly. I turned around, even though there was no one to hear. At the edge of the lot was a small unpaved field. I went to it and rubbed my hands against the stalks and the frozen grass. Some of the grease came off, but a film of it clung stubbornly to my hands. I would have to go inside and wash them.

I took the trays back to the car. When I looked up at the hall, I saw that Julie was standing on the front steps. She couldn't see me.

"Hello?" I called.

She put her hand above her eyes to try and find me. I stepped under one of the streetlamps. I stood there awhile, looking at her. I didn't want to go back inside. Finally I walked up the steps to where she was waiting.

"I'm sorry that happened to you," she said.

"Oh, it's all right." I looked at her skin, the darkness of it. Where her hair ended I could see, in this light, the soft down at the top of her back. "You mind sitting here a minute? I don't particularly want to go back inside."

I sat down on the steps and gestured for her to sit next to me. When she did, I heard the rustle of what she had on under her dress: the nylons; some underwear of a for-midable texture—maybe a slip?

"How can you stand to stay at home?" I asked.

She shrugged and looked down at the steps.

"Do you work?" I asked her.

"I'm a secretary," she said. She was still staring at the steps.

"Where?" I asked.

"Linco Tool?"

She spoke it as a question.

"Oh, yes," I said, seeing in my mind the squat stone building with its black-iron-gated window. I used to pass it often on my bike when I was little. I tried to imagine her there now, inside those dark rooms, light-bulbed, on certain fall afternoons, into a cozy glow.

"You didn't go to school?" I asked.

"No," she said. "I was gonna get married."

We sat there another few minutes, but it was starting to get cold.

"You want to go inside?" I waited, then said, "We could dance."

She turned to me. Her eyes and mouth had that anxious look again, a look I wanted to erase from her lexicon of expressions. She was a beautiful girl who had picked the wrong man, that was all—some doomed mechanic. She could start again. I took her hand and we went inside.

Uncle Billy was speaking into the microphone.

"Here's one B.J. had some luck with, and I guess the Academy thought pretty highly of it too."

Then the band struck up the first notes of "Raindrops Keep Fallin' on My Head."

I put one arm on Julie's back and with the other took her hand. Close to her, I felt a loss of excitement. The too-close proximity of aunts and uncles, the full, overheated room, and the depleted version of a hit song all seemed to make lust somehow a tawdry thing. What finally came of it? You made children, became a family, went to dances in big halls, got old. I worried, when Julie rubbed against me, that she could feel how small I'd become.

The room around us had gone more or less back to normal, the incident with the chicken wings passed over, though Lucy Ferrano sat at a nearby table recounting the details of the story to whoever would listen. Whenever she caught my eye she looked at me with an expression that suggested I had touched off some groundless, deep malevolence in her.

When Billy had finished with "Raindrops Keep Fallin' on My Head," Leo appeared from a wing of the stage and grabbed hold of the microphone. Laughter and scattered applause greeted him.

"What's this, Leo?" Billy asked from the stage.

"What do you mean, 'What's this?' This is a speech; what do you think it is? Tell your guys they can take a break, Bill. That's what you'd be doing in another two minutes anyway, right?" There was some laughter at this, not much. "Billy likes to take a break every two songs." Leo addressed the crowd now. "He thinks this is the annual meeting of the *vecchiarada*."

The crowd broke up at that. Julie, beside me, laughed along with them. Billy and his band moved slowly off the stage. Billy lifted his hand to the crowd.

"Go call Connie Stevens," Leo called after him; "tell her you can meet her early tonight."

Billy shouted something back, inaudible to the crowd. He was smiling hugely when he disappeared.

"Billy asked me to cosign a note before," Leo said, the information crackling over the microphone. "I said, For what, Bill? He said a piece of property in Philadelphia. I said. This is how you refer to Joey Heatherton?"

The crowd roared, and Leo dived into it with "And what a piece of property!," shaking his free hand lewdly and with the other, the mike hand, placing the cigar in his mouth.

"There's something serious we're here for tonight, though." Leo laughed as the crowd treated his line like another set-up. "And that's to honor John."

He paused, let them applaud.

"Now, Lucy Ferrano has already seen fit to honor John in her way."

The crowd erupted again. Lucy Ferrano pounded the table where she was sitting, her face in laughter becoming as dimpled and many-eyed as an old potato.

"Now, Lucy," Leo chided from the stage, "it's one thing to honor John, but oh, boy, if we don't get these windows open, you're also gonna be honoring the next five parties that come in here."

He looked around then at the crowd and accepted the applause they sent up to him. They were applauding Lucy Ferrano's having thrown up, I reminded myself.

"Now let's get down to business here," Leo said, removing the cigar from his mouth. "You all know John, and you all love him." He cut into the applause that had started. "And we thank God you're well and with us, Jackie."

He allowed the applause now, staring down sweetly at where my father stood with his head bowed, turning a deep color and smiling with his lips closed. Cousin Leo was the only one of my father's boyhood friends who still used the old diminutive "Jackie." Hearing it, I saw my father in leggings, curly-headed, following behind his cousin in a frozen field.

"But there's another person here tonight who we should also honor," Leo said, pausing. "Someone who kept things going and allowed us to have this kind of party tonight instead of a let's-all-pass-the-hat-to-help-John-pay-the-mortgage party. We often praise the man, but oftentimes there's somebody behind the scenes who's working as hard, and who does it without the thanks and praise that the head of the household gets."

My heart had started to beat fast.

"I mean Josie," Leo said, and the applause around me was suddenly deafening. I saw tears in the women's eyes as my mother stood up and waved. She went to my father, and the two of them put their arms around each other as if they were posing for a photograph.

"Your mother looks beautiful," Julie said to me, not turning away from the sight of her.

"May you always be safe from boilers that go kaput," Leo continued. "And may you live a hell of a lot longer. I think God was watching over you, Jackie, Josie." He winked and blew a kiss. There was virtual silence in the room. I watched my mother's lips form the words "Thank you."

"Now if we can get Billy unhinged from Sophia Loren back here, maybe we can get some more music going and continue the party." Leo waved and moved offstage to the final round of applause. Just below the stage, my mother and father began to accept congratulations, the crowd moving toward them as if they were statues at the front of a church. The Philly 4, minus Billy, took the stage again, and started into a peppy rhythm number. Some of the couples began to dance.

Julie looked up at me, expecting me to ask her to dance.

Her body swayed to the rhythm, in case I didn't get the hint. I stood still, watching my parents.

"Don't you want to dance?" she asked finally.

I tried not to look at her. I could feel her breath on me. It was the first moment of erotic stimulation I'd known with her, but it was too close, too suggestive of intruders, like making love on a bed full of other people's coats.

"I'm humiliated," I said to her.

"Why?"

"I got chicken grease all over your dress."

I'd noticed, just moments before, a stain the size and shape of my palm on the back of her dress.

"Where?" she asked.

"On your back. I'm sorry. When we were outside before, I'd just come from throwing out the chicken wings. I meant to wash my hands."

"It's all right. It comes out."

She looked mildly concerned about it, but anxious not to spoil things between us.

"No. It was stupid." I wasn't sure why, but I wanted her to go away, dance with someone else. I wanted to be left alone.

"What's the matter?" she asked. "It's not the stupid stain, is it?"

I looked down, away.

"Do you wanna go someplace?"

I looked straight at her then. The appeal she'd made was so direct it was almost frightening. Her eyes were clear and only a little bit hesitant, as if she were worried not about the suggestion itself but about her manner of phrasing it.

"Sure," I said.

Once we were outside, I kissed her in the doorway at the entrance to the hall. By then I'd realized, though, that we had no place to go.

"Do you have the keys to your car?" I asked.

"No. My mother drives."

I remembered I'd left the Oldsmobile open, but that the greasy trays were still in the back. It was the only place possible, though. I took her hand.

In the parking lot, three cars down from the Oldsmobile, an old pink Ford was moving, rocking on its hinges. I tried to direct Julie away from it, I didn't want her to see what was going on inside. When I opened the Oldsmobile door, though, I couldn't resist taking a peek myself. Uncle Billy's head had risen; the top of his hair was shaking like a jellied aspic. A skinny leg rose on either side of him. The shoes on these anonymous feet were white, institutional: one of the serving girls. I turned away. Julie was looking down at the seat, the greasy trays.

"Let me move those," I said. I placed them awkwardly on the floor. There was room now, but I saw that some of the grease had spilled off onto the seat. I rubbed at it with the arm of my coat. Then I took off the coat and laid it down on the seat.

"Go ahead," I said, too hurriedly. The words of seduction failed me. It was as if I wanted this to happen quickly, before disaster had a chance to befall us. She sat down on the coat and looked at me, marking with some disappointment my failure as smooth talker.

She let down her silk underpants, catching them on the end of her high heels before freeing them. Not knowing what else to do, she handed them to me. Then she drew me down.

Uncle Billy chose that moment to open the door of the

pink Ford. If he knew I was there, he gave no indication of it. I heard, distantly, the girl dressing herself, their muffled conversation.

"I can't," I said to Julie.

"Why?"

"Somewhere else."

We waited until my uncle and the serving girl were gone.

"Somewhere inside, maybe," I said. "There must be rooms."

We worked our way through the parking lot, up the stairs of the stage entrance, then up a narrow staircase we found, leading I had no idea where. At the top there was a landing, locked doors. A small window looked out on the parking lot.

I turned to Julie and fingered one of her pink barrettes. It was in the shape of a small plastic bow. I took it out and played with it, trying to focus on the moment when she'd put it in her hair. Had she done this for me—put this barrette in her hair for me alone? Seeing myself in this light, I felt lust disappear. It had started to leave a while ago, I thought, and this was just the end of it, going.

She drew my face to her and kissed me. All her need was there. I broke away.

"I can't," I said, and handed her the barrette. She accepted it, childlike. Her face had darkened, was about to crumple.

I ran down the steps and down the hall, past the musicians, into the party. "Nickie!" someone shouted, but I moved past whoever it was, and through the dancing and eating throng until I was outside again. At the top of the steps I breathed hard. My Uncle Al and Uncle Carmen were emptying a bucket of melted ice at the bottom of the steps. They bent over and waited for the bucket to be empty. Their thick bodies looked rubbery.

They came up the steps when they were finished.

"Nickie," Carmen said. He patted me on the shoulder and went inside. Al stayed with me.

He put his hands in his pockets and stood beside me.
We looked over at the pizza joint, the closed stores, and
then above them at the black winter sky and stars.

"You want to talk about something, Nick?"

I turned to him, my face hot.

"Go inside," I said. "Leave me alone."

I watched his face go slack, his mouth open. I had broken his heart and all he knew how to do was look stupid
and hungry. Finally he shambled inside.

When I was alone, I felt my whole body rack itself. It
was stupid to cry, I thought. I wouldn't do that. It was an
effort, but after a while I didn't feel anything but the cold
on my shirt sleeves. Then I stood there a long time,
breathing out and watching, with a kind of distanced curiosity, the size and shape of the space left by my breath
on the air.

2
LONGING

I returned to school and signed up immediately for a course taught by Mrs. Branner. The only one I was eligible for turned out to be a Theology course, taught on Fridays by her and on Wednesdays by Father O'Rourke, a priest I detested. The course was titled "The Cult of Fire: An Interdisciplinary Approach to the Study of Worship." Her half, the catalogue promised, would study fire as a literary symbol, offering "examples from imaginative prose and poetry ranging from William Blake to Jimi Hendrix."

My first sight of her in class was a disappointment. It was as though I had made her, in memory, more beautiful than she in fact was. It was the quality of obsession that had done it, I knew, and since I believed in my obsession more than in reality, I assumed she would return at any minute to the state of beauty in which I'd left her.

My roommate, Tommy Bevilacqua, insisted that I should be attracted instead to healthy Thomas More girls, blondes with gold crosses resting against plump, sweatered breasts. I had trouble explaining to him why this was difficult. He rejected my excuses and arranged dates for me, on which I sat sullenly and made stupid jokes. Such cynicism was not attractive. I walked these girls back to their dorms while Tommy commandeered our room, rendering it off limits for an hour or two. In class, I studied Mrs. Branner's movements with intense concentration, amazed sometimes that a being so deeply embedded in my own consciousness should display such autonomy. At night, on campus, the lights were faint and cold, the stars over the Bronx barely visible, but I kept warm, waiting for Tommy to be finished in the room, by imagining that someday she would walk with me; someday everything would be different.

I took every opportunity to visit her in her office, though, in fact, there weren't many. She had posted office hours, but frequently wasn't there when she said she'd be.

When I was in her office, though, I found I could hardly listen to anything she said. I'd appeared in the doorway and found her eating an orange. This transgression—this interrupting of lunch—troubled me to the point where I could hardly concentrate, so strong was the urge to apologize, to get up and go and leave her alone with her lunch. But underneath this was a happiness, a charge given to my daily existence that nothing outside of this office provided. I had never really returned, I thought sometimes. I was not here in the way I'd been before.

Toward the end of this meeting, I turned to the cork bulletin board beside her desk and saw a picture of a man pinned to it, a handsome curly-headed man in a flannel shirt, holding a big fish he had obviously just caught. The picture was dark, as though it had been taken just after the sun had gone behind the trees. He was smiling, and when I looked at him, I was jealous without reason, as though in my head life had escalated to a point well beyond the dreary facts of my existence. At moments like this, the simple truth came forward, and I felt mortified.

Most nights I kept to the room. I was expectant, though I wasn't certain anymore of what. Life had simply stopped; it was as though I were waiting, in a small air pocket in a cave, for rescuers to arrive.

One weekend toward the end of February, Tommy's father announced he was driving up from Providence. He was expected on Saturday, but he arrived, instead, on Friday night. I was in the room, studying.

"I'm sorry" were the first words out of his mouth when I turned from my desk and saw him.

"It's okay." I gestured for him to come in. He'd been standing in the doorway, denying himself permission to enter.

"This is Thomas Bevilacqua's room?" he asked.

He was a large, exhausted-looking man, but I could see Tommy in him right away: they had basically the same face.

"I don't expect him back till late," I said. "I'm Nick."

He nodded. "I'm Tommy's father."

"We didn't expect you till morning."

When he entered, he looked around the room as though this were in fact a seminary his son had enrolled in, and he had come prepared to find signs of the cloistered life. Finding none, he remained in the doorway as if, despite my assurances, he was not convinced this was where his son lived.

"Sit down," I said. "That's Tommy's bed there."

"You go ahead and study," he insisted, not moving. I saw now that it was his respect for the open book on my desk that held him back.

"No, this is nothing," I said, closing it.

"I know Tommy didn't expect me, but I got home from work tonight, I figured what the hell."

He lifted his hand, as if beseeching me, then broke the gesture, obviously thinking better of it.

"There's no cooking here, is there?" He held a paper bag in his hands.

"No. I'm sorry."

"Tommy's aunt fixed some food."

"Go ahead," I said. "Do you want to eat?"

"Yeah." He smoothed the paper bag, as if, before opening it, he wanted to free it of creases, then removed a thick sandwich and began eating. I turned away, went back to my book, continued studying until he'd finished. When I looked back, he was lying on Tommy's bed, and waiting for something from me as if for each action a separate permission had to be given.

"The bathroom's down the hall, in case you need it."

"Yeah, yeah," he said. "I'm just gonna lie here until Tommy gets back."

But in a little while, when I checked on him, he was asleep.

In the morning, I woke before him. Across the gap between the beds, I studied his profile. In sleep, he possessed an alertness, a troubled sense of attention, as if in the lap of a protracted boyhood where dreams needed to be paid strict attention to: if you didn't remember them in the morning, the nuns would slap your wrists. Underneath his close-cropped hair, the skin of his head looked pink.

"Good morning," I said, as soon as his eyes had opened and the look of panic appeared in them.

He sat up and brushed his hand through his hair, as if to tidy his appearance.

"Tommy never came back?" he asked, alarmed.

I wanted to tell him to lie down and rest, that nothing was expected of him today. He looked around the room as though necessity were a shoe hiding under one of the beds.

"No," I answered.

He seemed bewildered by the fact.

"You know where he might be?"

I tried to smile, to make light of Tommy's absence.

"He's a popular boy."

"So he sleeps out? Out of the dorm room?"

"Sometimes," I answered carefully. "Not often. There are lots of places to stay. If you're late, and it's too long a walk back to campus, there are friends who live off campus."

He looked at me, listening hard.

"There are, huh?"

"Yes."

He ran his hand against the terrain of his hair once again.

"The bathroom down the hall has a shower?" he asked.

"You can use one of my towels."

"Tommy doesn't have any?"

"His are probably dirty. Those are mine, hanging on the door."

I motioned, and, hesitant, he took one.

"You sure, now? I don't mind if one's a little dirty."

"Go ahead, take it. The maid comes in and replaces them on Monday."

He looked at the towel in his hands. It looked small,

too small to adequately cover even his shoulders.

Later, he stood, naked, drying himself, while the radiator steamed profusely against the cold. There were little puddles on the floor.

"How about breakfast, Nick? Let me take you out."

"No. That's all right."

"I insist. This is what I gotta do."

I wanted to laugh at the phrasing, but stopped myself.

"No, I insist, I insist. Here I come, wrecking everybody's plans. I got home last night, I had nothing to do, see? I said, Why go to Tommy on Saturday when I could see him on Friday? A man doesn't realize his kid's got plans."

"You don't have to take me out."

"You know a place?"

"Sure."

He started to dress.

Outside, he decided he wanted a tour of the campus. It was always embarrassing: the slow, oppressive pace, the stopping at every banal landmark to explain, in words that only made you want to move on, to hurry, to run for cover. And then too, there was the sad fact that Fordham was not Harvard. These yellow and brown stone buildings had been plunked down in the Bronx as if only half-conceived. No one had been inspired in the building of Fordham, and likewise, there was the distinct sense, even in the Jesuits' manner of teaching, that no one was expected to be inspired by it. It had the air of something begging to be converted into something else: a bowling alley marking time until it becomes a Hit or Miss. At any moment, the Jesuits might decide that the whole thing had, after all, been a bad idea, and pick up and move on.

Mr. Bevilacqua, though, was impressed. He kept stopping merely to stare, to marvel.

"This is a good school," he said, as we neared the Jesuits' residence hall. The word "good" was spoken with a depth of appreciated body and substance.

"I can see they keep the grounds nice, clean."

He turned to me. "I wanted Tommy to come here. He

had a scholarship to Rensselaer; I guess you know that. That's a good school too."

Each time he said the word "good," his eyes turned inward, as if he weren't sure exactly what he meant by the word.

"But here, I figured they'd straighten him out. You know, not so wild."

It was as if I were with him at the factory where he worked, both members of the grounds crew, and he could be sure of my sympathies.

"We had the hippies down in Providence, y'know. Jesus, the filth. Here, I see, you got none of that. The Jesuits wouldn't allow it. I see it's clean."

It was true: we seemed here still basically untouched by what was raging outside. The "hippies," as phenomenon, were now half a decade old, but most of the students who passed us looked as though they had read about all the big cultural changes in *Time* magazine but, failing to see how such changes applied to them, had gone on ahead with their lives just as they'd always done.

I was about to lead him off campus, but he'd stopped, seemed fascinated by the Jesuits' residence.

"This is where the Jesuits live," I said.

He looked upward, tilting his head slightly.

"They never marry," he said.

He'd phrased it not as a question but as a statement, pure and simple.

Mr. Bevilacqua was a widower, his wife having died five years before, when Tommy was fourteen. Tommy had learned domestic skills; he had attained the self-sufficiency of these priests. But his father—and this was clear even in the way his jaw set as he looked up at their quarters—could see nothing in womanlessness but a helpless groping. To *choose* such a state seemed amazing.

He was tired by now, and wanted to rest. We picked a spot, a circular garden surrounding an alabaster statue of the Virgin Mary. As soon as we sat he became fidgety again.

"Tommy's doing okay?" he asked.

"Oh, sure, he's thriving here."

"That's good."

He appeared to be weighing something in his mind.

"Not too much with the girls?"

"No."

"That's good." There was a pause. "I'm afraid, you know, since his mother died, Tommy's been a little wild."

"He's very mature."

He nodded his head.

"That's good."

"You'd be surprised."

I was going too far now, and I knew it. I looked away, over the white field beside us, wanting to make some forcible leap upward, out of this rut, to the place where I might be able to turn to this man and say, "Your son is insatiable. He thinks about nothing but cunt." But even that was laughable, like imagining Spencer Tracy saying those words in one of his priest's roles, where he's supposed to be giving succor to the wife of Clark Gable.

It was then that I saw her coming through the gates. She looked small, weighted down by bags, but her step was still light, and whatever else I may have thought of Fordham, it was transformed by her presence: its smallness, every ordinary detail had purpose now. I wanted to touch Mr. Bevilacqua, to squeeze his thigh and say, "Look!"

Instead, I remained very quiet, as if, sitting beside Mr. Bevilacqua, I could become invisible, disappear into the role of his custodian. He asked me a question about the clock tower and I quickly hushed him, so afraid was I of drawing her attention. She passed us. She opened the big iron door of Dealy. It has been as intense a series of seconds as I'd ever known; then, in its aftermath, I felt an anger directed at myself that I didn't understand. It seemed dimly possible—at the outer edge of things— that another boy, Tommy, for instance, might have acted differently, might have felt no guilt at abandoning Mr.

Bevilacqua and approaching her. But the old man was my charge; if I were to do such a thing, it could only be with his permission.

It was as if I'd chosen him for that reason.

Tommy appeared in the window of the restaurant, the letters ꓘOꓕIꟼAꓛ reading backwards across his chest. He wore a leather jacket, his newest affectation. He peered in through dark sunglasses.

"Tommy!" His father half-stood, one arm lifted; a forkful of egg fell onto his green pants.

Tommy opened the door and moved toward us.

"Jesus, where you been, Tom? You had me worried. You knew I was coming this morning, didn't you?" Mr. Bevilacqua had barely let his son come within hearing distance before starting.

"I just want to say one thing," Tommy said, sitting down beside me and removing his sunglasses. "Most guys, their fathers come visit them, they take them out someplace nice, someplace with a little class. You, I knew you'd come down from fuckin' Providence, right away you'd zero in on the biggest dive in the Bronx."

"It was Nick," Mr. Bevilacqua said. "I didn't pick this place. You ask him."

Tommy smirked.

"He said he wanted to take me out." I shrugged.

"You couldn't have waited five minutes?"

"We waited," his father said. "I got here last night."

Tommy stared at him a moment.

"When?"

"Around ten o'clock. I got home, I figured, what the hell, I'd surprise you."

There was no response. I felt as though I'd missed a beat.

"Where were you? Where'd you stay?"

Tommy looked off to the side, then said, "I was getting laid, Dad."

Mr. Bevilacqua's chin receded. He began fiddling with a saltshaker.

"Have something to eat," he said.

"Spiros!" Tommy called. "Lemme have two scrambled eggs, sausages."

The Greek waiter in the corner moved his head in assent.

"So you came without telling me."

Tommy's head was tilted now.

"I got bored at home." Mr. Bevilacqua touched his own head now. "I didn't think."

"You got bored." Tommy paused, the sides of his lips settled. "You got yourself a girlfriend yet?"

"No, no." He lifted the salt and pepper shakers, rearranged them on the table. "Come on, Tommy."

"Come on, what? You could be making some nice fat widow happy. Instead, what do you do, you watch TV."

Mr. Bevilacqua stared at the table. Tommy turned to me.

"I've been telling him for years he ought to get married." Tommy glanced up and down my face as though he was surprised at the way I looked now, in this proprietary stance with regard to his father. "He's got these pictures of Jesus up all over the bedroom."

Mr. Bevilacqua's hand started to go up in protest, but he must have thought better of it: he set his head in position, as if to endure this.

"My mother put them up in the bedroom and he won't take them down. He figures if he takes another woman to bed, Jesus is gonna see him and tell my mother."

He shifted in his seat. His father's head didn't move.

"Mom put Christ on the wall because of all her miscarriages, right? But look, I'm alive. I'm healthy. I made it to term. The deal didn't fall through, Dad. You were good, Christ gave you a healthy boy. Now forgive yourself, willya?"

Mr. Bevilacqua drew his coffee toward him. He looked at me. It was like he was saying, "See?"

"Why don't you say hello to your father nice before you start lecturing him?" I said.

Tommy reached over and tweaked his father's cheek. "Hello, Dad."

"Here are eggs." The waiter lowered Tommy's breakfast onto the table.

"Don't worry about me, Tommy. I been fine. Nick showed me around the campus."

Tommy, eating, nodded.

"I want to take you kids out tonight. Radio City Music Hall."

"Sure."

"You remember we went there with your mother?"

"Right. *To Kill a Mockingbird*. Jem and Scout. It marked me for life. Made me wanna grow up to be a fucking Southern lawyer."

"What's playing there now?" Mr. Bevilacqua asked.

"I don't know." Tommy scanned his father's face. There was a moment of uneasiness, as though he were going to start in on him again. Then he went back to his eggs.

"Okay. We'll go. We'll watch the Rockettes kick. We'll look at some leg."

"Nick'll come, right?" Mr. Bevilacqua asked.

"Sure," Tommy said.

"Yeah, go ahead, eat," his father said, as if Tommy had been waiting all this time for permission.

That night we watched *A New Leaf* at Radio City Music Hall. The picture looked grainy, inexpensive. Mr. Bevilacqua watched it as if he were worried that Walter Matthau would embarrass himself. Each time the audience laughed, he looked relieved.

We slept, the three of us, in the dorm room, myself and Mr. Bevilacqua on the beds, Tommy on the floor between us. I tried to be as quiet as possible when I masturbated. I'd waited till they were both asleep, till I could hear Tommy's quiet, even breathing on the floor, his father's snores. As quiet as I tried to be, though, I still managed to wake Mr. Bevilacqua.

"What is it?"

He sat up in bed, ramrod straight.

"It's okay," I whispered.

For a moment, he looked intensely frightened, as though by life itself, by the mere fact of being *awake*. Then he must have remembered where he was. He ran his hand back and forth over his head.

"It's all right," I said.

It was like coaxing a child back to sleep.

There were days when I would sit in class and watch Mrs. Branner move across the front of the room and feel an unexpected rush of pure bliss, as if this state—this inaccessibility of hers and my fevered waiting—were a satisfying, even desirable one, from which I had no wish to move on. After a while I made no more attempts to visit her, though each time I was near her office I couldn't resist passing by it, and looking in to get a glimpse of her. Once I caught her there, just staring above her desk in an attitude of exquisite boredom. She didn't see me. It made the waiting more real, somehow, to have this evidence of her distaste for her own life. I didn't know what the event would be that would change all this—push us into a new life. In truth, I couldn't imagine it. But I harbored a latent sense of power in me like a girding of the loins in preparation for battle, or like a physical practice one indulges without a necessary sense of its end.

There was an underside to all this, though. Occasionally, real life—the real life of others—would rise and smack me in the face. I would be standing in the room and look out across campus and see just that simple image of a boy talking to a girl—the shuffling movement of his thighs and the way she held her books—and something in me would rise to the surface, temporarily released and gasping for air. Or at night, when Tommy was off with a girl, and I would turn from my desk and look at his empty bed. As I imagined what he was doing, the light from my desk lamp suddenly became unbearable: I couldn't adjust it, or turn away from it without feeling the glare, so I would turn it off and fling myself on the bed, then think: what an absurd gesture, what an absurd life. One night, in the grip of this sort of tirade, I wrote to Julie Bonfiglio and declared my love. I was not exactly forgetting Mrs. Branner as I did it; merely assuming, in a way that seemed natural, that life could be lived on two levels at once. I mailed the letter before I could change my mind.

In the morning, there were doubts, but what could be done? I'd mailed it; I'd asked her to come. I had even made extravagant promises, told her she could stay in a hotel. There became something immediate to do: I had to find a way of making money.

The college placement service had something: a handkerchief manufacturer in the West Thirties was looking for a college boy to do "general office work."

"What the job is, mostly, is building boxes. Small ones," the woman who interviewed me said. She smiled apologetically. "We figure if we said that sort of thing in the ads, we'd never get the type of boy we're looking for. Aldo thinks college boys are the only reliable young workers around."

I stared beyond her at the thick, dust-laden air filtering in from Thirty-ninth Street.

"You know, and then too, we're always looking for young men to pose for our Christmas ad. We always run one in the *Times Magazine*, a sixteenth of a page, just at Christmas. And professional models are so expensive."

She reached into a box on her desk and extracted a large blue handkerchief, with a red border and a series of boxes, each a different shade of blue, leading to a tiny red box in the center.

"This is what we make. And here's the tag: 'Aldo of Milan.' That's where he's from, originally, Milan. The pay would be two dollars an hour, and we could use you, say,

twelve hours a week. Afternoons, whenever your classes
are over. Say, three afternoons?"
I said that would be fine.
"Oh, good." She appeared visibly relieved.
"We have one boy already; don't say anything, but
we're thinking of getting rid of him, if things work out
with you. Nelson's his name."
She raised her eyebrows dismissively.
"You can come in, first, when—tomorrow?"
"Sure."

The boxes came in flat sections of cardboard, which
had to be punched out, fitted together, then taped into
place. The work was relentless. The room we worked in
smelled as if horses had recently died there. From the
adjoining room, Aldo's Mediterranean voice purred into
the wires of a constantly lifted phone.
Nelson, the boy who taught me the job, seemed to develop an instant resentment in my presence—whether
because he sensed I was nosing him out of his job or
because I was college bred, and white, I could never be
sure. He showed me the work, and then was critical of
the way I did it, but never bothered to fix my misshapen
boxes. His responsibilities were larger—the getting of
lunch, delivery of orders—and he got huffy whenever he
was reduced to working alongside me.
When he did decide to speak, it was only to reveal his
obsession with the putative sex life of Mrs. Papandreou
(that was the name of the woman who had hired me) and
Aldo of Milan.
"He fucks her all the time," Nelson said. "I've seen,
and when I didn't see, I smelled." He would rub his nose
then, back and forth, as if that offended his sensibilities.
"The way she comes in here sometimes, you can tell. She
wiggles her ass: you watch."
If this was true, I figured Aldo would have to have figured out a way of doing it while talking on the phone. He
seemed attached to his WATS line, and could always be

heard from the workroom, touting his handkerchiefs, explaining the intricacy of a new design, complaining loudly of the cost of materials. He never condescended to speak to me.

The fact that it was a WATS line he was using had been proudly pointed out to me by Mrs. Papandreou the day she had hired me. "With this, you can call all over the country, and all you pay for is the lines themselves. This way, Aldo can keep up his contacts personally."

Often, in the midst of putting a box together, I thought of how easy it would be to pick up that phone and reach Julie at Linco Tool. Two weeks after I'd written Julie, she still hadn't answered. It was hard to understand why this should bother me, but it did. There was an implied rejection in her silence. Calling her at night was out of the question: Viola would answer, and I wanted none of that official courtship. I'd even left the return address off my letter to keep everything secret. One day I asked Mrs. Papandreou if I could use the WATS line to call Massachusetts.

She was handing me my paycheck in the office, and seemed taken aback by the request. Her mouth remained slightly open for several seconds; then she asked, "Is this personal, Nicholas?"

"I would pay. You can take it out of my next check. I just thought maybe I could make the call cheaper here."

"Well, if it's brief, I don't see that there's anything wrong. I'll ask Aldo how much he thinks it would be fair to charge you."

I expected that Mrs. Papandreou would leave the office, but she didn't. Instead, she opened a cup of yogurt and started to eat. Quickly, I secured the number of Linco Tool from Information, then dialed and heard a secretary's voice answer.

"I'd like to speak to Julie Bonfiglio, please."

There was no response at first from the secretary. I became worried that Julie didn't work there anymore. In the background, I could hear the faint whirring of machinery.

"Is this Nicholas?"

I had so convinced myself this wasn't Julie that the only logical response was to assume she'd passed my letter around the office; I was common currency in the secretarial pool.

"Yes."

Another silence followed.

"I got your letter."

Beside me, Mrs. Papandreou flipped through a rival's catalogue.

"I was just, umm, concerned that I didn't hear from you."

"I've been thinking of how to tell you."

She was speaking just above a whisper.

"Tell me what?"

"Well, I'm seeing someone else, Nicholas."

"That's all right," I said quickly, in reflex. "That's good."

She said nothing.

"You could still come."

"You'd still want me to?"

"Sure."

She had to think about it. I reflected on the way I'd said "Sure," and it was as if I were trying to convince Mrs. Papandreou that everything in this phone conversation was going just the way I wanted.

"I guess it would be all right."

There was a certain coldness in her voice. But why shouldn't there be? I had left her at the top of a landing, with the barrettes dangling out of her hair.

"I would stay in a hotel."

"Yes."

"When would be good?"

"Any weekend."

"Well, I can't this."

She receded, went far away for a moment.

"In two weeks I can come."

"I can get tickets to a show."

"That'd be great."

"Okay."

We both hung up a minute later, having said nothing more of significance. Mrs. Papandreou pretended not to have heard. I went back into the warehousing room, to fit together more boxes, and to listen to Nelson's latest theory on the sexual practices of his employers.

> *"In silent night when rest I took*
> *For sorrow near I did not look*
> *I wakened was with thund'ring noise*
> *And piteous shrieks of dreadful voice*
> *That fearful sound of 'Fire!' and 'Fire!'*
> *Let no man know is my desire."*

Mrs. Branner was reading at the front of the classroom, her head lifted, her voice clear if a bit uncertain, as though she were reaching for notes she hadn't recently practiced.

> *". . . coming out, beheld a space,*
> *The flame consume my dwelling place.*
> *And when I could no longer look,*
> *I blest his name that gave and took,*
> *That laid my goods now in the dust."*

The clear understanding of how much I wanted her had been suppressed lately; whenever the thought arose, it was as though a hand reached for it and pulled it underwater. Julie was coming in two days; it was Julie I was supposed to want now.

> *"No candle e'er shall shine in thee,*
> *Nor bridegroom's voice e'er heard shall be.*
> *In silence ever shall thou lie,*
> *Adieu, Adieu, all's vanity.*
> *Then straight I 'gin my heart to chide,*
> *And did thy wealth on earth abide?*
> *Didst fix thy hope on mold'ring dust?*
> *The arm of flesh did make thy trust?"*

Her voice had started to gather strength, but on "the arm of flesh" it broke off a little, and as it did some tight grip she'd held me in was loosened. It was as though, in that moment, I was seeing her from a distance, and it was so clear that the phrase hinted at sex—a cock, an arm of flesh—that hearing it was like receiving a slap: Yes, Nicholas, I have touched one, I have held one, I have even taken one in my mouth and *enjoyed* it. Involuntarily, I closed my eyes and found myself scratching at the edge of my desk so hard I came up with a splinter.

> *"Thou hast an house on high erect*
> *Framed by the mighty Architect,*
> *With glory richly furnished*
> *Stands permanent though this be fled.*
> *It's purchased and paid for too*
> *By him who hath enough to do."*

Suddenly, having lost the high excitement of the middle verses, she was laying the book down.

" 'Here Follows Some Verses Upon the Burning of our House, July 10th, 1666. Copied out of a Loose Paper.' Anne Bradstreet. What do you think?"

"Archaic," a girl said. "But sad."

"Sad how?"

"Oh . . ." The girl's hand gestured vaguely. Words failed her. Mrs. Branner waited, her look curious, testing.

"I don't think it's sad," a boy jumped in. "It's clear she's got her justification for it. She doesn't even wait for the ashes to cool before she's already justifying it. You know, it's God's, so God can have it. It's the whole Puritan thing."

"Meaning?"

"Well, they always had excuses, didn't they? They were scared of the Indians, scared of the country, so they clung to God."

She looked at him for several seconds, no expression on her face.

"She's an interesting woman," she said finally, pointedly ignoring the boy. "Maybe if you studied her, you'd find something more in the poem than you seem to be suggesting. Her father and husband were both governors of Massachusetts. She came here with a little rank, a soft life in England, and then—wham, the new world, with all its terrors. In addition to which she had trouble conceiving a child. Then, during one bad year, she lost three grandchildren and a daughter-in-law. All this in the midst of what she describes as a struggle with 'a carnal heart.'"

She did not look at me then. But I felt for the rest of the class that she was looking at me, holding the weight of my knowledge and teasing me with it. She seemed proud, defending Anne Bradstreet in front of us dolts. There was a sly look on her face the whole time she was talking, and it seemed to me as if she were not talking about a poem at all, but about some hidden underside to her life, the secret, eroticized part of it. I couldn't help but imagine it, and every time I thought of her with the man in the photograph I saw red for what seemed like minutes on end. I couldn't wait for the class to be over so that I could go somewhere and end my life. Surely it was not worth living. I had no idea how I would get through the weekend with Julie. Julie with her barrettes! What had I been thinking?

But by the time Julie arrived I'd convinced myself again that things were going to be great. I watched her step off the bus, and seeing her, only suffered a moment's bottoming-out before offering a big grin and shouting "Julie!"

It was clear from the start that Julie didn't share my lightheartedness. She offered her cheek, and then looked at me as if seeking out signs of mental illness.

"Here," I said, setting her suitcase down in front of the restaurant on Forty-fourth Street and handing her the hot dog I'd purchased from a street vendor. "You've heard of eating at Sardi's, haven't you, Julie? Well, here we are!"

She didn't find the joke very amusing, but made the

effort anyway. She sat on her suitcase while I stood, and
we ate our hot dogs in front of Sardi's.

She'd booked a room at the Hotel Consulate. Someone
from our local community had stayed there ages ago,
when it had been called the Hotel Forrest, and it had
become since then the preferred hotel for any one of us
traveling to New York. My parents had stayed there a
year ago, on their one visit to me. The black-and-chrome
elevator was familiar, as was the orange-and-black pat-
tern of the wallpaper in the hallways.

I sat in a chair beside Julie's bed while she unpacked.

"Do you want me to wait outside?" I asked.

"No. It's all right."

She unpacked only sweaters and toiletries. Her silk
underwear must have been at the bottom of the suitcase.

"I've got lots of things planned, Julie."

"That's nice." She was in the bathroom.

"I'm paying for this room; you know that."

"Nicholas." She appeared in the doorway. "You don't
have to do that."

"But I will. I'm working." It was a point of pride: I
might once have treated her cruelly, but I was at least no
slouch.

She smiled. "I'm glad you invited me."

I thought she stayed at the bathroom door a little too
long, as if waiting for me to say something she'd been
expecting, since her arrival, to hear.

The March light filtered in, hot and sneaky; I felt suddenly incredibly sleepy, like I wanted to curl up and take
a nap.

"I'll get ready and we'll go out, okay?" she asked finally.

We did everything that day that tourists do: went to the
top of the Empire State Building, then took the ferry to
the Statue of Liberty, and ended up at the U.N. "The
U.N.?" I thought, as the guide pointed out the closed

door to the Secretariat. Julie tried to look interested, and stifled a yawn.

We were too rushed for time afterwards to eat dinner. Julie wanted to change before going to the theater, and I had left this part of the planning to chance, assuming some quaint little out-of-the-way bistro would just turn up. We saw *Sleuth*, and I tried to keep my stomach from grumbling. I had no patience with the play and its "tricks." Somewhere in this city there existed a wild, liberating theatrical experience, but I couldn't blame anyone but myself for this choice. Whenever I entered the city proper, a green-tinted window seemed to go up in front of my face.

Afterwards, Julie professed hunger, and we had to choose from among the midtown coffee shops, all of which, I suspected, would be overpriced. I was on the verge of suggesting we walk all over the city until we found the out-of-the-way place I'd imagined, but she pointed out an unassuming hamburger joint near the Palace Theater, and I thought we might as well.

"The California Burger looks good," she said, consulting a menu heavy on cow imagery.

I watched her glance down the long list of hamburgers.

"Yes," I nodded, wishing suddenly that we could be different: that Uncle Billy had been able to keep it in his pants and therefore not have been found in the pink T-bird the night of my father's party. That Julie had never so much as seen a barrette, that she considered them tacky. That I were... well, what was the use? We ate our hamburgers and talked about her life at Linco, mine at school. She asked polite questions which I found it impossible to answer. "Mostly, I masturbate" would have been the answer to too many of them.

Afterwards, we rode the elevator up to her room in the Consulate and sat on the bed with our shoes off, watching Richard Harris, on a late-night talk show, sing "MacArthur Park."

"This is my favorite part," I said, when the lyrics to the song ended, and a long musical interlude forced Richard

Harris to dance around and think of things to do for what seemed like an hour.

When the song was over, and Richard Harris was explaining how hard it had been to film some of the scenes in *A Man Called Horse*, I turned to Julie and asked, "So who's this guy you're seeing?"

She took a moment before answering, started twirling a strand of hair around her finger.

"It's this guy at Linco." She paused. "I knew he wanted to ask me out after Lonnie died, but it took him a long time. He's real polite."

She wasn't going to offer anything more unless I prodded.

"So do you like him?"

"Yes."

"It doesn't sound like you're in love, or anything."

"No. I guess I'm not."

We watched a commercial.

"I've been thinking about tonight, you know, and what should happen, and I think on account of how rotten I was to you last time that you should make me go back up to Fordham and sleep in the dorm."

She said nothing at first.

"Make me prove myself," I said.

She continued to twirl her hair around her finger.

"And then you'd come back in the morning?" she asked.

"Yes."

"Okay."

She walked me to the doorway and we kissed. I ran my hand up and down her back, feeling the skin under her silk blouse, and then just feeling a moment's excitement. I looked at her and was unable to read her face. The room behind her looked large and neutral, a place you'd be afraid to fall asleep.

"You're sure you're all right here?" I asked.

"I'm fine."

Back in bed in the dorm, I lowered my hand immediately. I'd had hopes that a deep sexual desire for Julie would overwhelm me, but it was no use. The stroking actually became painful, forcing desire in one direction when it clearly wanted to go in another.

The next morning I was at her door well before noon.

"I had breakfast downstairs," she said.

"Alone?"

"Yes."

"Did you go to church, too?"

"No."

Her face darkened slightly: was this something I wasn't supposed to ask?

I took her on a hansom-carriage ride through Central Park.

"I'd like to take some pictures," she said, when we were not more than five minutes into it.

It would have been all right, but she kept getting out to take pictures of me alone in the carriage, and then having me get out to take pictures of her, until finally the driver offered to take pictures of the two of us together. While I was smiling into the camera, I kept thinking of how these pictures would turn up at her house, and Viola would see them, and in everyone's minds we would be practically engaged.

"I had a really good time, Nicholas," she said when we were back in the bus terminal that afternoon.

"So did I."

I wanted to touch her, to find the one gesture that would allow me to apologize for putting her through this weekend. Before I could find it, though, she stepped onto the bus.

I couldn't decide, as I searched for her face in the windows, whether to leap onto the bus and destroy her camera, or to get down on my knees in the aisle by her seat and offer to dedicate myself to the eradication of the memory of "Lonnie," whose stupid death had, in its way, made her vulnerable to the likes of me.

But as the bus was pulling out, I was thinking of neither incriminating photographs nor declarations of fealty, but of the amount of money her visit had cost: $30 for the theater tickets, $35 for the hotel, dinner, subways, and the hansom ride, another $30: in the end I could barely find the profit from all those afternoons putting together boxes at Aldo of Milan.

When I came out of this reverie, she was gone.

"Aldo's heart was broken last year at the opening of the musical *Coco*. You know, with Katharine Hepburn."

Mrs. Papandreou had her yogurt out, and had drawn up a chair next to where I was making boxes. Lately she'd been coming in to chat like this, unexpectedly. I thought I had a hint now of why I'd been hired: to play Ethel to Mrs. Papandreou's Lucy.

"You see, many years ago, he and Coco Chanel had a brief fling, in Paris. I guess all the young designers probably fooled around with one another in those days. Aldo's career since then has been disappointing. He's seen far lesser talents than himself anointed, and he's taken it hard."

She spooned yogurt into her mouth and seemed to allow it to fill every crevice before swallowing it.

"He really hoped, when he heard they were planning a musical of Coco's life, that he'd get some mention. Miss Hepburn might refer to a certain 'Aldo' with dreamy eyes, and business might get a little boost. He admitted afterwards that it was all a little foolish, buying the most expensive opening-night tickets, just on the *chance*."

She glanced out the window, through the filter of dust.

"But we went. I was his date. And every time Miss Hepburn, as Coco, started to talk about her past, I could feel Aldo start to sweat beside me. It was terrible to expe-

rience. It was like watching a man see his last chance for
real notoriety get washed away."

She sighed, and put her yogurt cup in the wastebasket.
I started another box.

"How does the place survive?"

"Oh, we do a lot of business at Christmas, Nicholas.
The ad always helps. And we're the whole staff."

She crossed her legs. Obviously, she intended to stay
here awhile.

"You'll be in the ad this year, Nicholas. Aldo and I
have already discussed it. Of course, you'll have to get
that hair cut."

I tried to smile; I knew I wouldn't last here till
Christmas.

"Would you do me a favor and just push the hair off
your forehead? Let me see what you look like when your
whole face shows."

This was stupid, but I did it.

"See? You're a handsome boy. Why do you want to
look like a hippie?"

"I'm not trying to look like a hippie."

"Well, what, then?"

Her hands were folded over her knee, and the crossed
leg swung.

"Would you like to see a picture of Aldo when he was
young, in Paris?"

Without waiting for my answer, she ran into the office
and came back with a black-and-white photograph. Four
men and a woman were gathered together in a garden,
two of the men slouched against a wall.

"That's Aldo there in the corner." She pointed to one of
the slouching men. The young Aldo held a cigarette and
peered at the camera with sexy, insolent eyes. He had on
a silk shirt.

"These are some of the young designers of Paris."

She spoke of them as though they were a club, like the
Jaycees.

"He was very handsome, wasn't he?"

Her leg was unmistakably rubbing against mine; for an instant, our hips touched.

"How long have you been working here, Mrs. Papandreou?"

She touched her glasses.

"Five years. Why?"

I shrugged, and lifted another of the cardboards, punched it into box shape.

"Mrs. Papandreou, I don't think I can work much longer."

"Are you tired?"

"No."

I could tell she was looking at me.

"No, I mean I'm going to have to quit soon. School-work's piling up."

There was a silence. I didn't want to look at her face.

"Oh."

Again, she adjusted her glasses.

"It will be hard on us, I can tell you that. You've been very dependable."

"Nelson can do what I do."

At first she said nothing. Then: "What about the ad?"

There was a small petulance in her voice, a little girl who's just been told some plan she'd counted on would have to be indefinitely postponed.

"I'm sorry."

"Is it the money?"

"No."

"I can't offer you any more."

It was horrible. She just stood there for several seconds afterwards, saying nothing. I still couldn't look at her face. Then she left, went into her office. There was a heavy silence in the rooms, interrupted by the sound of the radio—the Carpenters: "Close to You." She had left Aldo's picture in front of me, and while I made boxes I looked at it.

I decided I wouldn't come back, this would be my last day. I didn't tell Mrs. Papandreou this, though. When I said goodbye, she barely looked up, pretending to be busy at her books.

It was days like these that took up the semester, swallowed it, left me with nothing to show. Other boys, I imagined, were having adventurous lives; I was punching out boxes, moving on a guided tour through the United Nations, listening to Mrs. Papandreou chatter away.

Uncle Billy was calling, too. He was spending more time in the city, hinting at the presence of a woman friend. He'd called twice over the past couple of months, and I'd been able to put him off. When he called for the third time, I figured I had to meet him. "I'm in the city and I'm trying to see my own nephew," he'd crowed over the phone. "What do I have to do, make a reservation?"

We arranged to meet downtown, to have "brunch" (Billy's word) in a restaurant in the Village. It was a Sunday, and lower Manhattan seemed practically deserted. I found Billy sitting across from a woman in the window booth of the restaurant.

"Nicholas." He stood a moment, looking at me as if this were some big deal. "Nicholas, I'd like you to meet Judy Warrilow."

She waited to hear her name spoken before smiling. She reached over to shake my hand.

"My nephew," Billy said, a little floridly.

Judy attempted to light a cigarette. I noticed that whatever her face was doing, her hair remained perfectly in place. It was lacquered into a flip on either side, in the manner of women who worked in small-town beauty parlors. In this, and other particulars, she had the look Billy favored: the starlet look of the '50s, gone to seed.

"So tell me, what's up?"

It was clear from Billy's face that he wanted a stimulating answer.

"This and that."

He grabbed one of Julie's cigarettes and lit it. "Listen to him," he smirked. "This and that. Judy, this kid gets more pussy than Frank Sinatra."

"I bet he does." Judy looked delighted.

"Not really," I said.

"What are we eating?" Billy shifted in his seat. "Judy?"

"Eggs Benedict," she answered. "Order for me. I've got to use the Ladies'. Benedict, Billy, not Florentine."

"Benedict, right."

The restaurant they'd chosen looked like a hangout for theater types. There were posters on the wall smacking of the avant-garde: La Mama, Grotowski, those types. Judy's fanny wiggled on her way to the bathroom, but no one turned to look.

"What do you think?"

Billy's face now suggested one of those well-fed burghers in an old Dutch painting.

"She's very nice."

"Nice? Nicholas, she's loaded. You should see where she lives. She's got an apartment on Fifty-fifth Street that'd knock you out."

He shifted back in his chair, to gauge the effect this was having on me.

"You ride the elevators, ladies dripping with diamonds, pearls. Jesus, and all I gotta do is this."

He pulled his arm back at the elbow, then motioned rhythmically back and forth with his forearm.

"So things are okay with me," he said when he was finished. "How about yourself?"

"Oh, I'm just trying to get back into the rhythm of school," I said. I was uncomfortable, being grilled this way. I reached for one of Judy's cigarettes. "You think she'd mind?"

"Sure, go ahead," he said, leaning back now, surveying me from a distance. I lit a cigarette and watched the way Billy watched me light it. I rarely smoked, and he seemed to know it.

"Things are changing for me, Nicholas. No more here,

there, running around like a chicken with its head cut off."

He gestured with one hand to demonstrate the motion of a chicken with its head cut off. It looked, oddly, imprecise.

"I'm thinking of basing myself in New York, Nicholas. What do you think?"

"With the band?"

"Oh, fuck the band."

"Great," I said. The word sounded forced, empty.

Judy returned from the bathroom.

"You ordered Benedict?" she asked, her buttocks dusting off the chair as she sat.

"Benedict? Oh, shit," Billy feinted. "I thought you said Florentine."

Her mouth formed a long rigid schism. She looked ready to kill.

"Only kidding, only kidding, Judy. Benedict it is." He ducked under an imaginary blow. "The waiter hasn't even come yet, Judy." He winked at me.

Judy's expression took a while to change. She snapped her pocketbook shut and turned to me, rolling her eyes and shifting her chin toward Billy.

"Joker," she said.

When brunch was over, Billy and I went for a walk. Judy had no interest in joining us, so we called her a cab. Then we started uptown, heading nowhere in particular, stopping at Twenty-third Street to drink a couple of cups of take-out coffee on benches in Madison Square Park.

Billy looked happy as he stared up at the gray stone of the Flatiron Building.

"Twenty-three skidoo," he said.

I looked at him. He was huddled down in his coat, smiling, catlike.

"That's where the expression comes from, did you know that, Nicholas? Twenty-third Street, the wind used to blow the ladies' dresses up, cops had to keep the guys from congregating."

"Is that right?"

He was pleased by his knowledge.

"Judy's got some books around the apartment." He shrugged and looked around. "Great city."

The day started to turn colder. Something about Uptown cowed us both, I think, so we headed back down. At Gramercy Park, Billy tried the gates and found them locked. It bewildered him. A lady with a dog inside the park ignored Billy when he asked if she would open it. I was only embarrassed.

"C'mon, Billy, let's get out of here."

"No shit, what do they think they are—they're rich, they're better than me?"

He straightened his clothes, as if he'd been in a fight.

"Judy's got more money than these people, any day."

Then he hit me on the shoulder, as if to show it didn't bother him, and laughed his cackling laugh.

We walked down to Little Italy. Billy told me he was going to marry Judy. I had to work hard to offer up a convincing "Congratulations."

"You'll like her, you'll get to know her," he said.

I kept waiting for it to be over, the allotted portion of time finished so I could leave Billy and go back to my life. But then I thought, "What life?" All I could think of was the room in the dorm, and I didn't want to be there either. I was always rejecting things and people as if there were something so great I was protecting. But if there was, where was it?

On Mulberry Street, Billy stopped to speak Italian to a couple of men outside a bar. The door was open; there was a pool table just inside, several hangers-on. A sign over the door said "MEMBERS ONLY."

"Come on in, Nicholas," Billy said, after he'd spoken to the man.

Inside, no one moved. We drank shots of whiskey at the bar. Billy's energy was the only thing in the room that seemed alive, like a tank of tropical fish in a darkened living room. I looked outside at the movement on the streets.

"This is my nephew," I heard Billy say, but no hand was proffered, no head nodded. The whiskey went down easy, a little pit of warmth inside. One of the men went out, stood in the doorway a few seconds, then came back in.

"You ever been down here before, Nicholas?" Billy asked.

"No."

He huddled up closer to the bar. The wetness there stained his belly.

"Sure, you should come here." He threw his arm around me. "These guys, they're half-dead, but at least they'll let us in."

In the last class of the semester, Mrs. Branner asked us to bring in our record albums and read aloud the lyrics having to do with fire.

Listening, she gave the impression she didn't really like this idea, but was doing it to fulfill that part of the course description which had read, "from William Blake to Jimi Hendrix." As it turned out, no one brought in Jimi Hendrix. Eleven students brought in "Fire and Rain."

At the end of class, I went up to her desk and asked if I could take another course with her.

She was distracted. There were others waiting. She asked if I could come to her office.

Once there, she made a quick phone call, then just sat there, looking at her desk and touching her forehead, and I wondered if she knew I was there at all.

"What was it you wanted to talk about?" she asked finally.

"I wanted to talk about taking another course."

The way she looked now made it sound like the stupidest thing anyone had ever said. She reached for her bag, as if it were essential now that she be on her way.

"What is it you'd like to take?" she asked, when we were walking to her car.

"Anything you teach."

The baldness of it seemed plain and dull. And beside me, the way she lifted her head and faced the short breeze filled me with a sense of cosmic inadequacy. It seemed she was of another race entirely; her senses worked on a whole other level.

"I'm only doing two courses in the fall. A survey course and another one of these silly team-teaching things."

She went on, with a touch of anger, "I proposed a seminar on Simone Weil, and they practically laughed at me."

"I don't know much about it, but I've heard they let you do tutorials here."

Her eyebrows rose; meanwhile, something in me ducked, anticipating rejection, a stream of words coming from her, telling me exactly where I stood. I would accept them.

"Yes, they do. What were you thinking?"

"I was thinking of that poet you mentioned, the one you read from, with the burning house."

"Anne Bradstreet."

"Yes. Her. I went to the library and looked her up."

A lie. A moment before, I hadn't even been able to remember her name.

"I was thinking of doing something with her."

"Oh," she said.

"Do you think..."

"Write something up over the summer, why don't you. I'm sure I could get that approved."

When she found her car it seemed like she was going to go right ahead and get in without even saying goodbye. It was a Volvo, a pale color, tan. At the last moment she turned to me and smiled a little.

"So, are you doing anything exciting this summer?" she asked.

I wished she hadn't asked it. I looked down at the gravel of the parking lot and thought of the laundromat and then blurted it out.

"The one that blew up?" That she'd remembered at all astounded me.

"Yes. Well, it didn't exactly blow up."

Go ahead, I thought. Explain everything, as if even now you were not two hundred miles away but in the midst of it.

"I've been thinking of doing something else, though. Staying here. My friend Tommy drives a cab. I've been thinking of doing that."

She offered no reaction. Clearly now, she wanted to go.

"What do you think I should do?"

I leaned a bit closer, though we were not close. I'd got what I wanted, but now it was as though something in me had to beg for more. I watched her eyes scan my face and for a moment I thought she took me and my question more seriously than either deserved.

Then she let out a little half-laugh.

"You should do what you want."

I wondered what my face looked like as I accepted this answer and nodded and stepped back. She got into her car and started the engine, then turned to me and smiled, tapping on the window by way of goodbye. Then she left me there—while her car took on the traffic of Eastern Boulevard—to marvel at the idiocy of my life.

They were waiting for me in the arched entrance to South Station, stiff as the bride and groom on a wedding cake. Other parents had come running up to the train, eager to greet their offspring, but John and Josie remained set in their pose, as if they'd rehearsed this way and were determined to resist spontaneity.

"Nicholas, you look well," my father said.

"Yes. You too."

We hugged. I could smell my mother's lavender perfume, feel the starch on my father's shirt.

"Aunt Rose is waiting inside," my mother said. "She drove us."

Rose was sitting in the midst of the Memorial Day crowd, looking as though the busy throng, the festive atmosphere of the station were a personal affront.

"You know you can get off at the Route 128 station, Nickie," she said to me. "It's a lot easier for us."

We piled into Rose's Rambler. My mother's hand squeezed my knee.

"How was school?" she asked.

"It was good."

"I'm waiting to see those grades." Her gaze fell on the buildings of Chinatown. One hand reached out to chip away a bit of napkin that had stuck to my father's white, ashy skin. The remains of lunch. They had eaten in town: pastrami sandwiches, the three of them squirreled away at a corner table in a deli; I could see it all.

We drove home in a barely punctuated silence. Uncle Carmen had broken his wrist a week ago. We talked about that.

In the house, my mother and Aunt Rose went immediately to the preparation of dinner. I went into my room to unpack.

The room had, in my brief absence, taken on the aspect of a shrine: on the wall, just above my high school diploma, an 8x10 replica of my yearbook photo had been mounted. I looked too young, too happy for my situation. I looked at it and thought: Idiot.

My father came in and sat at my desk, watching me unpack.

"That's all—that's all you brought home?" he asked.

"I didn't take much with me, remember?"

"Where's your trunk? You sent that ahead?"

"No. I left it there."

He was looking at the rug, at the floor between us.

"You're not afraid?" he asked.

"Of what?"

"Somebody grabbing it."

"No."

I had my clothes all lined up on the bed now. I was uncertain where to put them.

"I'm moving off campus, Dad," I said. "My friend Tommy Bevilacqua and I found a place. The rent is a hundred ten a month. That's cheaper than the dorm."

This was all true.

"Off campus?" he repeated.

"Yes."

"That's smart?"

"Oh, sure. It's cheaper."

"What I mean is, you'll still get your studying done? Things won't get too wild?"

"No."

He nodded, studied the rug again.

After a moment, he said, "So your trunk is there now? Your friend, he's living there now?"

"Yes."

"All summer?"

"All summer."

Again, he nodded. This time he stood up as well.

"I've got to run down to the laundromat before supper. Relieve Ray so he can eat. You want to come with me?"

"Sure."

"You don't have to—I mean, if you want to stay, talk to your mother."

"No. I'll come with you."

"Okay," he said finally.

"Hey, Nickie," Ray said, the French-Canadian music in his voice rising and falling on the simple phrase. "Hey, you're back now for the summer."

I said nothing, but smiled and let him hit me on the shoulder.

"Cause your father here wasn't sure."

My father was looking out the window. The plate glass that had replaced the exploded window still, all these months later, looked newer, cleaner than the adjoining plate. My father looked as though he were inspecting it for flaws.

"You can go and have your dinner now, Ray," he said.

"Oh, sure, John. I'm just going in the back; you didn't have to come down."

"No, I know," my father said, "but this way nobody can bother you."

Ray took a paper bag containing his supper from behind the counter and left us. My father and I sat down on the front bench.

"You want some coffee?" he asked.

"No, thanks, Dad."

He got up and went to run a rag across the top of a row of machines.

When he came back, he said, "You sure about that coffee?"

"You want some?" I asked. "I'll get you some."

I went into the Mr. Donut and bought him a coffee. It was like walking across a map of my life.

Then I listened to my father drink the coffee. He drank with a quick slurping sound.

"We appreciated what you did last fall," he said.

"Oh."

"No, don't make light of it. We appreciated it."

I waited a moment: what was this a prelude to? He reached over and squeezed the skin above my knee. He used to do that when I was twelve, fourteen, usually after a period when he'd been lost in his own thoughts.

"What are your plans now, Nick?"

He took another slurp of the coffee.

"I'm going to drive a cab."

It was said before I could imagine myself saying it, and, probably for that reason, was accompanied by sweet relief.

He said nothing.

"I want to take care of things myself. I'm going to pay my own tuition."

I was aware now of going too fast. It was because I was trying to anticipate his every objection. Remarkably, though, he seemed to have none. He drank his coffee.

"This is in the city?"

"Yes."

He looked ahead.

"You got yourself one of those special licenses?"

"I'm in the process of getting one."

There seemed to be not a sound in the laundromat: not a dryer turned, not a sheet rippled. I thought if I listened hard enough I might hear Ray chewing. My father gripped the underside of the bench with one hand.

"How much can you make doing this?"

"Tommy says..." I stopped myself. Who was this child beginning his sentences with "Tommy says..."?

"I guess you can earn about a hundred and fifty a week, on the average."

He lifted his eyebrows slightly.

"Then you'll be paying your apartment..."

"I figure I can save better than a thousand. And tuition's only nine hundred. Then if I do it part time next semester..."

He tapped the bench gently.

"You're there to learn, Nick, not to make money."

There was nothing more to say. We sat there, very quietly, for several minutes. Then he got up and started sweeping.

He attacked the corners of each area, getting at pockets of dirt that wouldn't have been loosened in years of normal sweeping. He made neat patterns with the dirt, leading it all toward a central pile. Ray came out of the back room and sat down next to me, lit a cigarette.

"Your fadder," he said, "work, work, work, y'know?" He made a rowing motion with the hand holding the cigarette.

"Hey, John, I'm still on break, you know!" he called, his eyes squinting to accent the joke.

"Oh, I know." My father offered him a smile that showed his teeth locked into place too tightly; it could as easily have been a grimace of anger. Ray laughed back, though, heartily. The two of us sat and watched my father until he was finished. Then Ray got up and took his keys out of his pocket and carried the trash buckets to the back of the store.

"Just don't tell your mother about this cab business," my father said, putting the broom away.

We drove home in silence, attentive to the construction of houses at the side of the road, the presence of cars in the church parking lot, and a sale on native peas at the farm stand near our house.

In front of the house, Uncle Al's car was parked beside his wife's, leaving no room for us to reach the garage.

"Jeez," my father said, "Al comes here, he forgets we live here too."

As soon as I was out of the car, I caught the smell of my mother's tomato sauce, and wished she'd cooked something else, something American. I could too easily imagine the scene within: the relatives; the steaming sauce; their corner on reality marshaled, as if in their full awareness of its power. My father took his time adjusting the sprinkler on the front lawn. I thought of Mrs. Branner in the parking lot, the cool efficiency of her unspoken challenge.

"Hey, Uncle Al," I said, as soon as we were inside and I saw him at the top of the stairs. I reached up and touched his shoulder, remembering how the last time I'd seen him I'd insulted him, on the steps of the Sons of Italy Hall.

"Nickie," he answered, patting my hand almost before the words of truce were out.

"Everybody's here," my mother said. "Let's all sit down."

The big plates of thick spaghetti mired in my mother's pulpy, copper-tinged sauce made steaming pools on the formica table. My mother piled two meatballs and a thick red pork chop on my plate. Outside, in the distance, I could hear children playing. When I looked up, I was surprised to see that it was still light.

Above the table, my father stood jingling the keys in his pocket.

"Sit, John," my mother said.

He had to be called down from his high perch, whatever Olympus of small business he happened to be surveying the world from, making plans to fit himself, my mother, Ray. Once seated, though, he attacked his food like grim necessity.

"So how was school?" Al had turned to me, his big grin sending ripples up the sides of his face. "I bet you liked getting back, huh?"

"I did."

"You figure it out yet, what you wanna do? Any of those professors there help you out?"

The image in my mind was of a hand wrapped around a red, straining cock.

"Yes," I said. "It's getting clearer."

Dinner was silent for several moments.

"Nicholas has gotten a job in New York," my father said, not looking up.

My mother's head lifted.

"What's this?" Al said.

Rose was mysteriously silent.

I looked at my father. "On campus," I said.

"Where, on campus?" Al asked, as though he were familiar with the setup.

"In the Dean's office."

"The Dean." Al was impressed.

I hesitated turning to my mother.

"So who's gonna work in the laundromat?" Rose asked.

"Ray," I said quietly.

The name landed like a useless object among them.

"Your father's tired," Rose said.

"I know that."

Finally I glanced at my mother. Her face held a curious pose: as though she might be able to accept this if only she could find the logic behind it.

"We were expecting you," she said.

"I know that."

It was not at all the way I'd imagined it. But that didn't

seem to have very much to do with anything now.

My mother looked down at her plate of pork chops.

"He's got to live his own life, Josie," my father said from across the table. It hushed them, like an announcement that he had agreed to it, so all arguments became futile. I couldn't imagine why he was doing this.

"For the summer?" Al asked, several moments later, as though, having hit on this undetermined bit of information, he might be able to gnaw through to a solution.

"Yes. For the summer."

His head dropped an inch or two, and he went back to eating. The subject felt uneasily closed. I wished that they would fight more. I wished that whatever had to be going on underneath all this infuriating politeness would burst through. Instead, it sounded, and remained below the surface even after Al and Rose had gone. My parents involved themselves with Marcus Welby, and I lost hope that they were only waiting until Al and Rose had left to exorcise their anger. Watching them, I imagined how once, long ago, when they were newly married, they'd gone to see one of those old English movies—*Random Harvest* or *Mrs. Miniver*—and decided that if ever they were blessed with a son, this was how they'd behave toward him: civil, refined, undemanding, exactly like Greer Garson and Ronald Colman.

In the middle of *Marcus Welby*, I asked if I might borrow the car.

"Where are you going?" my mother asked.

"Just for a ride."

I drove to a pay phone and dialed Julie's number. Viola answered and I hung up. Ten minutes later the same thing happened. I drove to their house, having gotten the address from the phone book. It was a small house, crowded in by others, near a bridge in Newton. Which was Julie's room? I imagined throwing pebbles up at her window, waking her. I found a drugstore and called. Viola for the third time answered.

"Is Julie home?"

"Yes she is. Hold on."

It had been so simple. Why did I complicate things so?

She met me in the car, parked in front of the house next to hers, the dark one.

"Surprise," I said.

"Yes." She got in.

"Did your mother ask where you're going?"

"I told her it was you. I said you wanted to talk in the car."

"So no secrets."

She looked at me as though it was odd I should suggest that.

"I always come to you when I'm having trouble with my parents."

"That's all right."

I leaned over and kissed her neck, left my head there, in the soothing warmth.

"What's the problem you're having with them?"

"No problem. That's the problem."

I didn't want to talk. It required me to move my head.

"I'm staying in New York for the summer."

Then an unexpected feeling came over me.

"Christ, don't they want me to come home?"

I lashed out at the dashboard with one fist.

Julie waited a moment, then said: "Of course they do. But they respect you."

"Why?"

She said nothing.

"I'm not worthy of respect."

"Shh, Nicholas."

I kissed her. Then it seemed the appropriate, logical thing to put my hand on her breast.

"I only came here to talk."

She giggled.

"It's not funny."

"I know."

She wanted to be kissed, clear enough. I wondered who this guy was, from Linco Tool, that he could leave her so unsatisfied.

"It's you I want," I said.

"I know."

Her hand was on me.

"Oh, Jesus," I said.

In response, she started stroking. Then she unzipped my pants.

"This is nice," I said.

I was kissing her neck a long time, listening to her moan. Then it was over.

It was okay. I would clean it up later. This was all because I had wanted to rest my head on her neck. She was a girl who liked to do this, that was all. There was no reason for guilt.

We kept kissing, and in a minute I was hard again, but this time she took her hand away.

"I'm starting to think that any minute my mother is going to come out and invite you in for coffee cake."

This started us both laughing.

"You're right. I can see her in the window. It's Viola."

She laughed some more.

"You still seeing the guy?"

She scratched her forehead.

"Yes."

I wanted to kiss her now more than ever, I kissed her cheeks and her forehead and her nose.

"Let's do it, Julie."

"No. I'm getting worried, really."

"You want to go back?"

"Yes."

"Why?"

"Because I know she's going to start getting nervous."

"How come every time we want to do it, there's no place, and when there's a bed right in front of us, we don't want to do it?"

"I don't know."

I sensed a part of her had gone inside.

"Will you come visit me in New York again?"

"Yes."

"When? This summer?"

"Sure."

"I've got an apartment now."

She didn't say anything.

"You want to come inside and say hello to her?" She'd turned to me.

"Sure. Can I go like this?"

My erection was sticking straight up out of my pants. She didn't think it was funny, though. She even looked like it troubled her a little that I had suggested it in fun.

I kissed her again, and put myself away.

"Nicholas, what a surprise. Why didn't you come in in the first place?" Viola held the door open.

"I just wanted to talk to your daughter."

I was seeping into my pants. I felt an intense fear of Viola's antennae, her ability to see through me.

"Well, come in for coffee."

"It's late. I should go home and see my parents."

"Oh, I imagine they're asleep by now. We're the only night owls in the family."

Then she gave her daughter a look that let me know she wasn't used to having guests this late.

"Well, come see us again, then, will you? You're home for the summer?"

"No."

I watched the sides of Viola's mouth go down.

"But I'll try and come. Good night, Julie."

In a minute, the door was shut and I walked down the steps onto the street and looked up at the house, waiting for the light to come on in whichever of the rooms was Julie's. I thought of the things she would have to do now, wash her hands and the part of her shirt I had landed on, to rid herself of the smell and feel of me.

I drove home. I had at least somehow managed, with Julie's help, to forget what had been bothering me. I felt light. I cleaned up the mess I'd made in the front seat and then carried the wad of paper towels up to the kitchen to throw them away. My father was asleep in the den, with the light on. His mouth was open. The light shone on his head.

"Dad?"

I shook him.

"You fell asleep."

He rubbed his face.

"I was waiting up."

"Thanks."

I went to my room and took my clothes off. He came in, in his bathrobe. When he saw I had nothing on, he wouldn't look at me. He sat in the chair of my desk and looked at the rug.

"I wanted to ask you," he said.

He had to fight sleep. He looked tired.

"I want to pay your tuition."

His head shook from side to side.

"This is just something I want to do. Don't ask..."

He seemed to be addressing the rug.

Look at me, I almost said.

Every year, it seemed, he lost a little more hair. I thought, sitting there, that it was like the blanket of his life being slowly pulled back: that when there was no more hair, he too would go.

"That's okay, Dad. If it's important."

He yawned. I wondered if it had been as serious as all that.

He got up finally and went to his room. The doorknob turned, and there was absolute silence in the house.

"So you wanna go out to the airport?"

Tommy was sitting across from me in the Blimpie, in the eerie light coming from the blown-up photographs of overstuffed sandwiches. His face over the summer had taken on a little extra weight.

"No. I'm gonna hang around the West Side."

"The West Side's dead. Everybody's at the fuckin' opera in the park."

I shrugged. Tommy bit into his sandwich, came up with a mouthful of lettuce.

"What are you, afraid you'll get groped again?"

The week before, a man claiming to have been one of John Lindsay's prep-school roommates had made a pass, while handing over a twenty-dollar bill.

"Or do you keep expecting to see her? That's it, isn't it?"

He reached under the table and gave my thigh a squeeze.

"Higher," I said.

"Maybe she's out flagging a cab right now. Nickie, you might miss her. Better run. I just saw her—that was her! Her hand is up! Nickie!"

He showed me his teeth, wet with mayonnaise. He didn't need much from me when he started going on like this; I thought it would have been better if I'd never mentioned Mrs. Branner to him. I looked out the window to where our cabs were parked on Eighty-sixth Street.

"You want to meet a real girl?" Tommy leaned forward.

"What's a real girl, Tommy? One of those bimbos who like to lick your scrotum? This is your definition of a big deal?"

"Answer me this, okay? When you're with this Cynthia"—every time Tommy said the name, his voice dripped with contempt—"are you aware of the fact that you have a penis?"

I spread my hands out on the table.

"Because, Nickie, lemme tell you, you do not need in your life right now somebody who's gonna encourage the ascetic."

"What I feel for her is none of your business."

"No, but your physical life is, Nick. What about the nice Italian girl who jerked you off? Have you called her?" Julie was a source of guilt now: two months had gone by.

"It's wrong."

"Oh, Jesus."

"It *is*, Tommy."

"What is this, *Judgment at Nuremberg*? You think she did that to you because she hated it?"

Again, I looked away.

"You and my father, just the same. Sex is some shameful thing. Pleasure is a thing you gotta go runnin' to tell the priests."

"I don't believe that."

"No? Then what?"

He was waiting.

"I gotta get back to work."

"How much have you clocked so far tonight?"

"Thirty-five dollars."

Tommy put his shades back on, in the already dark Blimpie.

"Jesus, and you're not even making money."

It was true: I'd been called in twice by the dispatcher to find out why my totals were consistently less than the other drivers'. How could I tell them? I hugged the West Side like a familiar shore in thick fog. I scoured the streets for her. It was stupid, I knew, but done in isolation, there was nothing to keep me from it, no other voice, like Tommy's, suggesting alternatives. Some nights as I made my habitual pass down Ninetieth Street, I would become almost frightened by the weird extremity of what I was doing: as if I were closing down the world, reducing it to a street, a door, a woman; as if the borough of Manhattan were a store I could hide in the back of.

I knew her exact address, so I knew which building was hers: a nondescript reddish town house, mid-block. The block was usually quiet, but that night after leaving the Blimpie and passing up and down Broadway a couple of times in the guise of looking for fares, I saw in her building that a party was going on. It was taking place in the ground-floor apartment.

I drove by as slowly as I could, peering in at the three feet of exposed window; music filtered out. I could see the black backs of men, the shimmer of women's hair.

There was a space on Riverside I could just squeeze into, the cab's rear end a foot or so out in the street. I sat there, in the immediate silence after the engine had been shut off, feeling the way my clothes stuck to my body, the atmosphere of sweat and stink.

A few minutes later, I was sitting on the steps of the brownstone across the street from hers, watching a woman in a black dress eat a cheese snack, listening to the sound of a Leonard Cohen record, and the babble, the laughter of men. I was comfortable there. It occurred to me that I didn't have to go over and announce myself. I could just watch.

"Can I help you?" I heard a voice call from behind me in the next instant.

An old woman was staring at me from the top of the brownstone steps.

"I'm at that party," I explained. She pulled at the folds of her dress. Distrust, ancient and Old World, poured from her.

"So what are you doing here? You look like a hood-lum."

I started to laugh, willing it out of me. Her expression never changed. We had a brief moment of pure mutual hatred. I crossed the street.

Her gaze, searchlight-bright, never left me. I saw by her stance that she was on guard; I would have to either go inside or leave the block. Anger flared up in me. I wanted to *watch*, that was all.

Then a man came out of the door of the ground-floor apartment.

"Is he at your party?" the woman shouted, before I could say anything. This was awful, some childhood dare taken too far.

He was on the point of ignoring her when the woman shouted, "Mister!"

He turned, located her; his sullen mouth pouted; he disliked the assault.

"This fellow behind says he's at your party."

He turned now.

"This is Cynthia Branner's apartment, isn't it?" I asked. Expecting to hear the mistake confirmed, explanation of-fered, back to the cab.

"Yes, it is."

Then, oddly, to feel not surprised.

"Were you invited?"

"No. No, I'm a student of hers. I was just passing by."

"Oh."

Then a stillness, and a stench coming upward, and onto us, from the river in the heat.

He started off.

"Would you tell her I'm here?"

I'd said it before I could stop myself. It echoed after-ward, in my head, like a thing not actually said.

He turned and looked at me now, uncomfortable, wanting to be off.

The woman across the street called, "Is he all right?"

"I'll tell her," the man said.

He left me there, to wait in the hot, thick light, with the

woman still standing to receive some official judgment. I thought of running away—but no: here I was.

She looked at me when she appeared, as though there were some joke I'd never get, as though my density were a funny thing.

"It's all right, Mrs. Klein!"

She lifted her hand, and the woman slipped inside her door. The man, too, was gone now.

"So. We are not at the laundromat after all."

"How did you remember?"

She tottered slightly; reached halfway down, toward her ankle, as if a shoe were about to fall off. She was drunk.

"You know where I live. How?"

"The phone book."

A slight smile, almost inquisitive.

"Have you been snooping long?"

"No. I was just driving my cab..."

I pointed to Riverside.

"What made you decide?"

"What?"

"Nicholas, would you please look at me."

I did. I did not really want to be here.

"To drive a cab."

"It was what you said."

"I don't remember what I said."

Again, I turned away.

"How many times have you been here?"

"Lots."

"I've been away."

Inside the party, a glass crashed. I watched her flinch, was grateful.

"Would you like to come inside and meet my friends?"

"No."

"Why not?"

"I'm embarrassed."

"No need."

"Look at how I'm dressed."

She did. It did not appear to offend her.

"Come. There's something I want to give you."

She took my hand. I offered only the slightest resistance. We moved down the long dark hallway of her apartment. I expected any minute that her husband would appear. A dark-haired woman said, "Who's this?"

Mrs. Branner turned. "This is Nicholas Battaglia."

The woman, flat-chested, with thin, jutting shoulder blades, offered me an unpleasant look, as though I were distracting her friend from something urgent.

"Where are you going, Cynthia?"

"I have something for Nicholas. I'll be right back."

In the dark study, she lifted her arm up to where books lined the walls. The walls had been covered in red fabric.

"It's here somewhere."

"What are the walls made of?"

"Oh, don't ask. David's idea. We saw Bergman's *Hedda Gabler* last year in London. Some silly notion that if you surround a woman in red walls, you're making some profound statement about vaginal politics. Here."

She handed me a slim black volume, which, because she had just said the word "vaginal," I could not read for several seconds. Then I saw the title: "THE COLLECTED POEMS OF ANNE BRADSTREET." Inside the cover, the words "C. Cohen, 1965."

"I'm trusting you with it, all right?"

I opened it further, pretended to look.

"Study her deeply, all right? It would be nice if over the summer you could develop a point of view. A place we can start."

The words blurred. I understood, as if consciousness were a sudden wave of nausea, that I was in her house, that the deep red walls of this room were hers—even if a folly of her husband's, nonetheless...

"What's the matter?"

"I feel a little weird."

"Sit down."

I collapsed into a deep leather chair.

She went to an opposite corner and sat. From the party,

the clatter of glasses, disconnected voices, and Leonard Cohen. The room seemed to be getting darker.

I looked up and saw that Mrs. Branner was almost laughing.

"What's funny?"

"Nicholas, you look like you're having an orgasm."

"I'm not."

But I couldn't help but smile.

"Well, I should hope not."

She contemplated me a moment, this stranger, this boy in a chair, from a new perspective.

"Do you want to go back out? Maybe get something to drink?"

"No. I want to stay here."

She sat quietly in her chair, patient for reasons I couldn't even guess at. I was too aware of her knee, her leg.

"Do you have any interest in that woman at all?" she asked suddenly.

I looked at the book, surprised to find it in my hand.

"No."

"Then why go through with this?"

Something settled, in a corner of the room.

"To be near you," I said.

Her eyes opened slightly wider; then she looked down. Again, she appeared to be almost laughing.

"What is it?" I asked.

"In a Jesuit university, of all places."

But in the next moment, she was looking at me again, her eyes full of a kind of pity. "Nicholas, I'm going to pretend I didn't hear that, all right? Because no one else in that goddamned university is allowing me to do anything, and I would love to really teach you something."

And on the words "goddamned university" she again nearly laughed, as if the phrase had been so strange and wrong. Now she leaned back in her chair.

"The rest is your problem, I'm afraid."

I closed my eyes.

"Do you know I'm pregnant?"

I felt a plunging sensation, a deep voice in me saying: no.

I looked up, silent.

"Only a few weeks. I wondered if it showed yet. In my face."

She touched her cheek.

"Pregnant," I said.

"Yes."

In a room far away, Leonard Cohen was singing, oddly, of crucifixion.

"My baby will be born in April, midway into the spring semester, so I'll have to take that one off. I warned David to wait, but David would not be warned."

As she smiled, I imagined her husband, a curly-headed man in a rugby uniform, kicking a ball, kicking, running at the head of the others, at the head of a wild, raging pack.

"You look frightened," she said.

"No. I'm happy for you."

I looked down at the rug. I thought—and hated think-ing it—that in a situation like this, it was exactly what my father would have done.

"...the arm of flesh," I said under my breath.

"What?"

"Nothing."

"That's from Anne Bradstreet, isn't it?"

"Yes." I waited. "Where is your husband now?"

"He's away. He's an actor."

She sat further back in her chair. An actor. The fact of it only enlarged him. Playing what? Romeo? Troilus?

I didn't ask. In her, I thought of the seedy, colorless beginnings of a child, the mindless gropings toward the shape of a small hand.

"I'd like to go ahead with this." I held the book up. I didn't know why, but suddenly I was crying.

She held her distance.

"Nicholas, are you all right?"

"Yes."

"What is it?"

"Nothing."

I was over it quickly, thank God. Then, humiliated, looking for a place to rest my eyes.

"Are you sure?" she asked.

"Yes."

Anywhere but at her. Look anywhere else.

"Maybe you'd better go now."

"I guess."

Somewhere, in the distance, the Leonard Cohen record finally ended.

"You promised the tutorial," I said, finally realizing how deeply I must have compromised myself. To think I'd actually *cried.* The fact settled in, made it impossible to get out of the chair. At the same moment, I wanted to leap up, to eradicate my having come here at all. All these things she'd told me were things I didn't want to know.

"Do you think it's smart?" she asked.

"Yes."

I clutched the book with white fingers.

"I want to know about this woman."

Finally I looked up. Her face was heavy with concern. She glanced at my fingers.

"Well, good God, if it's that important..."

I breathed out, fingers relaxed.

"Will you have a boy or a girl?" I asked.

She looked at me curiously. I tried to breathe life into the question, to make it matter.

"I don't know."

She got up, went behind her desk and switched on the light.

"I think you should go now, Nicholas."

"Yes."

Still, it was difficult to rise from the chair, to leave the room, to pass through the noisy party and out into the street, the hot air, the cab, the devalued streets and world.

•   •   •

In Mamma Leone's, we waited, in the midst of the hot crowd, for a table. Women fanned themselves with programs for *No, No, Nanette!* A rat climbed on the low beams, among the rustic-looking strands of garlic, of twine. My mother, as if her training in the thick of the hot laundromat had given her a second skin, remained cool, remained fresh. Her head lifted above the straining crowd. My father studied the floor, the upholstery. A table was found.

"My name is Russo," my father said to the waiter, repeating the name, "Russo," when the waiter appeared not to understand. "We want the best."

The waiter nodded, and moved away. My father winked at me.

"Russo owns this place," he said.

"Do you know him?"

"Of course not."

In a corner of the vast dining room, a man traveled from table to table, in the company of another man carrying a mandolin. He was accepting requests for songs.

"So we understand you're dating a nice local girl," my father said, and winked again. Since becoming a "Russo," he'd attained a liveliness formerly missing.

"I wouldn't say we're dating, exactly."

His face closed in a fraction of an inch.

"No? That's what we were led to understand."

"She came to see me."

The men had begun to sing "Arrivederci, Roma" at the table of a couple across the room.

My father nodded.

"Do you come here with her?" my mother asked.

"No."

"Why didn't you tell us?" she asked.

My father reached for a breadstick.

"I didn't think it was important to tell you."

The singer segued into "Al Dì Là."

My mother's head moved back and forth, picking up on the rhythm.

"Remember this, hon?" she asked.

My father grinned, set his head backward.

"What movie was it from?"

He shook his head.

"It was from *Rome Adventure*, Ma."

She looked at me curiously.

"Suzanne Pleshette was the star," I said.

Of course she wouldn't remember.

"What are you having?" she asked.

I opened the enormous menu.

"We want to know everything; you know that."

I looked up at her and watched the way her earrings shook, the orange stones dangling. The singer was nearing our table.

"Everything looks good," my mother said. We ordered.

"You know, you should let this girl know"—my father leaned forward so that his head was over the table—"where you stand. Because this is not just any girl." Both hands were on the table now. "This has to do with family."

"Yes."

"You understand?"

"Yes."

"And Viola is so excited," my mother said, just as the food came.

"It's not Viola..." I started to say. But if not Viola, then who was important? Me? Only me?

"What's the matter?" my father asked.

"Nothing."

We ate from the big plates, saying little to one another, until the singer came to our table.

"We are taking requests for songs."

He had a big pockmarked face, too big for his body. His hair was cut in a thick, flat sheaf of bangs that fell against his forehead, like Moe of the Three Stooges.

My mother looked up, and wiped away the sauce that had clung to her mouth.

"Anything we want?"

The man nodded patiently, pursing his mouth a little.

"Ask for 'Quando, Quando, Quando,' " my father said, looking up on the end of it to add, "My name's Russo."

The man's big voice boomed across the table. Though the song was meant to be light and snappy, he sang as though he were begging funds for cancer research. My parents both were delighted. When he was finished, my father said something in Italian, and the singer, whose eyes until then had looked closed and half-dead, allowed his face to shape itself into a grin.

"Another?" he asked in Italian.

My mother requested "Non Dimenticà."

Again, the big voice rattled the glasses, shook the leavings on our plates. The mandolin player paid great attention to his strings. The singer stared at my mother throughout the song. Her head was still, at rest, like that of a cat who had found a spot of sun.

When he was finished, the singer still didn't leave.

"Beautiful," my father said.

The singer tilted his head in acknowledgment.

"Another?" he asked.

My father beamed. No one else had had three songs.

"Oh, I don't know. What do you think, Josie?"

She turned to me.

"Nick, is there a song you'd like to hear?"

The singer's head moved on the thick, stationary axis of his neck.

"This is our son," my father said, as if he and the singer were old business associates. "He goes to Fordham."

The singer regarded me. Once again, his eyes went dead.

"No, nothing," I said.

The singer nodded; in that single action, the energy left the table. I could see my father almost grasp for it, as if for the last remaining breadstick. The guise of "Russo" slipped; the singer moved on.

"I didn't know they did that," my mother said.

My father nodded, cutting into the last of his meat.

"It's a lovely idea," my mother said. "You couldn't think of a song you'd like to hear, Nick?"

"No."

They glanced at each other. My father shook his head, as if to warn her away from something. I leaned into my food, took a bite of the veal chop, tasted little.

Afterwards, they wanted to take a walk around midtown. The city frightened them. Something in their retreat made me walk faster, as Uncle Billy would have, as if this city were mine, as if I were on a first-name basis with waiters and maître d's.

I was relieved when they went upstairs.

I had told them that no, I'd rather the Hotel Consulate didn't make up the extra cot in their room for me, I had places to go, a place to sleep. But the city seemed hideously empty now. I walked to Ninetieth Street and sat, cold-buttocked, on Mrs. Klein's stoop. Where else? I made my vigil. But there was only a single light on in the window across the way. And that, most likely, only to fool the burglar.

3
PROVIDENCE

We met on Thursdays that fall—a regular hour-long appointment in the afternoon.

Cynthia was guarded now, in a new way, as though what I'd revealed to her in the closed room of her party had made her mistrust all but the intellectual side of these meetings.

"We have to have a title for this," she insisted. "We have to know where we're heading."

"All right, but when do we get to the good stuff?" We were enmeshed throughout September in Anne Bradstreet's early apprentice work. "All she does here is beg everyone's forgiveness, pardon me for writing poems."

"Which is understandable..."

"She's like me."

Her scowl was automatic: this wasn't what she wanted to hear.

"All right, a title. 'Seventeenth-Century New England as Laundromat: Being Stifled through the Ages.'"

"Very funny."

Undeniably, though, there was at such moments a sense of pleasure she couldn't hide. Whatever else she may have felt, she at least didn't hate having me here.

And how much I wanted to touch her!

Sometimes my fingers would glance across her fingers, and she would draw her hand back but refrain from speaking. To speak would mean she'd have to do something, she'd have to threaten me, and it was maybe the most exciting thing in my life in those days that she held back from doing that, from saying, "This much and no more." I could touch her and for hours afterward my existence felt buoyed up on some invisible cloud. I was separate from the rest of humanity. This was all I knew.

Then, at the beginning of October, she missed a Thursday, and on the following Monday, I returned to the apartment Tommy and I shared to find a note scrawled beside the telephone:

"My father died. I'm in Providence."

The spacing made it look as though Tommy had meant to say more, but had stopped abruptly. The top hadn't been put back on the pen he'd written with.

The next day I got on the train.

It had been a dry, torpid autumn so far, and the train was hot. I was annoyed with the weather, annoyed with Mr. Bevilacqua. His death had been inconvenient. It meant my having to stay with Tommy until he got over it, and that would mean losing another session with Cynthia, two in a row. On the ride, I tried to think past this basic selfishness, to re-create Tommy's father as he had been. But I had trouble holding him at center. I kept returning to the wording of the note I'd written to Cynthia saying I wouldn't be there—had the words been right? had they been too blunt, closed-off, unsolicitous? I'd assumed the reason she'd had to miss our last appointment had to do with her pregnancy, but strangely, in all the times I'd seen her since the night of her party, she'd never mentioned it again.

It was a short cab ride from the station to Tommy's house, one of a row of houses in a working-class neighborhood, with small gated yards, and front doors just a few steps from the street. The street had obviously been zoned for business: a Babson's Hardware was directly across from Tommy's house; a tire store lay in view just down the block.

A woman answered the door. I'd caught her in the middle of something.

"Ya?"

"I'm Nick. Tommy's friend from school."

It didn't penetrate; her whole face slanted, as though the information troubled her.

"Ya. I got the baby. You wanna hold on a minute?"

The door shut. I was left on the stoop, with time enough to watch a customer go into and out of Babson's, carrying a package on the way out.

"Ya?"

The door had opened again.

"I called, last night."

"They're all at the funeral home. Brasco's."

I held up my suitcase. "I've got this."

She looked at it like a handful of lint I was putting on display.

"The thing is, I thought I'd be staying here."

"Here?"

The suggestion seemed to frighten her.

"This is Tommy's house, right?"

It wasn't really that she was frightened. It was that every new thing I mentioned was like a bowling ball achieving a perfect strike; she needed time to reset the pins.

"You come from the Bronx?"

"Yes, from school."

Still she hesitated.

"Tommy's at Brasco's."

"I was just hoping I could leave my suitcase."

She stared at it another moment.

"Ya, sure."

Finally the door was opened.

Inside, the house had the thick air of rooms where the lights are infrequently turned on, the furniture kept covered, waiting for guests. I placed my suitcase in a corner of the foyer.

"You'll excuse me, I got the chicken on."

She was wiping her hands on her apron.

"If you could just tell me where the funeral parlor is, I'll go there."

"Ya, come in to the kitchen, I'll give you directions."

I followed her down the hallway. Her dark hair, worn long in the back, swung a little, like a girl's.

In the kitchen a much older woman, white-haired, sat at a table, folding long strips of dough, measuring them out with her fingers as though blind. There was a fragrance here almost too rich: fried breaded chicken, roast peppers, and some sweet maple-syrup scent. In the middle of the room, a boy baby hung suspended on an automated swing, gumming a bottle.

"Ya go out the street you came, down to the Citgo." She turned over the chicken. "Take a right at the Citgo, and follow that street all the way to Chalmers. You'll see it then. Brasco's is on Chalmers."

Another piece was turned. I looked at the golden breading. I'd eaten nothing on the train.

The baby dropped his bottle, started screaming. She wiped her hands again, to go to him.

"No, let me," I said.

I picked up the bottle and handed it to him, thinking he was capable of doing the rest himself. He threw it back at me, and kept screaming.

"Ya," I heard from behind me. "That's okay. You go to Brasco's."

Brasco's was located on a long commercial avenue, flanked on one side by a women's-hosiery store. Just inside the entrance, an usher came too close, half-blocking my way. He wore some perfumy after-shave against the hard grain of his skin. His eyes resembled those of an expiring fish, glassy and desperate for a drink. He spoke with them; nothing came out of his mouth.

"I'm with the Bevilacqua party," I said.

He pointed me down the hallway toward where a group of old, mostly short men, in shades of gray and black, stood clustered. There was, in this light, an odd delicacy to them. They barely parted for me. I had to squeeze through until I could see the coffin.

I had made my way through, so there was nothing for it but to go to him now, to kneel down and make the gesture of homage. Across the room, I could just see Tommy, in the thick sea of relatives and flowers, in his black suit. I'd dressed wrong. I was still in jeans from the train trip.

I knelt down. *In the name of the Father, the Son, and the Holy Ghost...*

Again, I tried to mentally pinch myself, to find the layer of feeling, but nothing here suggested life. A surfeit of images crossed my mind: his plate of eggs in the Capitol, his profile in the darkened Radio City Music Hall, laughing cautiously at Walter Matthau. It all seemed too effortful, as false as the thick, stubby dead fingers around which a rosary had been twined. And then, just before I

got up and went to Tommy, I caught a glimpse in his face
of a kind of eternal boyishness, the sense that he had
never quite grown up, or given up, had retained to the
last a boy's expectancy.

"Did you know I was coming?" I asked when I was
close to Tommy.

His eyes met mine for only a moment—a small spark
of light, then a snuffing; one hand reached out, and then
his view slid from me, as though it hadn't wanted to
stick.

He shrugged.

"I'm sorry, buddy," I said.

He pulled back a little, drew in his mouth, lifted his
eyes in acknowledgment, but wouldn't look at me.

Beside him, a bigger man, some cousin or uncle, made
his presence felt with a shifting of the shoulders, as
though he were acting as Tommy's bodyguard. I turned
and looked at him.

At first glance, he seemed much older, but the longer I
stared at him the more I realized he couldn't be more
than two or three years my senior. It was that his features, by their largeness, their harsh but undeniably
beautiful crudeness, made him look as though he'd been
cast in an older mold than either Tommy or I. He resembled those profiles of Caesar on old Roman coins: the
endless undulating nose, seasoned, skeptical eyes, the
forehead arcing backwards into hair that coiled and
snaked like something deflected over the massive scalp.

"I'm Nick," I said,

His eyelids lowered a fraction of an inch: it had been
wrong to speak, too loud, too rude an interruption. *Big
deal, so you're Nick...* He nodded.

Then I passed him, made vague conciliatory gestures
to the men next in line—the cousins, uncles, high-rank-
ing grieving parties—and found a place at the back of the
room.

I wasn't needed here.

It was five o'clock in the afternoon; the wake would go
on probably until nine or ten. Tommy didn't need me. He

had the big guy to lean on. What was I going to do? I
thought of calling Cynthia, telling her to ignore the note,
I could make it after all. Then I squelched it. At the front
of the room, Mr. Bevilacqua just lay there, the cause of so
much fuss, oblivious of it as a sleeping baby. Tommy's
head, lifting out of the dark suit, seemed etched now in
some harder metal. It was as though he'd done well at
some sport, and was being heralded for it.

A hand reached out, grasped my forearm.

I turned. An old man was sitting there. He was feeling
the muscle in my arm, touching it, judging it. He took his
hand away and stared into my eyes, unafraid of what I
might think, or of any way I might answer back; too old
for that, beyond it.

Then he smiled and turned away, and I turned with
him and saw Tommy's cousin doing the same thing: staring at me as though it were his absolute right to do so, as
though the Bevilacquas were a species separate and
apart, and a tribal code were asserting itself here. But
when, finally, he turned away, there was no moment of
release, no easing of tension. I'd felt, in that moment of
turning away, that casual averting of his big ancient head,
that he'd seen enough to reach a judgment that went
beyond the tribal—one that had weight, that counted.

At the house, afterwards, Tommy wouldn't eat.

The relatives had all come back after the wake, to eat
the fried chicken, the homemade pasta, the syrupy round
fried dough laced with raisins. It wasn't customary on
the night after a wake, but there seemed to be a general
consensus among this group that Tommy shouldn't be
left alone.

Filumena—the woman who had let me in—was holding a crusty chicken leg just a few inches in front of
Tommy.

"Go ahead. Eat. You don't wanna starve."

When did she relax? When did she let go of the intensity of that face?

"I don't want to eat."

"You want some gannoli?" She gestured, disparagingly, at a box of pastry nearby, store-bought.

"It's cannoli, Filumena. At least pronounce it right."

No offense taken.

"You want one?"

"No."

There was a babble in this room, laughter coming from another. A houseful of people. I sat beside Tommy, close enough to make my presence felt, though I doubted he much cared.

"Nick'll eat," he said.

She offered the drumstick, halfheartedly, to me.

"You want?"

I was starved, but didn't dare eat in front of Tommy.

"No."

"What am I gonna do with it?"

A young woman came into the room, carrying the baby Filumena had been watching this afternoon.

"Angie, Tommy won't eat."

"Leave him alone, Ma."

"Gimme the baby!" one of the old men shouted.

"He don't wanna go to you!" Angie said.

"How do you know?"

Her baby looked around, big unfrightened black eyes resting in a monkey's face.

"You wanna hold him, Tom?"

"Sure. Give him to me."

The baby gave himself to Tommy easily, started suckling on the collar of Tommy's shirt.

"He thinks it's a tit."

"Watch your mouth," Filumena said.

"You leave me alone, you hear?" He was fierce.

One of the old men approached him. "Lemme have him. Angie thinks I'll drop him."

"You will drop him," Angie said. She was eating the disputed piece of chicken. "Don't let him have him!"

"Come on! I'm not that old!"

"You drop him, you gonna give me another one just like him?"

The men in the room guffawed. The name Vito was repeated, in the midst of their first reaction.

"Never mind Vito; I'm gonna make you pay!" Angie said.

Then: "Go ahead, Tom, give him to him." She'd turned on a dime.

"I don't want to."

"Please." The old man crouched as much as he could, reached out with his arms.

Tommy handed over the baby.

The man remained in his crouch—he looked as if he would have difficulty getting out of it now—and jiggled the baby up and down. A jet of white liquid flew from the small mouth.

"See?"

Angie snatched the baby out of the man's arms.

Afterwards he just stood there a moment, confused as to what had just happened. His arms were out, as if the baby were still there. He stared down at the white vomit on the floor, at Filumena cleaning it. Then he looked around, a smile on his face. The men joined him in laughter.

The big cousin entered now, stood in the entryway to the kitchen. Angie, holding the baby, turned to him as if some explanation had to be made.

"Rookie made the baby throw up."

The old man's—Rookie's—hands went out to the sides.

"Nothing. It was nothing, Vito."

Below him, Filumena continued to work away at the floor.

"Here, give him to me," Vito said.

The baby was handed to his father, shaken a little bit, gentled. Vito held his son with effortless mastery, as if born to it. The room quieted several notches. Vito's big hands rested on the small back, seeming to move and not move at once, like a hand poised to catch a moving ball.

"Here."

He handed the baby back to Rookie.

"He likes to be on your shoulder. Settles the stomach."

"Like this?"

Rookie carried the baby like a sack of potatoes. He gestured to his compatriots in the corner.

"You see this?"

Vito looked past him, to Tommy.

"Is he eating?"

"He ain't eating nothing." Filumena was depositing the baby's mess in a wastebasket. "I tried to get him to eat chicken."

"What else you got, Ma?" Angie asked, opening some pots. "You want me to make you some plain spaghetti, Tom?"

Vito came close, leaned down to Tommy.

"Hey, whatsa matter? You gotta eat."

Vito looked over at me quickly, had no interest now.

"Angie, make him a pot of spaghetti," Vito said.

"I don't want—" Tommy started to speak.

"Hey..." Vito's hand touched his knee. Then he decided not to press. He turned again to me.

"I'm Vito." He held out his hand.

"Nick."

"Right." He looked me over a second time, as if to see if anything had changed.

"Hey, Vito, look, I'm doin' good!"

Rookie was getting the baby to sleep. At this sight, Vito smiled, and a few of the men applauded. Startled, the baby popped open his eyes. He started to cry.

"You bunch of assholes, you woke him up," Angie said. Already, she'd crossed the room and taken back what was hers.

Tommy didn't last much longer, and neither did most of the guests. He went up to his room. In a little while, I joined him.

He was lying on his bed, flat on his back, his jacket off and his tie falling across his chest.

I sat down on the bed, rested my hand on the place where his tie should have been.

"I'm sorry, Tom."

He closed his eyes. He looked as though he didn't want me to be there.

"What's the matter? I say something wrong?"

"Yeah. You said something wrong."

I took my hand away.

"What?"

He sat up abruptly. I could see the muscles on his back under his white shirt, heaving a little.

Then there was just the sound of his breathing.

Below us, someone was calling up to him. There were footsteps.

"Tommy, we're going."

Filumena was in the doorway.

"You gonna be okay?"

She toyed with a set of keys.

"I got the keys now, Tom."

He hadn't turned to her.

"I left the food. You can heat up the chicken. Just make sure it don't get soggy. Bake it till it's crisp. Feel it so it's hard."

In the darkness I could see her eyes swimming around in the broad face, looking for something, candles illuminating corners of a room.

"Ya."

She went.

Finally, Tommy spoke again. "I'm gonna go to sleep, Nick. You can do whatever you want. There's a TV downstairs."

"No. I'll go to sleep too."

"You can sleep in their room."

He hesitated a moment.

"I'll make up the bed for you."

"No. I can—"

He was already up. "Their" room was just down the hallway. He opened the door, flicked on the light, then entered, deliberately not looking around.

I remembered him chiding his father about all the pictures of Christ in here, and there they were: Christ in blue, Christ in red, Christ as a boy, among sheep, in the temple. They documented his life, as if Christ, and not Tommy, had been the child here.

"I don't want you to sleep in their bed."

He was staring at it now.

"It's okay," I mumbled.

"You can sleep in my bed."

"No. The floor—"

"Just don't argue with me, all right?"

Already, he was on his way out the door, carrying sheets. He flicked off the light, so that I was standing in darkness. In his room, he made up a bed on the floor.

"This is stupid," I said.

He took off his clothes and got into the makeshift bed.

"It's not right for me to have your bed."

He said nothing. He was under the sheets, curled to the side.

I couldn't sleep, and I couldn't tell if Tommy was sleeping either. We just lay there, and every time he breathed oddly, or made a noise, he startled me, as if he were going to get up and do something violent, if not to me then to himself.

It seemed like hours had gone by when I heard the latch opening downstairs. Then Vito was in the doorway, holding a bag.

Tommy looked up; he hadn't been asleep after all.

"I brought you some ice cream," Vito said.

Tommy leaned on his elbow, ran his free hand through his hair, just as his father used to do.

"You got some bowls?" Vito asked.

"Downstairs."

The transaction took place quickly. Vito was back in a couple of minutes with the bowls loaded up, and spoons. He and Tommy sat by the window in chairs. Vito left a bowl for me on the table by the bed. We ate without speaking.

In the middle of it, Vito looked up from his bowl, first
at me, then at Tommy.

"You got the other bed, Tom."

Tommy said nothing at first.

"If I go in there, I wanna tear it apart."

He scooped up a big spoonful of ice cream and downed
it. Vito waited to see if he was going to say anything
more, then did the same.

"So you don't wanna sleep there."

"No."

Vito held the spoon in front of him.

"You do honor to your father, you understand?"

It sounded odd, as if the word "honor" weren't one
Vito used every day.

Tommy didn't say anything.

We finished the ice cream. Tommy put his bowl down.
Vito picked up his napkin and wiped his own mouth.
Then he reached over and wiped Tommy's face.

"So what do we do?"

Tommy placed his hands at his sides, as if he were
about to get up. I could see the way his palms were sticking to his hips.

"What was I supposed to do—stay here?"

Vito just looked at him.

"You tell me."

Still Vito said nothing. Tommy's hands looked itchy
now, were moving.

"Tell me."

He reached out. It looked like he was going to hit
Vito. I knew he wasn't, but I knew just as surely that
that was how Vito saw it, and reacted. He blocked what
he thought was the punch and slapped out at Tommy,
hit him once hard across the face. This time Tommy
did try to hit Vito. There was a flurry of hands. Then it
was over.

Tommy was weeping now. His whole body was shaking.

"You stop, Tom."

Vito's hand went out, gentle now, but it stopped before it reached Tommy's face.

"You stop."

He got up, picked up all the dishes, took them downstairs. I could hear him washing them. Tommy was quieting down gradually.

"Hey," I said. He ignored me.

When Vito came back up, Tommy had stopped.

"You all right?" Vito asked.

"Yeah."

Before he closed the door, he looked once more at Tommy. He gave no evidence of guilt. I had to admire that in him; as if the very fierceness that allowed him to slap Tommy were evidence of an unquestionable sympathy—a blurring of the lines. He was not moons away, wondering what were the right words of consolation. He was *right there*, and the minute he shut the door, his absence was felt.

Tommy waited a moment, then got under the covers, and after a while I couldn't even hear his breathing anymore.

"When I think of the name Lou Bevilacqua, I think of the words courage, decency, family."

The priest stood talking into the mike, his shiny young Irish face like a full moon onto which a slanted, unhappy-looking mouth had been impaled.

"Because above all, Lou was a family man, dedicated to his son Tom, the memory of his beloved wife Connie, his sister Filumena, his nieces and nephews..."

At the front of the church, Tommy sat between Vito and Filumena, looking stiff and bored, but dutiful, waiting for this to be over.

"Now Tom's at Fordham," the priest said, "carrying on the tradition of what was best about Lou, his deep faith..."

Tommy's body seemed to absorb those words, to take them in and accept them. There was no irony in his posi-

tion, at least none obvious, and later, when the honor
guard presented him with the folded flag that had covered his father's coffin—Mr. Bevilacqua had served in
the Navy in World War II—he held it as if it were a pocketbook one of the assembled ladies had asked him to
watch for her while she ran some errand.

Afterward, he disappeared.

There was a large congregation back at the house, but
no Tommy. I hovered mostly at the edge of the room, eating a sandwich, drinking a Scotch Rookie had forced on
me. The old man who'd sat beside me at the wake sidled
up next to me.

"Who are you?" he asked bluntly.

"Tommy's roommate."

This made him smile, but it was as if he had earphones
on, was listening to a separate concert and reacting to it.

"Nicholas," I said, and held out my hand.

He took it, but not to shake. He could barely stand.

"I'm Louie's uncle," he said. "I gotta sit down."

I made room next to me. When he sat, he started to
shake, and I thought I was going to witness another one
of the big passionate Bevilacqua scenes. In the next instant, though, he was smiling.

"Go over there and get that picture," he said.

He nudged me, pointing to a picture on top of the
mantel. I brought it back to him. I could tell as soon as I
saw it up close that it was a photograph of Mr. Bevilacqua. He wore a Navy uniform and was standing very
stiffly. Beside him a young woman held a small bouquet,
wore a white hat.

"This was a beautiful woman," the uncle said, pointing
with one stubby, uncertain finger to the woman. His
finger ran a little against the glass.

"And this was a little squirt."

His finger was on Mr. Bevilacqua.

"A little troublemaker. I was the one who had the first
car around here. Nineteen twenty-seven. And this little
squirt, he broke the gearshift." He gestured with his
hand, as if there was more. "I'm telling you this."

He stopped suddenly. I don't know why I kept expecting him to cry. He had no intention of it.

"I had to give him a spanking. And did his father give me hell. We didn't speak for years." His hand went up.

He was silent for an eternity. Again, his hand went to my muscle.

Vito came over and stood beside us. The old man tugged at Vito's sleeve, and when Vito was close enough, said something in Italian that made Vito look at me, vaguely embarrassed.

"What did he say?" I leaned forward, smiling.

Vito shook his head.

When they were all gone, Tommy still had not come back, and there was some anxiety about leaving me there alone, in charge of the house.

"We could leave you the keys," Filumena said, "but then how would we get back in?"

"No, it's okay; I won't go out."

Everything I said, she treated with uncertainty.

"Leave him the keys, Ma," Vito said. Whatever his larger doubts about me, he'd apparently decided I was trustworthy. "Tommy'll come back tonight. We'll get the keys in the morning."

He was lifting the rented coffee urns, carrying them out to his car.

"He won't take nothing?" she said when she thought I was out of earshot. The keys were left on the front table.

I spent the night alone; Tommy never came back. I watched some TV, but it was too gloomy to do that for long. Mostly I sat, waiting, eating some leftover food I wasn't even hungry for. I looked at old photographs of Mr. Bevilacqua; his wife; Tommy as a little boy in a cowboy outfit, riding a mechanized Buckin' Bronco in front of the Stop & Shop.

After I'd gone to sleep I heard him downstairs. He was unmistakably with a girl. I heard her laughter, a high-pitched voice. I didn't go down, and they weren't there anymore in the morning. I waited an hour or so, then called the train station. There was a train at eleven. If I was lucky, I could make it back to Fordham by four, in time for the session.

The Department Secretary said I'd missed her by about fifteen minutes.

"Where was she going?"

Mrs. Underwood shrugged. She was busy squeezing the last of the liquid from her tea bag.

"I assume home," she said.

I went up to the apartment and deposited my suitcase. Then I got on the subway. In all this I was deliberately not thinking, just doing. I thought if I could keep thought at bay, I might actually accomplish something.

At Eighty- sixth Street, a good, cold breeze was coming off the river. It seemed a good day to be bold; the weather, at least, didn't argue against it.

When I rang her buzzer, a man answered.

It was David, of course, but there was so little superficial resemblance between this man—wearing glasses, looking bothered at the interruption—and the much happier, glowing figure in the picture she kept on her bulletin board, that I was thrown back at first.

"Is Cynthia at home?"

He frowned. One hand went up to push his glasses up the bridge of his small American nose. He had on a Ban-Lon shirt the color of pistachio ice cream. A yellow golfer teed off on his breast.

"Yeah." He disappeared. Then I heard him call her, and a far-off mumbling: "...some kid," I thought I heard him say.

Then he was back.

"Yeah, excuse me, who are you?" Said in the tones of jocks, the words that imply no effort.

"I'm Nicholas Battaglia." I started to explain. He looked at me with his head down a little, then interrupted.

"Yeah, that's fine."

He opened the door.

"I'm watching the game, if you'll excuse me..."

At the end of the hallway, just as he disappeared into one door, she came out of another.

It was the first time I'd seen her apartment in relative daylight—it was now just past five—and the shadows felt oppressive. She wore a black sweater, a cardigan, wrapped around her. Her hair looked uncombed, her face extremely pale. It was as if David, in closing the door behind him, had created a vacuum of energy.

"Nicholas."

She had to stifle a yawn. She didn't move from where she was.

"They said you had just left."

"Yes."

"You got my note?"

She waved off into the air with one hand. She yawned.

"Were you napping?"

She let out a small laugh.

"Is it that obvious? Come on."

"I've brought my book. I hope this is all right."

She scowled a little, to let me know it was. Then she led the way into her study.

"It was a funeral, wasn't it?"

"Yes."

"Whose?"

I sat in the big, overstuffed chair and explained.

She switched on the light.

Through the window I could see the cement courtyard, a gathering of birds near a feeder, a stack of old bricks.

"Your roommate's father," she said.

"Yes."

She rubbed at her eyes. I couldn't remember ever seeing her without makeup before. Her face seemed more pure, every trace of falseness, of effect, eradicated.

"Is it cold in here?"

"No."

She smiled at me, sounding me out, not quite trusting my motives.

"So you chased me down here."

I probably blushed; I don't know.

"I brought the book."

She glanced at it, as if she were thinking of something else.

I could hear the television in the other room: the rumble of an announcer's voice. Another voice—David's—occasionally participated.

"I was thinking today..." She was looking out the window. "There's really something basically wrong with an academic life. With sitting among books all the time, in neat, stuffy little offices. I don't know how men do it."

She stared directly at me a moment.

"Father O'Rourke, for instance. How does he do it?" Her upper teeth bit her lower lip; a moment's pause. "Does Father O'Rourke have balls, do you suppose, Nicholas?"

Was she trying to shock me? It was hard to tell; her eyes had a fuzzy look to them, as if she were several steps removed, but still interested in knowing something. It was too hard to guess what, so I just laughed. It seemed the easiest thing to do.

"Yeah, I bet he does," I said.

There was a silence afterwards. She looked disappointed. A little of the light went out of her eyes, as if she were becoming tired.

"What did you find in the Bradstreet?"

Then it was as if the book itself were what exhausted her.

"I was ready last week," I said.

"Yes. I'm sorry."

She closed off any further discussion of *why*.

"Mostly, these are more of the same. Her mind is very pedestrian when she's doing the accepted thing, when the emotions she's letting out are the appropriate ones. But I think in this one poem, David's lamentation, she breaks free of it for a moment. It's very exciting."

"Show me."

"In itself, it's maybe not much, but after those awful recitations of the virtues of Philip Sidney."

"Just read it."
"It's in the last lines."
I found the page and read:

> O lovely Jonathan! How wast thou slain?
> In places high, full low thou didst remain.
> Distressed for thee I am, dear Jonathan,
> Thy love was wonderful, surpassing man,
> Exceeding all the love that's feminine,
> So pleasant hast thou been, dear brother
> mine.

"Just that," I said when I was finished; "it's not much, but it's the first time I see her breaking away from words that could be written on statues."

I looked up and saw that a change had taken place in her face, mostly in the eyes, as though drops had been placed in them, the dark pupils enlarged. Her David was shouting something in the other room.

She had to be returned to what was going on in this one.

"What do you see in those lines?" she asked. "Different?"

"Well, for once you can see a human being."

I waited to be encouraged to go on.

"You know she talks about the carnal heart, about wanting to be virtuous and realizing there's something else in her, almost a bad girl inside her. But it's not 'bad,' it's not anything we'd think of as 'carnal.' It's just that she considers—I don't know—her soul, that part of her that responds in a perfectly simple, human way—carnal, wrong."

She sat, unimpressed, waiting for more.

"It's why she was ashamed of wanting to be a poet. She knew that part would come out sooner or later. It was why she wanted to be one in the first place."

By the time I was finished, I was talking excitedly, in

spite of her evident lack of enthusiasm for these ideas.

She pushed her hair back with her hands, and held it back, so that her face came forward.

"Have you written that down?"

"No."

"Well, do. It's a place to start, anyway."

"There's something else."

She liked that. Her eyes showed it.

"And what could that be?"

"It's the first time she's spoken in someone else's voice. It's because for a moment she thinks she's David that she's free to"—I paused now, not knowing quite how to say it—"to love men."

Her eyebrows lifted. Distantly I heard the word "Jesus" from beyond the wall. She heard it too, or picked up on my hearing it, and made a small, dismissive gesture toward its source.

"Go on."

"It seems to be important for her, an outlet. Maybe it's the guilty secret, maybe it's even what the carnal heart means. It's not something she can let out when she's talking about Philip Sidney, or her father. But in another voice, not her own, she can declare it to the world: 'I love men!' "

She smiled, but didn't seem to quite agree.

" 'Thy love was wonderful/ surpassing man/ Exceeding all the love that's feminine.' Not exactly erotic, is it?"

"No." I looked down now.

"What is it, then?"

"It seemed that way when I read it."

"Don't back down," she said, harshly.

"All right: I think the words say one thing and mean another."

"What do they mean?"

"I think it's something not quite mainstream erotic—she's not calling him a good lay, she's calling him something else. It's like she's talking about another dimension of love."

In another room, David shouted "Damn!" and the TV went off.

"All right. Good. Fine. Can you support it?"

"I don't know yet."

She leaned back in the chair, fell out of the light. She was looking out the window again. She looked tired.

There was movement in the next room. A portion of her face—the eyes—seemed to follow it. I tried to think what else to say.

In a moment we heard, "Cynthia, I'm going out!"

In the light, I thought I saw her flinch from it.

"Did your team lose?" she shouted.

There was no answer.

She got up and went to the door. "Where are you going?" She leaned into the opening.

"I'm going to watch the rest at Teacher's," I heard.

There was a pause. Her words afterward sounded defensive.

"They have a TV screen there?"

Before I could hear his answer, she'd closed the door behind her. I was alone in the study.

I couldn't hear what they were saying, but it seemed to be an argument of some sort. I tried to absent myself. I looked around the red room, darkening now. In the bookcase above her desk I found another picture of David. His dungarees were cut high on the calf; he wore suspenders and an open flannel shirt—some "hayseed" role or other: it was obviously a picture taken from a play, because he was looking petulantly at a girl in a long ponytail, as if he were begging something from her.

His face looked very young and soft, different from that of the man who'd answered the door. And looking at this picture—staring at his youthful face, handsome and clean, pure as a statue's—I thought there had to be some falling-off of love for what the man had turned out to be. The man at the door had been only *ordinary*, anyone's husband, with the look of a gym teacher nosing past his prime: the sort of man you see pushing a cart in a suburban supermarket.

I heard the front door slam, so I knew one of them was gone. I went and sat in the big chair. The only light in the room now came from the lamp. Finally, I got up and opened the door and called out, "Mrs. Branner!"

The long hall looked dark, empty. I thought maybe I was the only person left in the apartment. Then I heard a small "Yes" coming from somewhere.

"Where are you?"

"In the kitchen."

She was standing over a pot of water, waiting for it to boil. The kitchen was small, really just a linoleumed alley between the stove and counter on one side, refrigerator and sink on the other.

"Nicholas, I'd like you to go now."

She didn't look at me as she said it. She turned up the gas and folded her arms against her chest.

"We haven't finished," I said.

"I know that. I apologize."

The kitchen had a yellowish tinge to it, not overly clean. There were some spice jars, and a line of orange stain leading up the wallpaper over the stove.

"Why don't you let me make you some tea?" I asked.

"Is that what you're making?"

She didn't say anything right away. Her face bunched up. Then she turned to me. I had no idea what she was going to say, not a clue.

"I make real good tea," I interrupted.

An odd sort of half-smile appeared on her lips, as though I were on the periphery of things; as though she'd just been reminded of me.

"Didn't your parents bring you up to leave a person's house when you're asked?"

"My parents brought me up to leave *before* I'm asked. To anticipate every objection. To never give offense."

There was a silence. She wasn't looking quite at me: more to the side.

"Where are the tea bags?"

"I don't use tea bags, Nicholas."

"Then what?"

She held up a small silver ball and spooned tea inside it.

"I don't want you to stay very long, all right?"

"Okay."

"And I don't want to talk about poetry."

She went back to her study. I had won.

I didn't know, afterwards, how long you had to hold one of these tea balls in hot water before it made tea. When the water seemed dark enough, I called out, "What do you want in it?"

"Just the tea."

She'd hardly raised her voice.

I brought the cup to her in the study. She was lying on the couch, the sweater pulled around her.

"Here."

She looked at the tea.

"This must be when it hits you, huh—in the afternoon?"

"When what hits me?"

She sipped.

"...the baby," I said.

She sent me one of her mystified stares as if I had brought up something completely unexpected.

"How's the tea?"

"Fine." Pause. "Thank you."

"Am I doing all right with the Bradstreet?"

Again, her stare was curious, but detached. My manners, my politeness must have struck her as odd.

"You're doing fine."

She sipped another minute.

"I've got to tell you, this makes me a little uncomfortable," she said.

"You want me to sit farther away?"

I was sitting on the floor, right by the couch.

"Your being here is what I mean."

I got up and sat on a chair, a good dozen feet away. I folded my hands.

"You said, once upon a time, Nicholas, that there was

something else going on here other than this teacher—
acolyte bullshit."
She settled back onto the couch.
"In this very room, I think."
The cup was placed on the floor.
"Is there still?"
I sat there a moment, intensely nervous, looking at the
feeble light of the lamp.
"Yes. Sure," I managed to utter. Afterwards there was a
long silence.
"Is it difficult for you?" I didn't say anything at first.
"Or has it all been changed by my"—her mouth sud-
denly seemed to have gotten dry—"by my pregnancy?"
Still I couldn't answer. Finally, when I thought nothing
at all was going to come out of my mouth, I heard myself
saying, "I think about you all the time."
Now my hands wouldn't stay still. I rubbed my thighs.
I couldn't look at her. I looked out, at the courtyard,
where it was dark. Finally the silence was worse than not
speaking. I was afraid to see what her face looked like,
how she took these words.
"I love you," I said.
I looked around the room once more, desperate for any
object that could hold my interest. Finally, I settled on
her face. It had come forward, as if, more than anything,
she was interested in what I was saying.
"Is this really true?"
"Yes."
"And you can come here and talk about poetry?"
"Sure." I paused. "It's better than being alone in my
room."
Her eyes held me then for a long time. Finally she set-
tled back a bit on the couch.
"Tell me about your room."
"Why?"
She reached down and picked up the tea.
"Because I'm interested."
I waited a moment. I didn't know whether to start,

whether she was toying with me or genuinely wanting to know. She sat there, though, cup in hand, as though she were awaiting a good story.

"It's a white room. The person who lived there before painted it white. It's a little smudged now."

I could tell she was not bored, was envisioning it in her mind.

"There's hardly any furniture in the place. Tommy and I thought we'd have a lot of money from cab driving, but we never do. We picked up the front seat of a stripped car, that's our couch. We found it on Webster one night."

She leaned her head back a little, sipped.

"And then Tommy went out one night—morning, really, very early—and picked up the stacks of newspapers they leave in front of drugstores, all tied up. Those are our end tables." I paused. "August fifth, 1971."

She smiled.

"He calls the place our Mexican jail."

Then there was a silence. She watched her tea swirl.

"Tell me what you think, when you think about me."

She put her tea on the floor, then leaned back. She looked as though whatever I said was going to make her a little wistful, as though it were already deep in the past.

"Different things." I looked down at the floor, at my lap.

"Tell me."

"I can't."

We were silent.

"I don't want to sleep with other girls. When I think about doing that, it's almost like I think of you, being there, watching me, saying that's not good enough. Telling me I'm better than that."

I looked up, finally.

"I'm sorry. I shouldn't be telling you all this."

"It's all right."

Her curiosity had a troubled quality to it now; or maybe it was just that the light had shifted, and more of her face was in shadow. She looked up at the rows of books.

"Maybe that's all for now, all right, Nicholas?"

I sat there. I didn't get up. One hand went up to my mouth, an extended finger resting there, my right leg stretched out. I waited.

A long time seemed to pass in silence. She looked like I guess she'd look if she were alone in the room, a woman in a dark, comfortable place, thinking things over.

Finally she looked up. It was a moment that made me hold my breath, as if in the next moment literally anything could happen.

She looked at me.

Then she lowered her eyes and stared again into the bottom of her cup. I made the slightest of motions toward her.

I don't know for sure whether she actually said "No."

All I know is that was the moment when I knew I had to leave the room.

I he next session, the following Thursday, was the most difficult meeting we'd had. She seemed distracted, annoyed with everything we talked about, not alluding for a second to what had gone on the week before in that dark room.

Even the Bradstreet poems we talked about yielded little. There was one poem I was excited about, a short piece called "The Vanity of All Earthly Things." I read out the phrases I'd underlined: the ringing dismissal of all earthly comfort. Cynthia scratched the edges of her book, folded the pages back, looked as though she were thinking of something else.

"Do you want me to come back another time?"

"No. Let's go on."

She tried to concentrate.

I read: "The sensual senses, for a time they please, Meanwhile the conscience rage, who shall appease?" I paused. "My Aunt Rose could have written that."

Today nothing was funny.

I left before the ninety minutes was up. In my room, I tormented myself for ever declaring what was true and honest: subterfuge had been easier. Maybe she would cancel the tutorial. Maybe I would never get to see her again, just receive a note in the mail, from the Department Chairman, informing me not to show up anymore. Tommy still wasn't back from Providence, so there was no one even to vent this on. I pored over the Bradstreet poems, vowing never to joke again, never to reveal any of my feelings, to be the most serious, the most guarded of students.

Then, the next day, she began visiting my room.

That first time, I was cooking lunch when the knock came: a fried bologna-and-cheese sandwich.

"I bet you're surprised."

Surprised. Yes. She was standing on the landing, looking apologetic.

"Do you mind if I come in?"

"No. Please. Come on."

The kitchen was a litter of old newspapers and unwashed dishes. I cleared off one of the chairs.

"Here. Please sit down."

"Thank you."

I watched the way she sat at the table in her good red coat, perched there like some exotic bird that has wandered into a swamp. I wanted a different kitchen— cleaner, more worthy of her.

"Can I make you something? Tea?"

"Please."

"All I've got is bags."

She allowed a little smile.

"You don't mind?"

"No."

"It's really lousy tea. I gotta apologize. Big E brand. I bet you never had Big E before."

She shook her head.

"Well, it's very hip here in the Bronx."

Her being here made me clumsy with simple things, like getting the top off the old teapot. Such measures suddenly seemed very complicated; I wondered how I'd ever done them with ease before. Finally the tea was poured.

"I don't know why I'm here, if that's what you're going to ask," she said, accepting it.

The little Big E bag floated in the water, looking somehow inadequate.

"Do you want any sugar?"

"With this, yes, please."

I brought the sugar.

She looked up at me a moment. Impossible to read her
expression: a slight, very slight pleading that she be
given room.

"I didn't want to go home right away." She laughed a
little, as if to excuse it, lifted one hand to rub at her cheek
with the flat of it. Then she spooned the sugar, removed
the tea bag, and drank.

"How is it?"

"Horrible, thank you."

She put it down, looked at my table. The newspaper
was open to an ad for another Walter Matthau picture.

"You want something else? I was making myself a bologna sandwich."

"No. But you go ahead."

"Excuse the place."

For the hundredth time, it seemed, she tried to smile. It
was like my Uncle Carmen's smile, after his wife's funeral, while he was listening to me talk about my academic accomplishments.

"My roommate's gone, no one comes here, so you have
to get up a pretty good argument for washing a plate
when there are still clean ones in the cupboard."

I ate.

"Anne Bradstreet could come up with an argument, I
bet."

I wished she'd tell me. I was beginning to feel like a
jerk making these feeble jokes when there was obviously
something weighing on her mind.

She touched the edge of the table then, grasped it, let
go.

"Nicholas, did you tell anyone I was pregnant?"

She looked at me only a moment, her eyes like small
saucers around the edges of which some milk has
spilled.

"No. No one."

She looked down. She had both hands on the strap of her handbag, and was playing with the clasps.

"Good," she said. "That's good."

"Why?"

At first I didn't think she was going to answer me.

"I'm not."

It had been said just above a whisper, with her head down. Then, as if she didn't like this weaker version of herself, she cleared her throat and lifted her head.

"I didn't lie to you. I was pregnant, but I'm not anymore."

I had, at this exact moment, a bite of bologna in my mouth, which I now found it impossible to chew. I was sure it would be disrespectful to reveal myself gnawing on a hunk of meat while she told me this, but at the same time, I couldn't spit it out of my mouth. This was life, I thought: someone is telling you the most important secret of their existence, and all you can do is try to think how to dispose of the hunk of bologna in your mouth.

Finally (the hell with it) I swallowed. Her eyes were wet now. To avoid looking at them—they frightened me a little—I stared at the little gold balls of her earrings.

"Do you want another cup of tea?"

"No."

"Tell me what I can do."

"This is fine."

She folded her hands and looked down into her lap, but there was nothing contrite about the cast of her features: she seemed dissatisfied.

"Listen," I said, leaning forward, "if it helps, you can come here day, night, anytime."

It made her laugh: pure release.

"It's been a fucking difficult week, Nicholas. I'm sorry."

She wiped her face with her sleeve. I liked that, because I knew that somewhere on her, she had a handkerchief.

"If I was bad yesterday, it was because I was in no mood for Anne Bradstreet. For someone that *good*."

Her voice shook on the word and then changed, darkened; she was no longer laughing.

"I've got to apologize for the way I was. But I'm in no mood for virtue."

I pushed my sandwich aside.

"Look, I know this is completely beside the point, but I wanted you to know: I've never had a teacher say the word 'fucking' to me before."

She laughed again. This time her look was conspiratorial; differences seemed momentarily wiped away.

"Let's not be ridiculous, all right? You're how old?"

"Twenty."

"And I'm twenty-eight."

Now she reached into her coat for the handkerchief, blew her nose.

"So big deal. I think I should be allowed a 'fucking' every now and then."

Then she laughed louder.

"I feel like I'm in jail over there."

"Campus?"

"Yes." Her mouth set. "Priests."

The hand holding the handkerchief was lowered, rested amongst the crumbs, the dirty glasses.

"I had an abortion, Nicholas."

We were looking straight at each other. She didn't flinch, didn't seek to turn away or apologize. It was my vision that wavered, like the finger of the old man pointing at Tommy's mother in the wedding photograph.

"Are you shocked?"

"No."

"Of course you are. Look, you won't even look at me."

I did. I saw how disappointed she was.

"When?"

"Over the weekend."

There seemed nothing to say to that.

"Are you disappointed?"

"No."

"I'm sorry I told you in the first place." She had

stopped looking at me. "It was to put you off as much as anything."

"But it was true?"

She nodded.

"I wouldn't lie to you."

"Then, why?"

I had tried to hide it, but suspected it was there in my voice: I was heartbroken. I'd put a great deal of effort into imagining this child, had even come to envy him. If David had been there then I was sure I would have strangled him, hung up his balls to dry. He was not special enough to have done this to her. He ought not to have had the power....

"Everything was wrong."

A little wetness in the eyes, that was all.

Then we sat in silence a couple of minutes.

"Do you want me to go?"

"No."

"Of course you do." She didn't move. "It's very strange. I wanted to tell you." She pulled at her eyelashes a moment, as if there was something stuck there. "It's almost like I couldn't bear that association—you thinking I was like Anne Bradstreet—that *good*."

She shook her head.

"I'm not."

"It's okay."

"Are you disappointed?" I shook my head. There was a brief, tense pause. Then: "Do you still love me?"

She sounded shocked at having said it. One of her hands was up near her face. "Don't answer. That was stupid." She rubbed at her forehead.

"I will. I still do."

She looked at me, and bit at the edge of her thumb, then turned away.

"Please don't tell anyone, all right?"

"No."

Below her face and neck, her coat had opened: I saw the hug of her sweater, the shape of her breasts beneath. I thought all we needed was a nudge and we'd fall into some other world, be grappling, naked. But I couldn't be the one to start it. I squeezed the skin on my knees.

She stood up.

"No. Don't go."

I reached up and took her hand. Then she gave in, allowed it. I loosened my grip a little, kneaded her fingers. I wanted to know how long this could go on, how much I would be allowed.

"Let me see your room," she said.

"What?"

"I'd like to see it."

I sat back in the chair, confused, nodding to where it was.

She stood in the entrance to it. I knew what was there —mattress, books, discarded underwear—but there was no way of telling from the look on her face what it was she saw.

I stood up.

"And that over there is the living room."

The light made it look softer, more presentable than it deserved to. I leaned against the door.

She went in and sat on the old front seat, two shades of green.

"This is sort of wonderful," she said.

It disturbed some part of me that she could let go of her melancholy this easily. It made me like her less. But it was also unsettling to realize that that sudden dislike had nothing to do with tempering my desire.

"What is it?" she asked, studying my face.

I just shook my head; no way to tell her I felt slow, leaden, heavy in the crotch.

"Do you want to make me another cup of tea?"

"I thought you hated it."

She smiled, allowed a silence.

"But you're good at it. Go ahead and make me another."

I brought it to her and sat beside her and watched her drink. It had become the thing I did, this close viewing of her lips, throat. For a moment, it was enough to be this close.

"I'm sorry. I shouldn't have put you through all this."

"It's all right."

Her face considered something.

"There was no one I could tell over there."

She put the cup down. She looked drawn now. Her eyes were deep-set. She made a hesitant movement, her chin lifting; no more than the motion of a tree's branches when there's only a little wind—more a blurring than actual movement—and then an erasure of it, an unsureness. I had thought something was about to happen. Her motion had that edge to it. I opened my body to her, tried to make my chest as large, as pliable, yet as neutral as a pillow. I didn't want to create any awareness of sex, of desire—I thought that was wrong—but then it seemed unnecessary, too, because she seemed unaware of me physically, not paying any attention to that part. I could have been a woman or a friend. All she did was finish her tea. Then she stood up and went into the kitchen and washed the cup. It had to be the only thing in there that *was* washed; it stood alone on the drying rack. She looked across the distance of the two rooms—I couldn't get up, or wouldn't—and, drying her hands, let me know that she was grateful, but it was time for her to go.

After she left that day, life became a matter of waiting. At any moment she might appear at the door. It gave every moment a charge, significance. Waking in the morning was like breaking out of one of those deep erotic dreams—the ones where the thing most desired is magically accomplished—and not even minding that reality is different. To have come so close—to have felt the shock of accomplishment—gave energy to the day. I stocked up on good tea. I waited.

The first time she came back was on Tuesday, and it was quick, she had no time. It was as though she came here only to prove to herself that she could. She drank the tea, Twinings English Breakfast, and barely looked at me.

On Thursday, she stayed longer. I invited her back, after our meeting, for supper. On the chance she'd accept, I'd bought two packages of imported pasta, a can of Aunt Millie's tomato sauce with sausages and peppers, ingredients for salad. She had, it turned out, an appetite as big as mine; she ate noisily, unapologetically. I told her she would have gotten along fine at any Italian table, and she liked that.

We were becoming friends in a way I'd never have guessed.

"Don't you ever have friends coming in and out?" she asked.

"No. Not usually. Just when Tommy's here."

She broke a crust of bread, chewed on it thoughtfully, as if having a tough time believing I lived such an isolated life, that she was really so *safe* here.

Afterwards, when we were washing the dishes, she noticed her dress had been spotted by the sauce. I got a wet towel and began dabbing at the spots. They were just below her waist.

"Listen, where'd you tell David you were going?"

(David, unemployed now, spent his days mostly watching television, leaving the house only for the occasional audition.)

"I didn't. Now whatever the excuse I make up, it's got to involve sauce."

"No problem. Tell him you were heading up Kingsbridge toward the subway, you passed by Mama Louie's Pizzeria—be specific, say 'Mama Louie's'—and you couldn't resist going in."

I looked up. I was smiling to myself, feeling great, and I thought at first that I hadn't made sense, that what I'd said had come out disjointed, because she wasn't laughing.

We were close. I could almost feel the way it would be now: my hand touching her bare arm, and then that nudge into something else. I thought of her lips mashing against mine. But I must have been thinking too much, because in the grip of all this, I recognized that I wasn't doing anything. I was standing there, stupidly folding the wet dish towel.

"I'd better go now," she said.

Her smile looked phony.

"What?" I asked, and now I did touch her. But the skin on her arm didn't feel as I'd imagined it would. The air had changed radically. It had gotten cold.

She stepped back a fraction of an inch.

"Nothing."

Her arm lifted; one hand went up to touch the base of her neck. "Nothing, really, but it's time to go."

"Why is it time to go?"

Her face looked clearer now. Her smile no longer looked phony.

"Because it is. Now be a good boy and get my coat and walk me to the subway."

I tried to do as I was told. But when I was standing in my room holding her red coat, I wondered if I understood anything at all. If I let her leave now, would she ever come back?

We weren't really speaking when we left the apartment, were still silent as we rounded the corner of Kingsbridge, headed up the hill. She put her arm in mine, but it seemed a gesture from another time. Without ever realizing we'd possessed it, I understood now that we'd let go of ease.

Halfway up Kingsbridge, a figure became visible, directly in our path, walking slump-shouldered, carrying a bag.

"It's my roommate," I said, as if to no one, then shouted, "Tommy! Tom!"

He glanced up, not surprised at all. He was wearing an old felt hat that must have been his father's. His coat nearly dragged to the ground. It was his belly that gave him away—the way it dictated his walk—and the small, definite chin, which lifted now, revealing more of his face. He looked at first glad to see me. Then he took in Cynthia.

"Tom, are you all right? How you feeling?"

I thought I had to put on a veneer of feeling, to cover the dread his presence had started up.

"This is Cynthia Branner," I said. "My roommate, Tommy Bevilacqua."

She reached out and shook his hand. He looked like he was meeting her less than halfway.

"I'm sorry about your father," she said.

The sides of Tommy's lips went up, as if he were superior to the remark. She bristled at that, her eyes growing a little wider. Tommy let us know, by his silence, that if this was all we had to say, he'd just as soon move on and get settled back in the apartment.

I told him I'd be back in a minute, then watched him move off down the hill.

When we started walking again, her hand slipped out from under my arm. Her hands fell into the pockets of her coat. I wanted to say something, but I wasn't fully there.

"He's not taking it so great, is he?" I said finally.

"No."

She was looking at the ground.

"Something the matter?"

She didn't say anything. She closed her eyes. We were at the entrance to the subway.

"Listen, I'm sorry..." I started.

"Is that all you know how to say?"

"No."

I leaned over and kissed her.

For something so momentous, it was remarkably easy. I had finally gotten the nerve, was all. I knew she wouldn't resist. Her mouth partway opened; her hand went up and touched the hair at the base of my neck.

It was a shock to look at her when I broke away. I dug in again.

"I love you," I said, feeling detached from those words.

A very light rain had started up when we'd come outside, so everything was a little wet and misty, the ends of
her hair and the line of her forehead holding the drop-
lets.

I kissed the outline of her forehead where the rain
held. I thought about Tommy, trying to push him out of
consideration. It was like there had to be something at
the edge of this; it was too good. Life, you always had to
be reminded, was still a puppet show commandeered by
a god resembling Aunt Rose.

I wanted to just hold her there like that, looking at the
peeled paint on the banister, the lights on the Grand
Concourse.

"All right," she said, underneath me.

I laughed, didn't let go.

"No. I've got to go."

"Wait."

She looked up.

"Come downtown with me."

"Is David there?"

"Yes. Just partway. On the subway."

I went down and bought a token, then sat beside her in
the gritty station, feeling her happiness. The subway
train rattled in and we boarded. I felt protective of her,
didn't want anything bad to happen. I had gained size, I
was a hulk beside her. People would be afraid of me, and
let her alone. The lights kept flashing on and off during
the ride. Her small hand—not so dry now—found its
way into mine. Our two hands rested on the red coat. I
thought: if only this had happened yesterday, if only
Tommy had waited another day...

In the long tunnel between 155th Street and 125th, I
decided I couldn't put it off any longer. I had to get off
the train. I imagined Tommy by the window, Tommy
lying on his bed, alone in the apartment. The hand resting in mine suddenly seemed not as real as these images
of Tommy.

"I'll have to get off at this next station," I said.

"All right."

Her eyes looked bright, vivid. I leaned down and kissed her again. We were at 125th Street.

"Goodbye."

"I'll see you next week," she said.

The door closed behind me. The train carried her off. For an instant, I started to lunge for it. Why had I gotten off?

It was a Thursday night, not very late, but the station was nearly deserted. Down at the end of the station platform, a man turned and eyed me. I didn't stare, but I felt him, the whole time I was waiting for the train, and if he'd come up and murdered me, I wouldn't have been surprised at all; nothing tonight would surprise me. I stood there and prepared for death (I could believe it more easily than I could believe the scene with Cynthia would ever be repeated) until I heard, far in the distance, the sound of the train.

Whatever I'd thought—however I'd allowed concern for Tommy to darken the last half-hour—he was not waiting for me. He was there, all right, but not waiting.

I found him in his room, standing in his undershirt, choosing among three shirts, all lying in their cardboards, on his bed.

He looked surprised to see me.

"I thought you'd go downtown with your fancy lady."

"She's not my fancy lady."

He selected one of the shirts, opened it, started to put it on.

"Have you slept with her yet?"

"No."

"Why not? She was here, wasn't she?"

"How can you tell?"

"I smell her."

He stood there buttoning up the blue Oxford shirt.

"So why not?"

His face was dark, looking for trouble.

"Look, just because your father died doesn't give you a

lifelong permission to turn into an asshole."

"I can be whatever I want."

"Wonderful."

"So why didn't you fuck her?"

"Maybe she doesn't want that."

He scowled, dropped his pants.

"Nicholas, you get your conception of women from *The Donna Reed Show.*"

"I came back to be with you."

"Thanks. I'm going out."

"Where are you going?"

"What are you, my mother?"

I sat down, in the corner.

"No."

He finished dressing.

"How was Providence?"

"A million laughs."

"I mean it."

"It was fine. I'm selling the house. Should I sell the house?"

"Don't you want it?"

"What for? Which reminds me, you've got the keys. I had to leave Vito my set."

"You never came back."

"No. I went on a bender. I slept with every girl from my high school I could find. All the ones I was too afraid to ask out then. It's incredible what a couple of years and the loss of a father can do for a boy's self-confidence."

He finished buckling his belt and then stood there, a long moment, just looking at me. He raised his eyebrows; an old gesture—see how cocksure I am!—but there was something else in it now.

"I'd ask you to come with me if I thought you'd enjoy it," he said.

"Maybe I would."

He repeated his gesture: I understood what was different now. Tommy wanted me to believe he understood darkness.

"No, you wouldn't," he said.

• • •

He was back five hours later, drunk and alone. I heard him retching into the toilet, went in to help him; he waved me off.

After that, the weekend was torture: Tommy spent it exclusively in the company of a blond girl named Sue: a working girl (she had a job in Manhattan), a Bronx native. My presence didn't seem to make much difference to either of them. If I'd been a voyeur, it would have been paradise: they didn't bother to close the door to Tommy's room, and once, on my way into the living room, I was treated to a view of Tommy's big rump pumping away, Sue's legs on either side of him like andirons set at odd angles before a grate.

There could be no calling Cynthia over the weekend (that much, at least, was understood), but on Monday, I tried her office all day. I besieged the place: she was never there. The week started to fly by, a haze of missed opportunities. Uncle Billy called at midweek: his wedding was on for sure, Thanksgiving weekend in Judy's hometown on Long Island. They'd already talked to the minister. The family was coming, Billy was overjoyed, and when could I come for dinner? I made a date two Wednesdays away, leaving myself plenty of time to think up an excuse. Billy, on the other end of the line, sounded not quite real, as if he were coming from a world that had ceased to have credibility.

My single hope now was that Cynthia would come back, would visit the way she'd done before Tommy's return. But she didn't, and I wasn't surprised.

On Thursday, I burst into her office at the appointed time. She laughed at my eagerness, but I knew right away there was something different.

"I couldn't find you all week," I said.

"Yes, I know." She raised her eyebrows, as though I'd done something bad. "Sit down, okay?"

I did, but leaning forward.

"Nicholas..."

Now I could see that she was nowhere near as close to being carried away as I was; that she had done things in the interim other than *wait*. And it made me wonder if I had seen anything at all that night that had not been enlarged, magnified out of all proportion, in the days since.

"There are some things we have to talk about."

"You haven't come back."

"No. I can't come anymore."

"What's happened?"

"Nothing." She smiled at me. For me. "But there's business now. Father O'Rourke came in to see me today."

"And?"

"'What's going on with the Battaglia boy?' He calls you the Battaglia boy."

"What did he want?"

In my mind, I saw Father O'Rourke on an ice floe, stranded in the company of Mrs. Orr, in the North Sea. Sharks nipped at the edges.

"He wants to know what we're doing. He'd also like to know why you're here all the time, looking for me."

"And you told him?"

"No." She settled back. "But I have to give him some answer."

I didn't say anything.

"You have to come up with something. You have to *write* something."

Now I too leaned back. We were both in the same posture. I recognized, was surprised by, a new hostility on both our parts, as though we'd become enemies in some vague war. I thought of saying, We kissed on the train; you were so *happy!* But I knew how that would sound here.

Instead, I said, "Cynthia."

The sides of her lips went up, but it looked to be an effort.

"David's got a job," she said.

"He does? Where?"

"In a dinner theater. He's not happy."

She'd been playing with a pencil, running her fingers

down it. Now she put it down, leaned forward, opened her book.

"Please," I said. "I don't want to."

"Open your book, Nicholas."

She stood and opened her door a little, so that anyone who happened to pass by could view this innocence.

Reluctantly, I opened the book.

"I don't understand: overnight she's turned into a harpy."

The sides of her mouth went down, formed a lopsided smile.

"A harpy?"

"Yes. Making demands. Incredible demands. Her husband goes away and she goes nuts."

"And how does that fit in with your theory?"

"What's happened to the old dependable Anne Bradstreet?"

"How does it fit in?"

I looked up. She was biting her lower lip. I remembered how her hair had looked in the rain.

"She needs him."

Her hand smoothed the page.

"Your idea was that it was the erotic drive that forced her into poetry."

"Was it?"

"Yes. I think it was."

"Okay."

I'd said it sullenly, as though I were allowing her to put words in my mouth.

Now her look was hard.

"I don't know if it can hold water, but at least we can get it by Father O'Rourke. So let's do it; all right?"

"What about the train ride?"

I watched a pulse throb at the side of her forehead.

"What about what happened then?"

Finally, she turned, as if a decision had been made, one she'd finally decided to accept.

"Write the paper. All right?"

• • •

I waited for her at the gates to Fordham. It was raining again, the dull, dead rain of early November. I knew she'd have to pass this way on her way out. I knew also that nothing good would come of my being there; nothing good could happen in this weather. A luncheonette was open nearby; I could smell the hot dogs. They incited the opposite of hunger.

It was nearly five when she came down the walk.

"Surprise."

"Hello." Her voice was affectless.

"Now there's no one to hear. Can I walk you?"

"Yes."

She said nothing, all the way to the crosswalk.

"Well?"

I said it with the force of a man arguing for a cause he knows is lost.

"I told you. I can't come to your apartment anymore."

She held an umbrella under her arm. She tightened the button at the top of her raincoat. She was a woman on her way to the subway.

"I don't like the looks your roommate gives me."

"If you're worried about him, don't be. He won't say anything."

"Nicholas, this is a Jesuit university, and I am first of all a woman, and second, a Jew. I can just hear them if so much as a hint were passed. Overnight, I'd be the Harlot of Dealy Hall. They'd tar and feather me. I'd have to write the Pope for clemency."

"But nothing's happened."

She lifted the collar of her coat, opened her umbrella.

"No, nothing has. And you're an attractive boy, but I think we'd better leave it that way."

"What would happen? Would they fire you?"

She was detached enough to notice shop windows.

"I think they would, yes."

How I hated my own thickness!

"So where does that leave me?"

She looked at the wet sidewalk.

"I don't know."

"You don't *know*? How can you say that?"

She seemed to go away for a moment.

"You want me to go crazy?"

Quietly, she asked, "Are you going to go crazy?"

"Yes. I think so."

She made a sharp little grimace, which could have turned into a smile, but didn't.

"You're showing a remarkable degree of insensitivity in talking to a woman who's just had an abortion, Nicholas. Is it conceivable to you that your needs can't always come first?"

I thought she would have gotten really angry if her focus hadn't been captured just then by a man stepping out from the entrance to a rug store. He was a Jesuit, a small man; I didn't know his name.

"Dr. Bryant."

She stepped forward, calm and unfazed as a hostess who had expected this particular guest.

He was more embarrassed than we were, I think. His glasses were misted over in the rain, and he looked pretty helpless. A patch of hair was matted against his mushy-looking head.

"Were you buying a rug?" she asked, referring to the store.

"No. Oh!" He turned around, surprised, evidently, that that was where he'd been standing. "Good heavens, no." There was a very small giggle. "Just trying to keep dry. I had to go downtown and didn't take an umbrella."

"Here. Take mine."

She held it out.

"Oh. I couldn't."

"Please. I'm almost at the subway, and then it's only a block to my house. I can get it from you tomorrow."

"I couldn't."

"I insist."

She took his hand and wrapped it around the handle. I

wondered how long it had been since a woman had touched him. He looked undone by the act.

"This is most..."

"Really, it's fine."

"Thank you."

He was too embarrassed to stay now. We watched him wander down the hill, his rump making a part in the back of his coat.

"I think I can buy their loyalty, isn't that it? At my witch trial, I'll imagine him thinking, 'Once, she lent me an umbrella.' As if that makes any difference in final judgments."

"Now you're getting wet."

"It doesn't matter."

She walked, head down.

"Look, I didn't know you were so worried about losing your job."

"Yes. I am. I've done nothing but fuck up since I got here. Screaming at department meetings. Kissing a boy..."

She looked up, through the rain. Little rivers of it fell over her forehead.

"I can't do that anymore."

It struck bluntly at some internal organ to hear her say it, but it was several moments before I felt the pain. I was watching the way her face took the rain.

"So what are we supposed to do?"

"Write the paper, then we'll see."

There seemed any number of things I could have said. What I chose immediately sounded wrong.

"I'm not a eunuch."

"No. I know."

"I didn't mean to say that."

"Thanks for the place. Thanks for helping me over my deep trouble. See you next Thursday."

She disappeared into the crowd heading into the subway.

I was angry. I let her go.

I did try, all weekend, without success, to write the paper.

I even had a title. Pretentious as it sounded, I thought I'd call it "Eros in New England." But when I tried to apply *thought* to that title, all I could come up with was an image of myself masturbating in the bathroom of the laundromat, or being jerked off by Julie in my father's car. I didn't care about Anne Bradstreet. I wanted, basically, to be kissed again; but that event seemed cut off forever from the realm of possibility. Now I resented all the nights I hadn't masturbated, thinking she'd be coming the next day, wanting to have a store for her. All that private, blocked pleasure loomed now. The warm center of existence cooled; a filter broke loose.

Meanwhile, a mild flirtation had been going on in another of my classes, Shakespeare's Comedies. The professor, a layman named Dr. Sutorius, was a great butt for humor. He seemed unaware of the sniggers, the outright hilarity provoked by his desperate manual fumblings toward the correct gesture with which to express how Dante's notion of love infiltrated *Much Ado About Nothing*. The girl beside me, Carmella Buonanno, had been looking at me all semester suggesting, if I wanted to, we could see a movie, drink coffee in a small, well-tended kitchen, those things. But they had held no attraction until now.

In fact, they *still* held no attraction, or not much. It was that there was so little else to do. The apartment seemed too empty now, or, when Tommy was in it, not a pleasant place to be.

Carmella and I took to spending long hours after class in the cafeteria. I perfected my already hilarious Dr. Sutorius impression.

After a while I began to like the way she talked about her family—her father was a fireman in Queens—as though self-pity were a concept she was unfamiliar with. Mostly, I was consoled.

We happened to be together on the day I was due to have dinner with Uncle Billy. The coffee was finished, we were still having a good time, so I asked her if she wanted to come with me.

"Sure. Why not?" she said.

I picked her up at her apartment off campus, sat waiting for her on a red brocaded couch set in front of an artificial fireplace. The Bronx had stamped its habits on these old apartments. The girls who lived here had tried to hide the gaucherie of that artificial fireplace by placing a Chinese screen in front of it.

I'd decided to make a big deal of the evening: I would surprise Billy by showing up in a shirt and tie. Carmella appeared in a sweater and tweed skirt. I looked beyond her at the kitchen. Why were we going to Billy's? It was so *nice* here.

On the subway, I tried to warn her about Billy, how he might try to jump her on her way to the bathroom. The prospect didn't seem to bother her. She had a wry smile; she let me know you didn't grow up in a fireman's house in Queens without learning how to deal with that sort of thing.

A doorman let us into the building on Eighth Avenue. Billy opened the door of the apartment, dressed in a white silk shirt, open halfway down his chest, black pants that hugged his hips, a fringed buckskin jacket. His skin was the color of wet cement. He gave me his Cheshire cat grin after he'd taken in Carmella.

"Nicholas, you didn't tell me you were bringing anyone."

"It's a surprise. I didn't think you'd mind."

"No, what are you, kidding?" He winked. "This is a dish. Come on in, dear."

"Thank you."

Carmella Buonanno was a model of probity and tact. She would have been at home in the court of Monaco. And I had brought her to Uncle Billy's.

"Can I take your coat, dear? Judy—hey, Judy!"

Billy poured on the "dears," his hand briefly touching Carmella's neck as she removed her coat. Judy waddled in, a plastered smile of greeting on her lips that had nothing to do with the motion of her eyes as she took in Carmella.

"Hello, Nicholas," she said. "Who's this you brought?"

"My friend Carmella Buonanno."

"Carmella Buonanno," Billy repeated, as though it were the name of a delicacy he'd never tried. He put the coats away.

Judy was pregnant: it was evident right away. She barely sported a belly, but it was as if pregnancy were an unmade bed she'd been waiting all her life to lounge in. She was wearing a frumpy dress and no makeup, so that there were heavy, unmasked bags resting under her eyes.

"What's your poison?" Billy asked.

Judy's living room had the mahogany sheen of a furniture showroom; a liquor cabinet was central, Billy moved behind it now.

"Look at me, Nicholas: do you believe it?"

Judy pulled her dress tight against her abdomen, so that a very small hump showed.

"Scotch, Nicholas?"

"Sure."

"Carmella?"

"Bourbon, please."

"Bourbon? Mannaggia!" Billy let out his little cackle. "Straight or on the rocks?"

"On the rocks, please."

Judy was still waiting for my reaction.

"Billy never told me anything," I said, and patted it. That sort of intimacy seemed to be all right with Judy, though this was only the second time we'd met.

"My first boy," Billy said. "I'm sure of it."

"Don't be so sure," Judy said, and took a seat.

The gold medallion Billy wore swayed from side to side as he lifted the drinks; it looked uncomfortably heavy.

"Why do you want a boy, Mr. Battaglia?" Carmella asked.

"Billy," he corrected her, and handed her the bourbon. "I've already got three girls."

"But wouldn't you like another?"

His own drink in hand, Billy sat in a green leather chair placed directly under a standing lamp. On the reading table beside it was a copy of *QB VII*.

"My father says that men have this biological thing about wanting sons, but they always end up not really liking their male children, favoring their daughters much more."

Billy nodded vaguely in the direction of Carmella's comment, as if it needed translation, and offered her a glazed-eyed smile.

"So how's things, Nicholas?" he said, turning to me.

"Fine."

I sipped Scotch. I'd been hoping he and Carmella would get into a deep discussion of the relative merits of sons and daughters, and I could sit here, quietly getting drunk.

"We haven't seen enough of you," Judy said.

"No."

There was a brief silence.

"You go to Fordham too, Carmella?" Billy asked.

"Yes."

"I didn't think they allowed girls," Judy said, as though Carmella were trying to sneak one past her.

"Oh, for a long time now. Nicholas and I are in a class together."

"What's that?" Billy said. He liked to jiggle the ice cubes in his glass together when he wasn't sipping.

"It's Shakespeare's Comedies," Carmella said.

"Shakespeare." Billy sat up straighter. For a moment I thought he was going to embarrass me by lifting his pinkie.

"We got a couple of intellectuals here, Judy."

Judy had lit a cigarette. She smiled at the end of a long stream of smoke. Her legs were apart.

"Oh, I took Shakespeare, Billy."

"Did you?"

"A long time ago."

"When was that?"

"A long time ago."

"I didn't know that."

She sent him a sidelong look of mild controlled fury. A plume of smoke blew outward.

"'Whither is the rose,'" Billy said, and sipped Scotch, and cackled.

"What play is that from, Billy?" Judy asked.

"You know, 'Whither is the rose...'"

"No. I don't. I've read most of the plays of Shakespeare and I don't recall ever coming across the line 'Whither is the rose.'"

"You kids hungry?" Billy turned to us, patting the sides of his legs.

"Oh, yes," we both said, nearly in unison.

"We're going out," Billy announced.

The restaurant they chose—the Six Brothers Coffee Shop—was located only a couple of blocks away. Billy made a big show of knowing all the waitresses, of having his own "special table"; but the waitresses all greeted him as if he habitually undertipped, and our table was near the door, drafty.

"Somebody else is in the one we usually sit in," Billy apologized, then quickly changed the subject. "So what are you studying at Fordham, Carmella?"

She lit a cigarette. I hadn't known she smoked. She seemed more comfortable here than I did.

"I've got the standard dream of becoming an interpreter at the United Nations," she said.

"So languages?" Judy asked.

"Yes."

Judy snapped her pocketbook shut as if she hadn't heard Carmella's answer.

Billy's eyes misted a little in appreciation, then moved to take me in.

"And Nicholas here, Nicholas is gonna do what I never could."

I looked up, surprised.

"And what's that?"

He smiled. "Listen to him. 'And what's that?' "

"Come on, Billy. You keep making me out to be so great. I don't know what I do. I go to school. I'm sensitive. Big deal. I don't even want to be an interpreter at the United Nations."

"Billy thinks you're gonna do big things," Judy said.

"I wish."

I looked down at the menu. "What are we eating?"

For whatever reason, my words cast a pall on the conversation for several minutes. Everyone ordered. Billy got his salad: a bed of lettuce, no tomato.

"Jesus," Billy sighed. He raised his hand. "Miss, Miss!" He was ignored.

He turned back to us, "Who do you have to fuck around here to get a tomato?"

Carmella burst out laughing; a shred of lettuce she'd been chewing was expelled onto the table.

"What? What's so funny?" Billy asked, laughing too. "See, you'd better watch out, Nicholas, she likes my humor."

Judy's eyes darted sideways; her mouth tightened like a cartoon villain's.

"So will you be coming to the wedding, Nicholas?" Billy asked.

"Sure."

"Your folks'll be there."

I ate my salad.

The meal went on pretty uneventfully after that, except that when Judy's broiled fish arrived it was a crisp, fried little patty, and I thought her eyes were going to pop out of her head trying to explain to the waitress how deeply offensive this was to a pregnant woman. Her grievance left her with an empty place setting while the fish was properly broiled. She sat there fuming, while our food got cold.

"Go ahead, eat," she snapped.

During coffee, Billy placed a toothpick in his mouth, peered out the window, went into a short silence. Then he said the single word "Jilly's."

It seemed to animate him. He turned to me.

"Jilly's, across the street. Judy saw Frank Sinatra come out of there once."

Judy had to duck her head slightly to get a good view of Jilly's.

"I think it was him. You can never be sure."

She sipped her coffee. The two of them continued looking out the window.

Later, in front of their building, we said good night, and begged off coming up for a nightcap. Billy was full of insistence that we get together before the wedding, that I make certain I get good directions out to Long Island, though it seemed then that I'd be coming with my parents. Any mention of "the wedding," of "the baby" gave a visible lift to their spirits. Carmella kissed them both on the cheek and we watched them go into the elevator, Billy's hand placed absently, but still gently, on Judy's back.

In the subway train, she took my arm.

"He really respects you."

"Who?" I asked.

She scowled.

"I don't know why."

"Don't be a jerk. Let him respect you."
"Is it fair? I don't respect him."
"Why not?"
"Come on."
"No." She turned to me, suddenly serious. "Why don't you respect him?"
"You don't understand. He was my big hero when I was a kid. He had a band." I stretched out my legs. "He wore a pompadour."
I'd at least won a smile.
"The man has fallen."
The comment made her look down at her hands.
"Tell me," she asked, once she'd decided to speak, "do you see everything in terms of yourself?"
She folded her arms, I thought, the way her fireman father must have.
The lights went off in the car for several seconds. When they came back on, she was still waiting for my answer.

At her apartment, we drank bourbon out of 7-Up glasses. Her roommate came into the kitchen, dressed only in a long nightshirt. I could see most of her legs underneath, blond hairs on the back of them, a bruise on the instep. These simple pleasures I'd denied myself so long. Girls.
"The trick is," Carmella said, "to feel compassion for your folks, but not to be dragged down by it. To not feel like you're still them. If you're still them, then everything they are reflects on you. They've gotta be wonderful, or you're shit. Do you want to hear a record?"
She was not only witty, but wise. She had it knocked. What was I doing here?
"Sure. Do you have any Jerry Vale?"
"Do you understand what I'm saying?"
"Yes. In the words of Jerry Vale, easier said than done."
"No it's not. And what's all this about Jerry Vale?"
"I'm being humorous."

Carmella took a slug of bourbon.

"No, you're not. You're avoiding what I'm saying." She gave me a good long look. "I don't even think you know how much you're still in their clutches."

"But you know."

"Well, for one thing, look at your hair."

"What's wrong with my hair?"

"For another, your clothes."

"What's wrong—"

"I don't think you even try to be somebody else. You look like your mother still dresses you every morning, and you're trying to get over the embarrassment by hiding behind your hair."

"I think maybe I'll go home."

"Don't go home. Let me cut your hair."

She bit the edge of her glass, took a little bourbon in.

"You want to cut my hair?"

"All semester I've wanted to cut your hair."

"You have?"

"When Dr. Sutorius is being boring, I imagine a different shape to your head. I imagine what I'd do."

"This is surprising, Carmella."

"I know."

She poured a little more bourbon for us both.

"So why not, instead of being an interpreter at the United Nations, go into hairdressing?"

She frowned.

"You're not gonna let me do it, are you?"

"What are you going to make me look like?"

"You'll be very happy, I promise."

My resistance didn't last long. There was something too appealing about the idea, and her energy was right there, right out front. I did as I was told: took a shower, got my hair wet, then waited.

"Are you ready in there?"

"Yeah, just, what do I put around myself?"

"There's towels in the hamper."

I wrapped one around myself. "Okay."

She came in carrying a long pair of barber's scissors. They looked big enough to shear a lamb with.

"Go ahead. Sit down."

The bottom of the tub was wet.

"Isn't this the way to get piles?"

"Jesus God, I love this hair," she said, combing it straight back. "I didn't think I was going to get a crack at it this early."

This contact gave me an erection right away.

I tried to arrange the towel to hide it. Then I thought: Why?

"I'm gonna cut it short, so don't be freaked."

"Go ahead. I don't care."

She started snipping around the edges.

"And you'll see, you're gonna feel different."

"How?"

"Whenever I go home to see my parents, I make sure I put on a lot of lipstick. That way I know we're going to argue about lipstick. As long as the fights keep to the externals, they can't get to your soul."

"I see. So my parents and I are going to fight because I have short hair."

"Try going home in a leather jacket. Carry whips and chains."

"My mother would compliment me. She'd have me kicking myself within ten minutes."

"Bullshit. You can lift your head a little."

"You think I'm kidding?"

She clipped along the line of bangs: I looked at her through a shower of wet black curls.

"How'd you get so mature at the age of twenty?"

"My older sister took me aside, said, basically, 'Don't let them fuck with you.'"

She combed my hair back again.

"Also, it helps if your father never raped you, you weren't responsible, directly or indirectly, for your brother's crib death. Barring those sorts of things, not being able to go out into the world and make a reasonable life for yourself is probably your own fault."

She was snipping along my neck again.

"I mean, so what if my father didn't tell me he loved me every day of his life? So what if he forgot, or if he loved my sister better, or Mom most of all? That was his responsibility? I'm not Helen Keller. I'm this healthy person. I mean, we are basically this driblet of sperm who just happened to *happen*, and we act like a ticker-tape parade should greet our every move. You can stand up now."

I did.

"Now go ahead, look."

In the bathroom mirror (she held it open so I could look), my face stood out in bold relief: like it or not, there it was.

"What do you think?"

"I don't know."

"You look great."

"I don't know," I said again.

"Oh, come on. Take a shower and comb it back."

I did as I was told. Reflected in the bathroom mirror, I had to admit this was a new person, one who didn't necessarily have to carry the burdens of the old. Here I was, naked in a girl's apartment. This wasn't the laundromat.

"Maybe I should have left more here," she said when I met her outside the door. She touched the hair above my ears.

"No. I go on record as saying I like it."

I reached down and kissed her.

"Do I have to go home?"

"Yes."

I kissed her again.

"What's this thing poking into me?"

"Do I have to go home?"

"You can stay long enough for me to see it dry."

"Where do you sleep?"

"None of your business."

"Carmella."

"I think I should have left more over the ears."

• • •

We didn't go to class the next day. We stayed in bed until late afternoon, well after I knew I'd missed the appointment with Cynthia. When we finally did crawl out of bed and over to campus, it was with the superior, dissipated air of a couple of teenagers who've just tried marijuana for the first time.

I had gotten used to the haircut, quickly came to like it. The closeness of it, the sense of scalp, made me feel a little bit exotic, strange to myself, more capable of surprise. So had sex. Carmella told me I could do it longer than other boys, and that was nice to hear. I didn't tell her the reason: that it hurt. I was uncircumcised, and I'd thought I'd pulled it all the way back on a number of occasions, but never as far as being in her pulled it back; whole acres felt exposed for the first time. The pain was so bad it made me want to cry out, but I didn't. I let her believe it was all talent that kept me going. It was as if I were watching a movie where, overnight, Nicholas Battaglia had turned into a stud.

On campus, I imagined Cynthia in her office, looking at her watch, or staring at the door, waiting. Good. Let her. Let her come out and see me now. New hair, new girl. Let her see.

I stayed with Carmella for the weekend, until she kicked me out on Sunday night, saying she had a term paper to finish. Her roommate was getting annoyed. I wore Carmella's black T-shirt all day Sunday. It just fit.

Every time we made love I kept waiting for it to feel as good as it had felt just kissing Cynthia. It never happened. Inside Carmella, I found myself thinking of an old Robert Goulet song, about a tree that blossomed when the right people kissed. I wondered what a girl would think of you if she knew that while you were making love to her, you were thinking of Robert Goulet.

Then, all week, I wanted Cynthia to see us holding hands; I wanted things to come to something. Beyond the sex and beyond the banter, I was getting bored.

Finally, one day during the next week Carmella and I

were heading into the cafeteria, holding hands, just as
Cynthia was coming out. She held a cup of coffee in her
hand. I think she saw us before we saw her. There was
something rigid in the set of her chin, the way she held her
coffee.

"Nicholas. Hello."

I didn't know whether to drop Carmella's hand or go
on holding it. Which would draw less attention?

"Hello. This is Carmella."

They smiled at each other by crinkling up their eyes.
Each mouth was set.

"I missed you last week."

"Yes. I meant to call."

"Are you working on the paper?"

Carmella laughed, gave me away.

I focused on the Styrofoam cup she was holding: a part of
me became concerned, irrationally, with her health. I
wanted to point out to her the dangers of Styrofoam; how, if
it's left alone, the weight of evidence suggests hot water will
dissolve Styrofoam, will eventually *eat* it. I also didn't want
to look at Carmella. In just these few days, I'd forgotten how
beautiful Cynthia was. What was the use? My heart was
beating very fast.

"I'll be there today, okay?"

"Fine."

And in the next instant, I wanted to erase Carmella
from the scene, to let Cynthia know that none of it, not
the whole weight of our fucking, had ever come close to
the density of the movement of her lips saying "Fine."

She left abruptly, didn't say goodbye.

In the cafeteria, afterwards, I must have been a little
surly. After she finished her coffee, Carmella leaned back
in her chair and said, "Well, Battaglia, since we seem to
have run out of things to talk about, you wanna go back
to your fabulous Dr. Sutorius impression?"

I was in Cynthia's office at 3.

She was marking a student's paper, looked up with a

distracted air, and gestured that I should shut the door. She went on correcting the paper.

"I see you've got a new haircut," making a big red circle around a sentence.

"Yes. You like it?"

"It's very becoming, actually."

Finally, she looked at me fully.

"New clothes, too."

"Not new."

I was wearing a black turtleneck of Carmella's, and I felt the urge to defend it. Carmella, at least, had given me an idea of who I should be.

"No?"

She was going to pretend to be distracted again.

"All right, Nicholas, just tell me now so I can prepare for the future. Do I have a job here, or what?"

"I don't get it."

"When can I expect the paper?"

I looked down. I was leaning forward, hands on my knees. She still wasn't looking at me.

"Soon."

"What's soon?"

If it had been a pencil instead of a pen in her hand, the tip would be broken now.

"I don't know."

"I am so fucking *sick* of this." Finally she turned.

"No. Don't."

I reached out, but my hand was deflected.

Tears came out of her eyes then. There was a knock on the door.

"Come in," she said. Her arm was instantly up, blocking anyone's view of her face.

Mrs. Underwood came in and handed her a mimeographed sheet. The secretary had taken on the scent of the Jesuits, the suggestion of a poorly digested lunch.

"Thought you'd want this."

She'd noticed nothing; she left.

"Thank you," Cynthia called after her.

"I don't want to make you cry."

"Then don't."
I leaned forward. She let me know not to approach.
"Okay."

In quiet rage, I wrote her a paper.
I attacked the library stacks. I searched out every reference to the erotic life of Anne Bradstreet that I could find. I communed with John Berryman, Adrienne Rich; I scoured the poems as I would have a letter or note from her. When this was done, I would be finished. This would be it. I hoped for no more. I didn't want to make her cry. Beyond that, there seemed no possibilities. I had Carmella, and that would have to do. I'd hand this in and say goodbye.

Because I wanted so badly to be done with it, I worked through the night on Saturday. Tommy's woman groaned, and I combed the words of polite, restrained passion with which a woman of the seventeenth century felt free to speak. After a while, the tension got to be too much. "Say 'fuck,' Anne!" I wanted to shout. "Say it!"

> What can I more, in thy absence,
> But clutch those fruits from whose heat I
> bore?

Her life was so simple, really. Every fuck so potentially life and death. Before one of her children was born, she wrote a poem, certain she wouldn't survive the ordeal. Her concern was that her husband would forget her. She only thought of the child second.

I imagined her, with her vanity and her fears and her rage, lying in the small New England house in the middle of winter, Edward Bradstreet atop her, children in the next room, and a whopping orgasm rising up in her.

What did she do with it? Where did it go?

• • •

At about three in the morning on Sunday, Tommy came into my room. I was still typing.

"What are you doing?" he asked.

"I've got this paper to finish."

"Where does such newfound dedication come from, Nicholas?"

He was naked, drinking from a container of orange juice, munching on an apple.

"Why don't you dress proper once in a while?"

"The typing is bothering Sue."

"Oh." I leaned on the typewriter, unrepentant. "I'm sorry."

"You gonna stop?"

"No."

"Come on, Nick, don't be a—"

"Shut the door."

He stood there a moment, took another gulp, disappeared.

But afterwards it got to be too much and I lay down on the bed. I took myself in my hand and wondered what it would have been like if Anne Bradstreet had been able to have an abortion, to kiss any boy she wanted. Or if her husband had been an actor. I thought of her in my bed now, and how I would be able to do things to her that Edward Bradstreet couldn't do. Carmella had helped me at least this much. I would encourage her to scream; I would force her to rip past all the things that held her back. I spurted up onto the sheets and felt a loss like no other. If you couldn't make babies, what was the sense? They had at least that, Anne and Edward. I thought of David, watching a baseball game and sending his wife into an abortionist's. I felt crippled by my inability to prevent any of these things, to save any of these women. The hot stuff dripped onto me, useless, dying, growing stale. I decided to punish myself by getting up and finishing the paper.

• • •

On Sunday night, as soon as the last page was typed, I
got on the train, went directly to Ninetieth Street and
rang the buzzer. I didn't know what I was going to do if
David answered. Again, it was raining. I'd recovered an
old broken black umbrella from the trash on Decatur,
held it open to protect the paper.

She opened the inner door. I looked at her through the
grate.

"Yes?"

Her mouth had been the only thing that moved.

"I brought it."

She looked at the paper in my hand.

"Give it to me, please."

"Open the door."

She looked afraid of me. I couldn't imagine what I
must look like, two days without sleep.

"Who is it?" David called from deep within the house.

"It's Nicholas. He's brought a paper for me."

She opened the grate.

I had a moment of hesitation before handing it over, as
if I'd lived with it too long, was giving something of myself away.

"Thank you."

She could have gone then, could have closed the door,
and that would have been it. I had no power left, had no
right to demand anything.

She stayed, though. It seemed like hesitation more
than decision. The rain plastered my new short hair. She
stepped out into the rain, looked up at the sky.

"The rain's bad, isn't it?"

"Yes. Don't come out."

"You're soaked."

She touched the collar of my jacket. I shivered.

"Is it good?"

"What?"

"What you've written."

"Yes. It's good."

I leaned over and kissed her. It was our best kiss. I decided there was nothing like kissing in the rain.

I threw the umbrella to the side so I could feel both sides of her head. Just for a moment to feel them, with the pride of a surveyor, mapping chaos.

"That's enough," she said, and pulled back, but her eyes had grown wide, welcoming as hands drawing me in. I stopped feeling the shivering cold and the rain.

She lingered in the doorway, looking down.

"He'll be away for Thanksgiving," she whispered.

She stayed another minute, looking up only once—as if to be sure I was still there, still breathing; then she went inside, locking the door behind her.

My parents' words cracked and bleeped. I was losing whole syllables, as if the phone lines were a long track from which several of the ties had disappeared.

"We miss you," my mother said.

What I heard was "We mi- you."

"Yes," I said, thinking they heard "ye-." "Is this connection good for you?"

"We have no trouble hearing you," my mother said.

On another extension, my father's presence had been announced at the beginning of the conversation. Since then, his austerity had held forth in silence.

"You haven't been home."

"No. I've been busy."

An electronic gasp followed, brief, like a stage pause.

"This call has a purpose." I cleared my throat, made an aborted attempt to chuckle.

"Oh, what's that?" my mother asked.

"I can't come home for Thanksgiving."

There was a brief silence, a sound as if one or both of them were altering their positions.

"Oh, why not?"

"I can't."

It had the weakness of a flat stone, cast into water, which fails to make the skip.

"We thought we'd all drive together to Billy's wedding."

"Yes. I know. I don't know if I can make it to Billy's wedding either."

My father cleared his throat.

"He'll be disappointed," my mother purred.

"Now what's this?" my father asked, the phrasing odd enough, for him, that I wasn't sure right off what he was talking about.

"I've gotta be here."

"Oh, why?" my mother asked, as if, for her, the conversation had not yet moved far off from the realm of pleasant chitchat.

I hesitated. "There's a girl," I said finally. "A woman." Then, as if I were talking into a vacuum, the connection broken off: "I've gotta spend the day with her."

"Well, can't you tell her you have to go home for Thanksgiving?"

"No, Mom. That's the only time I can see her."

I stopped short of announcing, "She's married," though the impulse had been there.

"Doesn't she have parents?"

"She's much older, Mom."

It silenced them.

"She's an older woman," my father said, as though the remark had no validity until he'd announced it, and this was somehow a way of translating it to my mother.

Finally she sighed in agreement.

None of this had the effect I'd expected; not even a momentary thrill of liberation was involved. Instead, there was the embarrassed feeling a son gets while listening, in the next room, to his parents discussing, in hushed voices, the facts of his hormonal changes.

"Al and Rose will be here," my mother said.

"Mom, they're always there."

I shouldn't have said it; their silence took on an injured feeling. Al and Rose being there was not meant to be a bragging statement, merely a fact of life.

"I'm sorry," I mumbled.

They chose not to answer. I had a sense of them drawing into themselves, becoming one.

"I don't know, maybe I'll be able to make Billy's wedding," I began. "I just don't know yet."

"What will you eat?" my mother asked.

"What?"

"On Thanksgiving. Will you go out to a restaurant?"

"I don't know."

"Or the girl, will she cook for you?"

The girl.

"I think maybe she will." Then: "She isn't a *girl*, Ma."

"She has no parents to go to?"

"They don't live here in New York." I'd never asked about parents, about an earlier life. It seemed inessential.

"You could go to Mamma Leone's," my mother suggested. "We'll send you the money. I bet they have a nice spread."

"Sure, turkey cacciatore," my father said. My mother started to laugh. It took me several seconds to accept the fact that he'd made a joke.

"I saw Billy, you know," I said.

"Oh?"

"I had dinner with him. And Judy."

"So you know why they're getting married." My mother laughed.

"Josie," my father said, abruptly returning to the Calvinist mode, where a moment before he'd been Milton Berle.

"It's no *secret*," my mother protested.

"Maybe Nick doesn't know."

"I know," I said. "Billy's proud of it."

"See?" my mother said.

The conversation had narrowed down to the two of them, as if they were playing a game of one on one, using their son as backboard.

"So no more Julie?" my father asked abruptly.

"No, Dad."

"You two didn't get along?"

"We got along fine."

He didn't ask for any more, but I felt called upon to explain.

"We only saw each other a couple of times, Dad. It's not like this was some big affair. There was just the party and then the time she came to New York."

And the hand job in the front seat of your car.

"I don't think she's exactly pining for me."

"No, she has a boyfriend, Viola said," my mother added.

It fell off then, whatever energy our statements had managed to generate up till now.

"It makes for bad feeling, that's all," my father said, but his disapproval no longer had weight. I sensed his attention wandering, perhaps to the TV pages, to see what movies were on tonight. His only weakness, really, was that he had to say his formal goodbye before he was free.

"Let us know if you change your mind," my mother said.

"I will. But I don't think I'll be changing my mind."

"That's fine," my father said, without irony. He hadn't been listening.

"Make sure you eat," my mother said.

"Ma, it's Thanksgiving. How could I forget to eat?"

"And we'll see you at Billy's."

Would they? Or, more to the point, was it worth arguing? I let it stand.

On Thursday, Cynthia held the paper before her, clearly waiting for me.

"Well, it's got energy, nobody could deny that."

She was leaning back in her chair, making every effort, I thought, to look detached, uninvolved with the paper's author.

"It's written as though you were in heat."

"I practically was. I stayed up late to write it."

She laid the paper down, rested her hand on it, shook her head.

"The tone is desperate, as though if you don't get it right, and you don't get it right *fast*, someone's going to come get you." She breathed a mock sigh of relief. "Anne

Bradstreet has been dead for three hundred years, Nicholas. I think she can wait another couple of days for you to get things straight."

"I thought I had to do it fast or you wouldn't forgive me."

She eyed the partway-open door.

"You thought right."

"Well?"

"I've made notations. Mostly it needs to be slowed down and filled out."

She handed me the paper: a study in red scrawl against black type. I was resistant to looking at my own words, couldn't remember, in fact, what I'd written, what secrets were announced here to the world.

"Take your time now, all right? I'll pass a Xerox of this on to Father O'Rourke."

"I thought this would be enough."

"Nicholas, I'm still your teacher, all right? I do retain some illusions that you'll come out of this with something more than the piercing insight that because she couldn't scream out her orgasms, Anne Bradstreet had to write poems."

"That's not bad, though, is it?"

She smirked. "I've heard worse. Given the competition, you could probably manage to squeeze a career out of it."

"What about Thanksgiving?"

"We can't talk about that here."

The smile had dropped; her face was clear, devoid of expression.

"It's just, my uncle is getting married that weekend. I'd like to be able to tell him—"

"I can't tell you anything."

She turned to her desk, made a circle of a group of paper clips.

"I'll have to call you, when I'm free," she said. "I don't know what that weekend will be like."

"You mean I should just wait?"

She sent me a brief look that I didn't understand.

"Is that too much to ask?"

"No."

"All right, then..."

"Are you all right?"

There were footsteps in the hall. She'd dropped a paper clip, sent it flying—clumsily; she hadn't meant to.

"Yes, fine."

"And you'll be free, won't you?"

"Shhh." One hand went up, brushed away her hair. She whispered, "Yes," as if afraid someone would hear.

I couldn't get anything more concrete out of her in the next session. Thanksgiving was now a week away. I decided to write Uncle Billy rather than call. Writing would give me a chance to be more hifalutin about my reasons for missing his wedding, though I suspected if anyone understood it would be Billy.

While I was posting my letter in the Campus Center, I ran into Carmella. She was not exactly waiting for me. I found her near the entrance, leaning against a wall, talking to a boy.

"Battaglia!" she called, lifting one arm a little extravagantly. Then she took her time finishing the conversation.

"So?" she asked, when she was done. She continued leaning there, like a girl on the cover of a paperback novel with a title like "Restless."

"'So' what? I've got a letter to mail."

I'd tried, in Dr. Sutorius' classes, to remain friendly while letting her know I was no longer available.

"I see you're back to dressing like Mama's little boy."

"You want your turtleneck back?"

"I want you to *wear* it. I thought we were making real progress."

"It's in the wash."

"Who's the letter to?"

I held it up.

"My Uncle Billy. Remember?"

"This has become an epistolary relationship? You and Uncle Billy?"

"No. I had to write and let him know I can't come to his wedding."

"He'll be crushed. Why not?"

I looked around. The Campus Center was crowded. I didn't want to risk running into Cynthia here.

"You want to go get a drink?"

At a dark back table of the Killarney Rose, Carmella held her bourbon up to the light, half-listening.

"I can tell you this because you're a sophisticated woman and because I know you're not in love with me. There's someone else. There's always been someone else, but I didn't know it was reciprocal until last week."

She drank, held the liquid in her mouth for several seconds, slanted her eyes at me.

"Come on, don't be mad," I said. "We had fun, didn't we?"

"Are you paying for these drinks?"

"Yes."

"All right, we had fun. Except it's heartbreaking to see you turn back into your old self again."

"What's wrong with this? This is a good shirt. These are good chinos."

"You were a wild man for approximately twenty-four hours. It did you good."

"But you weren't in love with me."

"No. I just liked how long you could do it."

She flipped through the metal pages of the table jukebox.

"Can I tell you something? The only reason I could do it that long is because I'm not circumcised and you're the first girl I ever did it with."

She leaned back into the cushion behind her.

"Sure."

"It's true. As soon as I get used to doing it, I'll probably turn into a premature ejaculator."

"Right."

She squeezed an imaginary ice cube between her teeth.

"Come on, Carmella. Ask my roommate. Ask Tommy. You are the only person in the world who ever considered me a stud. Tommy would laugh."

"How would he know?"

"Maybe the reason I'm wearing these clothes is I know who I am. Just because I've got a sore dick, you think I'm Porfirio Rubirosa."

"Who?"

"He was supposedly a great—"

"Buy me another drink, all right?"

I looked at her a moment. She was in no hurry, so neither, I decided, was I. The bar had a good feel to it, mostly empty, a pocket outside of the world. I thought what was probably happening was that we were finishing this in the only way we could. I went to the bar and picked up the bourbon and brought it to Carmella.

"I also am in love with someone else, I might as well tell you," Carmella said.

"Oh. Who?"

She sipped.

"His name is Dirk Tubridy. He's a fireman at Engine Company Eight; he works with my father. Thirty-three years old, two kids; there's not a chance."

The shot was gone.

"But I've been in love with him for ten years."

"You were ten ten years ago."

"I know."

Later, in her room, in the unmade bed, in the soggy yellow late-afternoon light, all the beer eased my pain considerably, and the sexual prediction I'd made pretty much came true.

She shifted under me, as if her body was unwilling to believe it was over so fast.

Then she let out a long sigh.

"What a falling-off was there. Hamlet," she murmured.

And, as if completing a couplet, I said, "Whither is the rose."

She let out a big guffaw; her body shook and expelled me.

"Whither indeed."

"It's still there."

"I've got no more use for you, Porfirio."

She turned over onto her stomach, her big soft behind pointing up a little. I patted it.

"I was drunk."

She murmured dismissively.

"Hey. Doesn't one get forgiven in this world?" I asked.

She spoke half into her pillow. "I spend too much time in bed. When I get bored with somebody, I imagine he's Dirk Tubridy. It's just depressing to wake up from that."

She lowered her behind, getting more comfortable.

"Is that who you imagined I was?"

"I didn't have time to imagine. Imagining takes several seconds."

I got up and went to her window. It looked out onto a dull brown street, a church on the corner. I had wanted to fail. But now, looking out onto the brown street, I became afraid, as if for the first time. The whole size of what I wanted to accomplish appeared huge to me.

I looked back at Carmella on the bed. One of her eyes was open, glancing at me, perhaps hoping I'd become aroused again.

"You had such promise," she said, and, closing her eyes, pulled the covers up over herself.

There was a message waiting when I got home. It was scrawled in Tommy's handwriting across a paper towel, attached to the door of my room with a bit of masking tape smeared with something that looked like butter.

"Tommy, are you here?"

I found him lying across his bed, writing in a loose-leaf notebook propped up against his lifted thigh. His underwear looked gray, soiled, wearing through at the edges.

"When did she call?"

He didn't stop writing, or take his eyes from the loose-leaf.

"Tommy?"

He squinted, as though he had to concentrate harder.

"She called..." He wrote something. "...a while ago."

"When?"

"A while."

I dialed her number. My hands were shaking, I couldn't tell whether from rage at Tommy or nervousness over what might happen.

David answered, and I hung up.

"Did she leave a message." I was back now in the entrance to Tommy's room.

"I think so."

"Well, what was it?"

"I do believe our Nickie is in love. Has the pork hit the fat yet?"

He lifted one eyebrow and looked me up and down.

"You are such a jerk."

I sat in the corner, facing him.

"She said she'd call." He went on writing. "Not to call her."

"Which is what I just did. Thank you."

"Well, she wasn't clear. She knows I disapprove."

He lifted one cheek, to let out a fart.

"Jesus."

"Hey, if you don't *like* it..."

"What are you writing?"

"A poem."

"She said *she'd* call, right?"

"I think so."

"Tommy."

"I think so. I'm concentrating on this."

"When did you start writing poems?"

"It's for Sue."

I let that pass.

"You know, maybe I've got some literary talent here. I'm selling the house; maybe I can finance a career as a writer."

"Have you given up going to class?"

"Pretty much."

He put down the loose-leaf and propped himself up on his elbow.

"Sue's coming over after work. We're gonna make some Tuna Helper. You gonna be around?"

"I'm staying right here until I get that call."

I was still a little drunk, and smarting from Carmella's sexual insult. I knew the thing to do was get up and go to my room, but I didn't.

"Look at you—you lie in bed, you're waiting for some Bronx girl so you can lie in those sheets and fuck her all night. Is that all you want to do with your life?"

He waited a moment.

"Is that the best you can do?" he asked.

I looked down.

"Is that the most savage indictment you can come up with, Nick?"

"I'm holding back."

"Well, don't."

"All right. I think Sue's a tramp. I think she's not worth you. I think I'm worth you, and you won't give me the time of day. Everybody's father dies, Tommy, it doesn't make you special."

It still didn't seem enough. It didn't get to the heart of anything.

"I just hate it that it makes you give up."

He stared at me afterwards a long time. When he finally spoke, he started slowly and carefully.

"You got your little celibate affair with your English teacher, so you got life knocked, right, Nickie boy? You go to class, you take your little notes, you have your fancy discussions with her about Henry James's penis size, or whatever the fuck it is you two find to talk about. You think because she's married it's somehow more important than what everybody else is doing, and because she's got her Ph.D. she's better. Let me ask you something, Mr. Nicholas B. Jerkoff; if it's all so great and important, why isn't she here now?"

"Come on."

"Why isn't she?"

"She's got a husband."

"You want me to tell you something? You're not gonna like to hear it. If there was anything real going on between you two she'd be here right now, she'd be on her knees on this floor with her twat flying sky high, saying Give it to me, Nick, shove it right in. *That* is real. These secret fucking phone calls are not real. You're lucky I even told you."

"I wish to God your father hadn't died, Tommy. I wish to Christ that somebody could point out to you that this new philosophy of yours is not the be-all and end-all of human existence. Your father didn't do it enough, so he died. And you think if you do it enough, you're gonna live forever."

He lay back then, laughing.

"Brilliant. Oh, brilliant. That is just what I'm doing. I'm gonna get a bust of you, Nickie, put it up next to Freud and Kierkegaard. Great insights into human motivation."

"Shut up!"

"No!" He sat up. "The only good thing that ever happened to me was having my father die. What was I doing here? What was I gonna *become*, Nick, a teacher? An engineer? What road was I on, huh? You and me, we follow this stupid little treadmill because our fathers didn't have balls enough to deny us this wonderful thing, this college education. They weren't smart enough to know what was good for us."

I could hear his breathing when he stopped.

"You think somebody like Vito—my cousin Vito—is running around right now calling up married women, waiting breathlessly for them to call back? If he is, it's because he's going to fuck them, that's all, just plain and simple stick the old rod in. But for you, it's not that, is it?"

"No."

"Do you even know what it is?"

"Yes, sure."

"Do you?"

"Why don't you tell me?"

He waited a few seconds.

"I think Nickie thinks he's gonna be changed. Put through the mill and come out different. The beauty parlor of class, and old Cynthia's the beautician. But what happens when you finally get down to it and you find out it doesn't make you any different?"

His words hadn't gotten through. I thought what he was saying didn't really touch what was going on. It was a desultory game of tennis we were playing, each of us with our own notion of where the net was, a little annoyed that the other wasn't returning our serves.

"You really think you could be like your cousin Vito, Tommy?"

"No, I don't."

"So what is this crap?"

"Don't call people tramps, all right?"

There was something strange about his mouth now, as if it were all bunched up in defense of Sue.

"Okay."

I thought there'd be more, but strangely, there wasn't, as if the point about Sue subverted things. We had finally been getting toward something, but this small parliamentary matter prevented us from going on.

I went into my room to wait for the call. Sue came; they ate; I tried to keep out of their way. Tommy and I were stupidly polite all evening, as if we were afraid of fighting in front of Sue. Later they made love. I listened to them, wishing the sounds of lovemaking would grow predictable. They never did.

It was very late when she called: one, two in the morning.

"Are you awake?" she asked.

"Yes. I was waiting."

"I'm sorry about this."

"It's okay."

There was a silence.

"Your roommate told you I would call."

"Yes. Are you all right?"

"He wants me to come with him."

"Where?"

"To Warwick, for Thanksgiving."

"No!"

There was a hollow silence.

"No," I said, more weakly.

"I know, I promised. But I'll be here all of December and he'll still be there."

"It's not the same."

Then, as though I were ashamed of it: "I've told my parents." And then, to cover the stupidity of that remark: "I told my uncle I couldn't come to his wedding."

"I'm sorry."

"Don't keep saying that."

Silence.

"I told them about you. I told them I was in love. I can't just show up."

Still nothing.

"Why can't you just tell him you can't come?"

"For what reason?"

"Make one up."

"He's feeling bad about the abortion. He's thinking maybe if he'd been working, it might have been different."

"Well, that's just too bad for him."

A moment later, she said: "He's sleeping, I've got to go back."

"No. Don't."

"I've got to. He could wake."

"Wait."

"Nicholas."

"Where is Warwick—"

A click, as though she'd hung up.

"It's in Rhode Island."

"It is?"

"Yes. Goodbye."

"No, wait. What if I could get there?"

"To Warwick? *No.*"

"To Providence. It must be close. Rhode Island is the smallest state in the Union. Could you get there?"

"I don't know."

"Could you?"

"Nicholas, I've got to go."

"*Stay on the phone.* Stay. I'm sorry. No, shit, no, I'm not. If I can get to Providence, if I can be there that weekend, all four days, you could come for one, couldn't you? You could get away."

"I don't know."

"You could."

"Maybe.... We have *all* December."

"No. Not good enough."

I waited.

"I don't believe you. I think you'll just make up another excuse. I think you're tired of me already. I think you've just been using me."

She said nothing.

"Do you hear me?"

"Yes. I've got to go."

"I'll be in Providence."

I heard the click, definite now.

I lay in bed an hour, stupidly believing it was possible for sleep to descend on a body in revolt. Then I got up and went to the door of Tommy's room, knowing I'd have to ask him eventually. He and Sue lay wrapped in each other, a pink, hairless *Laocoön.* Up close, their bodies looked soft, childlike. I touched Tommy's leg to rouse him.

He blinked awake.

"What is it?" he asked.

"I need to talk to you," I whispered.

His hand covered his eyes.

"So talk."

"Not here. We'll wake her."

"Can't it wait till morning?"

"No." Then: "I can't sleep."

"I can."

"Please."

He looked askance at me, then sat up, annoyed.

"*What?*"

"Come into my room."

"Jesus."

In another minute, we were sitting on my bed.

"Are you going home for Thanksgiving, Tom?"

Again, he rubbed his eyes.

"Jesus, is that what you woke me up for? You want to discuss turkey recipes?"

"No. Just tell me. Are you going home?"

"I've got no home."

I braced myself.

"Can you give me the keys to your house for that weekend?"

"What?"

"The keys. Can I stay there that weekend?"

"Why?"

I touched the sheets on either side of me.

"We were supposed to spend the weekend together. Her husband's in Warwick. He's in a play. Maybe if I'm in Providence she'll come."

"You want to fuck her in my father's house?"

I paused, tried to think of arguments.

"Yes."

He didn't say anything, just looked at me.

"It's up for sale, you know."

"I know."

"So why don't you just buy it?"

"Tommy."

"I can't let you have the keys."

"Why not?"

"I don't *like* it."

He started to get up.

"Please."

I grabbed his knee, to hold him there.

"Let go of me, okay?"

I did.

"Look, there are all kinds of places you can fuck her, Nick. There's here. There's her place."

"I told you. She's going to be in Warwick."

I was still sitting on the bed, and he was standing, so that I had to look up at him. I was begging.

"I don't want to do it."

"*Please.*"

"No."

He started to go.

"Jesus God, didn't I ever do anything for you?"

He stopped in the doorway.

"No. Not that I can think of."

"I was there when your father died."

"Well, aren't you the good boy."

"I was there, goddammit."

"Yeah, you were there, the star attraction."

He left, went back to his room. I followed him.

"I will not touch her in your parents' bed, if that's what you're afraid of. I will bring my own sheets, we'll do it on the floor, all right?"

"I don't care where you do it, Nick. Just not in my house."

He lay down beside Sue.

"All right, fine, give me the name of a motel in Providence."

He laughed.

"I mean it."

"I'll give you the name of a motel in Providence. I'll give you a dozen names. In the morning, all right?"

"All right."

It would have to do. I didn't relish spending four days in a motel, and besides that, I would have to pay my hack's dues and drive a cab from now until Thanksgiving to pay for it. But it would be better than going home, better than admitting that defeat.

Then, when I approached Cynthia with it, she said no. She would not meet me in a motel in Providence, it was out of the question. I pleaded with her, but we were in her office, and there were limits. I made up my mind to badger her until she agreed—I felt certain I could win. But a couple of days later, when I got back to the apartment, Tommy had had an unexpected change of heart, and the keys were lying on my bed along with a note:

> *Don't make a mess. Watch out for Vito.*
> *Eat at Joe's.*

Then, at the bottom:

> *This does not, by the way, mean I love you.*

I took the late train Wednesday night.

I'd driven the afternoon shift in the cab for a solid week, and was traveling with two hundred dollars in my pocket. Cynthia had directions—exact as I could make them—to the house in Providence. She'd never exactly promised she'd come. It always remained in the realm of "if it's possible." But when I boarded the train I didn't allow myself to think it might not be.

It was late—well after midnight—when the train reached Providence.

The key stuck in the house's lock. I was a long time working at it; meanwhile, the dark street (all but a very few lights were off, the only real light coming from streetlamps) seemed to absorb the sound unnaturally. Finally the lock turned, the door gave, opened onto the black foyer, objects coming into view as if whitened by shock, invasion. No one lived here.

I turned on every light in the downstairs. I checked closets; I was frightened. There was only a jar of olives in the refrigerator, and it was too late to go out. Tomorrow was Thanksgiving; what would be open?

I sat on the couch in the living room, inadvertently thinking of my parents. All the confidence of the past days, the days since Tommy had given me the keys, vanished.

I made my bed on Tommy's floor. I'd tried his bed, but wasn't comfortable there. I turned off the lights, piled blankets over me, hid there, shivering. There was not a chance she would be here even tomorrow; Friday the soonest, she'd said. So why was I here? Why couldn't I have eaten Thanksgiving dinner with my parents, taken the train here Friday morning? I imagined the turkey, the smooth gravy, the moist buttery stuffing. Potatoes. I thought of the creamy pies. I wondered what I would eat here, where to find food tomorrow. Maybe it wasn't too late to go home.

In the morning, it was easier—just seeing things in the light, even if it was a gray, overcast Thanksgiving light. I got dressed and went out to buy food, heading in the direction of the station, where I knew things were. I found a breakfast place open, ate a skimpy plate of eggs, another. I read the Providence *Journal* front to back. I was the only customer in the place.

Then I walked back to the house, stopping only to buy bananas at an open grocery store (I couldn't make up my mind about anything else). There was still the day to get through. On television, Ronald Colman, a blind painter, had his masterpiece destroyed by Ida Lupino. There were old copies of *Reader's Digest* and *Field and Stream* lying around. I read an article called "Surprised by Grizzlies" —the accompanying picture showed a pair of fishermen dropping their rods, just as a fat salmon had been hooked, while behind them a pair of brown monsters raised their claws; then a profile of Bob Hope. I lay in Tommy's bed and started to masturbate, but decided against it. What if she came just as I'd finished? Besides, it had depressed me to read about Bob Hope, to hear him talk about "the boys" in Vietnam, and to remember that a

war was still going on, a war everyone kept expecting to
be over any second yet which still went on, and here I
was, in an empty room in Providence, playing with my
dick. I went into the Bevilacqua room, looked at the pictures of Jesus getting dusty. When I switched on the light,
every object seemed to blink. I touched the bed, I looked
at every picture. When I went downstairs it was not yet
two o'clock.

When it was dark, I went outside and called my par-
ents from a pay phone. Mr. Bevilacqua's phone had been
turned off.
   "We missed you," my mother sang.
   "Yes," I said.
   "What did you eat?"
   "Oh. Turkey."
   "Mmm. Not as good as ours, I bet."
   "No. I don't think so."
   My father picked up the other extension.
   "Nicholas."
   He used his jaunty party voice to address me. He'd
probably just been making jokes. Aunt Rose was proba-
bly right now peeing in her pants.
   "Hi, Dad."
   "You all taken care of?"
   What did that mean?
   "Yeah. I'm fine."
   "You don't sound it," my mother said.
   "I'm just tired. I just called to say Happy Thanksgiving,
that's all."
   "Oh."
   They were silent a moment.
   "Al wants to say hello," my mother said.
   "How you doin', Nicholas?" Al said.
   "Good, Uncle Al. How was the turkey?"
   "Delicious. Your mother, she's a genius."
   There was a clatter in the background, some laughter.

"Is there more company there, Al?"

"No. Just us."

But they were having a good time.

"Well, it's good to talk to you, Nicholas. Will we see you at Christmas?"

"Oh, sure."

He hung up, and I was about to, but I remembered my father was still there.

"Dad?"

"How about Saturday? Will you be at Billy's wedding?"

"I don't think so, Dad."

We both endured a silence.

"You understand," I said, as if to no one.

"Well, you continue enjoying the day," he said.

It was worse after this conversation; the house seemed even emptier, the hours impossible to fill. I went out to try to find food, but everything was closed. Then I imagined her coming here, arriving at the house, finding me gone. I ran all the way back.

In the kitchen, I huddled over the can of olives, eating them by hand from the can. I went to bed before nine, and slept for thirteen hours.

I was awakened on Friday morning by the click of the latch, footsteps. I ran down the steps in my underwear, certain it was her, to confront Vito, a strange couple, and a little girl. Vito, startled at first, finally recognized me, but the couple continued to stare, aghast.

"What are you doing here?" Vito asked.

"I'm sorry." I started up the stairs. "Tommy didn't tell you?"

He had already turned to the couple, started to apologize.

When I was dressed, I came back down.

"Nick, right?" Vito shook my hand as though he wanted to convince the other couple everything was on the up-and-up. "You're staying here?"

"I'm surprised Tommy didn't tell you. Just for the weekend."

The woman was examining the kitchen drawers and cupboards, as if she half-expected to find something hiding in each of them. Her little girl took it as a game, imitating her mother.

"Stop it, Melissa," the mother said.

The man turned his face toward me: small-time racketeer, hit man, he could have been any of them.

"They're looking at the house," Vito said.

I heard them upstairs, afterwards, going through the bedroom. Vito was probably making some joke about my bedclothes on the floor. What if she came now? I suddenly wished there was coffee, food. I'd finished the bananas yesterday, so there was nothing. My stomach gnawed, my head ached from too much sleep—and for no reason I could imagine, I had an erection.

"You're staying how long?" Vito asked, as he was ushering the couple out.

"The weekend," I said.

I could tell he didn't like that. He nodded. The little girl skipped down the steps, fell, started screaming. I closed the door.

When they were gone, I knew I had to get food, so I searched the house for paper and pencil to leave her a note. Each of these seemed unfindable until I thought to look in Tommy's old desk. There was a notepad labeled BOSTON RED SOX and a pen from—I had to look twice—Brasco's Funeral Home. I wrote the note. Then there was the problem of Scotch Tape. The Bevilacquas had none, anywhere. I searched the house so many times my head started pounding from the hunger. I tried just licking the back of the paper and sticking it to the door, but that didn't work. In the basement I found a hammer and nails. I nailed the note to the door, making a big gash in the wood. Too late, I realized I could have just stuck it in the doorjamb, leaving enough visible for her to see.

At the nearest bodega, the derangements of hunger made wise choices impossible. I came to the cash register with a jar of coffee and a box of Cocoa Krispies, as if, out of all the available foods, these were what connected most deeply with what I desired.

"Oh, excuse me, I forgot milk," I said to the clerk, and on the way back, only because I happened to notice them on the rack, picked up a jar of peanut butter and a box of Jello instant pudding. I didn't look at the pudding directions; I didn't think about what I would need to add. Who had time for that? I would eat it out of the box; it looked that good.

I was eating at the kitchen table when Vito came in. I had a spoonful of Cocoa Krispies up to my mouth, and a cup of coffee and the open jar of peanut butter were on the table. I'd forgotten to buy bread.

Vito had his son in his arms.

"How you doin'?" he asked.

"I'm fine."

"I just talked to Tommy."

He sat down. His son started to cry. He said, "Shh, shh" and put the baby far up on his shoulder, carrying him high, the way he'd shown the old man, Rookie, after the wake.

"He says there's a woman coming here."

"You want some coffee?"

"No. Is this true?"

"Yes."

His finger went back and forth across the table. As I watched it, my heart sank. I'd been detached enough from conventional morality to believe that Vito might approve, might like me more for this.

"You gotta go somewhere else. I got people comin' in and outa here all weekend."

"I can't."

His face started to turn red, and I made a movement to try and halt the flow of his thought. It was shameful to envision things from Vito's perspective. It made me want to absorb his life, to find, on the instant, the strength to say no to Cynthia.

"Tommy wants me to sell this house." He turned away

from me. "During the night, I don't care. But during the day, it looks funny to people."

"I don't know when she's coming."

The baby started crying again. Vito shifted him, and then, for a moment, the boy was quiet, looking around.

"What do you mean, you don't know? Call her up."

I looked down at my food, the little world I'd made here, so defenseless now.

"I can't. Please," I said. I felt desperate enough to say that. It was as far as I thought I could go. "Please don't kick me out. Just tell the people I'm a friend of Tommy's. They'll understand."

He said something in Italian, mumbled it. His son was bawling now, so he got up and started walking him around.

"I find a woman here, I throw you both out, you understand?"

I was standing in the kitchen, watching him as he passed into the living room. I felt half his size.

"Sure," I said.

"So don't let me find you."

He looked over his shoulder at me, to make sure I understood.

"Tommy really looks up to you," I said.

His look was quizzical. I didn't know if he properly heard. It seemed a stupid thing to say, anyway. He didn't seem to have the kind of ego that would be flattered. He was just Vito. His mastery was offhand.

After he'd gone I found it difficult to go back to eating. Instead, I waited. I sat at the window, looking out at the gray Providence street, at the customers going in and out of Babson's. This morning I'd had a hard-on, but now I felt about an inch long and retreating. If she came now, what would be the point? I thought if I could have, I would have called her, told her not to come. The day passed that way. It got dark.

That night, famished, I ate the rest of the peanut butter and made another pot of coffee. I made the pudding, too, but I must have gotten something wrong; it came out watery, and I had to throw it out. At ten, I went up to bed. She hadn't come.

It was raining in the morning. I thought that was a hopeful sign. Vito brought another couple to see the house; when I heard them downstairs, I folded my blankets, made myself presentable, and greeted them as though I had full legitimacy here. After they were gone, I made coffee, breakfast. I put everything in order, as if this was my life here, this was what I did every day.

It rained throughout the morning and afternoon. My head was in a fog from loss of human contact. At mid-afternoon, unexpectedly, I thought of killing myself, how easy it would be. Mr. Bevilacqua's straight razor was still in the bathroom, silver and shiny, ready for use. I looked at myself in the mirror and thought, what was the point? But then there seemed no point in doing it either, and what if Vito found me and was carrying his baby at the time?

I went back to the window and looked at the rain. I made plans: #1) Never do this again. #2) Go to Warwick, find the dinner theater, find her, rage, scream. #3) Find out what it was in my life that ever made sense and go back and do that again.

It stopped raining late in the afternoon, got hazy; the house felt damp. I called the train station to check on trains leaving in the morning. That felt better: at least, to have a definite plan, a time to leave. But even with that, when I went into the bathroom, I couldn't resist holding the straight razor to my wrist, until it drew blood.

I pulled it away as soon as I saw the blood start to come. I said aloud, "At ten o'clock tomorrow morning, the train leaves; at ten o'clock..."

I held toilet paper to my wrist, watched it bleed through. It required a lot of toilet paper, finally two Band-Aids, and still there was a red blotch, leaking through. Underneath the sink I found cotton, held it to the outer edge of the Band-Aid, watched it sop up blood.

I knew I was doing things backwards, but it didn't seem to matter. I sat on the couch, in an entirely dark room, waiting for the blood to stop pulsing. My fear was no more real than a child's is, when he's contemplating an event weeks in the future. Finally the bleeding stopped. There was only a red mark there. The future was a blank slate, filling me with a kind of easy hope. The rest of life couldn't be so bad compared with this.

At eight o'clock, I felt hungry enough to eat another bowl of Cocoa Krispies.

At nine o'clock the doorbell rang and it was her.

She had chosen Tommy's parents' room, and it had not been a time to argue her out of it. The covers had been pulled back and the sheets were crisp, mint green: someone had changed them. Neither of us had thought to turn on the light, so that as we lay there, the only visibility was provided by a flood lamp positioned over the neighbor's driveway.

Her head lay against my shoulder now, but in a plastic dullness, as though she existed in another dimension, had an extra layer of skin. Above us, the pictures of Jesus presided. An ancient Catholic notion of sin opened, engulfed us. Nothing that had happened since she'd come had been real. I couldn't afford to allow it to be.

"You feel terrible," she said.

Idly, I passed my hand along the side of her rib cage.

"You must."

"No," I answered. The truth: she hadn't come here; all this was imaginary.

"I'm sorry I made you wait so long. Was it that?"

"No." Then: "Yes, maybe. I'm very hungry. I never knew when you were coming, so I never got a proper habit going. I couldn't even go out to get food."

"Silly. I would have waited."

She rolled over onto her stomach, resting on her elbows, preparing to leave. I watched her rump rise, little mounds of soft hills, igloos, orange halves.

"Like now?" I asked.

She looked down; her lips touched my chest.

"I'm sorry," she said.

"No."

"I told him I was seeing a movie in Providence."

"What one?"

She laughed a little, rested the smooth skin of her cheek against my chest.

"I'll have to make one up."

A hole in the center of me knotted up, tightened. At the same time an ache started, without focus, that was like a convulsive longing for another body, to lose the skin of this one and find something underneath, machinelike, of use. Perhaps the only thing that had kept us going this long was the network of illusions that clothes allow.

"We'll have lots of other times, Nicholas."

"No, we won't."

"Oh, now, don't."

"We won't." I shifted, hoping to lose her, but she clung. "What'll it be like? I'll come to your house, all we'll be thinking about is will I be able to do it."

"Why don't you forget that?"

"I can't."

Her hand came up, bunched the skin of my belly.

"I bet David never has this problem."

She didn't answer.

"Huh? I bet he doesn't."

She kissed my chest again.

"Do you want an honest answer or do you want a lie?"

"Don't bother."

"David has other problems. Not this one."

Her hand slid down and grasped my penis. One of her fingers ran the length of me. Then her hand reached underneath and cupped my balls. She squeezed lightly, then touched the tip of me, tickling. Something stirred.

"Life," she said, almost laughing at the word, and started lowering her mouth, first to my belly and then to the root of my cock. Then she lifted it all the way up and closed her mouth against it, shoving it in until it made her gasp, then pulling down so hard on the root I cried out a little. She continued, her hand pulling, her mouth not letting go. When she did release herself, it stood there, reddish, half-hard.

"Better," she said, and went back to work. The pain of it helped. The pain allowed me to work past shame, past all thought. What was happening now was all that had happened: the past blurred, consciousness became a mouth, and then there was the onset of another kind of desire, separate from the first.

She lifted herself up, and not letting go her grasp, lowered herself onto me. "There," she said, smiling, immediately lifting herself again, coming down hard, the bush of her somehow softened, ripened, turned red, viciously wet; her eyes half-closed. I bit down on my lip to feel pain again, to deny myself pleasure. Her arms, thin, white, suspended on either side of me, became things to bite. I looked up and saw her eyes gone mostly white; she rode all the way up and down me and I wished I could see her ass doing it. I'd never felt this big, this huge, this capable of filling her. It was a shock to realize I could touch all of her now, take possession. I reached back to feel the spread of her ass, the wide net in which I was captured. Her breasts hung, lost their shape. I wanted more than this, suddenly. She was crying out, collapsing on me. I wanted more.

I turned her over so that she was under me and started thrusting as though it would be impossible to hurt her. She wore a thin smile; her eyes were closed. She wrapped her hands around my buttocks and pushed me farther in.

Above me, the pictures of Jesus seemed lost behind a film, bled free of color. Emboldened, I thought we were pushing past David as well. He was nowhere in this room, this house. The net spread wider. I thrust and made him disappear from the city, the state. Soon the world. Inside her, I touched a hot center that could have been either of us. Skin nudged against skin, the effect like a rose being pulled roughly to its core, the sweet center there shying and folding inward against unexpected light. There was no end to her, I thought. I could have climbed up myself, I felt that large, and yet there was no filling her, or reaching the end. That was fine. I would keep doing this, I would never come, so she would never go.

Her hand was under me, though, pulling, unwilling to let go, cupping the testicles. Her smile was full of appreciation; it softened the rest of her. I thought of small mammals gone to pulp under the effects of a spider's poison. I could ingest her now.

I lowered my mouth and closed it around a breast, felt the wholeness of it fill me, the nipple starting out, rising at the prodding of my tongue. She groaned, and I tasted something, some odd liquid that made me think she had lied, was still pregnant, all of it a lie. I pulled away and there was another kind of groan. She'd wanted me to stay. I tried thrusting harder again, but something different was at work: the sense of the lie, the hint of deception made a weakness in me, an ungirding in the balls, the desire for some splashing release, a wetness like punishment. She encouraged it, hands, mouth. I felt the things flying from me. Things, as though each were separate, nothing to do with one another, or with the act, sudden visitants, and a thick closing of her inner hand to catch them.

Later, she is sitting on the bed, dressing. Pulling on stockings. I run my finger up her column of vertebrae, watch each stand out. The cup of her ass lifts; I imagine the thin line beneath, mentally trace it, and want to go in there again.

"One more time," I say.

"No. The movie's long over."

But it is like this—I have a new member of my family, this thickness between my legs. And though it's always been there, some shyness has held it back, kept it in a corner, kept it silent, while we talked and talked. It is as simple as this: I am no longer telling it to shut up. I am sitting back. I am letting it speak.

"Please."

I place it against her vertebrae, watch the way it leaves a diaphanous stream where it goes. Its redness against her whiteness like a mark made in anger against a wall.

"Please." Then: "Will you come back tomorrow?"

"You know I can't. I'm leaving tomorrow."

"Can I drive with you?"

"I'm already driving someone. Another of the actors' wives."

She stands then, turning so that I can see the front of her. In stockings only, with the bra hooked around her, not yet clasped. She has taken a shower. Her bush hangs wetly, fronds sweating in a tropical heat.

A separate heat, a rising, convulses me. I must put my mouth there. When my hands reach out, she pulls back, slapping a little, but on my knees I can reach her, with tongue, taste a mediciny husk that gives way to salt, some tart, invigorating center. I can lap, mindless as a dog, oblivious even of the fact that she allows this, has her hands in my hair, is saying underneath, "It hurts." So I pull her down onto me, holding her open, and she slides onto the hot stranger—this oddity, this unexpected *power*—and I watch her go all white now, even the eyes, just because it's *in* her. She is doing things that nothing else on earth could make her do, and all my life I have been *blind* to this. Look! her lips against the cleft of my shoulder, her lips against my chin. She comes again and again and then says, "You, please, now," but I can't, I am too hard still, and I have no desire, until energy falls off just a little, something held up by both of us collapses suddenly and she is lying against me, having given up. There is no sense, now, I *want* to come, and then it is as if she knows this, because she lifts off it and lowers herself, and with sweet kisses surrounds it, and out of deep time —a former life—I think, "Mrs. Branner," remembering a boy in a class, his silence and fear of what he is, his holding back from her as if she were a separate, gleaming world he has no right to, and as she kisses the tip of him, he spurts up, onto his own belly, his claim to a maleness separate and distinct from everything that is specific about him, everything he hates, and now she smiles as she once did, in a time when he thought such smiles were dismissing of him, and with a finger spreads the essence on his belly, forming continents and seas, and stands above him until he opens his eyes, struck by a vision of beauty he finds it unbearable to accept, thinking nothing will ever be the same, it is all changed now, nothing will ever be the same.

4
A SON

On Christmas morning, after the presents had been opened, my mother fetched a cup of tea and started telling me about Uncle Billy's wedding.

"You should have seen the dress Judy wore," she said,

moving to a position on the couch from which she could survey a greater portion of the neighborhood.

"Of course, she couldn't wear white. I don't know how many times she's been married before. Billy says just once, but I don't believe him."

My father wasn't listening. He was intent on getting at the pieces of cellophane tape that had stuck to the rug in the hubbub of unwrapping presents. It was his habit, in the middle of that ritual, well before the last present had been attacked, to begin cleaning up the discarded wrapping paper. Quietly, at a moment impossible to predict but somehow recognized by him alone, he would go into the kitchen and retrieve a large shopping bag, and while my mother oohed and ahhed over the latest treasure, would begin his steady, serious cleanup. Only when he felt his participation in the festivities was absolutely required would he turn his head to us and, exposing his teeth in a strictly local smile, nod and say "Terrific, terrific."

"It was purple," my mother said, spreading her lips and looking down at a spot on the couch between us.

"It wasn't purple, Josie," my father said. He'd been listening after all.

"No? What, then?"

His face settled a moment, and after continuing his scan of the rug for hidden particles, he quietly reached into the bag of wrapping paper and removed a fragment of fuchsia-colored paper, carefully ripped a square, then held it up.

"It was more like this."

My mother studied the paper a moment, then turned away, as if dismissing it.

"Ya, that was the color," she said. And, on the end of a sip of tea, added, "Purple."

My father looked at her, trying to make up his mind whether to pursue this, finally deciding against it.

"Of course, Billy wanted you to be there," my mother

said, turning to me. "He kept asking for you."

"I was sorry I couldn't be there."

"Oh, I wouldn't worry about it." She picked up her tea and looked out the window, as if even the least consequential event going on out there was capable of dwarfing Billy's marriage in social importance. "He's gotten married before, he'll get married again." She let out a small laugh.

"That's not the point, Josie."

My father stood now. Under his blue cotton pajamas, his form looked incomplete, as though it had still not returned to its fullness since the explosion.

"Billy thinks the world of Nick. Whether it's his second marriage or his sixth, Nick should have been there."

He lifted the bag then and took it down to the basement. My mother and I sat in that silence, the hole created by his scolding. Two or three wrapped boxes remained beneath the tree, and it was to these that she turned her attention.

"Why don't you open another present, Nick?"

After church, we rushed back to the house. Al and Rose were coming, and my mother wanted to be sure the "hors d'oeuvres" were ready when they arrived. In the kitchen, she worked quickly and with fixed concentration, mixing chopped pimento olives with cream cheese, stuffing mushroom caps with sausage and bread crumbs, arranging a potful of tiny meatballs in one of the special holiday bowls that were taken out of the hutch once a year.

When they arrived, Al and Rose climbed the steps in the hushed awareness that they'd become, overnight, "the guests." Biweekly visitors at their most antisocial, they were now required, by everyone's sense of the day, to forget all that, to behave as if they'd been here rarely, if at all. Rose kissed me with stiff formality, then went into the kitchen to join my mother. "You have such lovely dishes, Josie," I heard her say, as though she hadn't eaten off, hadn't, in fact, *washed* these same dishes, more times than she could probably remember.

My father and Al took up positions by the Christmas tree. Already, the artificiality of the day seemed to be wearing them down.

"Take in the hors d'oeuvres to Al and Dad," my mother called, handing me a bowl of meatballs.

This changed things. When Al saw the meatballs coming, his face opened. Giving me a big, welcoming grin, he speared one of the little meatballs with a toothpick. But the toothpick's grip was insufficient; it broke in half, and the meatball fell to the rug.

"Oh boy, oh boy," Al said, and got down on his hands and knees after it, followed by my father, who studied the rug anxiously after Al had retrieved the meatball, then went to the kitchen and came back with a damp towel. My mother and Rose were behind him, looking worried.

"It's only a little meatball stain," Al said to my mother, but her attention was firmly on my father's steady scrubbing of the rug.

"That's fine, hon," she said, covering the real concern in her face; "it won't stain." She tried to give Al a look of reassurance.

When my father returned from rinsing the towel in the kitchen, the motion of the four of them was like a jerky push forward.

"Here, have another meatball, Al," my mother said.

"This time be careful," Rose piped in.

Al was careful. He ate as if his mind was nowhere except on the taste of the meatball. He looked to my father for encouragement, but my father was still studying the rug for signs of stain. When he glanced up, he saw what Al wanted, and tried to give it to him. Al didn't search beyond the tendered smile. Mirth returned to his face, and he enjoyed the second meatball.

The day passed sluggishly after this.

Once the big meal was finished, my father sat in the den watching Jimmy Stewart in *The FBI Story*. In the midst of trimming the tree, Jimmy Stewart was called away on business; he picked a fight with his family, to cover his real disappointment. My father seemed to be watching his own version of this scene; I caught him glancing up at the wall phone as if *wishing* it would ring, so that he too could feel a busy man's annoyance at all the things that would prevent him from enjoying the pleasures of family life.

It wasn't likely to happen. The laundromat was closed; Ray had gone off for the week, to visit his daughter in Canada.

After finishing with the dishes, my mother had gone into their bedroom to lie down, and the "guests" now sat in the living room, adrift among the presents.

"Why don't you open ours, Nick?" Rose suggested, having found the large present she'd brought unopened beneath the tree.

Al leaned forward, as I began to unwrap, anticipating a mild bit of excitement. The present was a pair of brown cotton pajamas.

"Pajamas," I said, giving them an appreciative look. I held them up, not knowing what else to do with them.

"I figured you could use them at school," Rose said, scrutinizing them to make sure nothing had gone wrong since they'd been wrapped. "You live in an apartment now, right?"

"Yes."

"So I figure it must get cold." She didn't look at me as she said this, but at some image of a frosty garret.

Al continued to lean forward and smile, making an effort to keep the moment going.

My father, having been roused by the sounds, appeared at the edge of the living room, his hands in his pockets.

"Nick opened his present," Rose said. "Pajamas."

I held them up again. My father offered a dim smile.

"Why don't you try them on?" Al suggested.

I shook my head, trying to fold them back into their box.

"Go ahead. Suppose they don't fit," Al said. "Rose'll have to take them back."

"It's true," Rose put in. "I could take them back this week. This is the week for returns. Otherwise they run out."

I looked at their faces, shrouded in expectation, and held the crisp pair of pajamas in my hand. I fully intended to say no. Instead, I went to my room, where there seemed nothing to do but try them on.

They were waiting when I returned, nearly in a line: Al and Rose seated, my father standing. When I looked at Al, I thought I could have appeared in a dress, it wouldn't have made any difference: it was all *event* to him. My father's eyes, on seeing me, seemed to retreat, as if embarrassed by the spectacle of his grown son appearing at midday in pajamas. For a moment I thought he might turn to Al and Rose and apologize. But then he seemed to focus on the pajamas, as though himself considering whether to buy them.

"Good," he said, fingering the lapels. "Good quality."

"Ya," Rose said, looking flattered, "they ought to be." Then she recited the brand name, "Carter's," with absolute faith in its integrity.

"How's the fit?" she asked.

"Fine."

I watched her eyes cling to my answer for a moment, as if looking for a place to go.

"Did you show your mother?" my father asked.

"No."

"Oh, go show her," Rose said. "What's she doing, lying down, John?" I was certain Rose knew exactly what my mother was doing.

"I'll go see if she's awake."

In another moment, he motioned for me to come.

"This is what we gave him, Josie," Rose announced from behind me.

My mother, from her position on the bed, looked at the

legs of my pajamas and smiled. "Very good," she said.

"Come in, Rose," she said.

Their bedroom was heavily mirrored and draped. I'd always thought it could have served as a pretty good set for *Dial M for Murder*, with plenty of room for the killer to hide behind the drapes. Rose hesitated to go in, but I didn't blame her. When she finally approached the bed, she looked uncomfortable, in a scene that provided no cue for appropriate behavior.

"How are you feeling, Josie?" she asked, opting for the concern of the sickbed visitor.

"I'm fine."

"You do too much. It's too much. Next year at our place, huh, John?" She glanced up, but didn't wait for my father's agreement. She made this gesture every year.

I went to my room then, got back into my clothes, and stared at the phone. Cynthia was spending Christmas in Warwick; David's show was scheduled to close the day after New Year's. I wanted suddenly to hear her voice, the assurance of it. I wanted something on this day other than the feel of new pajamas and the silence and the fetid heat of the hours yet to go before we could call it quits. More, I wanted to assert all the things I knew about her, the tiny knowledges I had gained during the month of December, when I'd visited her apartment an average of three times a week. It was as if I wanted the day to contain another surprise present, left mysteriously at the door, that once opened, would bind us all in a kind of awe: this is what life is, not meatballs and special bowls.

In a little while there was a knock on the door.

"Come in," I said.

Al entered with a smile on his face that begged pardon, as though this were a bathroom but there was no need for me to leave, he would not require privacy.

"So how's things going down in school, Nicky?"

He ran his hand over his scalp, ruffling the wisp of white hair on the top. At the end of his question, he had to suppress a yawn.

"Going fine, Uncle Al."

"You got a girlfriend yet?"

"Sort of."

Hadn't my parents told him why I wasn't here at Thanksgiving?

He reached under his collar. A vaguely troubled look came over his features. He yawned again, then remembered me.

"Nice day," he said. "Nice day." He managed to send me a tired smile before his longing glance rested on the bed.

"Would you like to lie down, Al?"

His hands lifted off his thighs, then rested there. "That's what I came to ask."

He raised his chin, and smiled. "There's no need for you to go, though, Nick."

He removed his jacket and folded it carefully over the chair. Then he lay on the bed, and within minutes was snoring.

As soon as it was dark, my mother announced supper: turkey sandwiches. Al rose from his nap, the only one of us actually hungry. We went through the motions. It was barely past five o'clock, and we'd eaten dinner at two. As we sat there, I wondered if my mother hadn't rushed this completing ritual just to get rid of Al and Rose early. If so, Rose responded perfectly. As Al was finishing his second sandwich, she looked at the clock and said, "You better hurry with that, Al. It's time we got home."

Al looked at her, then at the other faces at the table, as though he'd missed something important. He started eating his sandwich as if he were nursing a grudge: All afternoon with nothing to do, now an honest-to-God *activity* and I'm being given the bum's rush. Rose looked as though she were clocking him. Before he was finished, she got up and went to the closet for her coat.

"Come on, Al," she said.

He looked up, his mouth full of turkey, as if asking, "What are we going to do at home?"

But he suppressed this. Dutifully, smiling as though

the pleasures of the day would never be forgotten, he got into his coat and wished us all good night, Merry Christmas.

"You gonna wear those pajamas tonight?" he asked me.

His mouth was partly open, grinning; his eyes retained the glow, the repressed energy, of banked fires.

I promised him I would.

Cynthia was at the bottom of the stairs.

I watched her from the landing. It was midafternoon.

"You're sure he's gone?" she asked when she reached the top. She didn't wait for me to kiss her, even. I did that now.

"He's got a job, I told you."

Tommy had dropped out of school just before finals, was working downtown in Sue's marketing-research firm. The apartment was empty during the day now.

I closed the door behind us, and kissed her again.

"Do you want some tea? I've got soup, too."

We stood in the hallway, neither of us making a move. I reached out and grasped her shoulders and drew her toward me. I thought we both were a little afraid, still, of going beyond this.

"What kind of soup?"

"I don't know. Some kind of crap."

She was laughing.

"The kind with the little meatballs in it."

I emptied the can into a saucepan and turned the heat on under it. She was sitting at the table. I had cleaned up some, so the place looked decent, but there was still a difference. We'd always met before at her apartment, with its sparkling glass, its kitchen smelling of expensive coffee.

"I told David I was only coming to turn in grades."

"That's all right. You can tell him there were a bunch
of students waiting, and they all wanted to complain."

She wasn't looking at me.

"You can take off your coat."

"Yes."

"I'm kinda nervous; how about you?"

"Yes," she said again.

We hadn't slept together in nearly a month.

"You wanna forget this soup?" I asked.

"No. If we do things in order, it'll make it easier, I
think."

"It's taking forever to boil. Goddammit, soup, come on,
hurry up!"

I turned the heat up. The broth was obstinate.

Finally I saw a thick bubble rise. That was good
enough. I poured.

We ate for a little while in silence. I wanted to say
something but it had to be important or what we were
doing wouldn't be.

"I feel sometimes too good lately," I said.

She raised her eyebrows.

"I see other boys, I don't know, I feel superior to them."

She looked down into her bowl.

"Isn't that called a swelled head?" she asked.

"No. I think it's something else." I waited a moment,
not sure whether to continue. "It's like this gift I feel I've
been given. And I can't touch it or hold it or anything, so
I feel like it's going to go away."

She was silent. I didn't know why my story hadn't
gone over the way I expected.

"What have you been doing all month?"

"Oh. David's home."

That seemed to mean something. I didn't press.

"Did you turn in my grade?"

"Yes."

"What'd I get?"

She smiled.

"You're going to have to go over there and find out."

I touched her neck.

"Do you want more soup?"

"No."

I reached over and kissed her. I tasted the soup and then I tasted her. I could tell she was nervous.

In the bedroom, as soon as I had her dress off she shuddered with cold. Then I embraced her and felt, from the way her body shook, that it wasn't cold so much as her total impatience with preliminaries.

I began to make love to her with the slow, quiet skill she'd taught me during the month of December. At first I thought it was different because we were doing it on my bed. But then I realized it wasn't the bed; she was too eager. She bore down before she was ready to. She kept losing it.

It was up to me now. I had to guide her, to quiet her, to get her to allow me to do more. It was always a revelation when she came, as though I were laboring on a solitary project that I suddenly discovered I had a partner in.

I kissed her cheeks afterward; they were wet. Then, because I didn't think we could do any better than this, I let myself come as well.

When we made love, her body—the whole size of her —seemed manageable to me, small enough to hold in one hand. Afterwards, I made an effort to keep her that way, huddled beneath me. But as if sensing this, she stretched out, looked at me as if from a distant place.

I bent over and kissed her.

I held myself back.

"I got your letter," I said.

She just raised her eyebrows. At the beginning of the week it had come, a Xeroxed copy of Chekhov's "Lady with Lapdog," with, at the end, a note in her script: "This is like us." Then a longer note, crossed out, illegible. Finally: "I changed my mind. But read it anyway."

"You want to explain?" I asked.

"No. I thought I needed to know what we were doing. I thought for a moment I'd found a way of defining it. Then I realized it wasn't anything like that."

She squinted, and crinkled her nose.

"You know what I'd like?" she asked.

"What?"

"Cigarettes."

"*What?*"

"I'd like to sit here and smoke cigarettes."

"I don't have any."

She didn't have to say anything.

"You want me to go out and get some?"

"Yes."

"Will you still be here when I get back?"

"I might."

I put my hands on both sides of her waist and squeezed until she laughed.

"You'd better be," I said.

"Why?"

"You'd just better be."

I got dressed and went down to buy the cigarettes.

The air outside was cold. Great blasting gusts of wind ripped down Decatur. I had a coating of residual heat on my body, and in the store it changed my sense of things. I could still feel her body on my fingers as I touched the packet of cigarettes. It made them feel almost alive.

Then, when I was outside again, and looking up at the windows, I remembered how it had been when I'd driven my cab along Ninetieth Street, watching for her.

I didn't want to go in yet. I wanted to remain as long as possible in this moment before. I stood there and I remembered Christmas; I thought what I wanted more than anything was to meld the two parts of my life, to find some way of bringing her home, to present her in a way that wouldn't be messy or complicated.

I ran up the stairs, and when I reached the apartment and entered my room, I saw her sitting with her back to the wall, her legs gathered up, the sheet just covering them. It was a relief—almost a surprise—that she was still there.

There was still light in the room, and under the sheet, in the place where it fell away, I saw the way her vagina opened, the dark hairs and the pinkness, like a piece of fruit, lush in summer, begging you to pick it. Without taking off my coat I knelt down at the side of the bed and put my tongue there. God, how I loved that! It was the thing no one ever told you about before you did it. In its way I thought it was better than fucking, possessing an intimacy that didn't even require you to be male.

She opened for me, and while I was in there she touched my hair lightly, as though she were absently stroking a cat's fur.

We smoked the cigarettes afterward. I sat next to her on the bed. Our backs were both against the wall, and the smoke gathered around us in the air. We were neither of us expert at smoking. I'd taken off my clothes, so that we could be even.

She stared down at the sheets as she smoked, not looking at me, not communicating. The change was sudden.

"What is it?"

She shook her head.

"No. Tell me."

Again, she shook her head, but this time decided to speak.

"I spend too much time thinking about this."

She breathed out and covered her eyes with the back of her hand so that the smoke curled over her forehead.

"You're not supposed to think about this? What are you supposed to think about, then? This is the best thing in the world."

"It's the *way* I think about it."

"Oh, come on."

She looked up at the ceiling.

"It feels exactly the way it felt when I was fifteen. Like I'm exactly the same."

She snorted, as though she were letting out a pocket of compacted air.

"What were you like at fifteen?"

"You don't want to know."

"Of course I do."

"I was a *bad* girl."

I laughed, and then, surprisingly, so did she.

"I'd fall in love with a boy and then become absolutely obsessed."

She hesitated a moment, touched one of her eyebrows with a long finger, looked as though part of her was enjoying this.

"Not with *him*."

Her eyes scanned the room before her.

"One night I was with a group of girls, we were all fifteen, we were all very drunk, and I was in love with this boy from the vocational high school. I had fantasies of sleeping in his undershirts and rolling the sleeves up the way he did and sticking a pack of cigarettes there. I took a piece of chalk and wrote in the middle of the street, '*I Want to Blow Buddy LaSalle.*'"

She covered her mouth, as though surprised again by the act.

"I didn't sign it. Imagine what he must have thought, walking to school one day and finding that written in the road and knowing that somewhere in the school, a girl wanted to do that."

She covered her whole face in her hands.

"And did you?"

"No. Of course not. I didn't want to blow him. Christ, I wanted to *be* him."

She looked straight ahead now.

"The stupid limitations. Fifteen-year-old girls. They don't have lives yet, so they think they can go get a life through sex, or whatever. And the thing is, even sometimes after you have a life, you feel as though you're still looking for one. Some boy comes along, you might as well be fifteen again. You might as well take a piece of chalk in your hands and write it all over again. The little declarations. The little wanting more."

I put my hand on her ankle nearest me, rubbed the skin there.

"And please don't think this is because you're so wonderful or anything."

"Thanks."

"No. Don't take it that way either."

She looked away.

"I used to think how nice it would be to be you." She lit another cigarette, nervous with her fingers. "Maybe it was the way you talked about your room, or the way you talked about me. Maybe it was the idea of passion I fell in love with, just the fact of it. A boy in his room. It was like it had nothing to do with me."

She shook her head.

"What am I saying? It had everything to do with me. With the way I saw myself in your eyes."

Suddenly she covered her eyes with her hands.

"I'm sorry."

"No," I said.

"I'm so ashamed."

"Of what?"

I couldn't see her eyes. I could see the wetness escaping her hands, though. It had all been very quick.

Finally, she let go.

Clear-eyed, she said: "For what I've done."

She got up.

I watched her ass and her back and her hair as she moved out of the room, heard her distantly in the bathroom, then waited for her return. There was an absence in the room more palpable than her simple failure to be here.

When she came back I watched the way her breasts looked in the last light.

She crawled under the covers, suddenly cold, and, I could tell, in a different state from the one she'd been in before. I had a sense by now of her fluid ability to escape into the erotic. What was new—what was revealed to me now—was the desperation of it, and the ease; she had a much greater facility than I did to become her own body. Her hand was on me now, the fingers gently beckoning, and her lips were on my neck.

"I've gotta go too," I said.

I did—it was true—but there was another reason why I left. I'd become a little frightened. The thing she was

ashamed of, the way it suggested sin, and made me understand immediately that I was her accomplice. I tried
to block it out. I peed.

But I was still thinking about it on the way back. I
didn't understand whose hand was pushing us together,
but someone's was. I didn't understand, either, why she
looked at me that way, with that simple hunger and appreciation. But it was easy now to imagine her at fifteen,
with a piece of chalk in her hand, writing on a street.
Imagine her wanting to be me.

One morning—it was late in February now—I found
Tommy in the kitchen when I woke up. It was hours after
he usually left for work. He was stuffing oranges into a
backpack.

"What are you doing?" I asked.

"Packing."

I could see a notebook, and a small pile of clean underwear near the top of the pack.

"You going on a trip?"

I turned on the gas under the pot, to make instant coffee.

"That's right."

He wasn't looking at me.

"Care to tell me where you're going?"

"I'm just going, that's all."

He disappeared from the room for several minutes.
When he came back, he carried a tube of toothpaste.

"You're out of this stuff, okay?" he said, holding it up.
"This is the tube I bought."

"What is this, a divorce settlement?"

He stuffed it in, zipped the pack.

"No."

"So tell me."

"I'm going to Florida."

He hefted the pack onto his shoulders. "Jesus, this is
gonna be heavy."

"What's in Florida?"

"Maybe I should eat these oranges first, rather than carry them."

"Tommy, come on, explain this."

"What, you want a rational, pedantic explanation, Nicholas?"

"Yes."

"Okay. I woke up this morning, I felt like my imagination had fucking died, that's all. I mean of all the things I could be doing in my life right now, working nine to five asking questions over the phone isn't anywhere near the top of the list."

"So do something else."

"Right! Exactly. You got it. Only I want to do more than something else. I want out of winter. I want sun. I want . . . who the fuck knows? *Something.*"

We'd been yelling. It took a moment to recognize this.

He started toward the door, then stopped.

"How cold do you think it gets in Florida this time of year?"

"I don't know. Wait."

He stood in the doorway.

"How you getting there?" I asked.

"I'm gonna hitch a ride. I thought I'd start down at the Deegan, see if I can get across the George Washington Bridge first."

"Can I come?"

"To Florida?"

"No. To the Deegan."

He waited a moment.

"Suit yourself."

We had to stop in the bank first. Tommy removed his savings: something close to three hundred dollars. He handed me fifty-five for February's rent.

"That may be the last you get out of me. If I like things down there, I may not come back."

"Tommy, what do you think Florida is? You think it's this place you go and there's a beach chair and a piña colada waiting for you? It's a *state.*"

He put on his sunglasses. It wasn't warm, but he'd decided to walk and save the bus fare as far as the Deegan. He said, too, that he wanted to get used to the weight of the pack.

"What about Sue?"

"What about her?"

"Did you tell her?"

"I left a note."

Sue had been staying over more and more often lately. They had their routines. At night they drank beer and watched television together, like any working couple.

"What's it say?"

"It says, 'Dear Sue: Have gone to Florida. Will write. For all your sexual needs, please contact N. Battaglia, first door on the right past the kitchen.'"

"Come on."

"That's basically what I told her. Nicholas, you have no idea of the ambitions of that woman. She lives, breathes, eats, and sleeps Marketing Research. For her, dick is just a metaphor for Marketing Research."

He stopped to buy some gum, popped a stick immediately into his mouth.

"You know, you didn't have to drop out of school."

"Oh, come on, are we gonna go over that again?" He tweaked my cheek hard. "I hope the priests teach you something, Nicholas. For me, this whole world is dead. It's like a bone sticking out of the ground. It's like the fucking Shroud of Turin. Seventeen hundred guys guarding it on the chance Christ might have wiped his face on it. You know, Nick, you die, you go to heaven, God isn't gonna give you extra credit 'cause you went to Fordham."

I didn't laugh.

"What are you taking this semester, anyway?"

"You'll just make fun, why should I tell you?"

"Tell me. Come on, you might never see me again. It would be a shame if I didn't know your curriculum."

"I'll see you again," I mumbled.

"What are you taking? Come on, out with it."

"Russian history."

"Beautiful. Tell me about your literary endeavors."

"I'm taking Pope and Dryden," I offered hesitantly, knowing what was coming. He didn't say anything at first, though. He was thinking it over.

"He makes a good tomato paste, Pope. Dryden I don't know about."

He stopped, to let a woman cross in front of him. His manner was deadpan.

"Next semester, why not take Ragú and Aunt Millie?"

"All right. Enough."

We had crossed the Grand Concourse now. Tommy's pace slackened a little, as if he'd suddenly decided he wanted to notice more.

"So how's things with the Lady of Shalott?"

"Fine."

" 'Fine.' " He shook his head. "Mr. Communication. You see how I take a serious interest in your life. Which is more than you do in mine."

"Oh, sure, it's me who's been ignoring you. Don't give me that bullshit. We haven't had a discussion that hasn't ended in a fight since September."

He practically winced. It had been stupid to refer to his father's death that way.

"I'm sorry," I said.

"It's okay."

"Things, if you really want to know, are incredible. I haven't been this happy ever. I don't even know if I deserve to be this happy."

"I can answer that. You don't."

I waited a moment.

"All right. I don't."

"Just do yourself a favor, all right? Don't be stupid."

"What's that mean?"

"Just don't be a jerk. Don't go whole hog for something that isn't going to have a happy ending."

"How do you know anything about it?"

"You think you're what she wants, Nick?"

He stopped and looked at me. I didn't say anything.

"Come here."

There was a Nardi Discount Clothing on the corner, with a mirror built into the supporting pillars out front. He positioned us so that we could see our own images. There was distortion, but you couldn't tell what kind, exactly. The impression was that we'd grown shorter and stockier. We also looked criminally young.

"Look at us," Tommy said. "Young Sacco and Vanzetti. Delusions of grandeur."

We might have moved away, but for some reason we didn't.

"You want to see the future sometimes," he went on. "You want to believe that you're the actor in the movie playing Young Tommy, Young Nick, that your responsibility only goes so far, and then some other actor, some big star, comes along to play you as an adult. What's depressing is that we gotta watch these two all the way through the movie. Later on, they get gray in the hair, they put on old-age makeup, but you never quite believe them as adults."

Then: "You honestly think you're what she wants?"

I looked at my face. I said we should move on.

When we got to the overpass above the Deegan, Tommy stopped and looked at me again.

"Listen, you big jerk, you'd only slow me down, but do you want to come with me?"

I looked down at the traffic.

"I still don't have any idea why you're going."

He looked over the abutment and spit. Then his chin went up, like he was sniffing the air.

"Sometimes I think there's a direct correlation between the way I was brought up, the choices that were made for me, and the way my family ordered in Chinese restaurants. One from Column A, two from Column B. Fordham was the Moo Goo Gai Pan of my existence."

He smiled.

"Now I want to order from inside the menu. See what's there."

He looked away, back down at the moving traffic.

In another moment, he put down the backpack and unpacked the oranges.

"I'm going to fucking Florida, what the hell do I need
with oranges?"

He handed them to me.

"Go ahead, try and stop me," he said.

"You've got all your reasons. Moo Goo Gai Pan, and so
forth."

He squinted at me, hoisting the backpack onto his
shoulders.

"I bet you think this is real easy for me, don't you? Old
Tommy can do this sort of thing with his eyes closed."

I didn't say anything.

"Head out for parts unknown. Embrace orphanhood.
What the fuck."

"No. I know it's not—"

"You see this?"

He lifted his hair and showed me a thick worry line
across his forehead. The joke was that he didn't need to
lift his hair.

"Right," I said.

He looked at me through his sunglasses.

"Okay, so I'll write you," he said, and started down the
ramp.

At the bottom, he opened his pack and took out a small
cardboard sign. On it was printed the word FLA. He held
it up.

It took ten or fifteen minutes before he was picked up.
He looked relieved when it finally happened, and waved
to me before getting in. The wave was perfunctory, like
he didn't want to risk keeping the driver waiting.

I watched the car—a brown Buick or Oldsmobile—
until the traffic absorbed it and Tommy was out of sight. I
was still holding the three oranges in my hand.

I waited outside the building where the gynecologist's office was: a low, squat red-brick building on Downing Street. Cynthia had come to my room, but refused to undress, told me she couldn't stay, she had this appointment, it was necessary. She hadn't wanted me to come, but I'd insisted. Now I sat on one of the benches near a park.

She was inside more than half an hour, and looked no happier coming out than she had going in. She sat down beside me on the bench. It was turning cold, though the sun was strongly visible.

"Well?"

She waited a moment before speaking.

"Someone had better be more careful with me," she said, and stretched her long legs and squinted unhappily at the sun.

"What does that mean?"

"I've got cystitis."

"Is that bad?"

"No." She smiled at my ignorance. "No. It just means we have to abstain from prolonged sex for a while." She flattened her coat against her, and stared down at her body. "Especially from behind."

I still couldn't get used to her talking this way, the freedom with which she discussed such acts, out in the open.

"There's a place that gets bruised, apparently."

She rubbed her forehead with one hand.

"Okay, whatever. I'm sorry."

I put my hands down between my legs. The gesture made her laugh a little.

"Oh, don't be so contrite. It's no *shame*."

"It was me?"

"No one else has been making love to me with much passion lately."

There was a silence. I could tell she was somewhere else now.

"Something else is bothering you."

"Yes."

I reached out for her hand.

"It's none of your business."

I turned away slightly, stung.

Then, as if I weren't there, she began talking.

"The last time I was here was just after my abortion. She gave me an examination then. I don't know if it's me or her...."

Her cheeks flared bright red.

"She's this old Germanic woman, no nonsense, very cut-and-dried, totally without judgment. She was the one who told me I was pregnant."

She lifted a hand to push back her hair.

"And now I'm back because my sexual appetites have gotten the better of me. And still she offers no judgment. Just a lecture. A suggestion of abstinence. Which fills me with total rage and confusion. I want people to have *opinions*. If she thinks I'm wrong, let her say so. Don't make *me* tell myself I was wrong."

She sat forward on the bench, looking a little ahead. I took her hand.

"Come on, let's go somewhere," I said.

"No. Just home. Call a cab or something."

"It still hurts you to talk about it, doesn't it?"

"Of course it does."

In the cab, I watched her lay her head back against the seat.

"Maybe you want a child," I said.

She looked out the window.

"Maybe that's what all this craziness is about, that you want it but you're not allowing yourself to."

"Of course I want one," she said. It was a bit strong, as if she were telling me I was wrong. "The question is, who's going to give me one?"

"I would."

She lifted her head as if to see something better.

"Did you hear me?"

"Yes."

She continued looking ahead. I assumed that was that. I was disappointed.

"What makes you think you could do that?" she asked.

"I don't know. I guess I could."

She turned to me finally, as if she were looking me over. Then she stared ahead again.

The odd thing was that we were talking calmly, our voices flat, and my heart was beating suddenly very fast. I looked out the window at the crowded green and yellow buildings of the garment district, workers on the street pushing racks of covered coats—It occurred to me that there were moments in life that were one's own, a mute and abbreviated possession of time, when the molecules became briefly scrambled and you could reorder them.

And then, in the same flat tone, I said, "You could come and live with me. I've got room. That way you could have what you want, and we could be together."

I spoke this way because I thought I was negotiating a difficult passage.

"Right. Wreck a boy's life so that the woman can be made happy," she said.

"It wouldn't wreck my life."

"No?"

"I wouldn't care about school. I could go out and work."

She settled farther back in her seat.

"No, I don't want a child. I just don't want to feel guilty all the time."

We sat quietly while midtown descended on us.

"Maybe you don't know what you want," I said, then waited a moment. "I saw you when you were happy."

"When was that?"

"That night in your room, when you told me you were pregnant."

She didn't respond.

"I remember the way your skin looked. It made you look so full. Now I see how David makes you mad all the time. He makes you bitter."

Still, she didn't respond. I looked at the barely perceptible throbbing of a vein in the side of her neck.

"I think you should be with somebody who's younger than you, because whoever you're with you're going to be stronger than and better than, and if he's younger that'll be easier to take. Somebody who worships you."

I put my hands on my knees. I didn't want to look at her now.

"But I'm nothing. I know I'm nothing. I could just be somebody who's not afraid to do this one thing for you."

She shook her head, then moved it forward so that it was resting on one of her hands.

"You don't know what you're talking about."

"I know what I saw that night."

"What did you see?"

She had turned to me, her eyes wild, looking angry.

"Don't make me put a name on it."

"Why not? Putting a name on things makes them real, takes them out of this fog, this romanticism."

"I saw how you would love him, all right? I saw what the whole thing would look like, what *he* would look like and what your breasts would look like and I saw his face there and I was jealous. I was jealous of *him*. But Christ, it wasn't even important, my jealousy. I believed in him more than me."

Her head went back a second; she looked at me differently.

"Of course it would be a *he*, right? Right, Nicholas? And look like you."

"No. I don't care about that."

"The pure romantic image. A woman carrying your child. An older woman."

"I don't care about that. It's not for me."

"No? And what makes you so certain it's what I should have?"

"Because what you're doing isn't good enough. The life you're living just isn't big enough. You're capable of this incredible passion, but you live with this man who won't even let you breathe. He made you get an abortion. God knows what other ways he represses you."

She closed her eyes, rubbed them.

"So you're my Savior."

"Nothing like that. Jesus, just the opposite."

We sat in silence a moment.

"You're wrong, you know." She had turned away. "It wasn't just David. I lie, Nicholas. I lie all the time."

I looked at the back of her head.

"I don't believe that," I said.

She turned and stared at me, looked deeply into my eyes. Whatever she saw there kept her from saying the next thing.

She looked out the window again.

"It's the next block," she said to the driver. "You can let me off at this corner."

When she stepped out, I followed her.

Her anger at this surprised me.

"What are you doing? Are you coming with me to my house?"

"No. I'm just walking you—"

"You come too *close*. I want to be left alone a little." She was gasping a little, as though the words wouldn't come out right. "Don't just destroy my life, all right? Leave me something."

She started running. I watched her, not following, and after a while she turned and saw that I was not following and slowed down.

I went to the corner. The city was losing light now. I could see her walking toward Riverside Drive, where the last of the light was. I couldn't help thinking her life on this street was eclipsing as well. She closed the door behind her, and I waited another moment before walking away.

We abstained, first for a week, then two. She insisted.

We still met in the afternoons, in the cafeteria, in coffee shops. We did not allude to anything I'd said in the cab, as if there were an unspoken agreement to let it alone. I knew she was going way beyond what the doctor had ordered, but it didn't seem right to insist. It was as if I were going for something much greater now, and to insist on this lesser thing would be a mistake.

I spent the nights of my abstinence mostly in bars, growing to like the feel of them, or the idea of myself sitting there, imagining out of the noise and the smoke a vision of the future whose absolute purity dazzled me. I believed, on the basis of nothing she'd said or done but on some bedrock sense of its rightness, that she would someday ask me for a child. It was as though I'd finally found a use for myself.

Cynthia had plans to go to Vermont with David over spring break. When we met for the last time, I wanted to bring her to one of the bars where I'd been feeling so confident, but she insisted on the cafeteria. It was always awkward there. Though her fear of being caught by Jesuits had slackened some, it seemed they were all around, coming in for coffee, passing us on their way out and nodding their heads hello. The cafeteria made us understand our situation all over again.

We sat and drank coffee and talked about her plans. She was going to a town called Burleigh, for a week. They had friends there; they were trading houses. No, she wasn't looking forward to it. The cafeteria was overheated, as though whoever was in charge hadn't realized a season had turned.

After a while, I said, "Come on, let's take a walk. There's a place I've never taken you."

She finished her coffee. "Where?"

"You'll see."

We had, in fact, explored very little of the Bronx together: never been to the Zoo, or the Botanical Gardens, both of which bordered Fordham.

We took a path through the gardens leading away from where the greenhouses were. It led across a field, then into the woods, and finally to a stone bridge arching over a thin, rushing tributary of the Bronx River. On the other side of the bridge was a fortlike stone structure. I'd never known what it was used for.

I led her up to the highest point on the bridge, the arch, where the river was more than a hundred feet below us. You couldn't see any part of the city now.

"This is where I'm going to jump, when you betray me," I said.

She peered over.

"How deep is that water?" she asked.

"How should I know?"

"You should find out before you jump," she said. "You never know, you might survive."

She continued looking down.

"I'd make sure I didn't," I said.

She turned and looked at me. It was an off-center look, as if she were more interested in the condition of my ears, or hair.

"Have you thought anymore about what we talked about?" I asked, looking down into the water.

"What's that?"

"In the cab."

She turned so that her back was against the abutment. She stared at the stones that cobbled the walk.

"We didn't talk about anything. You talked about it."

"Well, have you thought?"

"Please don't. This is our last day."

"It's not our last day. It's only a break."

"Right. But I'm going away with David."

"Maybe I could come."

"Oh, yes."

"You could visit me the way you do here."

I leaned back so that I was beside her, looking down at the stones, at the same place she was.

"We could make a baby."

She closed her eyes.

"I don't want you to talk that way. Please."

"Why?"

I put my hand on her neck, drew her to me.

"Do you think anyone will see us here?" she asked.

"No. I want you to tell me why."

"It disturbs me."

I held her face away from me, my hands on either side of her head.

She wouldn't look at me.

Finally, she broke away and started down the bridge.

"Come on, let's go over and see what that building is," she said.

"Why?"

"Come on."

There was a landing in front of the building, a kind of deck. Tables and chairs had been stacked at one end of it. The water pooled out here; there were ducks.

"It must be a restaurant or something," she said. "In the summer."

"Who would come here?"

She looked inside one of the windows.

"There's someone in there," she called.

I had gone to where the chairs were stacked.

"Do you want to sit down?"

She continued looking in the window, so I dragged over a table and two chairs. She came and sat.

"He'll see us."

"Who will?"

"A man."

I held her hand at the table. It was as if she were resisting such moments of intimacy, while I wanted them badly now.

"What are you doing?" A man appeared at the door in shirt sleeves. His accent was Eastern European, maybe Russian.

"Do you mind if we just sit?" Cynthia asked.

He looked at us.

"Do I mind?" he said, as if translating.

"We won't disturb anything," Cynthia said.

He threw a hand at us and went inside.

"Do you think he minds?" she asked.

"Yes."

She let me hold her hand.

"Maybe he's a Jesuit," she said.

"He's moonlighting."

"Are there Russian Jesuits?"

"Russian Orthodox Jesuits, yes."

I touched her fingers.

"You must be the only twenty-year-old in the world who wants a baby."

There was a strange moment afterward. Her fingers, still entwined in mine, felt damp, and she made a sudden, odd movement with her face that was like the way she had of giving in to things: a softening, an acceptance. I looked up at the high bridge to our right and into the deep green woods across the cool, dark water, and it was as though I were not here anymore, but remembering it.

"Since you are here, I might as well make money. We don't open for another week."

The Russian man was carrying two small boxes, which opened to reveal harlequin ice cream inside. In his back pocket were two spoons and two napkins. He laid them out.

"You pay me two dollars when you are finished."

We didn't seem to have any choice but to eat the ice cream. He stood over us while we did.

"We seat a hundred people out here in season," he said, and smiled, as though he were showing off.

His presence made things easy for us. We didn't have to talk about the great subject. So long as he was here, it was free to submerge, travel underwater.

We walked a little, afterwards, along the edge of the river, past the pool, where it was deepest. At a place where there was a natural grassy incline—a place to rest —we stopped. Cynthia lay there and I skipped stones into the water.

The sun was full out now, after a day of ducking behind clouds. My stones made long, erratic journeys, skipping two, three times. Cynthia lay with her face in the sun.

I turned and looked at her, then at the water.

"I dreamed about this place the other night," I said.

"Did you?"

She was lying down, eyes closed. I was remembering the dream. It had been longer than two days ago, and though my remembrance of it was vague, I was certain now that I had dreamed of a place that looked exactly like this.

I stood there and threw a few more stones. Then I went and sat beside her a moment. The day was warm.

I stood up and took off my shirt. Then, as though it were the most natural progression in the world, I removed my pants, then my underpants, and rolled them into a neat ball and placed it beside her.

She opened her eyes and blinked.

"Nicholas. What..."

I stepped into the water.

It was cold, icy, and the bottom had a squishy feel to it. I hoped it led to some depth, and it did, but very gradually, so that I was in the middle before I was even up to my waist.

"What are you doing? You'll freeze!" I heard from the shore.

I turned and smiled at her.

"No," I said, very quietly. Then I went under.

It was the strangest feeling, summer's first immersion, with all of summer's exaltation, and yet the vaguely guilty feeling of pushing things, or pulling time down with me. I could see nothing, only a murky film of green, and I wondered—detached—how long I could stay down. When I broke water, she was on the edge. One of her arms was extended.

"Nicholas! Come out!"

"It's all right."

I felt the water dripping off me, and the cold air. I was full of some unspoken dare. I thought: I am naked and alive, and in that instant I couldn't understand why the human race knew a thing like misery.

"Come out!"

"No."

I was beginning to shiver, but there was no call to worry. I wrapped my arms around myself and went under again. I thought with envy of boys who drowned, who offered to a lover the accident of their deaths. It couldn't be deliberate, though.

"Nicholas, come out! You'll freeze!"

"I'm happy," I said.

She let that go, then moved back a step, merely watching me, even smiling a little, as though she were capable of appreciating this as a gesture, and that congealed the moment for me, made it less than I wanted it to be, as though the center of it had passed. There was a wind now coming down from the trees. I started the ascent out of the water, electric at the moment I stood before her, naked, cold on the shore. I wanted a photograph of this. I wanted more than memory was capable of.

She took off her coat and wrapped it around me.

"God," she said, and "God."

"Where does the sun go when you need it? Here. Dress. We'll run back to your place and get you into a bath."

I was in no such hurry.

She helped me into my clothes and we ran over the bridge and through the gardens. She tried to hail a cab on Eastern Boulevard, but they were all full. I insisted on walking the long way around Fordham.

"But you're freezing."

"No. I don't want anyone to see us."

I was thinking of her.

· · ·

She ran a tap for me when we were inside. I settled
into the hot, steaming water, hotter than any I'd been in
before, and it was comfort, but it was somehow less than
what had come before it. I had an awful chill, but it
didn't matter.

"Come in with me," I said.

"No."

She drew a hot cloth over my forehead.

We made love afterwards, and I listened to her cry as
though something were breaking in her.

D
April 2, 1972

ear Nickie,

I have arrived at a definition of perfect bliss.

I am sitting, as I write, in a lovely room in the Wrangler's Inn in Fort Worth, Texas, watching a blood-red sunset and sipping a Lone Star beer. From this advantage, it is hard to believe my life once consisted of subway rides and foolish longings for repressed Northern women. I have ordered from inside the menu, and let me tell you that it is Good.

The night of the day I left you on the Deegan, I wound up on a road in Virginia, just outside of D.C., when this big black Ford pulls up, loaded down with kids, all of whom proceed to just pile out, leaving this one guy at the wheel. So I tiptoe up, not even sure he's stopped for me, and I find myself staring at this huge ugly guy, this guy whose face makes you think this is what would happen if Ernest Borgnine fucked George C. Scott and this was the baby they got—and he stares back at me with his big bloodshot eyes and says in this thick Philadelphia-Italian voice, "So whaddaya say, kid, ya comin'?"

Well, I got in, I rode with this guy, thinking he couldn't be going very far—he rides down the freeway like he's playing some gigantic game of bumper cars, with a dozen

open beer cans lining the dashboard—but surprise! he's
going all the way to Daytona! I've hit pay dirt! So I try to
settle in and enjoy this if it's possible, but Jesus, the guy
even embarrasses me when we stop in Georgia to get
some food and he asks the waitress to sit on his face.
This is Georgia, for Chrissake, rural Georgia, and I've got
these images of lynch mobs in my head, but no, the
waitress just laughs, says not tonight, and brings Frankie
his black-bottom pie.

Fat Frankie Fallazzo, this is actually the guy's name.
And before we're finished with our coffee he offers me a
job. What he's doing the next three months, he says, is
selling hot dogs for a private concession company that
travels right along with the PGA tour, setting up these
little tents on the grounds, catering to all these hungry
golfers. After that, there's three months of state fairs,
doing just about the same thing, and then it's home free,
Jack, $1200 a week easy, and in six months you're a rich
man. So I gulp down my coffee and say lemme think
about it.

To make a long story short, Frankie's bumper-car style
of driving didn't bother me so much after that. By the
time we were out of Georgia, I'd accepted the job. Now
I've been to Tallahassee, New Orleans, and this week
Fort Worth, and asking waitresses to sit on my face has
come to seem a commonplace. Some of them actually
say yes, Nicholas, and the honesty of such interchanges
still dazzles me, as well as teaching me a little about
Northern manners and their imperfect relation to the real
stuff of the world. Down here it is basically sun and
twat, Nick, appetite and getting appetite taken care of. I
am enclosing $55 for March's rent, but you better start
searching for a new roommate.

Let me try to describe our days. Every morning Fat
Frankie and I get up in the dark from the motel where
we're staying and go out onto the golf course just before
dawn to pick up supplies and set up our tent. From then
on, we're lords of the 7th green, all day long. I've sold
hot dogs to Bob Hope and Glen Campbell. They call us

Fat Frankie and Skinny Tom (which, considering my
health and general appetites these days, is not strictly
accurate). At night, we dine on the South's best: chicken-
fried steak, mostly, and nothing has ever tasted better.
Then there's the evening, cool and full of roads and
women's legs. There is nothing like the evenings here.
What you want, if you're going to have paradise, is the
sense that *anything can happen*, and they've got it here,
in excess. It's not just the nights, though. I love the cool
green afternoons when everybody's just starting to sweat
and I fetch them Dr Peppers with ice. I love the size of
Texas and the speed and the hot blacktops and the
weather. I like seeing my life in these terms now, as this
long stretch of cool green days and hot nights and money
coming in (not quite as much as Frankie promised, but
not bad either) and nothing to do but spend it. It is good
to be young in America, Nick. You can quote me on that.
    As for you, my fine feathered friend, I think you should
come down here and join me—pronto. It'll shake you
out of all that crap you've been enmeshed in as long as
I've known you. But could you take advantage of these
sweet things as much as I do? Are you close enough to
the click—to not hearing your father's voice inside you,
saying no, no, no? The one thing I can tell you is your
friends Mr. Pope and Mr. Dryden are not going to be
better guides to the reality Olympics than my Mr.
Fallazzo. (It might be an interesting switch, actually, to
get old Alexander Pope down here broiling a few dogs,
and let the Jesuits institute a course in Elementary
Fallazzo.)
    I hope your ladylove is either putting up or shutting
up. Whatever, I guess it was important for you to go
through the boring old routine of first love, but it got a
little sickening to watch, and what little I've seen of the
lady in question makes me not quite trust her. Let Nickie
make his own mistakes, I said. It just got hard, that's all.
When I got off the train after my father died and found
you standing there on Kingsbridge, with her arm in
yours, escorting her like such a proper little squire, I

wanted to scream at both of you. You seemed to be *aping* something, not doing it. But I guess that's the way you go about things, like a fucking pint-sized version of the Prince of Wales, always sprucing up for the throne, but never quite taking hold. It's like you think you have to wait for whoever's on it to kick the bucket. Well, lemme tell you what Tommy's learned, Nick: there's nobody on the throne. It's empty, it's waiting, it just takes a little balls to go and claim your rightful place on it.

Lest that sound too profound, chalk it up to the final glow of the Fort Worth sunset as it dips over the Bonanza Steak House across the way. I'd like to hear from you but don't know how you can reach me, since we move around a lot. I often entertain myself by thinking how you'd do down here in this world, which I guess is a form of homage. Whatever you're doing, and however you are, I remain

> Your wised-up friend and ex-roommate,
> T. Bevilacqua

I read Tommy's letter while I was cooking for Billy and Judy. They'd called the week before, said they'd had a large request to make that needed to be made in person. I'd invited them to dinner.

The letter was propped up on one side of the stove. On the other, I read from the back of a Mueller's Egg Noodle package: Easy Beef Stroganoff. I was stirring sour cream into the mixture when Tommy compared me to the Prince of Wales.

I was wearing a bathrobe, and there was an excess of steam in the room. Diving into the Bronx River had given me a savage cold. I had this notion that steam was good for it, so I boiled two pots of water and let them blow off. I needed them to cook the noodles in anyway.

Billy and Judy were already late, but I didn't feel the urge to get dressed. When the buzzer rang, I went out onto the landing to greet them. They made jokes all the way up the stairs about my living in "Seventh Heaven."

"Jeez, you believe in the casual look, don't you?" Billy said when he'd made it to the top.

"I've got this cold..."

Judy nearly reeled backwards when she heard that, and wouldn't come close enough to kiss me.

"It's not German measles, is it?" she asked.

"No. I think I know the difference between a cold and German measles."

"Well, just the same, Nicholas, I'm not gonna kiss you. You understand."

"I'll kiss you for her," Billy cackled, then, once he was inside, shouted, "Jesus, what do we got here? Smells like the Ritz."

"I made a little Stroganoff."

"Stroganoff?" Billy's face looked impressed. "Hey, Judy, should I go home and put on my tux?"

"Stroganoff with meat?" Judy's face screwed up.

"Beef. Sure."

"I hope it isn't fried, is it, Nicholas?"

"No. No." I held up my hands: innocent.

"What'd you do, broil it?"

"Yes. In the broiler."

She smiled broadly, as if not unaware of the stock character she'd been playing. Too late, I realized Judy had developed a sense of humor about herself.

"What do you think of this, Nicholas?" Billy patted Judy's belly, now large, pointed, but still compact.

"You're almost there, huh?" I asked.

"I tell you, Nicholas, sometimes I think I'm giving birth to an elephant."

I led them into the kitchen.

"Hey hey hey," Billy said, apropos of nothing, staring at the pan of bubbling meat on the stove.

"This is the kitchen," I said.

"You're kidding? This is where you live?" Judy asked.

"Sure."

She looked into the bedroom with distaste.

"It's a student apartment," Billy said. "Nicholas is a..." He started snapping his fingers. "A bohemian."

Judy had no interest in Billy's classification of me. She surveyed the living room.

"Where do you *sit?*"

"There. There's our couch." I pointed to the car seat.

"Do your parents know about this, Nicholas?" Judy asked.

"No. They've never been here. They stay downtown when they come." I smiled. "I think they like to pretend I live in some swank hotel for boys."

Billy sat down on the car seat. He patted the seat next to him.

"Come on, Judy."

"I can't sit there."

"Why not? You afraid we'll take off?"

Finally, she sat.

Billy looked delighted. "Home, James," he said, and cackled lightly.

"I've got hors d'oeuvres," I said.

I brought in cheese and crackers. Billy dug in immediately, but Judy held back.

"What's the matter?" Billy asked. "You're not hungry?"

She smiled, trying to be polite. "Where do you buy your cheese, Nicholas?"

"Jesus." Billy leaned back in the seat, sending Judy upwards a little. "What is this, the third degree? It's *cheese,* Judy, same as we get in Manhattan."

He turned to me.

"And I might add, delicious. Maybe a little dry. You got something to drink, Nicholas?"

"Oh, Christ, I forgot."

"No. No problem." Billy held his hand out. He looked taken aback, though, like he'd expected more of me.

"I thought you guys would bring."

I lost eye contact with Billy.

"I could run out and get something."

"Stay where you are, Nicholas," Judy said. "You've got a cold, and Billy could stand a night off the sauce."

She picked up a cracker, removed the cheese, and ate it.

"So what's this big thing you had to tell me?"

Judy's eyes misted over.

"We'd like you to be the baby's godfather," she said.

At first I didn't know how to answer. They both sat there mutely expectant, like Al and Rose waiting for me to unwrap my pajamas. And though this was something I might have anticipated, I hadn't.

"This is an honor," I said.

Billy shifted in his seat, happy again.

"We searched and searched all our friends," Judy said, "and we landed on you as the one who could best—God forbid we should die—bring him up with some values."

"Basically, we searched and searched all our friends" —Billy was leaning forward, serious—"and landed on you as the one who could maybe recognize a value if he tripped over it."

He laughed loudly.

"Ignore him," Judy said. "So you accept?"

"Yes. Of course. I'm honored."

We sat there in silence a few moments.

"Of course we're not gonna die, so all you really have to do is hold him while the priest splashes water on him." She smiled. "But the whole thing has great symbolic value."

"Right," I said.

"Billy wants to do it back at home."

"Just a gesture," Billy said.

He shrugged, took another cheese and cracker.

"I tell you, Nicholas, sometimes I think Billy wants to take our whole life and perform it in the Sons of Rome—or whatever the hell it's called—"

"Sons of Italy," I said.

"Italy, Rome, whatever..."

Billy stood up, with his hands in his pockets, and looked out the window.

Judy seemed more comfortable now that she had the car seat to herself.

"Billy's gotten a lot of respect in his life, Nicholas, as you know. As a musician, as a..."

Judy had started ticking things off on her fingers, but she decided to stop at "musician."

"But it's like now, none of that's worth anything unless he gets it from Don Corleone."

"Eh, it's not that." Billy gestured vaguely with one hand.

Judy ignored him, her eyes still on me. "Your father, and that crowd."

"It's just, I want to show them, I'm proud, they're not the only ones..." Billy directed this to me, but as soon as our eyes met, the old look of amusement came into his, as though he considered it laughable to be discussing his motives in this room.

"Is that meat burning?" he asked, to change the subject.

It wasn't, but I served anyway. Judy only moved her food around her plate, barely touching it.

"What's the matter, Judy?" Billy asked. "You don't like it?"

"I'm not so hungry."

"You were starved on the street."

"He's got a *cold*, Billy."

It was as though I were gone, they were on their way home, reviewing the dinner. Then they both turned to me at the same time. A soon-to-be family. It was hard to believe. I couldn't think of them as any older than me. I thought the three of us should be in some car somewhere, hot-rodding around, looking for our lives.

"So you're actually due when?" I asked.

Again Judy's eyes misted over. The subject of her pregnancy seemed the only one she was comfortable with.

"May."

"May. Right around the corner."

"So come June, you'll be a *compare*," Billy said, pronouncing it in the Sicilian way. Then he resettled himself in his seat, as though forgetting we were finished with dinner; his posture had the anxious, hungry manner of someone waiting to be served.

We watched a little television afterwards (Tommy's portable still worked); then Judy began to yawn loudly and Billy got the hint. I got dressed and walked them to the subway. It was a brisk, windy night.

"Be careful with that cold now, Nicholas," Judy said.

"I will."

She finally agreed to kiss me, but on the cheek, and she didn't look too happy about it. She'd decided, though, that you couldn't ask someone to be your child's godfather without kissing him.

"Compare," she said, pronouncing it in a way that displeased Billy.

"*Compare*," Billy corrected her, and laughed, and kissed me too.

Then the two of them went down into the subway.

The next morning, I was awakened by a call.

"Is this Nicholas Battaglia?"

The voice was a woman's. She'd mangled my last name.

"Yes it is."

"I'm sorry if I woke you. My name is Sharon Glass."

There was a singsong quality to her voice, as though she were imitating, to some obscure purpose, the cadences of a child.

"I'm a friend of Cindy Cohen's." Then, after a moment: "Branner. Sorry."

It was enough to jolt me awake.

"Yes. Sure."

"This is really embarrassing."

"Go ahead."

"No. It is. Anyway, I'm on the Cross-Bronx Expressway, I've got a flat tire, and I'm afraid I'm gonna be killed."

"Are you serious?"

"Sort of. I'm in this phone booth, only there is *no glass*. There is also no cover on the receiver. I am talking into a wire."

"How'd you get my number?"

"Oh, that's right. I should explain. I'm staying at Cindy's apartment this week. She gave me your number in case anything went wrong." There was a pause. "Well, something went wrong."

"Your flat tire."

"Right. I know I'm not supposed to be calling a man to help me out with this, but this place freaks me out. Everything's in Spanish. What's an abogado?"

"A lawyer. Tell me where you are."

"This is a lawyer's office? Why are there old spare tires out front?"

"Tell me where you are and I'll come help you."

"I'm right under the Cross-Bronx Expressway. I can see my car from here but I couldn't help but notice all the way up this road anytime there was a car left abandoned, there were no tires left on it. Do you suppose that's where this abogado got all his tires?"

"What avenue is it?"

"Oh, it's...hold on."

She came back a full minute later.

"Someone just told me I'm on Webster Avenue."

"All right. That's good. You're close. Wait in your car, all right? I'll find you."

I dressed, and, because it was the quickest way of getting there, ran down Webster. I found her car a little ways down the Expressway. A small green Beetle. She was already out, had the jack in place, was unscrewing bolts.

"Hello!" I called.

"Hi. I got brave when I knew you were coming. That was the only thing. Changing a tire doesn't faze me. It's these images of the Spanish underworld descending on me, turning me into an abogado or something."

She removed the tire deftly. She was a small woman, whose hair was the widest part of her—a great frizzed-out ball around her head— with a mousy face, and no hips at all. She wore jeans and a denim shirt.

"I hope you don't have a real busy schedule this morning, cause I'm going to need you to help me find a tire store. This one's a demonstration model, and I don't imagine there are too many tire stores in Cindy's neck of the woods."

She snapped it into place, tightened the nuts.

"You could buy from the lawyer."

"You've gotta be crazy."

She put on the hubcap, wiped her hands on her ass and then offered one for me to shake.

"All right, hello," she said.

"There's a Sears down the way. I think you can get tires there."

"Oh, God, Sears would be a shot of sanity. Come on, get in, I'll give you a ride home."

We drove down Webster, her car making an odd, rattling noise that didn't seem to bother her at all.

"I can't believe there's a Sears in this neighborhood. I can't believe there's *anything* in this neighborhood. You go to *college* here?"

"Yes."

"And Cindy teaches? And it's the Jesuits? Oh, well, that makes sense. They tried to tame the Indians, didn't they?"

"The Sears is up ahead."

"I see it."

She bought four new tires and a hundred dollars' worth of auto accessories, claiming she believed certain events were harbingers of bad luck, and paying cash for the whole thing. The Sears people were going to put the tires on for her, so she had time to kill.

"Listen, I'm starved. Show me a good place for breakfast. My treat."

"What are you doing with all that cash?" I asked her in the greasy spoon I took her to. "No wonder you were afraid up on the Cross-Bronx."

"That'd be the least of it."

She slapped open her menu, ordered eggs and then looked around the place.

"This is your academic atmosphere, huh?" A Muzak version of "In the Year 2525" was on the sound system.

"It's all right."

"You're Cindy's prize student?"

"No. Not anymore. Just a friend. How do you know her?"

"We went to Iowa together. Graduate school. I couldn't get a job teaching afterwards...no that's not true, I did teach for a year, but it was so boring, I celebrated when they didn't renew my contract."

She wolfed down her eggs as soon as they arrived.

"So what do you do?"

"I'm a potter. That's why I've got these wads of money."

She smiled.

"Only kidding. My husband's a psychoanalyst. We live close to Bennington, so there's plenty of business. I'm here for a crafts show at a building I hear is so monstrous I'm going to go running back to Vermont as soon as I see it. But who knows? Maybe I'll sell some pots."

She wiped her mouth.

"So your house is the one Cynthia is staying at."

"Right. And what's-his-name."

"David."

"Right."

"You don't know him?"

"Oh, sure I know him. He was at Iowa too."

She sat back and folded her arms.

"What's the matter with David? You don't like him?"

She smirked.

"Ask her sometime how she fell in love with him. She tells this great story about watching him in *Desire Under the Elms*. What's the character's name? Eben, Evan, something very O'Neill."

"Eben."

"Right. I always think if O'Neill had named his characters Joe or Hank or Bill, nobody'd be doing his plays anymore. Anyway, we all went to see this great actor, this kid she thought was so great."

"You didn't think so?"

She shrugged her shoulders.

"Go ahead. Tell me."

She looked at me curiously.

"No. I gotta respect this student–teacher crap. You're not supposed to know too much about your teachers. Besides, she's a friend and that's all, really. He's a nice guy. You just can't hold a conversation with him for more than ten minutes. I always get the feeling he walks into a room, the first thing he's looking for is an electrical outlet, for a TV or a radio or something, like there's always some *game* going on somewhere, in Iceland, or Finland, and he'd rather be listening to it than listening to you."

She sipped coffee.

"We're not great friends anymore, even. This week just worked out. I had the crafts show, and Jonathan's going to see his mother in California, so it's a perfect place for them to go and do whatever you have to do..."

She left that open.

"And do what?"

"Nothing. No more."

She turned away. I leaned forward.

"No. Tell me. Come on, I'm not her student anymore. I'm her *friend*. This is a side of her life she never tells me about."

"Maybe she doesn't want you to know."

"I feel like I could help her more if I knew things."

"Listen, thanks for the help, they might be ready with the tires now."

"No, please. They're not breaking up, are they?"

She grunted.

"Far from it."

"Then tell me."

"It's *nothing*. They're up there for a vacation, all right?"

She signaled for the check.

"No, you said before, they had to go up there to do something important."

"Did I say that?"

"Yes."

I reached for her wrists. I couldn't believe I was doing this. Neither could I think of any other way of getting what I needed from her.

She was very calm.

"Let go, all right?"

"Please tell me. That's all. I'm her friend."

"Let go."

I didn't.

"Let go and I'll tell you."

I agreed.

I tried to smile, to make light of it.

"Listen, whatever it is, she must have wanted me to know. Otherwise, why would she have given you my number?"

"I don't know."

She started to get up.

"You're supposed to tell me. That was the bargain. I kept my half."

She took the check to the counter, paid. I followed her out onto the street.

"Come on. You made a promise."

"I think I would have been better off letting the Spaniards get to me."

"No. I'm safe. Honest."

"You're in love with her, aren't you?"

"Yes."

She paused. There was a light she had to wait for.

"Don't be," she said.

"Why?"

The light turned. She started to walk.

"Jesus Christ, don't give me this," I half-shouted. "I'm not gonna let you just go off unless you tell me."

I grabbed her wrists again. We were out in the middle of Fordham Road.

"Tell me."

"Let go."

"No. Not unless you tell me."

"All right. Jesus. They're up there trying to get pregnant. It's no big deal. It's just not something I think every Tom, Dick and Harry should know. Now let go."

Finally I did. She started off immediately. I didn't move. I didn't think I could. When she was on the oppo-

site corner, she turned, as if expecting me to be right behind her. I was still in the middle of the street. The lights
had turned.

"What are you doing?" she shouted.

The cars had started. They were all going by me now,
some of them very fast. She looked cool on the opposite
curb.

I was aware, peripherally, of a blend of colors, people
staring, and a lot of cars honking. I was aware, too, that it
was a hot day. I thought: Go home and write a paper. Do
some work. Locate the thread of your life. I took a step,
and a car nearly hit me.

"Sorry," I said, very quietly, as if to no one, an apologetic young man on a city street.

I didn't have to know.

That was the thought that kept playing in my mind, on the bus to Burleigh. It had only been chance, a flat tire on the Cross-Bronx Expressway. Otherwise, it was conceivable she wouldn't have told me, not for a while at least. As bad as that sounded, I would have preferred it.

The bus stopped in a dreary succession of depots—New Haven, Hartford, Springfield, Holyoke, then a two-hour layover in Brattleboro. I sat in the Brattleboro station and nursed the heaviness in my stomach. I couldn't read, or find any means of distraction.

The bus pulled onto Route 9, passed a movie theater where *A Clockwork Orange* was playing, then up a short hill, past an empty Memorial Park. It was the middle of the night.

We rode along a highway on which there seemed to be nothing but fence posts. Burleigh was a white inn illuminated by floodlights, a gas station, a store with a Coca-Cola sign out front. I wouldn't have known to get off unless the driver had announced it.

It was 4 A.M. I quickly reasoned that it would be a waste of my limited supply of money to get a motel room now. Better to work off the night, wait for morning. I sat on a cement stoop in front of a white building that could have been a church or a town hall, and waited.

After about five minutes, there seemed to be nothing at

all between my ass and the cement. My cold felt like it
was coming back. There was a white haze on the ground.
In one of the rooms of the inn, a single light shone. I
thought: Thank God it isn't raining.

At one point during the next couple of hours, I realized
that all I had to do was locate a phone book and I could
find her. She was staying in Sharon Glass's house.
Sharon Glass would be in the phone book. I imagined
throwing pebbles at a window, like in a movie. It seemed
I was always imagining things like that, and they got me
nowhere. Still I kept thinking of her coming out to explain to me, some very simple explanation, and the two
of us standing on a wet lawn with mist on the ground. I
thought these images were coming out of some soft
underlayer in me that had nothing to do with the world;
still, I was drawn to them. I was here to convince her of
something, but standing there, I couldn't imagine what.

A car passed through town, its headlamps low, shining
on the ground, the inn, the store, illuminating paint and
wood, hard ground and cement. The weight of the unac-
complished settled on me, pressing. I thought of Tommy
in Texas, and wanted now to talk to him, for him to be
here. I thought of how his father had died, how I'd never
really said anything to him, or asked for details. It was
what I ought to have done, but I'd been lost in something.
Here it was, its end. It was cold.

In the morning I found a motel and tried to check in,
but they told me you couldn't until eleven. There were
plenty of rooms, though; I didn't need to worry. It would
cost eight dollars.

I went into town and got some food. I ate standing up,
on the grass near the inn. I watched people coming out,
dressed for traveling.

I hoped I didn't see her now. I was eating breakfast on a
public lot, with a day's growth on my face. I did not appear a worthy candidate for fatherhood, or for anything
else.

Afterward, sleep felt wonderful. I took a bath first, lay in the deep old dirty tub in scalding water, not caring that some of the dirt came up off the bottom and formed a scud on the surface of the water. I lay in bed afterwards and thought that if this feeling of relief—of physical exertion and release—was all I'd come for, it would be enough. I thought: you are twenty years old, it doesn't matter, you have years to become a father. Then I imagined someone else saying those words to me, someone whose life had been marked by disappointment. I imagined Uncle Al on the bed: Forget it, Nick. Let's play miniature golf. I saw, like a detached but essential part, the side of me that would say yes, all right.

I dreamt of her. The imagery by now was constant: water, pregnancy, the white slope of her neck like a piece of familiar territory recovered from childhood, with that charge. Her hair rose off her neck and she sat up on the bed. Her skin was the color of new peaches and bleached bone: near-consumptive.

When I woke, I actually thought she'd been there beside me. My hands had the feeling of having recently touched her. I lay there and looked at the side of the bed where she would have lain and made an indentation there in the general shape of her body.

I thought that was silly.

I went out to find her.

Before I left the motel, I checked in the mirror to make sure I looked all right.

It was absurd. I looked fine.

I'd shaved before with soap and hot water without really looking at my face. Now I thought she'd be able to study it and think there was nothing wrong.

I went out.

I had no plan for finding her except to wait. Sooner or later she would have to shop at the Coca-Cola store. Sooner or later they would go to dine at the inn. I could

have gone directly to the house, but it seemed wrong. I
didn't want to barge in.

Even for us to talk in this town would be wrong. We
would have to go somewhere else; otherwise, she'd be
thinking of the milk she'd come to buy. The discussion
we needed to have should be conducted naked. There
should be a river to leap into—some gesture like that.

I watched people go in and out of the store. Each car
that approached I imagined as her Volvo, that she was
alone at the wheel. I felt the cold starting up my body,
almost from my toes. Still, it wasn't raining. You had to
be grateful.

She never came into town that day.

When it got late, I went into the inn and asked for a
phone book. It surprised me that they let me see it.

I looked up Sharon Glass's address, and then asked the
desk clerk where South Main Street was. She showed
me a map of the town. It was given, free, to guests of the
inn.

I found the house without difficulty. There were no
lights on.

I walked to the back, making as little noise as possible.
A room sloped out in the rear, a more recent addition.
Then there was a stream that ran behind the house. I
couldn't see inside the house. I was afraid of going too
close.

I waited.

Finally a car pulled into the driveway, and I heard
them. They were speaking to each other, but saying nothing of importance. David told her to be careful on the
walk. Then there was the sound of a door closing, and in
another part of the house, a light came on.

It was possible now to go from window to window, and
watch them. In the kitchen, David made popcorn. He had
his glasses on. He adjusted them with one hand while
with the other, he shook the pot. I looked at the size of

his shoulders. There were hairs on his wrists that looked reddish in the kitchen light.

He brought the popcorn to her in the living room. He shook salt on it and turned on the TV. She watched awhile and then picked up a magazine. There was a smiling woman on the cover.

You imagine the most outrageous images of passion and violence, and this is what you see: a man watching television, a woman reading a magazine. I thought that if I was the child they were trying to make, I would not want to be born: it would be too heartbreaking to sit in that room with them. It was easier imagining Billy and Judy having a child than them. Judy would know how to usher out heartbreak: she would give it a disgusted look. But I thought this of Cynthia: She is walking into fire. She is punishing herself. Still, here I was, and the windows weren't being broken. I wasn't picking up a rock and throwing it. They were being allowed this night, and I couldn't imagine why.

I slept through the night and woke up the next morning and checked out of the motel. I didn't have enough money to stay another night, but that hardly mattered. I knew I was going to see her today, and anything after that didn't matter.

Today there were clouds in the sky. I thought: What the hell. Go ahead. Yes. Rain.

I had forgotten to eat the day before. When I'd gotten back to the motel, I'd bought a dollar's worth of Jax Snax and eaten them on the bed. I'd been ravenous. I'd wolfed them down on the bed: the peanut butter cheese crackers, the roasted peanuts. I didn't care if I got crumbs on the bed and then had to sleep there. That sort of thinking seemed needless, an effect of overcultivation. I slept naked, and the fact of the crumbs and the wrappers under me made me think I was sleeping on pine needles and stone.

Then, in town, I bought more food: sticky buns and

Hostess fruit pies. I spent all my money and stood on the town green and ate, and I thought if I went into the inn now and asked for a phone book, they would refuse me. Someone would come and clutch my arm and ask me to step outside. The thought pleased me. I wanted my whole being to rage against the inn and all it represented: order, decorum, the world founded on a genteel mode of detachment. I wanted women to look out the windows of the inn and, finding me, think: yes, there is a passion more beautiful, wild, disorderly than anything I have known. I wanted Cynthia to come and, seeing me, not say: here is a good-looking healthy young man who has come here because he wants to be fucked, but instead: here is my Redeemer, mad, barefoot, standing in the rain.

But it had not yet rained.

Nor had it started up when, early in the afternoon, I saw the Volvo pull into town and stop in front of the Coca-Cola store.

I watched them through a window, my face obscured by the racks of paperbacks and children's coloring books that had been placed against the wall. David was buying wine, and taking a long time, looking at bottle after bottle, reading what it said on the back of each, feeling the weight of them as though testing bats before going into the on-deck circle. Cynthia wasn't interested. She looked at stacks of bread. She glanced through magazines.

Her face may have been slightly closer to mine than David's was, but I couldn't watch her, couldn't look at her. Her face was closed off to me, as though she had taken something back.

It was easier to look at David, to stare at the lines on his face and chart out the places where he was no longer young. He was still young in the eyes, though. His eyes were blue and looked sharply, critically at the wine. His hands were different from mine, too. He had long fingers and strong hands, and the ring of gold looked small on them. I imagined what it would be like to be in love with him. It scared me to think that way, but I could do it. He was solid. Whatever else you wanted to say about him, he occupied space in a way most men didn't, and the way he stood, you knew he was rooted to the ground.

These thoughts rushed by as if I didn't know who had had them, and I thought: he is *David*, and tried to pile up all the negative thoughts I'd ever had about him. Except they weren't there anymore. Now it was only a man buying wine in a store, and I knew what it would be like for her to turn and look at him and catch the look of his profile and the set of his mouth and think: yes, it is okay to do what I am doing. Not walking into fire, but simple fact.

Then David chose his wine, and Cynthia, though she couldn't see him, at the same instant picked up a couple of magazines and moved to the counter.

When they came out of the store, I was standing off just a little from where their car was parked, so they couldn't fail to see me. But there was self-absorption in the way they walked—David carrying the wine, Cynthia a loaf of bread in addition to her magazines—an attention to some invisible bit of business going on between them, as though they were brother and sister involved in a game requiring intense mental concentration.

Cynthia opened the door on her side, and it was only then that she saw me. Her look was at first neither surprised nor angry, and then both. She dropped one of the magazines and immediately bent to pick it up. When she had it in her hand again, she got into the car and shut the door.

I moved to the other side, where David could see me too. It wasn't premeditated, but seemed the natural thing to do. He looked up at me. He'd already started the car.

Cynthia was staring at the dashboard, her head gone a little forward. It was the sort of position you'd be uncomfortable in if you were the least bit conscious of it.

David said something to her.

I think she nodded her head.

Then he shifted the car into gear and they were gone.

• • •

I waited until nightfall.

I kept expecting her to come back, but of course she didn't. I thought I could have gone to Sharon Glass's house, but what then? What was in my mind was the image of the two of them in the store, and their precise mutual understanding of when it had been time to go.

I thought of her as she'd looked in the store, and it became difficult to believe I'd ever done more than speak to that woman, and then haltingly.

Then I thought of her on the bridge near Fordham, in the Botanical Gardens, and how funny it was to have believed all the things I'd believed when now it was over and you could see what it had really been and how much she must have been holding back all along.

And still I expected her to show up at any minute. Still I expected the words of consolation and reprieve. It was all some misunderstanding. I waited, and then it started to rain.

At first it was light, and made a splattering sound on the ground. The combination of dark and rain made me dizzy. I had no money for a bus. You couldn't hitchhike in the rain; that is, you could, but given the way I felt now I thought I'd probably die if I tried to do that. Dying didn't sound like such a bad idea, but I was hungry, too. With food in my belly, I thought I could go stand in the rain and hitchhike, and maybe she'd drive by and see me with my hair matted down by the rain and understand what my passion had been. I lay down on the stoop and fell asleep.

When I awoke, my head was cold from resting on cement. A fierce shivering overtook my body, and also a fierce happiness. It takes a while for the facts of your life to catch up with you after a dream. I'd dreamt again of her.

I sat there a moment, cold and hungry. Then I got an idea.

I crossed the green and walked into the inn. It was a short walk, but the rain was coming down now, and drenched me. I asked to be seated for dinner.

The hostess looked at me. I was hot and shivering, and my clothes were wet. She picked up a menu and took me to a table behind a pillar close to where there were heating trays full of food. The room was barely half-full. She asked me to wait there.

I looked across the room and saw that there were flowers on the other tables. There was the ritual of dining. I was full of envy. I wanted to lay my head down on the table and just rest awhile. I could smell turkey and squash. I thought of the movie *Splendor in the Grass*, where Warren Beatty is mourning Natalie Wood in New Haven, and a waitress named Angie finds him in her café and takes care of him, brings him into the kitchen, feeds him. Eventually they marry and have a child. I smiled at the memory, as if it were my own. I thought: Any moment Angie will come and take me into the kitchen. It will smell of sauce. She will introduce me to her family. They will tender smiles of instant and total acceptance.

The hostess appeared at my table. A man was beside her.

My head was resting on the table, on the warm dish.

He asked me if I would come with him. I said no.

He asked again. This time I felt a nudging on my arm. I knew the man was aware of the other diners. I could tell from the quiet of his voice. There was more than a nudge. I felt his hand close around the muscle of my arm.

"I don't want to be kicked out!" I said.

What I heard was "Idonwannabekiktout."

His grip tightened, and I freed my arm, wildly, knocking everything off the table.

There was that silence after something like that happens.

I sat there a moment, and when he came toward me again I got up and shoved at him and ran past him and the hostess. I was going to shout something to the other diners, too. I didn't only because I couldn't compose a decent sentence in my head quick enough. I ran out into the rain.

I ran all the way up the hill to the road I'd turned onto the day before, then continued until I came to the house.

The light was on in the back room.

I didn't care about making noise. The ground was muddy, and my feet made squish-sounds as I walked to the back.

The light was on, and through the back window I could see everything. Her legs were lifted on the bed, opened wide, and David's strong back towered over her. I could see the muscles and vertebrae on his back. Looking at him was like looking at a man when you are a small boy and you think of men as a foreign country you are condemned to emigrate to some day. I was amazed by his power and his will: it was like he was trying to push a baby into her. I watched them, barely aware of my own position, and because they looked, in that instant, so beautiful, and their enterprise so large and noble, I was filled with an extraordinary flood of happiness. I only thought he was trying too hard, that he should ease off a bit. It was as though he wanted something too badly, and would never get it that way. I thought I was as close to him now as a ghost would be, or a guardian angel, and I wanted to help.

I needed to tap twice before I had their attention. The second time was loud.

I don't know why I expected them to be grateful.

Their faces looked large and hard and red and frightened. David came out into the rain and punched me in the stomach. I hadn't expected him to—his anger was totally shocking—but I didn't mind either. He punched again. Words welled up, but I had no breath to speak them. My mind registered that he was naked. His body gleamed in the rain. I was proud of him.

He hit me a third time and I went down. I could see her in the window now, her breasts flattened against the glass. The rain made an odd plunking noise against the ground and the roof of the house, separate noises for each.

He turned, finally. I watched his naked back in the rain heading into the house. As he did, she moved away from the window, so that her breasts were not squished against it anymore, and she was just a woman standing in a window with the rain making a film against the glass, only her outline visible.

When I opened my eyes, I saw my mother on a green metal chair, sitting next to a radiator.

She had on her plum-colored dress, and I could see the way the makeup stood out on her face, like she'd put on too much, and her face resisted it.

I didn't have to ask where I was, because I knew. I had perfect recall of the night before, sitting in the Burleigh police station—it was one room—shivering on a bench and telling them my address in the Bronx. And hearing them say that was no good, they couldn't send me back to college in this condition, and what were my parents' names and where did they live.

It took my father four hours to drive there. Meanwhile, they gave me a blanket and told me to lie down on the bench. As soon as he came into the small, dark room, my father brought with him an energy, a sense of the bustle of life that made me see everything I had done as a large and selfish indulgence. I sat up on the bench and threw off the blanket.

I wanted to leave right away, but the officer took his time explaining to my father about the incident in the restaurant, and afterwards with David. He used the word "trespass," and it seemed to have a different, more complex meaning than the one I knew. I watched my father nod, letting the officer know they spoke the same language.

We drove the four hours home mostly in silence. He seemed to understand what had happened as well as he wanted to. The only questions he asked were if I felt all right, and did I want to lie down in the back? I didn't. He stopped for coffee near the Massachusetts border and without asking, brought me one as well. We drove as we'd driven years before, when I had been his son and we'd gone on errands together, when he had not found it necessary to tell me where we were going, and I had not found it necessary to ask.

When we arrived home, it was just light; we sneaked into the house, quiet as soldiers breaking camp. We were returning home from a night fishing trip in which we'd caught nothing. We were anticipating my mother's disappointment.

She looked at me, then waited a moment before saying, "He's too sick to stay here."

We'd accepted her certainty. My father stood with his hands in his pockets as though he'd failed at something.

"I'll take him to the hospital," he said.

Then, while I sat on another bench, he listed the facts about me to the woman at the receiving desk. I wondered if he was embarrassed, bringing me here. I'd gone into another room then; there'd been no need for him to stay longer. He held his hat in front of him and said something like, "You'll be all right, then?" I knew it was time to open the laundromat. He'd gone a night without sleep, and even if he hustled now, he'd still be late; somebody might already be waiting outside the door.

Now my mother smiled at me from her seat beside the radiator.

"How are you feeling?" she asked.

When I sat up, my lungs felt like bags filled with sand, drawing down the muscles of my chest.

"Fine," I said.

"You have pneumonia."

There was something that came after the word, an audible residue. She and her sisters talked about certain diseases that way. Words like "diabetes," "heart attack."

They'd grown up in a world where you didn't survive those words, at least not as you were: they envisioned, automatically, the wheelchair, the grave.

"Pneumonia's nothing, Mom. I'll be fine."

"Ya." Her voice caught.

Aunt Rose came in, carrying two large paper cups, with straws protruding. She seemed unpleasantly surprised to find me awake, then looked guiltily at the two cups in her hands.

"I thought you'd be asleep," she said.

"It's okay, Rose."

"I would have brought three."

"It's all right. I'm not thirsty."

"He can have mine, Rose," my mother said.

"Don't be silly, Josie."

Both cups landed on the tray beside my bed. Neither of them would drink.

"I told you, I don't want any," I said.

I got out of bed to hand them their drinks. I didn't realize that the hospital johnny didn't cover me.

Rose turned away. My mother stared. I got back into bed.

"All right, take them, will you?"

Finally Rose got up and took the drinks, and then the two of them sat there with their mouths around the straws.

When my mother finished, she excused herself to go to the bathroom. Alone with Rose, I watched her eyes flare, just as they'd done when I'd met her here in this hospital the last time. For her, we were the most exciting of families.

"What happened up there, Nickie?" she asked.

She sat there trying to look accusatory with a straw between her lips.

"They said you were peeping on a woman."

"Is that what they said?"

"Yes."

I suddenly felt very hot.

"That's not how it was," I said evenly.

My mother came out of the bathroom and I repeated it. "I knew that woman, Mom. I wasn't any Peeping Tom."

She looked at me.

"Lie down," she said. "Don't get yourself excited. It's bad for the pneumonia."

I watched the way she looked at my eyes. Then she smoothed back my hair.

"Lie down, Nick."

She went back and sat on her chair next to Rose. Then there was nothing but the radiator hissing.

"They said you were trespassing, Nick," Rose said. "What were you doing there?"

My mother turned to Rose with a solemn look on her face. She shook her head.

"It was the strain of school, I think," my mother said. I watched Rose nod, her dark eyes growing large, as though she were deciphering a message written in code.

There was a silence afterward. The two of them sat there as if in the lap of an agreement.

After a few moments they got up to leave. The fact of having been restrained from digging for the truth had seemed to tire Rose. I wondered at first why I wasn't resisting my mother's fabrication more, but as I watched the two of them pass by my bed on their way out, an answer of sorts came to me. I thought I could feel what the tenor of the next few weeks and months would be like, and in the light of it, my invalidism appeared to me as a balm, an inspired guess, something I ought to have been grateful for. "Pneumonia" would do as a punishment. No human hand or voice would have to be raised against me; bacteria would do nicely. As the door shut behind them, I had a distinct sense, too, of my own participation in this process. In my weakness, I was allowing—even desiring—them to take me back.

I stayed in the hospital another two days before they sent me home.

Then I lay in bed in my old room under the bright

acrylic painting of a sailboat that my mother had put up in my absence. I had time now to think about such things: the paintings and furniture chosen for rooms in which a son had once lived, the books placed there, the old set of encyclopedias. I found comfort in this room as I never had before.

Three times a day my mother brought me meals. A portable television set was hooked up so that I could watch it while I ate. I found myself studying "sons" as they existed on television, on commercials. The enterprise of sonhood seemed marvelous to me now: a grand undertaking I had never taken seriously. "Sons" were always coming in doors, wanting to borrow cars. They were lanky and wore sweaters, were handsome and bold and complete unto themselves. All this while they slept in upstairs bedrooms, ate at the parents' table.

They had girlfriends. They talked to their parents as if they were from the moon and would never be understood. Yet this was comical, this was small. In the end, they got the car keys; they said things like "Thanks, Dad." All was well.

I watched all this in amazement, as if I were growing monstrous there on my childhood bed, splitting the seams of my pajamas, my body oozing water, hair falling out in clumps. I thought I could no more hope to become "a son" again than a dwarf or a humpback could successfully impersonate these boys in sweaters. It was like watching an inheritance fly away at the exact moment you become aware of it.

But at other times, I found myself slipping into this new-old role with remarkable ease. The recent past reared its head, and it seemed like some grotesque object I had clung to out of some delusion I could no longer even name. Here I was, on this bed, I thought, and gave up the struggle, easily, to believe I belonged elsewhere.

One day my father came in to clear away the lunch dishes. After he had stacked them, he didn't leave the room as he usually did, but placed them on the bureau beside the TV and then sat at my desk. The two of us watched a *Dick Van Dyke* rerun. He didn't say anything to me, just watched the TV with his jaw set and his mouth pointed like he was listening to a question being put to him.

When *Dick Van Dyke* was over, he leaned forward and turned the knob to Off. The picture shrank to a white hole, and then the room seemed dark.

"We called Fordham," he said.

The word sounded strange, and filled me with dread.

"I wanted to let them know what your situation was."

I thought of some dark office at Fordham, and the secretary who would pick up the phone. I could hear the name "Battaglia" as she would hear it, unpleasant-sounding and Italian, one of a million names from the great void outside that came and interrupted her from finishing her tuna fish sandwich.

"What did you tell them?"

He stared down at the rug.

"I told them you were sick."

He looked at me now as if to ascertain the fact that he hadn't lied to priests, as if I should look sicker than I did in order for him to accept his own report.

"What'd they say?"

"They said if you're too sick to come back, you can write to your professors."

Then he reached for a thought, and finding what he'd been looking for but still not being sure of it, said, "They can give you an Incomplete."

I could tell he didn't like the way the word sounded.

"Did you ask them about the money?"

He looked at me as if he didn't understand the question.

"About a refund."

Then he looked down at the rug.

"That was what I thought. What I wanted to know about. But they said this Incomplete would be better. This way you won't lose anything."

But I had no intention of going back, ever.

"Maybe you could write them today," he said. "And I could mail them."

"Sure."

But he didn't move.

"You mean now?"

He nodded.

Then he waited, as if only with the letters in his hand would he understand anything at all.

He handed me a sheet of paper he found on my desk. The letterhead read "LEO GALLITANO INSURANCE." I didn't know why it was there.

"Here," he said. "I've got to make a quick call to Ray, see how he's doing. I'll be right back."

My hand started to shake as soon as I began writing.

He was back very quickly. I felt as though he had betrayed me, forced me to make amends to a world I no longer believed in, and which he ought to have had sense enough not to believe in. The pneumonia ought to have been punishment enough. He ought to have believed that, as my mother did.

His face settled as he took the letters. When he left, I got up and stood at the window and watched him go out to the car, stopping to scrape something off the dashboard. He had the four stamped envelopes in his hand. He adjusted his fishing cap before he got into the car. He looked like Glenn Ford going off on a mission, in a jeep, all intensity and forward thrust. The enemy was at the Maginot Line. Suddenly everything was important.

After he had gone, I didn't want to go back to bed. I understood, dimly, that "healing" was supposed to be my business now. It was what my father's trip to the post office was all about. He would guarantee something for me. I imagined his speaking to a crony about me: "Yes, he's sick now, but we fixed things up for him at school; we got him the Incompletes." The word would become a reprieve. I would lie in this room in all the depths of my failure and a network of words and reassurances would buoy me up and suspend me in their world. They would create a net.

I stood at the window and looked out over the brown wet lawns of the neighborhood, and the new well-tended houses, and thought of myself as existing in the bedroom of one of them, wearing a pair of brown cotton pajamas (the ones Aunt Rose had given me for Christmas).

When I turned and looked at my image in the mirror and saw what I saw there, it was not a surprise, but the personification of everything I'd been thinking. This person who stared back at me could not possibly have been loved by the woman in his imagination, and so that possibility—that last delusion—flew off. I understood only after it had gone that it had still been there; that even as I'd thought with cold logic about "the boy in brown cotton pajamas," there had still existed the possibility that I might turn to the mirror and see someone else, someone who might surprise me. The only question now was How had she stood it so long? How had she humored me such an ungodly time? Hadn't she seen that this was what I was, these acrylic sunsets on the wall and these old encyclopedias and this room?

I crossed to the bed, but before I got there I knelt down beside it with my hands clasped over the covers. It was an attitude preparatory to prayer, but the prayer itself didn't come. I was going to live. I'd been punched in the stomach and the rain had given me pneumonia, but these weren't the things that killed you: you had to participate a little if you were going to die. I had not gone that distance. Instead I had stood there and seen David and Cynthia buying wine and had wanted to say Forgive me.

As soon as I was well enough, I went back to work in the laundromat. The work was easy and pleasant. I liked being there, out in the world again. That this, the laundromat, had become "the world" was not a contradiction I chose to play with much.

My return to work displaced Ray—he was reduced to fewer hours than my father indicated he was happy with—but I could tell both my parents were glad to have me out of the house, and in some occupation; I was glad to oblige.

The only problem was that my father, once I was well enough to work, began getting on my back about the Incompletes he'd arranged. He understood the concept well enough now to see that the stamped "I" did not hold life in abeyance forever, that it expected something in return. But I was still not ready to write to my professors for the work, to resume that old life. Just imagining that sort of activity weakened me. I used that for an excuse, and for a while they let it go.

Then they decided, both my parents, that I should transfer to Boston College. It was Jesuit. It was nearby. They could "keep an eye on me"; I could live at home. There were no good arguments on my part against it. In fact, the idea solved so many of my problems, I grew to like it. My father called and made an appointment with the Dean of Students.

It was a Wednesday when we drove in. Early June now, and the campus was pretty much empty of students, but there were enough of them still around to make me deeply self-conscious. Boys lounged on the steps of the Library, on the walls in front of red-brick buildings. They seemed to embody a freedom I stood in awe of. My mother smiled at them; at any moment I expected to hear her say, "Here's Nick, he's going to be joining you next year." But she didn't, mercifully, say anything, only smiled at them as though she couldn't conceive of the possibility they might consider us an oddity. She'd dressed up for the occasion. Beside her, my father stepped grimly over the green campus, as if he were delivering me there, as though I were a letter he had come to mail.

The priest who greeted us looked sharper, more keenly critical than any of the Fordham Jesuits. For a moment, looking at him, the idea of a real intellectual education seemed just the ticket. No groping after Anne Bradstreet here; something harder, less forgiving.

I hated my parents' discomfort in this office. They refused the priest's offer of coffee. When I looked at my father, he was staring down at the priest's rug. Then he glanced up at me and sent me a smile that seemed to embody all the helplessness I had ever seen in him. For his sake, I wanted this to go well.

My mother didn't take long to make herself comfortable. She began talking about the laundromat. She told the story of its inception and its rise, claiming full credit for the latter. The priest nodded, his little Irish smile twisted into a pucker. My mother was fully at home now. She had found her subject.

When the priest's eyes started to glaze, my father interrupted her and said, "That's enough, Josie. We've come here to talk about Nick."

Then the priest looked at me. I knew right away he found my mother, for all her solipsism, more interesting. If it had been she who was applying here, he'd have accepted her on the spot. She knew how to "speak up."

He asked me what had happened at Fordham.

They were all expecting me to answer, and when I didn't right away, my father started in for me. "He had a little problem there," he said. "Came down with pneumonia."

"So he had to come home," my mother said, and then smiled at the priest as if he would understand, he had children of his own.

The priest repeated the word "pneumonia," and it sounded absurd to me, like something I hadn't really had, but which we had all *agreed* I had. This priest had the hardness of one who doesn't take disease as a cause, but as an excuse, and Fordham seemed to stand now in his mind like a castle whose defense I had let down because I had the sniffles.

He said he would need to see my transcripts. I told him I could have them sent, but I could just as easily recite every grade I'd ever received in college, which I proceeded to do. I could feel my mother beaming beside me, but I thought—though I couldn't be sure—that my father was vaguely troubled by what I was doing, as though I were making an inappropriate display. At the end, it was like I'd been reciting the accomplishments of some beloved older brother whose absence was now felt.

The priest continued to stare at me after I was done with this recital, until the silence was terrible. My mother finally broke it by saying, "He did beautifully in high school, too."

This time, when the priest offered coffee, we took it, and my father and I also accepted the slices of cake his secretary brought in. I thought we were accepting these things only for the chance to stay in his office a bit longer, to pick up the thread we had misplaced, to find the words that would redeem us. My recitation of grades loomed large; I was red at the thought of it. My father bit at his cake. I was embarrassed by his teeth and the way his tongue had to reach out to lick the crumbs off his lips and his gums, endlessly, when he was through chewing.

As it was, the priest paid little attention to us. My mother was giving him advice on how to care for his plants. He seemed interested.

However disastrous this meeting might have been in reality, the Ministry of Propaganda went to work on it and turned it into another Battaglia triumph. I heard my mother on the phone assuring some relative or friend that the priest had said I was a "shoo-in." Even my father, in the laundromat, liked to tell people there was "an excellent chance" of my being accepted into B.C. Among ourselves, the topic never came up; I assumed they had convinced themselves of the logic of their excuses, and I certainly didn't want to disturb the balance. What an effort it must have been to present an image to the world of a son whose life was on track! At night, I imagined them secretly wishing they'd had other children, that the burden wasn't so relentlessly on this poorly made Nicholas. After a while, it got so I believed myself that my showing hadn't really been so bad, or that my mother's expertise with plants might have made up for it, so that any day now there might be a thick letter in the mail.

Then one day Tommy arrived.

I was sitting in the laundromat, leafing through a stack of old magazines on the table in front of me, when I looked up and saw him, standing on the other side of the glass window, tapping on it. I knew him by his belly; otherwise, Tommy was so changed I wouldn't have recognized him. His black hair had grown long, and fell in waves all the way to his shoulders. His skin was close to the color of a green olive. His big round face was split in half by dark sunglasses, and his chin looked stronger, dusted by a few days' growth. Only his belly, pushing out formidably at his green T-shirt, seemed unchanged.

"Jesus Christ, you skinny thing, what are you doing here?" he asked when we were close. He even smelled different, darker, vaguely tropical.

"I'm here. I'm just here. What about you?"

He looked at me a moment as if he had to interpret my words. But he wanted to keep smiling.

"I got some dirty clothes. Laundromats in Texas suck. Can I do 'em?"

"Sure."

We hugged now. It was as if I'd been afraid to up till now, and he'd picked up on that.

"How'd you get so skinny?"

"I've been sick, Tom."

"How?"

"Pneumonia."

He smiled.

"That's all?"

"Yes."

"Come on, there's somebody I want you to meet."

There was a girl in the passenger's seat of Tommy's van. The van was big and black and had been pulled right up in front of the laundromat, where there were crossed yellow lines warning against it.

"Tommy, you're not supposed to park here."

"Meet Jolene."

"Hi."

She was a small girl with stringy black hair plastered against her face by the heat. Her green T-shirt was identical to Tommy's, like they'd both gone shopping in the same Army-Navy store.

"I'm gonna get in trouble if my Cousin Leo finds out you're a friend of mine."

Tommy just kept looking at me.

"You want me to park the car someplace else, Nick? I come all these thousands of miles to see you and you're worried about my parking space?"

"No. Fuck it. Come on in."

But I felt even this small rebellion as something that would stick to me, whereas Tommy would go, would drive off, blameless.

We sat on the front bench and drank Cokes, the three of us. Tommy talked about Jolene with great pride—she had been a cheerleader in San Antonio and was headed for Vassar in the fall, but she had stood up to her daddy, a wealthy San Antonio lawyer, in running off with Tommy. Tommy said all this with a slight twang in his voice— San Antonio was "San Antone"—and Jolene just sat there, sipping at her Coke.

"So? Can we do our wash?"

Tommy went out to the van and dragged in two enormous loads of laundry, one of them in an Army green burlap bag, the other loosely wrapped in a stained white sheet. He kept dropping things out of this second one, and it didn't seem to bother him that the floor was littered with his underwear, and Jolene's. I ran around quickly picking them up, because my father would be here eventually, and...well, my mind stopped at the other reasons, but they seemed to be good ones.

"What's the matter, Nick? My underwear embarrass you?"

I helped him stuff it into a washer.

"You want me to tell you a secret?" He came close and whispered: "Everybody in this place wears underwear, Nick. Even the girls."

"You got quarters?"

He grasped me by the shoulders.

"What's the matter? You don't like seeing me here?"

324

"I'm afraid of my father coming, that's all."

"I told you, I saw him at your house. I did my Eddie Haskell routine; it's okay. Your mother even offered me and Jolene some meatballs. Come on, ease up."

He kept looking at me with that disappointed look, which made things harder.

"What happened, anyway?"

"We split up. I got pneumonia."

I shrugged. I honestly wished he would go. His presence here was doing me no good. I had my life set up: B.C. in the fall, this place until then. He wasn't staying, so there was no chance for a long-range examination of things, not that I wanted that. It was mostly that I didn't want the questions. It had been easier to open a magazine to read "10 Tips for Keeping a Husband" by Zsa Zsa Gabor, which is what I'd been doing when Tommy appeared at the door.

"I'll tell you what," Tommy said. "Come with us to Providence. I sold my house; I gotta go sign papers. Maybe if I get you outta here, you won't be so worried about my spilled underwear."

When my father did show up, Tommy poured on the charm, saying things like, "Gee, Mr. Battaglia, you wouldn't mind it if we took Nickie to Providence with us tonight, would you?"

And my father, hands in his pockets, looked down and tucked in his chin as if he were thinking about it, and said, "Oh, sure, I guess it would be okay, as long as you get him back here for the night shift tomorrow."

We drove to Providence. The city looked small, diminished from the size that memory had given it, and the summer night air made it seem calm and benevolent, not at all the place where I had chased around in my mad search for bananas and Cocoa Krispies.

We ate with Vito and Angie. Angie was pregnant again, though not yet showing. They wanted us to spend the night there, but Filumena lived with them, and it would have been the three of us on a couch, so we begged off.

Instead, Tommy drove the van to his father's house and parked there.

"Are we going in?" I asked, not wanting to.

"I don't even have the keys anymore."

Tommy looked at the house a few moments, and said, "I don't even feel sad, that's the crazy part. I'm getting forty thousand dollars for it, and I want to give it all to Vito's kids. I've got this new life now, and I don't want to be carrying around all this money; it just complicates things."

He stared at the house another minute, then climbed into the back of the van and lit up some of the pot he and Jolene had brought from Texas. I took a couple of tokes, but it never did anything for me.

When we settled down to sleep, they started to make love.

"You want me to wait outside?" I asked.

"Suit yourself," Tommy said, barely pausing, then looking up and smiling at me, as if it were a good joke.

I waited on the sidewalk with the van rocking behind me. It was warm, so they could take their time. The problem was I had to look up at the house, and looking at the house made me remember things I had forced out of my mind for too long.

To counter these thoughts, I tried to return to the way she'd looked in Vermont, buying wine with David, but it seemed impossible now to go back to that mood of self-denial. I wondered if I'd ever been fully alive to what had gone on, or if the net had been there, always, to suspend me. Instead of hearing the high, clear voice of passion inciting me to achieve things or die, there had always been a darker, calmer, compromising voice inside, and in the end, it had been the one I had listened to.

I'd stood outside the window and marveled at them as if it were a surprise that people, that *anyone*, should behave like adults. And while this adult world shimmered brightly from its depths and in its colors, I'd thrown rocks at a window like a boy in a movie. For all Cynthia's cruelty, I thought I had done worse finally. I'd been false —not to myself, for I knew the compromising voice was as much "myself" as anything else, but to another self, the brief and stunning glimpse of which she had given me; the gift. A thing to aspire to, which I had let go.

The baby blinked its eyes open while the water fell across its forehead. Its mouth was open a long time before any sound came. Then the sound seemed distant, only a gesture toward sound—I wondered if something was wrong with this baby's larynx, something we would discover only now, in the baptismal nave—while the face turned very red, but not a full dark shade, more the color of boiled lobster. I said something like "All right, all right." The priest looked at me as though it was my fault, and for a moment like he didn't like babies and didn't like being a priest. His hands fidgeted as he went on with the Latin words.

The church was hot. Uncle Billy looked hot. He leaned against the polished wood of a pew, his eyes a little glazed, his arms crossed and feet tapping gently. He looked as though at any moment he would say, "Hey, Father, who do you have to fuck around here to get some air conditioning?" Then he would look at his son and something else would come over his face, something very un-Billy-like. I searched for the resemblance between them, but the baby looked only like a baby: as though, briefly, the slate had been wiped clean, and the race was beginning anew.

The priest had been annoyed with us from the moment we'd appeared. To start with, there was no godmother. The woman Billy and Judy had asked was unable at the last moment to make it. At first my mother was going to be the proxy, but then she thought she would be better used in going to the Sons of Italy Hall to make sure everything was all set for the party. Some arcane law forbade Judy from setting foot in the church.

When it was over, the priest shook Billy's hand and moved quickly up the side aisle, walking steadily but a little crookedly under the stained-glass windows, toward the pastel representation of a conference of angels at the front of the church.

Billy watched him go, took his son away from me, and stood there as if he were in no hurry. It had not gone well, but he hadn't seemed to notice. He grinned, and hit my shoulder with his free hand.

"The water bothered him, huh?" he asked.

"Yeah. I guess."

"You did good."

My mother had done good too, in the Sons of Italy Hall. The food was all set out, but where were the guests? The serving girls waited at the side of the hall, bored because there was nothing to do, but standing there anyway. Judy sat at a table with Aunt Rose, looking hot and puffing on a cigarette, while Rose stared at her as if she were a piece of exotic statuary on foreign soil, one she was standing beside just long enough for Al to snap a picture.

"How'd it go?" Judy called, when Billy was in the hall.

"Went fine. Where is everybody?"

"Oh, they'll be here." My father stood, with his hands in his pockets, in the center of the room. "Some of them'll be late, that's all."

Beside my father, a shorter, slighter man stood, dressed in a suit that looked like it had once fit him, but no longer did. I had to stare a long moment before I recognized Ray. Who'd invited him? My father must have known that the crowd would be sparse. Ray lifted his hand and smiled at me.

On the stage, a pair of second cousins, high school boys Billy had hired for the occasion, were tuning guitars, while behind them a third set up drums.

"We all set?" Billy called.

No one seemed to hear him.

"Oh, they should all be here soon," my mother called from her table. The way she said it made me doubt it. "Ray, have something to eat," she said, and Ray, hands in his pockets as though he were imitating my father, shrugged and moved to the table of food, my father's eyes following him, as if even here Ray couldn't be trusted, but had to be watched lest he get drunk and embarrass us in front of this handful of people.

When the doors finally opened and a scattering of guests arrived, they were greeted as though their arrival were a lifting of the plague. Food was forced on them, and Billy leaped to the stage to get his little pickup band in tune. The days of the Philly 4 seemed legendary now, and this a fall from grace. Billy's first number was "I'm Gonna Sit Right Down and Write Myself a Letter." The band seemed not to know it, but Billy carried on. Ray held his plate of food and swayed slightly to the music. Al asked Rose to dance, in vain. She sat at her table as if she had decided it was her duty to protect Judy, to keep her from the anxious hands of all those guests just now making pilgrimages in the direction of mother and child.

Eventually more guests arrived, so that the room was half full. I sat at the table with my mother and Judy and Aunt Rose. I looked through the swirl of cigarette smoke and hoped no one would come and ask me anything about my life. I had not been accepted at B.C., as it turned out. We hadn't said much about it when the letter had come; it was just one possibility less. At dinner that night, my mother had perked up. "How about B.U.?" But my father hushed her. Maybe he didn't have the heart to sit in another Admissions Office, listening to his son recite his glorious academic record. I didn't blame him.

Then Tommy had come and told me I could drive back to Texas with him if I wanted, and sell hot dogs. It was two weeks after his first visit, and he was getting ready to go back. We'd sat in a Burger King on the highway, and he'd said, "Come on, Nick," and put his hand on my shoulder in the way he had, and it was like he'd had the best idea in the world.

But as I sat at this table in the half-filled room, I was not certain of anything anymore.

I looked past my parents into the dancing couples and saw Julie Bonfiglio. She was dancing with a young man I didn't recognize. I hadn't seen her come in. Maybe she'd seen me and stuck to the opposite side of the room. I got up immediately when I saw her, and only a second later realized it was inappropriate. Worse, it was crazy. The young man was her boyfriend. He had short hair and glasses, was even handsome in his way, with blond hair and only the big nose to show he was Italian. I could see him having children with her—I could see him as a father just as I'd been able to see David as a father; it was a fixation of mine now, one of the world's natural divisions. Still, I was seized by the desire to dance with Julie. I wanted my chance again.

I crossed the dance floor and tapped Julie's young man on the shoulder. He looked at me with slight belligerence; a tough guy. I said something like "Could I . . ." and I saw that he didn't want to, but Julie, whose eyes lifted no higher than the level of my chest, nodded her head and touched him very gently on the shoulder. Then we were dancing.

Beyond her, I could see Viola looking nervous, her eyes disappearing behind her glasses. The young man came and stood next to her, and the two of them stood there watching us like a pair of bouncers.

My hand was on the back of Julie's dress, and either the dress or my hand was damp, I couldn't tell which. All I knew was that suddenly I thought Julie was the most desirable woman on earth, and I would have given anything to be that young man she was dancing with, with a girl in my arms and a future assured. Why did everyone seem so blessed to me now, so capable of splendid lives? I didn't know. Before I could think, I whispered in Julie's ear, "Come with me." She acted at first like she didn't hear, so I said it again. This time she let go of the tenuous grasp she'd had on me and went back to Viola and her boyfriend.

At first I stood there, not quite believing she had done that. Maybe she was only going back to tell her boyfriend it was over between them. But then she stayed with them, not looking at me, and finally whispered something to her boyfriend that made him look hard at me, with his mouth closed tight.

I went back to the table where Al and Rose were sitting. Al grabbed my arm and smiled, but I didn't want that. I walked up the stairs at the side of the stage and found the room where the musicians had taken their breaks last time. I sat there, wishing they were all back here, those seedy men who had been Billy's band. I wanted the one with the pencil-thin mustache to give me the name of a girl, Debbie Nuttings of Tenth Avenue, a number I could call. I wanted someone to act like I had a future.

I looked up after a while and saw my father standing in the doorway. I'd been sitting there, just rubbing my thighs and staring at the floor, I didn't know how long.

"Are you all right?" he asked.

He was holding a drink in his hand. I wondered if he was even a little bit drunk.

"Yes. Fine."

I looked at him, as if waiting for something, and then looked away, because the nakedness of my gaze made his own eyes retreat.

"Billy's turnout is a little disappointing, I'm afraid," he said.

"Yes."

Then he just stood there a moment and looked down the hall, as if he were waiting for someone to show up, someone whose presence would change everything.

"I guess," he said; he was fumbling for something, I could tell; "I guess the news from B.C. was pretty disappointing."

He jiggled the ice cubes in his glass.

"Sure."

He nodded. We had been serious about it. Something had passed.

"Well, Fordham's still a good school."

"Yes."

We both nodded now. It was as if each agreement was an increment toward some goal. Except I didn't know what the goal was.

He was smiling now in that glazed-eyed way of his, as if he were about to make some pronouncement that rendered the world a certain way, however it really was. "We have a very close-knit family," I'd once heard him say to guests.

"Okay, Dad," I said, as if to let him know he could go if he wanted.

Then Ray appeared beside him, looking jaunty.

"You having a good time, Ray?" my father asked.

"Oh, sure, John." Ray smiled and fell back on his heels. "Hey, Nickie, what's the matter with you? There's some sweet French Canada pussy down there. What are you doing by yourself back here?"

I looked at my father's eyes after Ray said "pussy." His eyes were shocked, in retreat. It made me want to laugh.

Then he looked at the floor, while Ray carried on, blissfully unaware of his latest faux pas.

"Myself, if I was twenty years younger...eh, John?"

My father made a gesture toward mirth, toward rakishness. It was enough for Ray to settle deeper into this company. I could see he felt comfortable, accepted. He took a long swallow from his drink.

"I better see how things are downstairs," my father said.

"Oh, don't go on account of me, John," Ray said.

But my father had started down the hall already.

"What, were you two havin' a father–son talk?" Ray asked me, looking concerned.

"No. We were finished."

He looked like he knew he'd done wrong, but it would only take a word from me to settle things.

"It's okay. We really were finished."

He took a seat across from me.

"You want some of this?"

He gestured with his drink toward me. I said no.

"Your Uncle Billy, he's done a nice spread."

Ray nodded, as if he were impressed by Billy. I looked into his face. It had that youth in it still. Like Billy. Like Mr. Bevilacqua.

"So you'll be going back to college in the fall, Nick?"

I hesitated a moment.

"Yes."

Ray's feet shuffled back and forth under the chair.

"Cause I can use the work is the only thing."

He looked at me, a little needy, and I said "Yes" in a way that I thought would reassure him. My decision would give him more hours in the laundromat. It would at least do that amount of good.

I left the room and went down into the party. As soon as I was visible to him, Billy called me up onto the stage.

"Nicholas and I are going to sing a song," Billy said, throwing his arm around me. I could smell the mix of his sweat and his aftershave and I remembered how, when I was younger, Billy's peculiar smell suggested an adult world richer and more pungent than that of my parents; it suggested a world you could go to.

"What song, Nicholas?"

He was enjoying himself, having a good time.

"No. No song."

I tried to move the mike away so that my words wouldn't be amplified.

"Come on, name one."

"No. Maybe I'll say something."

"All right!" Billy addressed the crowd. "Nicholas wants to say something."

When I took the mike and looked out at the room, I realized only about a quarter of them were listening— maybe seven in all. My father stood at attention, waiting. I thought of all the words I might say—the words of love and fealty that had never been ours, but that were strangely more appropriate in rented halls—and knew I would never say them. I still thought there might be something truer and closer to the bone in declaring my loyalty to the events leading up to the Burleigh police station than to the world of this room. But here I was now, nowhere else but here, and as I watched my father standing there, looking small and tender, with a drink in his hand, I was able to name a part of my loyalty to him. Not enough to speak. Just enough to gain a small understanding of why it had been so difficult to become someone else.

I looked up at the windows and saw that the light was changing. The party would be over soon. It seemed silly to be holding up what was left of it this way. I said—I blurted—"To William," and watched those few people who were listening lift their glasses. My father lifted his, I thought, with a mixture of disappointment and relief.

When this was done, I handed the mike to Billy and walked down off the stage and across the floor to the big doors and pushed them open and walked outside.

Across the street, I passed the pizza parlor where the Italian boy had cooked my mother's chicken wings. He wasn't there now. Someone else was.

I could hear Billy singing faintly inside the hall, though the song was indecipherable. It was dark enough in the window of the pizza parlor so that I could see my reflection. I reached up with one hand to touch my face, and saw that act reflected in the window. I saw the planes and outlines of their faces, all the people in the hall: my parents and Uncle Billy, the too-familiar noses and mouths, the cramped foreheads. Then the boy behind the counter looked up, and self-consciousness overtook me. I moved on.

I did see Cynthia once again, although not that fall when I returned to Fordham. She was not there then, or for the rest of the time I spent there. I asked once, and they told me she had resigned. There was no indication that she had gone on to another school, or that she was pregnant.

Years later, I lived in her neighborhood, twenty blocks north. In the evening I liked to run in the park, usually just before sundown. I was lonely then—I was married but lonely—and when I saw her sitting on a bench at the place where the gravel and the runner's path met, I couldn't be sure whether my interest was solely in recognizing her, or in seeing a woman in that pose, looking the way she did, alone on a bench with her eyes downcast, as if she were thinking of something. I didn't stop—it was only in the moments after I'd passed that I understood who it was. My heart had started to beat very fast, and I wanted to turn around, but something kept me from it. I reached the end of the park and then turned around and started back. I told myself I would stop when I reached her this time. My heart was still beating very fast and I was composing words, composing a face with which to greet her. I was not beyond imagining a resumption of things. I was still young.

When I got to the bench, it was empty. Perhaps she'd seen me too, and moved on. My body, though, couldn't accept this assumption, and ran to the top of the park, to where her street was. There I saw her, standing at the curb, and beside her, David, in his white runner's uniform. Neither of them seemed to have aged much, but there was still a sadness about them. They moved differently. What had happened to them was subtly manifested. They had no children: I knew it instantly.

I didn't follow them. The light was fading; my wife was waiting. I watched Cynthia's hair in the red light. I watched the way they clasped each other in the red light as they crossed the street and disappeared.

Then I turned and went back down into the park.

About the Author

ANTHONY GIARDINA is the author of the novel *Men with Debts*. In addition, he is a playwright whose work has been produced by Playwrights Horizons and the Manhattan Theater Club in New York, and by regional theaters in Washington, D.C., Philadelphia and Seattle. His essays and articles have appeared in *The New York Times Magazine* and *New England Monthly*. Currently, he is on the faculty of Mount Holyoke College. He lives in Northampton, Massachusetts, with his wife, Eileen, and daughter, Nicola.